Kate Griffin was born within the sound of Bow bells, making her a true-born cockney. She has worked as an assistant to an antiques dealer, a journalist for local newspapers and now works for The Society for the Protection of Ancient Buildings.

Kitty Peck and the Music Hall Murders, Kate's first book, won the *Stylist*/Faber crime writing competition. It was shortlisted for the 2014 CWA Endeavour Historical Dagger. Kate's maternal family lived in Victorian Limehouse and Kitty's world is based on stories told by her grandmother. Kate lives in St Albans.

Praise for *Kitty Peck and the Child of Ill Fortune*:

'A twisting and turning historical thriller that captures the grit, grime and teeming life of nineteenth-century London and Paris.' *Sunday Express*

'This fast-paced historical mystery with its cleverly contrived twists and turns is a worthy follow-up to Griffin's debut ... *Kitty Peck and the Music Hall Murders* was shortlisted for last year's CWA Historical Dagger. This clever sequel combines the wit of the music halls with a great action story full of shades of light and macabre darkness.' Crime Review

Praise for *Kitty Peck and the Music Hall Murders*:

'Terrific debut novel ... Victorian London has never been better illustrated ... if this standard keeps up, we have a major new talent on our hands.' *Sunday Express*

'Occasionally a new writer bursts onto the scene with almost explosive force ... [Griffin's] hugely entertaining debut, set in the squalor, filth and depravity of Victorian Limehouse is all things to all readers – almost gothic in its intensity, but full of shades of dark and light, combining the macabre and wit of the music halls with a rattling action yarn which will appeal to historical readers, crime readers and people who just like a really well-written adventure story ... the book is an absolutely first-class read and I shall be surprised if there's a better debut this year.' Crime Review

'Kitty's narrative voice ... is sharply memorable and deserves to be heard in a further adventure.' *Sunday Times*

also by Kate Griffin

KITTY PECK AND THE MUSIC HALL MURDERS
KITTY PECK AND THE CHILD OF ILL FORTUNE

Kitty Peck
and the
Daughter of Sorrow

KATE GRIFFIN

FABER & FABER

First published in 2017
by Faber & Faber Ltd
Bloomsbury House,
74–77 Great Russell Street
London WC1B 3DA

Printed and bound by CPI Group (UK) Ltd, Croydon CR0 4YY
Typeset by Faber & Faber Ltd

The right of Kate Griffin to be identified as author of this work
has been asserted in accordance with Section 77 of the Copyright,
Designs and Patents Act 1988

A CIP record for this book
is available from the British Library

ISBN 978-0-571-31520-8

FSC
www.fsc.org
MIX
Paper from
responsible sources
FSC® C020471

2 4 6 8 10 9 7 5 3 1

For Stephen, John and Michael
– my 'boys'

Prologue

Against the brightness of the day, the Thames ran black and sleek as a mourner's band.

I closed my eyes, threw back my head and stretched my arms out to the sides so I could feel the sun on my skin where the neck of my cotton dress gaped wide. It felt like a kiss.

The air was so heavy I could wrap it around me like Nanny Peck's old plaid. I wriggled my fingers and felt the heat in the palms of my hands. I was minded to wade into the river and let the cooling water soak through the fabric. I took a step forward and something curled around my feet. I went further and the thin dress clung tight and damp to my skin. The water was warm as the day and thick like the air.

I was in deeper now, but I still didn't feel the benefit of it. My scalp itched and a trickle of moisture slid from the dip of my throat and under my bodice, tracing a sticky path between my breasts.

'Fannella!'

The voice came from close by. I shook my head. I was safe here. He didn't need to look out for me. My brother Joey had the meat of it when he said Lucca Fratelli was an old woman. I lowered my hands to the water and trailed them around. At first the feeling was a pleasant thing, but then they got caught up. I tried to pull them free but it was like they was tangled in weed. I tugged hard but something held them, bound them.

A small hand slipped into mine. Cold fingers wound over my knuckles. I opened up and looked into the water. A pale face surrounded by floating strips of raggy brown weed stared up at me. After a moment things came clear. The weed was long, thin hair the colour of a mouse.

I knew that face.

It was little Edie Strong down there holding onto my right hand. Her eyes were blank and grey like old bottle glass tumbled against stones in the river.

Edie?

There was something wrong, I tried to catch it but it slipped round a corner in my mind. I pulled away but Edie gripped tighter. And now another hand clamped onto the left. I say hand, but it was more like a great bear paw crushing my bones.

I looked to the left. There was a man in the water on the other side to Edie. His face was long and angular, and the black hair spreading round his head like a dark halo had a single streak of white in it. I recognised him straight off. It was Amit Das, the big mute lascar.

I shook my head. It wasn't right, was it? There was a reason – a bleedin' good one – why they couldn't be here in the water with me. I tried to work it out, but tracking it down was like trying to feel my way home through a fog.

Think, girl!

The pair of them began to pull so hard I feared I might go under. I jerked back, but my hands didn't come free. A dozen foot ahead a gleaming patch in the water began to spin. I couldn't take my eyes off the twisting ripples – faster and faster they went, the ring spreading wider until the scummy froth of it circled my waist like a frowse of old lace.

2

Of an instant, the spinning stopped dead and a shape began to rise from the river – a head then broad shoulders. The shape was dark against the sun. I couldn't see who it was, but there was something familiar about the man standing there with his back to me.

Joey? It had to be him.

Thank Christ he was here. I needed . . .

What did I need? The thought slipped from my head like an eel.

He raised a hand to push the sodden hair from his eyes and droplets of water scattered about him, glittering like diamonds in the sunlight. Then he spoke.

'I waited such a time for you, Kit.'

That voice made my belly wring up tight as a dish rag.

It wasn't Joey after all, but I recognised who it was standing there. That was when I knew it wasn't possible. None of it. Big Danny Tewson couldn't be paddling in the river in front of me because he was a dead man. Same went for Edie and Amit.

They were all of them dead because of me.

'No!' I tried to shout, but my tongue was glued to the roof of my mouth. Very slowly, Danny began to turn. Just for a moment, I saw the cut of his handsome profile, black against the sun. I shut my eyes, I didn't want to see his face. Sharp little nails dug circles into the skin of my right palm and my wrist burned where Amit's hand clamped fast like a manacle. The pair of them began to drag me forward into deeper water, closer to Danny.

'Fannella!' Lucca's voice came again.

I flailed about and tried to open my eyes to see where he was but the lids were stuck fast. I felt the river slap against the underside of my chin. My lips were wet now; a bitter sweetness was trying to force a way between them. Christ! I was about to drown out here.

Lucca – he'd make it all right. He'd stop it. I opened my mouth to call out to him and began to choke.

'Kitty!' A warm hand gripped tight on my shoulder and shook me about.

'Kitty. Wake up!'

Chapter One

I heard the snap of fingers right in front of my face.

'*Che follia!*' Lucca muttered beside me. I coughed again as an arm caught me round the shoulders and dragged me upright. Something sweet dribbled from the corner of my mouth to my chin. I still couldn't open my eyes but I felt Lucca swipe whatever it was away with a bit of cloth. He wasn't gentle about it.

'Wake up!' The clicking came again, so close to my face now that a thumbnail flicked at the end of my nose. The sudden sting of it made me open my eyes.

Dark shapes shifted around me. Nothing had a form I could rightly put a name to. There was just a soup of shadows. I swallowed down another sour cough and tried to wipe my mouth but my hand was coiled up in a knot of cloth. As I struggled to free it, the woven pattern seemed to loosen from the fabric and float off somewhere. I watched it unravel itself in mid-air and disappear.

I blinked – it was coming right now.

I was huddled on a low bunk piled with cushions and stacked against a wall. My hands had twisted themselves into the fringe of an embroidered shawl laid out beneath me. Indian it was, scrolled over with feather-like curls. My trousered legs were caught up in a thin blanket that had wound itself round my feet. At first I thought it was patterned like the shawl, but then I realised it was plain stuff spattered with black stains.

Of an instant, I knew most exactly where I was – and I was ashamed. Not to be there, mind. I'd been here often enough. No, I was ashamed by the fact that Lucca had found me.

I rubbed my eyes. My hand caught against the edge of a cap, knocking it askew. Immediately Lucca pulled it down tight again over my hair.

'Not here.' He hissed the words and turned about sharp to make sure no one had noted me. I almost laughed. Fact is, Queen Victoria herself could do the dance of the bleedin' seven veils down here and no one would care.

The room rushed in at me, everything coming up so fast and close that I thought it might squeeze the breath from my lungs. Then, just as sudden, it billowed out, everything quivering like leaves on a tree stirred about by the wind.

I squeezed my eyes shut and opened up again. After a moment, the room settled to a hazy stillness.

Smoke fugged the low brick ceiling arching above. There was a glow over to the left from a candle or a lamp on a small table. In the dim I made out a familiar row of mounded shapes ranged against the far wall. More lamps were set between them. Occasionally there was a flicker of red in the gloom. The room was clammy – the air laced with that tell-tale floral scent which couldn't mask the stench of unwashed bodies. It was quiet, but just occasionally there was a cough or a mutter as someone fidgeted in their nest.

Lucca slipped from the pile of blankets and cushions to crouch beside me. He had a face on him like he'd taken a bite from a cookshop pie and chewed on a mouthful of roach backs.

I couldn't look him in the eye. I turned to face the greasy wall and the room swayed like a river barge. He reached for my hand again, his touch more gentle now.

'Why, Fannella?'

Now, that was a ripe old question, wasn't it? I cleared my throat and felt a ball of bitter glue move into my mouth. Without thinking I spat it out. Something black and foul and shiny fell onto the blanket. Lucca moved his hand away and stared at the spittle.

'I thought you were better than this.' The good side of his face was rigid. His eye didn't catch the light of the oil lamp set beside my own pile of cushions. I wanted to answer him but I couldn't find the words.

Right on cue another voice went off.

'So, he's come awake at last, has he? I'll be taking for five pipes' worth, unless you want to join him for another. I'll do it for half again seeing as how he's been so eager.'

Lucca glanced up at the small woman now standing directly behind him.

She flicked a blackened finger at me. 'You his pastor then, sir? Nice little piece you got there. Keeps them sweet and amenable, don't it? And it don't do no harm neither – not like the gin. If you're running him you done the right thing letting him come here. There are some places that don't bear thinking about, but Nanking Nancy'll look out for him.'

Her voice was loud. She spoke as if she was putting on a performance for the benefit of the others lying about the room. Not that any of them was likely to be paying attention seeing as how they was all lost in their own black dreams.

Lucca stood up. Nancy's tiny black eyes widened behind her gold-rimmed spectacles as she took in the scarred half of his face. Her painted lips screwed themselves into a knot, but she masked it quick.

'We get all sorts down here – mostly female as it happens, so you needn't worry about damaged goods. I always keep an eye out, and like I say, I run a clean establishment. Do you want to fill another, sir?'

She flapped a hand at the opium pipe lying on the floor beside me. There was a long yellowed feather beside it with a ball of black stuff smeared around the end of the quill. Nancy bent down, took up the feather and rolled it between her fingers. It reflected double in her specs, the pale vertical line in each circle of glass giving her the eyes of an old sheep.

She twiddled it about and squinted at the tip. 'There's still some more here for the bowl if you've a mind for it. Waste is a terrible thing.'

She dandled the feather above me like she was tempting a kitten with a fishbone. The nail on her smallest finger was long as a match. Of an instant, she put me in mind of Tan Seng back at The Palace, but at least he was the real thing. Despite the dyed black hair, the loose embroidered gown and the flaking lines of paint round her eyes behind the glass, I reckoned the nearest Nanking Nancy had ever come to China was the saucer she slurped her morning tea from.

She started up again. 'You've paid for it. I run a fair business – and don't never let no one tell you I don't.'

I stared at the feather, at the sticky pea of sweet black opium at the point of the quill set ready for the pipe.

I wanted it.

Without thinking I reached up to take it from Nancy's hand, but Lucca dashed it away.

'No! I think you've had enough.' He folded his arms. 'We are going. You are coming with me now.' His voice was clipped. Nancy stayed quiet for a moment, her black eyes flitting between us.

'That'll be two and six then. It's finest Persian and that costs.' She spoke loud and turned to take in the room again like an old theatrical, then she pushed the thick panes higher on the bridge of her nose. 'I think you ought to know, sir, that your ... *lad*'s got quite a taste for it. Been here before *he* has, several times – I make it a point to know my customers.'

'How many times?' Lucca's good eye burned like the bowl of an opium pipe.

Nancy shrugged. 'Several is several. More than a hand's worth, less than a dozen.'

'*Poco stupido idiota.*' He grabbed my hand and pulled me roughly to my feet. The room swam again. My legs folded and I slumped back down onto the pile of cushions. There were words in my head now, only I couldn't wind my tongue round them.

'S . . . sorry.' I could hardly get it out.

'Are you?' Lucca took my chin in his cool hands. I could smell turpentine and paint on his fingers. He tilted my face to his. 'Are you really?'

My eyes slid to Nancy's slippered feet. The flowers embroidered at the toes were wearing thin, little threads of brilliant silk coming loose. The pattern had an unnatural brightness to it. The more I looked, the more it seemed to have movement too, as if the flowers were growing and winding about her ankles.

I slipped from Lucca's grasp and fell back against the wall. My head bumped on the bricks.

'Fannella!'

Immediately he knelt on the bunk and held me against him. I took in the smell of his skin beneath the thin cotton shirt – soap mingled with the salt of his sweat. It was a good, clean scent. My eyes prickled with tears that weren't caused by the smoke. I buried my face in his shoulder and he rocked me back and forth like a child.

I heard the sound of Nancy shuffling about.

She cleared her throat. 'So you'll be taking her ... *him* off then.'

'*Sì*. I'll pay what is owed then we can leave this ...' Lucca finished off in a jumble of rapid Italian and stared angrily at the others slumped about the room. The points of red were the bowls of the opium pipes glowing up as Nanking Nancy's clients sucked their fill.

'You don't pay me. Not for ... *her*.' She bent close to whisper. '*Not for The Lady.*' I looked up and caught Nancy exchange a look with Lucca. He nodded.

Nancy clapped her hands. A curtain at the far end of the chamber twitched aside. A scrawny Chinaman, the real thing this time, leaned forward. Nancy sang out a stream of words that sounded like the yowling of a cat on heat and pointed at me.

The man took me in, nodded and closed the lid of the black lacquer table set up in front of him. He pulled the curtain a little wider to allow a new customer – a woman dressed finer than you might expect – to step down into the arched room. The painted skin round Nancy's eyes pleated like a concertina as she peered at the new arrival.

Lucca helped me to my feet and steadied me against the wall. The room bulged again while he bent forward to tug a boy's jacket free from the jumble of cushions and rags. There was something about that jacket, something important ... I watched as he rolled the rough thin stuff into a ball. He turned when Nancy tapped his arm with that single long nail.

'Water – lots of it.'

He nodded.

'As much as she can take down. And then she'll want sweetness.'

She stepped back and waved at the well-dressed woman. 'Over here, my peach. There's a bunk come free.'

Chapter Two

The sun woke me.

The brightness burned through my eyelids so that when I turned away and opened up, my sight was full of floating shadows. I lay there for a moment waiting for it to clear. When it did I saw I was lying on a bed pushed up against a panelled wall.

The wall was covered with pencil drawings, sketches and little paintings on squares of card. There were scores of them overlapping each other and pinned to the wood all the way up to the ceiling. Men, women, children ... all of them trapped in a lively moment by Lucca's clever hand.

I reached up to touch a face I knew – Peggy Worrow. A scrawl of dark curls tumbled over her shoulders showing up the line of her neck and her rounded jaw. Her pretty, heavy-lidded eyes looked at me direct. Lucca had caught her true. There was a faint line between her brows and her teeth bit into the edge of her full lower lip. She always did that when she was thinking. I pulled my hand back like it was scalded. I knew only too well what Peggy was thinking about. It was why I couldn't face her, not even on paper.

I looked up at the people crowded above me. I recognised nearly every one of them. They were from the halls – the hands from the workshops, the girls from the chorus, the little ones who served the tables, all of them my people.

Lucca worked fast and bold. He could capture a fleeting

expression in just a few perfect lines and smudges. It came to me that every person pinned to that wall seemed more alive and vital than I felt. Lucca Fratelli was wasted as a scene painter in my halls. Hall, I corrected myself. Only The Carnival was what you might call a going concern now, seeing as how The Gaudy had burned to the ground two months back and The Comet was in need of a new plaster ceiling.

I closed my eyes, but I could feel them all staring down at me, judging me.

See, it was like this. Less than a year ago, my grandmother, Lady Ginger, had left me her empire on the banks of the Thames. She kept her blood in the business. But Paradise – a name that must have been chosen by someone with a rare sense of humour – wasn't the sort of family enterprise a girl could take a pride in. As it turned out, my inheritance was a filthy tanner's pit of every vice and crooked trade you had a name for, and some you most likely didn't.

I was one of the Barons of London. Kitty Peck from the halls – one of the great and secret Lords who controlled every stinking foulness that drove the City like an engine.

My own grandmother had put my hands to the levers and now they were black as pitch.

There were moments while I sat alone with her ledgers when I fancied that if I listened hard enough I could hear the machinery running. I could feel it too. The thrum of evil from every piss-streaked corner of Limehouse rose through the soles of my boots and jangled my nerves until I wanted to open my mouth and scream it out.

There wasn't a way back now. And there wasn't a way forward, neither.

They say the sun never sets on the Empire of our Queen on account of the fact that it stretches so far round the globe that it's always daylight somewhere in her lands.

The sun never rises in Paradise. My empire is a thing of the dark. It runs from the docks in the east, where every second man, including the customs, is in the pockets of my skirts, to the grand houses up west where the toolers and jemmy boys on my books are in the distribution trade. That is to say they distribute their nightly takings among my pawny men back east.

It all goes around and about – it's neat work. On a shady day a proper toff might pay a sly visit to Uncle Fishman's shop on Rose Lane to buy a little gold piece for his skirt, who, as it happens, is most probably a girl I have the running of. Without looking at the ledgers I could tell you her worth to the nearest farthing.

These days I can give you a price for everything. Women, men, girls, boys – and more, if you've a mind to imagine it. There are singular houses in the warren north of Penny Fields where a type can buy the flesh of any living creature by the hour, but that's not the half of the skin game.

I didn't know how sour a *gentleman*'s taste might turn until I studied my grandmother's books in the company of her man of law, Marcus Telferman. There was a morning in his dusty office in Pearl Street when I'd asked him what exactly was on offer in the premises in Severs Street listed as *Domus Cadaver*.

I wish I could un-know that, but I can't.

There's a lot of things I wish I didn't know. Christ! It comes to something when you think of a gang of toolers as the clean side of the trade.

At the beginning, not that long ago, I thought I could do it different. I reckoned that even though Paradise was mucky as a dockers' easement I could shine it up and let some air in. I was always good with a mop and a bucket in the halls. Now I know there are some stains you can't wash away.

The Gaudy, The Carnival and The Comet and the people who worked them were the only part of my inheritance I took a care for. They were where I came from before Lady Ginger claimed me as her own, but now I'd failed them too. I'd failed everyone pinned to that wall.

I rolled over. The window shutters had been hooked back. Sunlight bounced off the square glass panes and sliced across the bed.

Lucca's bed.

I sat up and the thin cotton sheet fell away. I was naked. I wasn't bothered by that. These days Lucca was the closest I had to a brother, and besides, I wasn't his type.

No, what bothered me was the fact that I was tucked up in bed in his room, not back at The Palace. It surprised me that I'd actually begun to think of that soot-pitted pile off Salmon Lane as home. When she went off to Christ knows where Lady Ginger left her house to me, along with everything else.

'Lucca?' His name grated in my throat. My mouth was foul as the floor of Jacobin's cage – my grandmother's mangy old parrot had come with The Palace, along with her Chinese servants, Tan Seng and Lok.

I rubbed a hand over my sticky forehead. Tan Seng would be wondering where I was and he wouldn't be happy. Being a servant, he wouldn't say as much, but I'd get the treatment all the same. His long grey plait would flick about behind him like the tail of an angry cat.

'Lucca?' This time it came out as a rasping croak.

I pulled the sheet around me and slipped off the bed. My legs were weak as the pins of a newborn foal. There was a tin basin half-filled with murky water on the floor next to the bed, a small pile of rags mounded beside it. The sight of the water made my throat burn. I wanted to lift that chipped white basin and drain it to the last drop. My lips were rough and papery to the touch. I tried to lick them into life, but my tongue rolled about in my mouth like a fat-bodied moth. Surely Lucca would have something clean to drink here? I scanned the room. There was a clouded glass on a wide deal table drawn up near the hearth. I gripped the sheet and stumbled across the boards. The glass was dry.

I doubled over as a pain gnawed at my belly. I had to steady myself against the table until it passed. There were piles of papers stacked across the wood. More drawings – mostly animals and birds this time – but on top of a pile nearest the hearth there was a face.

I pulled the sheet closer. Lucca had drawn himself. He hadn't turned to the side or hidden behind a curtain of hair, instead he looked out direct. If you was to cover the bad half of the picture with your hand, he was beautiful. It's a peculiar word to use for a man, I know, but it was true.

The other side was a different story.

Years back he'd been in a fire and it had marked him for life – inside as well as out. Lucca had drawn what he thought everyone saw. On the right, scars pulled his skin, sealing one eye behind a knot of melted flesh. The side of his mouth and nose were crimped together, the damaged skin spreading into a mesh of ridges that stretched to his ear and down his neck to his shoulder.

The drawing was a cruel thing. There was a naked quality to it that made me feel like I was eavesdropping on a private conversation.

How could anyone love a ruin?

He asked me that once and I didn't have an answer. I'd never known Lucca to look any different. Tell truth, over time I'd lost the knack of seeing the scars. I saw him instead.

I put the drawing back on the pile and then, after a moment, I moved some others on top of it, so it was hidden.

I turned from the table to take in the room. As I moved it was like the steam hammer at Grand Surrey was working double time between my ears. My neck was clammy with sweat and I could smell the grease in my hair. I tried to remember how I came to be here but it was all a fug. Every time I caught an echo of something it fizzled out quicker than a Lucifer.

I wrapped the sheet around me and went to the window. Lucca's lodging was on the second floor of an old-time merchant's house with a view out to the river. At one time this must have been a grand room with its high ceiling and wide marble hearth. The fat merchant must have sat at this window watching for his trades to come in. Now the house was split and rented by the yard.

I'd wanted Lucca to come and live with me at The Palace, but he said he needed the light for his art. I reckon the truth of it was that my grandmother's house gave him the fear.

I pressed my forehead against the glass. It wasn't cool.

17

Today the Thames was almost as blue as the sky. Tall ships, sails furled, were moored in rows out across the water. The river was so still they hardly moved. Their ropes hung slack and silent. I couldn't see a soul on the decks or on the quay stones below the window. As I stood there a single bell started off nearby. The dull sound matched the tolling in my head. I counted for the hour, but the bell carried on. Perhaps it was ringing out for a wedding? Given the leaden tone it seemed more likely to be calling mourners to a funeral.

There was a rattle from behind and the sound of a key in the lock. I turned to see Lucca standing in the open doorway, juggling a set of keys with a brown paper package.

'Lucca!' It was hardly more than a whisper but he looked up. He stepped sharp into the room and slammed the door behind him with his foot. I was surprised when he put the package on the floor and turned to lock the door again.

'How long have you been awake?'

'I . . . I . . . Not long.' My tongue felt as if it might shred as I tried to make the words. He bent to take up his package.

'You will be thirsty.' It was a statement, not a question. Instead of coming to me he set the package down on the table on a pile of drawings. Then he went to the far side of the hearth and opened up a cupboard set flush in the panelling. I watched him stretch up to take down a brown jug with a square of beaded material draped over the rim. As he moved I saw grey moons of sweat beneath the arms of his white cotton shirt. The summer was fierce as a Bengal tiger.

The splash of water into the glass made me swallow hard. My throat creased up on itself and I started to cough.

'Here.' He came to the window, still holding the jug, and

handed me the glass. I took a gulp, but couldn't force it down. It felt as if my throat was stuffed with pages from a cheap family Bible. Water dribbled from my lips.

Lucca shook his head. '*Lentamente* . . . slowly.'

The tiniest sip filled my mouth. I managed to squeeze it down and took another sip, then another. I found I could move my tongue now.

'More . . . please.' I pushed the glass into Lucca's hands and he filled it again. This time I tipped it back and finished the whole thing.

'Very elegant, Fannella.' Lucca stared at me, his lips twitching as if there was something more he wanted to add. Fannella was his name for me. It came from the times when he heard me singing in the gallery at The Gaudy – I was a slop girl back then. In his language Fannella means little bird. It was meant as an affection, but there wasn't a deal of warmth in his brown eye now.

'Are you hungry?'

I recognised the griping in my belly. I nodded. Lucca went back to the cupboard and took down a painted china plate. He loosened the brown paper package and emptied half a dozen golden sugar-dusted buns over the blue and white flowers.

'Here.' He sat down, gestured at the chair opposite and pushed the plate towards it through the stacks of his drawings. I didn't need asking twice. Without thinking about the gaping of the sheet wound around me I ran over, sat down and tore at the buns, cramming my mouth with doughy, currant-studded sweetness. Lucca refilled the glass and watched as I switched between the water and the food. When the last of the buns was gone he spoke again.

'She was right then.'

'Who was?' I ran my finger round the plate, licking the last of the sugar from my fingers.

'Nancy.'

I looked up.

'That's where I found you, Kitty. In Nanking Nancy's pit in Shambles Passage off Broad Street. Or don't you remember?'

The room was suddenly so quiet you could hear a mouse fart in the skirting. Of an instant, it all came crowding back. Nancy's den, Lucca finding me there and most particularly why I went that evening.

I had to get going. There was someone I needed to see.

'Where's my gear?' I looked at the bed expecting to see my jacket and breeches folded up neat nearby. Lucca was most particular about his rooms. The clothes weren't there. I stood up abrupt, knocking the spindly chair over. It clattered to the boards behind me.

'Where's my jacket? And ... And the rest?'

Lucca didn't answer. He scrunched up the brown paper and tossed it onto the unlit hearth behind him. The cotton sheet slipped and I had to scrabble at my shoulder to keep myself decent.

'I've got better things to do than sit around here. Tan Seng will be—'

Lucca cut me off. 'He knows exactly where you are, Kitty, and why. He's known for the last four days.'

Four days? I stared at the bed and at the bowl and the rags.

'Tan Seng told me where you go and how often. He's

worried. That's why I went to find you.'

I pulled the sheet around me. I felt like an exhibition now.

'He had no right. Where I go is my business and you can keep out of it, Lucca Fratelli. The whole bleedin' lot of you can mind your own. You're a pack of old women, only you're the worst. Joey always said . . .'

Joey? The thought of my brother made my belly ball up tight as a knuckler's fist. He was the reason, part of it least-ways, why I went to Nancy's pit. When the thoughts came swooping in like gulls mobbing the lines of Billingsgate gut girls, I needed something, somewhere to make it stop. But not for this long.

I stared at the door. It came to me how Lucca had locked it behind him.

'You say it's been four days you've had me here?'

He nodded. 'Today is the fifth. It is Sunday. The bread is from Zaelman's – the only bakery open. I went there after mass. I knew you would be hungry when you came to yourself again.'

'But you locked the door. What am I, a prisoner?'

He shifted some of his drawings about on the table, moving pages to different piles. 'You ran a fever. When I found you I thought it was the opium, but it went deeper. I brought you back here and I've been with you all the time. Do you remember anything?'

I didn't answer. He started to neaten the stacks so the ragged edges of the papers lined up square. 'Even if you hadn't fallen ill I would have kept you here. We agreed.'

'We? Who's this *we*?'

'Tan Seng and Lok.' Lucca carried on sorting. I noted he

didn't look at me. It was deliberate. '*We* thought it best if I kept you here and persuaded you that your ...' He came across the drawing of himself, paused and pushed it further into the pile. '... *excursions* were dangerous. It would be for the best. The brothers thought I could convince you to stop.'

I saw it clear now and it riled me. I was angry but, worse than that, I was ashamed. I stepped closer to the table. 'So that's it, is it? You kept me here under lock and key thinking that one of your holy Roman sermons might sort me out. Is that why you've been to mass today, to get inspiration? You must think me a fool, Lucca.'

'Aren't you?' His lopsided mouth tightened 'What is happening to you?'

He stared at me expectant and I turned away. I didn't need to be a stage mind-reader like Swami Jonah to take in what Lucca was telling me. But he was wrong. I wasn't like them other weak souls in the dens. I chose when I went and what I took – and it was my business, no one else's. I was perfectly in control of myself.

Five days? Turns out I wasn't.

Lucca's voice clipped up. 'It has to stop. Do you know what I am saying, Fannella?'

I didn't answer.

'Do you understand?' His voice was soft and low. It was the tone of it, concern dipped in disappointment, that fired me again.

'Of course I do! But I reckon you should understand that I can do what I bleedin' well like.'

Lucca reached out and caught my hand. He tried to thread his fingers into mine, but I didn't let him in.

'Kitty, you mustn't let it destroy you.' He held tight. 'I don't mean the opium. Something happened, I know it. I saw you return from that first meeting with the Barons. Since then you have become a different person. Now you are *una cosa vuota* . . .' He paused for a moment searching for the English. 'A hollow thing.'

Sweat trickled down my forehead.

'I know you too well, Fannella. I've watched you. It is as if a light in you has been . . . *estinto*,' he snapped his fingers, 'is gone.'

'What did you expect? I'm a Baron, don't you know what that means?'

Of course he didn't. But he was right about darkness in me.

My head filled with shadows as he carried on talking. 'You made a promise, Fannella, to all the people in the halls. You promised to deal with them fairly and they believed you. Now The Gaudy is a ruin and The Comet won't open again until spring next year at the earliest. Fitzpatrick is . . .' he grimaced, '*un porco grasso* and that fox Jesmond needs to be watched, but they know the business. You should listen to them. Jesmond is in profit at The Carnival so at least one of the halls is providing work, but it's not enough. People are worried – there's talk. We need *you* to lead us. We look to you.'

Something Lady Ginger told me went through my mind. I heard her sour sweet, little-girl voice clear as if she was sitting in the room.

Paradise is more than three theatres. They are merely a painted facade.

Now I knew the truth of it. I closed my eyes. A pain was

gnawing at the back of my head.

Lucca pulled a sheet free and held it out. I took the page from his hand and stared at the drawing. The girl on the paper had dark circles beneath dull eyes and sunken cheeks. It was me.

'Peggy says you have become too thin.'

'Oh, she says that, does she? I'd like to know how she—' I broke off. Tell truth, I hadn't seen Peggy in a good while. Not since Danny. I couldn't bear to look her in the eye.

Lucca sighed. 'She was at The Carnival three weeks ago when you were in the office with Jesmond. One of your increasingly rare visits. She'd come with some costume repairs. She hid from you because she was afraid – afraid that you would turn away and reject her – *again*. Peggy says you've ordered Tan Seng to refuse her at the door of The Palace. She thinks it is because you don't want her to find out.'

'Find out what?' I couldn't hide the tremor in my voice.

'That you are ill. She is like me, Fannella, one of the few people who can really see you. And besides, she needs you. She is not . . .' Lucca shook his head. 'She is not strong. The business with Danny. We all knew he had debts, but to abandon the mother of his child . . .'

He went quiet for a moment. I watched him work at a knot in the wood of the table top with the tip of a finger. I was relieved when he started up again on a different tack.

'While you were sick, you . . . you spoke aloud, Kitty. I know things have changed since you became one of them, became a Baron, I mean. *You've* changed . . . But . . .'

He stopped tracing the pattern and looked at me direct.

'I never thought of you as a murderer.'

Chapter Three

Lucca folded his hands together. There was green paint scuffed on his knuckles.

'Amit Das and Edie Strong – in the fever you called out to them over and over again and begged them to forgive you.' He stared at me. 'What did you do?'

I bit at some dried skin on my lip. Amit Das had been my protector, built like a great dark bull. The last time I saw him he was slumped against the wall in a burning theatre with a knife in his back. I never heard the big lascar cry out: Amit Das was a mute. When I found him it was too late. Little Edie Strong vanished the same night when The Gaudy burned to the ground. Fourteen years old and scrawny as a sparrow, Edie was a slop girl like I'd been. They never came across her body when they sifted through the wreckage. I didn't murder them, but I was . . . responsible.

'Well?' Lucca's eye was round as an owl's.

I bent to right the spindly wooden chair, more because it gave me the chance to avoid his look than because I wanted to sit down. The last thing I wanted to do was stay here, not when there was something I needed to do.

'They died in the fire, both of them. You know that, Lucca. It must have been the fever talking.' I pushed the chair closer to the table. 'The truth of it is they're on my mind, both of them. Amit has, *had* . . .' I corrected myself, 'a brother and

Edie lived with her mother. I've been meaning to go to them both, Amit's brother and Edie's mother, to pay my respects, but . . .'

'But you haven't been?' Lucca's voice was flat.

I shook my head. 'There's not been time.'

'You mean you haven't made the time.' He muttered something I didn't catch. 'Yet you have plenty of time for Nancy, it seems.'

'Don't!' I sat down heavily. 'Don't you play the saint, Lucca Fratelli. We both know it don't suit you. I'm a Baron like you say, but it's not what I thought. It's not like being a fairy in a pantomime. I can't jingle my skirts and make things come right. You haven't got the first idea what I've . . . All the things I've . . .'

'All the things you've done?' Lucca finished that for me.

'I need another drink.' I snatched up the glass and reached across the table to the jug.

'What did you do to Danny Tewson?'

The glass slipped from my fingers and shattered on the boards.

See, it wasn't fever talking there. Big Danny Tewson, what was left of him, was in a pit beneath Great Bartholomew's Church at Smithfields. I'd sealed him into it with my own hand. It was the test the Barons set for me when I joined their ranks. And I'd passed.

I *was* a murderer.

Broken glass glittered on the pitch-coated boards like diamonds on a jeweller's cloth. Something else Lady Ginger said to me the night when she delivered me to the Barons in her own black carriage came back. My grandmother had reached out in the darkness and plucked at the satin ruffles sewn over my heart.

You must be cold and hard as a diamond . . . You must be dead here.

Part of me died that night. I don't know how long Danny cried in the dark beneath that flagstone at Great Bartholomew's waiting for someone to come and lift his broken body into the light. I prayed it was short – that he'd suffocated quick down there or died from the fall soon after the sealing. But I don't know.

Ever since, pictures keep leaking into my mind of their own accord. And when I think of Danny I think of Peggy – my dear, kind, good-hearted friend – carrying his child. My mouth goes dry and my eyes scorch with tears I can't seem to shed. I keep it all locked away inside, but the memory rises like bile. The pain is sharp and real as the canker eating my grandmother alive. And the worst of it was that for a moment, for a single second that night at Great Bartholomew's, I'd been glad it was Danny kneeling there begging me to help him, not Joey, my brother.

Some days I hated my brother, and others the loss of him ached like a rotten tooth. I thought about that jacket again; about the note hidden in the lining.

Five days was too long. I had to see Telferman.

'Fannella?' Lucca's question brought me back. 'I asked you about Danny. What happened to him?'

'I don't know what you mean.' I could hear the lie. I brought my fingers to my lips to wipe it away.

Lucca's eye narrowed. 'You sat up straight in that bed, pointed at someone only you could see, then you spoke to them. Let me tell you your exact words. "Don't look at me like that, Dan. I didn't mean to kill you.'"

I reached down to gather the broken glass together. A tiny sliver sliced into my thumb.

'Kitty!' Lucca grabbed my hand in his. The green paint on his knuckles mingled with flecks of fresh wet red. 'Tell me. What happened to him? You know, don't you?'

I shook my head. The room was unbearably hot. The sheet stuck to my skin like fly paper.

'I didn't know what I was saying. It didn't mean anything. You . . . you said it yourself, I was feverish.'

Lucca gripped harder. 'Peggy's mad with worry. If you know anything about Danny you have to tell her, for the sake of their child. She's your oldest friend, Kitty, doesn't that mean anything?'

'Let me go!' I pulled my hand free. 'If you want the truth, I can't see her because I . . . I'm . . .' *What was I?* It was a question that kept me awake night after night. What had I become? Across the table Lucca waited for an answer. I pressed the heels of my hands into my eyes.

'I'm ashamed of myself. That's what it is. I can't face her knowing all the things I do – all the dirty things I have to do to keep Paradise square. She's good and kind and decent. She'd hate me if she knew what I'd become.'

'I don't hate you, Fannella.'

'Don't you?' I looked up.

He shook his head. 'I am frightened for you. That is quite different. You are not the girl you were. But I know she is still here somewhere.' He reached across and rested his fingers over my heart. 'She must be.'

My eyes swum with tears. I covered his hand with mine.

'It's bleedin' lonely being a Baron, Lucca.' I caught an odd expression flit across the good side of his face. 'I mean it. If it wasn't for you looking out for me, I don't know what I'd do.'

He stood and took another glass down from the cupboard.

'Why do you go to that place – to Nancy's den?' He filled it again from the brown jug and handed it to me.

'Because . . .' I took a sip. 'Because it makes me forget. Just for a short time I can shut the world out and I can make the voices in my head go away.' I stopped myself short. It was Danny's voice I heard most often, pleading for me to save him while the rest of the Barons, those cold-eyed, arrogant bastards, watched us.

Lucca nodded. I caught a wariness in his look once more.

'Promise me you won't go there again, Fannella. I won't always be . . .' He went to a battered leather trunk by the window. 'I won't always be able to come to you.'

He threw back the lid. 'Your clothes are here. Another thing, you cannot go about Limehouse dressed as a boy, it is dangerous.'

That was ripe coming from him. 'Seeing as how you taught me how to go about in breeches, you're hardly in a position to complain when I do. I gave a false name – Jimmy Riley, if you're interested – which I'm sure you're not. I tied my hair up small under the cap and dressed plain. It's so dim in there Nancy wouldn't have recognised her own mother.'

Lucca crossed himself. He bent down and took out a neat folded pile.

'Are you strong enough to go back to The Palace?'

I nodded. Tell truth, I felt like I'd been trampled by a pair of dray horses, but I'd already lost too much time. He pushed the pile of clothes into my hands. There was a pale blue dress on the top.

'Where are my things?'

'These are your things. Tan Seng sent them over from The Palace.'

'No. I mean the things I was wearing that night.' I shrugged at the sheet to keep it draped over one shoulder. 'The boy's things you don't approve of.'

Lucca blinked. 'I burned them, Kitty. They reeked of the den, and besides, by the time we got here they were almost stuck to your skin.'

I thought of the note tucked into the jacket lining. I could remember it, every word. Then again, I wasn't likely to forget it. Lucca was right. I was a fool. I badly needed to straighten myself out.

He moved back to the table. 'I have something else for you.' I heard the scrape of wood as he opened a drawer and the rustle of paper. He unfolded a sheet and began to read aloud.

Lady Linnet.

It has been more than two months since our meeting and yet still you have not answered our question concerning Joseph Peck.

I assumed, perhaps wrongly, that our enthusiasm to re-new acquaintance with your brother was made clear at the Vernal session in what, I hoped, was a most compelling demonstration of our interest in those close to you.

I have every certainty that you will meet the terms of

our request at the Aestas session. If you cannot produce the living body of your brother at the next meeting of the brotherhood, we will accept information that leads to him.

The completion of this task will assure us of your fitness for the role you have recently assumed.

We will know when you have accomplished this simple matter. Your grandmother left Paradise in your hands, but I must warn you, as a Baron to a brother, that it needs a firmer grip. My man Matthias is ready to teach you a valuable lesson in mastery if you cannot control your holding.

There are three weeks until we meet again. The Aestas Court will assemble in the first week of August. Your man Telferman will, as custom, communicate the details. I assure you of our continued concern for those you hold dear and enclose a keepsake to remind you. Wear it and think of us.

K.

When he'd finished Lucca held out the letter. I snatched it from his hand. Next, he reached into his pocket and took out a small gold locket. He flicked it open with a thumbnail. I looked away. I didn't want to see that lock of dark hair curled beneath the glass. It came from Danny, I was certain.

'The letter fell from the jacket when I put you into my bed. This was wrapped inside it.'

He swung the open locket on the chain.

'Who is this *Lady Linnet*? Why was a letter and a trinket

for her hidden in your clothes – and why would she know where Joseph is?'

I hugged the blue cotton dress close as if it might ward off the words.

'You already know, don't you?' I tried to take the locket off him but he stepped back.

'I want to hear it from you, Fannella.'

I watched the locket sway like a pendulum. After a moment it stilled and began to twist about. I saw Danny's black hair curled into the gold.

'All right. *I'm* Lady Linnet. It's the name the Barons gave me when I became one of their number. It's one of their games, their secrets. K stands for Kite – Lord Kite. I don't know his real name – I don't know any of them, but Kite's the worst of the lot and Matthias is his fist. We . . .' I bit down hard on my tongue, '*They* . . . meet each quarter. They call it holding court. It's when I have to report to them – prove I'm worthy, show how well I'm running things in Paradise. The letter and that . . . thing . . .' I jerked my head at the locket, 'came to me the day I went to Nancy's den. It's why I went. Don't you see?'

Lucca frowned. Of course he didn't see. How could he? That package was thrust into my hand on a dusty crowded street. I didn't even see who passed it. The noon sun burned hotter than the furnace at the Whitechapel Foundry, but when I read Kite's note and opened that bleedin' locket, of an instant, it felt like a January night.

It was the fear that made me go to Nancy's, fear and disgust. The thought of seeing the Barons again, the grey ones, the tall ones, the old ones, the joined ones, the one whose grossly distended body had so many folds of unreachable, un-washed flesh that for days after I couldn't get the stench of him out of my nose; the thought of standing among them; the thought of being counted as one of their number, re-minded me of what I'd become. I couldn't have fallen lower if I'd tumbled out of that cage Lady Ginger hooked to the ceil-ings of her halls.

Just for a couple of hours, that's what I told myself. All I wanted was to lose myself in the smoke, rest in the dark and wipe my head clear. Then I could straighten myself up and deal with it. But the truth was that Nancy's place had become what you might call a habit. It was where something like sleep came. It didn't come often otherwise.

Lucca couldn't see it, I was certain, but I caught the mean-ing of that letter straight off. It was a threat to everyone I cared about. The hair in the locket and the words underlined in a cruel black stroke made it very clear that unless I handed my brother over to the Barons of London, people I knew would suffer like Danny Tewson. It was simple as that.

Only it wasn't.

I had no idea where Joey was. I hadn't seen him since the week The Gaudy burned to the ground. He'd stood there in my parlour, dressed in that fancy French gown, a plaited mouse piled on his head, and he dragged me to stand next to him in front of the mirror to show how very much alike we were. He was frightened that day. I saw it in his fine blue eyes despite his talk.

Oh yes. My golden brother had so many complications weaving through his life it was a wonder they didn't knot around his throat and string him up. In the past he'd done something to the Barons, and Kite wanted him, but I didn't know the what or the why of it.

There was only one person who might be able to help.

I wasn't even sure if she was alive.

Chapter Four

Marcus Telferman had been my grandmother's legal creature and now he was mine. He stared at me through gilt-rimmed half-moon spectacles and drummed his fingers on the desk. After a moment he looked down at the ledger between us and sighed. I caught irritation rather than regret in the tone of it.

'We have been through this before.' He tapped the page. 'Come, there are other matters to discuss – many other matters. In the past weeks you have repeatedly ignored my requests for a meeting and yet now you arrive without prior warning. You are aware, are you not, that I cannot progress your interests without your assent? I am merely your servant. You must take control and, perhaps more pertinently, be seen to take control. There have been . . .' he looked direct at me, 'laxities. To be frank, I am disappointed in you.'

I folded my arms. 'I asked a simple question, Mr Telferman.'

He sniffed and his spectacles hopped on the bridge of his long nose. A strand of oily grey hair unhooked itself from behind his left ear and dandled in front of his face. It quivered on his breath as he started to talk rapidly at me.

'When Captain Houtman's boat arrives tomorrow you will need to be ready. It is a new arrangement from a trusted source. The meeting will take place just after sunrise. The heft has been dealt with – two lascars have been paid to carry.

I trust you will be in attendance. You need to take the measure of the man. The decision must be yours and yours alone. I say only this: I understand from my contact that there is likely to be a fat profit in any future transactions. The gin run offers a healthy return.'

He didn't look up as he rattled on.

'Houtman's ship, the *Gouden Kalf*, will be berthed at Shadwell New Basin until the end of July. Some repairs to the machinery and the paddles are to be undertaken by the mariner smiths.' Now he paused. His nose twitched and the little golden specs rose again. 'The story of the Golden Calf is not favoured by my people. I do not understand why such a name should be used for a boat. There are some who might consider it a blasphemy.' He ran an ink-stained finger back and forth over the words in the ledger as if it might rub them out.

'I don't see what's wrong there.' I quizzed at him.

The Beetle looked up from the page and peered at me through them spectacles as if I was something very small and very far away. 'It is taken from the Old Testament, the Book of Exodus. I believe your own Bible refers to the "molten calf" – an image worshipped in idolatry?'

Of course, I knew it now. I reckoned there was a deal of ripeness to the fact he was sitting there giving me a lecture on the Ten Commandments, when the book open between us broke every one of them – and a dozen more old Moses hadn't thought of.

If Telferman saw the joke he didn't let on. There was a dry rustle as he rolled the tips of his thumb and first fingers together. 'Then there are the items supplied by Madlock and his team. I have made arrangements for the gold to be

36

smelted after-hours at the Whitechapel Foundry. The ingots will be marked by Selzman. He is the best, no questions will be asked. He has proved himself loyal in the past.'

The Beetle – that was me and Joey's private name for Marcus Telferman, mostly on account of the way he crept about and for the sake of the sheeny black gear he wore at Ma's funeral all them years back – ran a dirty nail down the list of names and figures in the ledger.

'Madlock is good, but he has been so diligent in recent weeks that he may draw attention to you. I have asked him to wait for a month or so before sending the team west again. You agree?'

He turned the page without waiting for an answer.

'Customs Officer Skimple informs me that a shipment of China silk and tea will arrive on *The Windhover* in two weeks' time. The Redmayne warehouse at King Edward's Stairs will be made ready. Your portion amounts to a little over a third of the whole. Skimple's discretion is costly, but I am certain you will agree to the usual sum? Half in advance and half on delivery – he prefers coin. I will arrange it.'

The Beetle hooked the straggling hair back over his ear and scuttled on.

'Mother Baxter's house has been closed for a fortnight. Were you aware of that?' He didn't pause for my reply. 'It was thought that one of her girls had contracted smallpox. Fortunately it turned out to be chicken pox, which, I understand, does not pit the skin severely. Trade will not be damaged, in the long term, but I think you would be wise to allow the women time to regain their . . . vigour. With your permission I will send word.'

He flipped the page.

'And here we have the halls . . .' He pursed his lips. 'Perhaps I should use the singular. The Carnival appears to be satisfactory, which is something, but the work at The Comet will gnaw into the profits. You must make a decision on the future of The Gaudy. To rebuild would be a costly undertaking. The site, however, is of some value. Your managers Fitzpatrick and Jesmond do not rub along together, but they both have their value. You must make a team of them. Do you understand me?'

I rolled my eyes. 'Perfectly, thank you, but you don't seem to understand *me*, Mr Telferman. Anyone would think I wasn't talking London. I'll try again. Where – is – she?' I said the last three words loud and deliberate.

The Beetle slammed the ledger. Dust flew up around him, tiny flecks of it dancing in the sunlight doing its best to cut through the gloom. His front window hadn't seen a cloth since the Charge of the Light Brigade.

'Now, Katharine, there is another matter, something of troubling importance, I wish to discuss. Recently . . .'

'No!' I stood up abrupt. 'Didn't you hear me? I told you I want to see her!' I planted my hands flat on the desk. 'You will tell me where I can find her. I give the orders now, don't I? I'm a Baron.'

Marcus Telferman didn't blink. Fact is, he didn't move at all. From the greasy strips of hair hanging down each side of his face to the faded brown eyes swimming behind the thick glass, he was still as a rat when a cat's on its scent. Tell truth, the way he held his ground made me uncomfortable. After a few seconds had passed without so much as a twitch of an eyelid from him I sat down and clasped my hands in my lap. I felt like a child caught in a tantrum.

He watched me across the desk and I tried to imagine what he saw. My head still ached from the fever and my hair was limp and dark and plastered to my scalp. The girl staring back at me from the mirror this morning had rings around her eyes that didn't come from a stick of lamp black.

After a moment the Beetle sniffed.

'In most matters that is correct, Katharine. However, in all affairs relating to your grandmother I continue to take my orders directly from her.'

'She's still alive, then?'

Now he blinked. I could see him calculating whether he'd said too much, but he couldn't take it back.

'I believe that death, when it comes, will be a kindness.'

I almost laughed out loud at the thought of a kindness connected to Lady Ginger.

'You'd better giddy up then, before it's too late. Her address, Mr Telferman.'

'We both know that is not possible. I can send a message to the effect that you wish to arrange a meeting and, *if* your grandmother is prepared to see you, she will reply in due course. That is the best I can do.'

'If that's your *best* it's not bleedin' good enough.'

The Beetle steepled his fingers. He was still trussed up like a mourner today. Despite the heat he had a broidered waistcoat on under a long black coat. The room was airless. It smelt of mouse, moth and something medical, which I put down to the preservation of the dead. On the mantle behind him a large pale bird, with eyes like golden marbles, spread dusty wings in a wide glass case. Of a moment I had the distinctive impression the wings were attached to Telferman, not the owl. The arrangement gave the Beetle the look of a shabby celestial. He patted his fingertips together three times. All the while he never took his eyes off me.

'You will recall that she has made it very clear that her place of residence is not to be divulged – to you or to ...' Something flickered across his face, but he wiped his expression clean quicker than a mumper snatches a penny. 'To speak plainly – I cannot tell you where she is. As her representative I am bound to respect her wishes. I am legally constrained in this – as, I might add, are you.'

I thought about his reply and sifted something out. I'd come back to that later. For the moment I was interested in the legals.

'Constrained by what?'

Telferman's eyes slid to a chest in the corner between the window and the marble mantle. There was another glass-domed case set on the top covering a bird the size of a crow. The creature was a comical thing with splayed yellow feet and a beak streaked three different colours. It was mostly black except for its white front and face where sad eyes marked out with dark lines put me in mind of a clown.

I nodded at the case. 'I've never seen that one before. New, is it?'

He nodded. 'The puffin is not native to London. In the far north its flesh is considered to be a delicacy among sea-faring people. It tastes of rotten fish, I am told.'

'Why eat it, then? There's not even any meat on the thing.'

'I believe it is partly for the challenge.' He rose and fiddled

40

in his coat pocket. 'The birds live in clefts high on rugged cliffs. It is dangerous to harvest them. I believe there is an element of bravado in their flavour.' He stared at me. A muscle worked now beneath his left eye. 'Bravery, Katharine, and defiance. It sweetens the taste.'

I looked from the puffin to the owl. Over to the left, high in the corner resting along the top of a half-open cabinet there was a shrivelled leathery creature with a gaping mouth. It wasn't under glass.

Telferman didn't much go in for housework. I could see more dust on its knobbled back and a cobweb strung out between its evil teeth. There were no eyes, just wrinkled hollows sewn shut with crude stitches. The crocodile – that's what I took it for – was blind as Lord Kite. His lids weren't sewn together, mind. Kite's blank eyes were white and wet as milk. That night at Great Bartholomew's, in the flicker of the candles, they put me in mind of silver pennies laid on a corpse.

Sweat crept under the collar of my dress. I reached up to pull it loose and opened the top button.

'Why do you keep all these dead things around you?'

Telferman drew a ring of keys from his pocket and went to the dome containing the miserable puffin. Taking the base in both hands, he lifted it free and placed it gently on the bare stone floor. He jangled through the ring and bent to unlock the wooden chest. The threadbare seat of his breeches shone through the parting in his shiny coat tails.

'As a boy, I had a great interest in the natural world.' His voice was muffled by the wooden lid of the chest and by the rustle of papers as he rummaged about. The thought of the Beetle as a child was a new one. He continued to ferret among the documents while I digested the idea. It was as ridiculous as chewing on a puffin. Then again, the thought of Marcus Telferman with an interest in anything except papers and ribbon-tied contracts was hard to swallow.

'Animals, is it? Why don't you get a dog or a cat – something alive? If it's birds you're interested in, I've got a parrot I'll gladly let you have.'

'Jacobin lives? Remarkable.' Telferman carried on delving. 'A most vicious and disagreeable creature. You have my sympathies, Katharine. I never understood why The Lady . . . your grandmother was so fond of it.'

'She can't have been that fond or she wouldn't have left it behind. It went for me this morning. I wouldn't stand in your way if you sent it to the dermist.'

'Ah, here.' Telferman's bones clicked as he straightened up. He turned to hand me a familiar document. It was the first paper I signed that day at The Palace when me and Lucca answered my grandmother's summons. She was gone, but the Beetle had been waiting for us in the gloomy hall, a stack of ledgers at his feet.

I signed my soul away for Paradise that day.

I looked down at the close-packed script on the paper in front of me. My signature was at the bottom, the letters round and bold. If only I'd known then . . .

'If I may bring your attention to a clause, halfway down.' Telferman jabbed at the paper. 'Just there. Her intentions are quite clear.'

I moved the sheet to catch more of the light struggling through the smeary panes.

The donor demands the right of privacy at all times. The signatory (as below) will not make physical contact or enter into correspondence with the donor except through channels appointed and good services rendered by the donor's sole representative in this matter. The donor's sole representative shall be Marcus Telferman, hereafter referred to as 'the executor'.

The donor reserves the right to contact the signatory (as below) at any time or place or in any ways fitting to the purpose. The signatory (as below) accepts that she . . .

I read that line again. Despite the fact that the words were crammed tight as herring in a barrel, I could see the alteration. The word *she* had originally been *he*. The extra 's' was scratched into a space so narrow it couldn't be mistaken for anything other than an afterthought. I ran over the rest of the page – it was the same everywhere, most times not as plain.

I realised then that the deed of transfer – the document by which my grandmother had given me charge of Paradise and everything and everyone within its boundaries – had been drawn up for my brother. I always knew it was in her mind, she'd told me so herself. But I hadn't realised how close she'd come to it.

Telferman moved nearer. Old moth bait caught in my nose. He ran an ink-stained finger down the paper. As he leaned over my shoulder the naphtha mingled with the scent of clove oil and grease from his hair.

'Just here. Do you see, Katharine?'

I nodded slowly. 'Very clear, now, thank you.' I whipped

around so fast he started back. 'She was giving it all to him, wasn't she? It was all ready – you'd drawn up the transfer. This was written for my brother, for Joey. It was never meant for me.'

The Beetle tried to snatch the paper from my hands, but I sprang up and moved out of reach. 'I want some answers. What made her change her mind at the very last moment? I know she spirited Joey over to Paris to keep him safe from the Barons, but I don't think anyone's ever told me the real reason why. What's my brother done to make Lord Kite hate him so much?'

Telferman brought a hand to his lips. It was a gesture of silence, as if the mere mention of that bastard's name could summon him into the room with a flash and a shower of sparks. But I wasn't going to button it.

'I haven't told you about my first meeting with the Barons at Great Bartholomew's, have I?'

Telferman backed away, moving round to the opposite side of the desk, like there was a safety having it between us. He didn't look at me as he answered. 'As it has been so difficult to persuade you to attend to the affairs of Paradise, there has not been an opportunity to discuss the details of your . . .' He faltered.

'Do you want to know the details? How it went that night two months back?'

He pushed some papers around and still didn't look at me. 'Some things are best left to the competence of the Barons themselves, Katharine. It was always this way with your grandmother. My safety depends on my ignorance. I do not need to know the place. I do not need to know—'

'I'll tell you what you need to know.' I took a step forward. 'I acquitted myself well enough. I gave my report at their Vernal Court and I did it from memory. I had it all here . . .' I tapped the side of my head. 'Everything in Paradise – weighed and valued, right down to the last sparrow. I'll give you credit for that because you helped me work it through – showed me what I needed to offer my first parable. Funny how they wrap everything up in Bible words – perhaps it makes it seem clean? Anyway, I put on a good show, just like she told me to. Christ! I was even pleased with myself when I finished up. Do you know what I thought?'

Telferman sat down heavily. He removed his specs and rested his forehead in one hand so I couldn't see his face.

'I thought it was easy – that's what. I reckoned it was less trouble than hanging up there performing in that cage in the halls night after night. I actually felt safe. That's the joke of it.'

There was a long silence while I waited for him to say something. After a moment he cleared his throat.

'You returned, Katharine. You must have passed the test. Just as she knew you would.' He still didn't look at me. 'I tried to dissuade her. I argued that you were little more than a child, but she said . . .'

Telferman clenched his fingers into a jagged bony fist – brown spots stretched across the skin of his knuckles. 'When I changed the title document Lady Ginger told me that she was mistaken in your brother. She regretted it. She said that she had been foolish to trust him when you were the one with the mettle for the task.'

I thought of the moment when I sealed Danny into that pit. They'd tricked me into it, but I'd done it all the same. Was that the mettle she meant? My eyes stung, but I blinked back the tears. I certainly wasn't going to spill over in front of the Beetle. I screwed the paper tight in my hands.

'You knew too, didn't you? You knew what was going to happen – not the detail, perhaps. But you knew they'd do something. You knew I wouldn't come out of there the same girl who went in.'

He looked up now. Without the specs I could see his eyes clear. The thick lenses made them small as the head of a dress pin and sharp with it, but in reality they were large and sad with grey pouches slung beneath.

'I have been waiting for this conversation. To be frank, I have thought of you often since the night of your ... introduction to their number. Did they ... *hurt* you in any way, Katharine? I can ask Dr Pardieu to call upon you, he is most discreet. He worked for your ...'

'For my grandmother, I know. As I understand it, the old crow was treating her for the canker before she went away. And the answer is no, they didn't hurt *me*.'

Of an instant, an odd thought occurred. 'Did they hurt her? My grandmother? Is that what you're saying?'

Telferman shook his head. 'Not in all the years I have served her. But she ... In the past ... In the early days when she was tested, as you have been, I believe that something—' He stopped himself and stared up at the ceiling. It was heavily plastered in the old way with curling scrolls whipped to decorative points. It would have looked like a fancy wedding cake if it hadn't been grey with cobwebs.

His eyes roamed around up there like he was searching for a place to hide.

46

'Something what?'

He brought a hand to his mouth and pinched the fleshy bottom lip between his thumb and forefinger so I could see his lower teeth, both of them.

'Go on – what happened to her?'

He shook his head. 'I do not know.' He saw the look on my face and raised his hands. 'That is the truth, Katharine. I swear it on the faith of my father and his father before him. She never spoke of it to me, but she carried a shadow.'

'Perhaps it was her conscience. You know how she ruled Paradise.' I jerked my head at the window. 'There's not a man or woman out there who wasn't terrified of her.'

'She was a Baron. Having seen them, having heard them, having walked among them, can you tell me, truthfully, that you do not understand why she acted the way she did? She was one of them. I know very little of their ... constitution, and I confess I am grateful.' The muscle worked beneath his left eye. I saw the tic in the sallow skin as he stared up at me. 'You, however ...'

He faltered and reached for his specs. He knew he gave too much away without them. 'You too are a Baron now.'

The only sound came from the clock on the mantle, dripping time like a leaky gutter. Another trickle of sweat slid down between my shoulders. I tugged again at the neck of my dress; it was so close in the room I could hardly get the air down.

Telferman didn't move. The glass of his specs caught the sunlight so I couldn't see his eyes.

I took a breath. 'Lady Linnet – that's the name they gave me. That's who I am. And if you're asking me what they're

47

like, I'll tell you – they're monsters, the lot of them. The things I heard that night when I became one of them, the things I saw . . .'

Danny.

I dug my nails into my palm to stop the tears. 'If that's what it means to be a Baron, I don't want none of it. Here, you can take this back to her.'

I ripped the paper in two and flung the halves on the table. After a moment, Telferman reached out and carefully fitted them together again. I watched as he smoothed the frayed edges into place and flattened out the creases I'd made. The base of my spine prickled where the sweat collected in the sticky dip above the cotton waistband.

'It's not as simple as that, is it?'

He shook his head. 'You were chosen. You accepted. And now you have become one of their number. There are two ways to end the . . . association. One is to choose a successor, as your grandmother did. The other is . . .'

In the long pause that followed, I understood what the other way was. It was a curse – what kind of woman could do that to her blood? I stared at the blind crocodile on the cabinet and thought of Kite's letter. My brother was her blood too, but when it came to it she didn't trust him.

'I need to see her. She gave me a warning for Joey; much good it did because he didn't listen. He came to London two months back and then he disappeared again. I learned a lot of things that night at Great Bartholomew's, but I still don't understand why Lord Kite—'

'No!' Telferman shook his head in alarm, but I went on, repeating the name slowly and deliberately.

'. . . *Lord Kite* wants my brother. She must know why. Even if she didn't trust Joey she cared for him enough to try to keep him away. But I have to know . . .'

I remembered the question that crossed my mind earlier when the Beetle was explaining that he couldn't tell me where to find her.

She has made it very clear that her . . . place of residence is not to be divulged – to you or to . . .

Of an instant, I knew what he'd stopped himself from saying.

'You've heard from him, from Joey! Don't deny it. You nearly gave it away earlier. "Her placc of residence is not to be divulged to you or . . . *to your brother*" – that's what you were running to, wasn't it?'

'I cannot discuss this.' Telferman folded the torn papers together.

'But I am right, aren't I?'

He rose and went back to the open chest. When he'd stowed the papers inside again he closed the lid, locked it and lifted the puffin in its glass dome from the floor. As he pushed it back gently into place he spoke quietly.

'You asked earlier why I surround myself with the dead.' He came back to the desk and stood opposite from me again. 'There is a certainty in death. These creatures . . .' he looked around the room at his mangy treasures, 'will never surprise me or trouble me. I cannot say the same of your brother.'

'So you know where he is!'

'I do not. However, recently, I forwarded a message from Joseph Peck to your grandmother.' The Beetle pushed his specs up to the bridge of his nose.

My heart started up under my bodice. 'What did he say?'

'I did not read it.' The Beetle frowned. 'Two weeks ago a woman knocked on my door and pressed a letter into my hands. It was sealed and addressed to Lady Ginger. I recognised your brother's script.'

'Why didn't you bring it to me?'

'Because the letter was meant for your grandmother.' He sounded like a school master explaining a simple fact to a very dull child.

'This woman, did she say anything?'

'No. She turned and walked away without uttering a word.'

'And you didn't even think to mention this to me!'

Telferman raised an eyebrow. 'As you have not responded to my messages – any of them – there has not been an opportunity.' He swallowed and his prominent Adam's apple made his collar ride up his neck. 'You have clearly been . . . occupied. I am telling you now. Besides, it relates to the matter of importance I mentioned earlier this morning. Last week the woman's mutilated body was fished from the Thames.'

'What do you mean – mutilated?'

'She had been tortured, Katharine. Her body had been ripped apart. It was most singular.'

The hairs rose on the back of my neck. I would have put it down to a draught in the room if it hadn't been hot as a glass house gloryhole in there.

'Singular? What's that supposed to mean?'

The Beetle flicked at the edge of a ledger. 'The newspaper report did not go into detail – and it is little wonder – but I have since learned more and . . .' He faltered, clearly unwilling to say any more.

'And?'

He didn't answer.

'Tell me.'

'You do not need to know the detail.'

'Tell me. It's an order.'

Telferman cleared his throat. 'The woman's tongue had been cut from her mouth and forced into … a part of her body. Her left breast was found crushed into her mouth. There is more. Do you wish me to continue?'

I shook my head. I wiped my palm round the back of my neck. 'But how do you know she was the one who gave you the letter?'

'After I read the reports in *The Illustrated London News* I made discreet enquiries among the lightermen who found her. I am satisfied that the woman taken from the river and the woman at my door were one and the same.' He opened a drawer to the left of his desk, dropped the keys inside and took out another book. 'There cannot be many redheaded women in Limehouse who stand over six feet tall.' He closed the drawer. 'Now, I believe we have kept Mr Fratelli waiting outside in the hall for longer than is proper.'

As if he'd planned it, the mantle clock cleared its throat and chimed twelve times.

'Do I have your assent to the interests we discussed earlier?'

'You mean Madlock, Selzman, Skimple and Mother Baxter's place?'

The Beetle nodded. 'They are the most pressing matters. You will remember Captain Houtman too. The appointment is set. There is more here requiring your attention.' He held the book out to me. 'I have listed every trade, every arrival, every agreement and every debt agreed in your name since our last meeting.' He paused. 'You will need this information when you offer your parable at the Barons' Aestas Court.'

I looked at the black cover of the book in his hand. It minded me of the ledgerstone closing slowly over Danny's howl at Great Bartholomew's. I snatched it from him and thrust it into my bag.

'Aestas?' I recognised the word from Kite's note, but I didn't know its meaning.

Telferman nodded. 'Summer. The summer meeting of the Barons. You will be summoned in the usual way in the first days of August. You must be ready.'

He came round the desk to open the door. Out in the hall-way Lucca stood up from the boot bench where he'd been waiting. The Beetle held the door wider. I took up my straw bonnet and hooked my bag over my arm.

'I'll deal with it. And I'll deal with this Houtman too. Don't worry, I haven't forgotten – sunrise tomorrow at Shad-well New Basin. I'll be there. You will write to her, to my grandmother, today – it's an order. Ask her about Joey – ask her where he is.'

I thought about Kite's note and that locket full of Danny's hair.

'How long will your letter take to reach her?'

'I cannot tell you.' The Beetle made a sweeping motion with his hand. He wanted me gone.

I clapped the bonnet to my head and tied the ribbons to-gether. 'Can't or won't? Is that part of the contract too?'

'I can say only this: I will contact your grandmother on

your behalf. I believe it would be judicious to do so. Whether she will reply . . .' He paused and shook his head. 'Whether she will be *able* to reply, that is a matter for a higher authority than even you, Lady Linnet.'

Chapter Five

'Well?' Lucca pulled the brim of his straw hat down and pushed up his collar as a couple of sailor boys stumbled towards us. When people caught sight of his scars they didn't, of a general rule, stint at allowing themselves the luxury of taking an eyeful. The pains Lucca took to shield his looks always made me sad for him, but I felt it most keenly today when my dress stuck so close to my flesh it was like the cotton had been coated in honey.

Despite the hour, I could smell rough liquor as they pushed past. For the past three weeks the streets of Limehouse had been filled with shipmates kicking their heels. There wasn't enough wind to fill a thimble so the clippers couldn't put out. Only steam ships like the one coming into the basin tomorrow could move about on the river.

'What did Telferman say?' Lucca took my arm and shepherded me past an old man slumped against the wall.

'Pity me, miss.' The words were little more than a whisper as if the speaker had given up hope of ever being heard. I looked back. The man was dressed in rags that might once have been fine gear. The material of his breeches on the left side was knotted in a greasy ball that swung just above the place where his knee should have been. A wooden crutch was propped against the bricks.

I opened my bag and took out my purse.

'Here.' I pushed a couple of coins, couters, into his grimy palm. Then I closed his fingers up tight. 'Get yourself something to eat. You got a place?'

The man shook his head. I dug into my purse again. 'Take this too. It'll buy a bed for a month at least.' Confused, he stared at the coins and then at me. I could see lice moving in his beard.

'Why, Miss?'

That was a question, wasn't it? I wanted to make Paradise a better place and I had enough chink in my purse to give him three times the amount I'd pressed into his hand. It was dirty money, though – it came to me through all the trades in the Beetle's ledgers. Passing it on made me feel better about the way I earned it.

'Just hide it away now, for safety's sake, and get yourself off the street.'

The old man gazed up at me, then he peered at the coins again. He thrust them into the folds of his tatty coat. As he scrabbled in the rags, the stench of his body frowsed around us. I would have covered my nose if it hadn't been an indignity. He roused himself, took up his crutch and stalked away, moving faster on one leg and a stick than you might have thought possible. As I watched him go he minded me of one of them soot-stained pigeons with broken feet.

Lucca sighed. 'That was a kindness, but it won't help, Fannella. He'll be heading for the nearest stand-up. Those coins won't buy him shelter or meat.'

I knew he was right, but I didn't want to hear it. I started off up the street again.

'The money was heavy in my purse. I won't miss it. If

it buys that poor sod an hour of pleasure then it was well spent.'

'Is that what you think about Nancy's den?' Lucca's voice behind me was tight. He hadn't said as much, but I could smell disappointment rolling off him in the way you get the tang of old liquor off a lusher.

I whipped round, shielding my eyes against the sunlight slanting off the windows of the warehouse opposite. The broad brim of the hat shadowed most of his face, but I didn't need to see him clear to know that just now his lips were knotted up tighter than a cat's arse.

'What's that supposed to mean?'

'You know very well, Kitty. You . . . you won't go again, will you? It's important.'

'I gave you my word yesterday, didn't I?'

It was true. In the cab on the way back to The Palace, I'd had another lecture. At the end of it Lucca had asked me to promise him that I wouldn't go to Nancy's place again. He was most insistent about it. He'd dug a little silver cross from his pocket and asked me to swear on it. The cross was a gift from his mother, he'd said.

'Don't you trust me, Lucca?'

I caught that guarded look again. Since I woke in his rooms yesterday there was something in his manner that I couldn't rightly put a name to. Guilt might have been the word, or maybe it was closer to sorrow? I loosened the strings of my bonnet and pushed it back from my head to get a better look at him.

'You all right?'

'*Sì*. Of course. It's *you* I worry for, Fannella.'

'Well, you don't have to. I swore on your old mother's cross, didn't I?'

He swallowed. 'Your grandmother. Did Telferman tell you where she is?'

I shook my head. 'He's not allowed to – it's legally binding. He's going to write to her for me – and he's had word from Joey.'

Lucca's eye widened. 'He knows where Joseph is?'

'No – that's the point.' A coster boy pushing a trolley loaded with cabbages trundled between us and we stepped apart. 'He passed a message on to her, a message from Joey, but Telferman says the woman who put it into his hands was fished from the Thames a fortnight back. He said there was no mistaking her. And it was no accident, she was murdered.'

I didn't tell Lucca the details. The thought of poor Red, how they found her, made my lights shrivel.

'*Il buio lo segue.*' Lucca crossed himself. We flattened up against the wall now as a brewery dray rumbled past. The flanks of the horses were foamy sweat. When it was clear we clipped off again. My bonnet bumped on my shoulders as we jostled through the sticky yapping crowd.

'What was that you said, just then?'

Lucca glanced at me. 'Your brother is not . . . not a lucky man. He brings trouble, even when he is not around. Do you think your grandmother will tell you what you want to know – about Joseph, I mean?'

'From what Telferman said, I'm not sure if she's in a state to tell night from day. But she's the only chance I've got. I don't know what else to do.' I bit my lip. The skin was still cracked and flaking from the fever and the opium.

'Even if she does know where Joey is, what then? I can't just hand him over. If I can find out why Kite wants him so bad, that might be a start? Perhaps she can shine a light there and then ... then ...'

'And then what, Fannella?' Lucca prompted quietly. It was a good question.

I stopped walking and faced him straight. 'I'm scared. You're the only person I'd admit that to. I'm not frightened for myself, not exactly, but for all this ...'

I looked at the street around us, at the people going about their business. Kite's note threatened those close to me, but it went further than that.

'Christ knows this place is poorly named, but if I fail ... if someone, another Baron I mean, takes Paradise off me ...'

The thought of them all, and what I knew they were capable of, made my throat close up tight as a drawstring pouch as if to stop the words coming. I loosened another button in the lace at my collar, pulled a 'kerchief from a pocket in my skirt and swiped at my neck. I changed the subject.

'Is the heat like this back home, in Naples I mean? If it is, I don't know how a person could bear it.' Lucca didn't answer. He pulled off his own straw hat and started to fiddle with the brim. It was a habit of his when he was worried about something.

'What is it?'

The circle of straw turned between his fingers. 'I have ... You need to ... You need to be very careful, Fannella. You mustn't go about alone. Even Lady Ginger never went anywhere without protection. Your position ... it's dangerous.'

'I know that. Tan Seng's lectured me enough. He's found

someone to walk me on a regular basis, like poor Amit used to. God rest him.'

'That is good to hear.' Lucca nodded. 'Very good.'

'I still need you with me, though.' I took his arm. 'You're good at reading people, getting the measure of them. You're better than me most times. Point of fact, I want you to come with me to a meeting. It's important.'

'When?' Lucca started turning his bleedin' hat again. Round and round it went.

'Tomorrow – early. There's a boat coming into Shadwell New Basin. Gin racket. Another dirty trade for Paradise.'

Chapter Six

The great paddle wheel rose over the side of the quay like an unblinking eye. It must have been fifteen foot across. I could see weed and slime caught between the slats. The tide was coming in fast now. The black metal hull of the *Gouden Kalf* clanged against the stones as another barrel was rolled from the deck and down the swaying gangway to join the stack rising just behind us.

Tell truth, the rising of the paddle made me feel noxious. Every time I caught a glimpse of the scummy water between the quay and the boat, the movement made my belly slip about in time with the swell. I had to look away sharp as another barrel bumped down to the quay.

I was grateful that Lucca was counting them off. It gave me the chance to be watchful. Telferman was right; it was important for me to be here this morning. This was a new trade and I needed to get the measure of it.

I already had the measure of Captain Houtman.

I watched him strut along the quay. His neck spread thick and red above the crumpled collar of his blue jacket and sunlight caught on the stray fair hairs clinging to the back of his bald head. He turned as if he'd felt me staring at him.

The captain's blue eyes crinkled up at the corners, but there was no warmth in them. There was something else there, mind. I folded my arms conscious that it wasn't my face that interested him. I shifted my right arm to shield my eyes against the lights sparking off the water, but I kept my left arm crossed firm over my bodice.

It was early morning at Shadwell New Basin, but the sun was already high. Apart from Houtman's shipmates and a couple of big lascar boys Telferman had sent along for the job, the quay was unusually quiet. We wouldn't have trouble from the customs – they looked in another direction when one of my trades came in. I paid them well for the benefit of a blind eye.

I heard one of the lascars mutter something to his mate as the pair of them hefted the last barrel into place. There was silence for a moment and then the two of them started to chat fast and foreign.

Houtman dragged his eyes from the pearl buttons on my frock and stared at the lads on the quay. He hadn't sullied his vision by bothering to acknowledge them yet. Of an instant, he frowned and jangled the coins in his pockets.

I knew his type – he didn't like dealing with women and he didn't like dealing with men he considered to be little more than animals. When he caught sight of Lucca's scars – and he'd taken a good bold eyeful like he was enjoying a penny curiosity – his lips had twisted into a sneer.

I made up my mind there and then. Even if the captain's gin was cheaper than horse piss I wouldn't deal with him beyond what was already agreed. I didn't like the smack of this arrangement, even if there was a fat profit in it.

Houtman barked out an order in Dutch. Another man, tall and fair where his captain was bald as a turkey cock, appeared up top with a ledger in his hands. He swayed down the gangway to where we was all standing. Houtman coughed out something in his lingo, pulled his hands from his pockets and took the ledger from his mate. The fair man nodded and went back up onto the boat, disappearing again beyond the deck rail. All I could see up there now was the smoking funnel stack.

Houtman licked a finger and flicked through the pages until he found what he was looking for. He held it out to me and pointed to an entry halfway down.

Twintig vaten jenever

He grinned wide, a big gold tooth glinting in the front of his mouth. He snapped the ledger shut, nodded at the stack of barrels on the lip of the quay and held up his hands, the thick fingers stretched apart. He repeated the gesture, spat into his palm and held out his hand.

'*Twintig.*'

I stared at the ball of yellow spittle. I didn't want it on my skin. After a moment Lucca nudged me. I turned, but now he was looking back at the lascars. They were still gabbling away together, the words peppering the air like gunshot. Houtman slid a glance at the pair of them, then he thrust his hand forward so it was almost under my chin. It felt like a threat, not an understanding.

'*Zoals overeengekomen.*' His voice was as flat and cold as his eyes.

I shook his sticky hand once, letting it drop almost as soon as I touched it. He tucked the ledger under his arm and jerked his head at the barrels.

'*Het is van goede kwaliteit.*'

I reached into the folds of my skirt and drew out a leather pouch. He snatched it from me and emptied the chink into his hand. When he'd counted it out and was satisfied I'd played him fair he pushed the coins into the pocket of his striped breeches. Then, without another word, he tossed the pouch into the water, turned his back on me and swaggered down the quay to the springing gangway.

He called out something and the fair-headed deck hand appeared above us again with another cask in his hands. This one was smaller than the ones on the quay. Houtman went back up on board to take it. He said something to his ship-mate then turned to me, raising the cask between his hands.

'A gift for you, to mark our new arrangement.' His English came perfect now. There was something familiar in the tone of it as he went on. 'I will place it with the others, yes? But remember – this is yours.'

He came down the gangway with the cask and pushed past Lucca, moving towards the stack. Houtman winked at me. 'It is special . . .' I didn't catch the end of what he said as the bellow of the ship's horn ripped through the air. It came so sudden and so loud that me and Lucca bent forward and covered our ears.

The funnel belched out a cloud of steam as that bleedin' horn went off three times, each blast louder than the first. I swear I could feel the stones shifting underfoot. As the last note faded I heard Houtman laughing.

'To mark our agreement. I make my lady sing for you.'

I coughed up a lungful of soot and straightened up. There was a rumbling sound from behind. I swung about, my eyes smarting. Through the billowing black smoke I saw a couple of the gin barrels judder and topple slowly from the stack. There was a yelp and then a splash as something tumbled into the gap between the *Gouden Kalf* and the quay.

At first I thought one of the barrels had gone over, but of an instant the yell became a wail of terror and then a scream, broken apart by spluttering gasps for air. One of the lascars had lost his footing. He'd gone over the edge and now he was thrashing about in the water between that paddle wheel and the stones. Houtman was crouched on the quayside reaching down.

I ran across and knelt beside him. We were joined by the other lad who stood behind me calling out over and over. At first I couldn't see anything down there on account of the smoke and the shadow, then a dark head and an arm broke through the scum and the foam. The fallen lascar choked as he tried to fill his lungs and the screaming came again. Houtman stood up and called to his shipmate on deck.

The other boy fell to his knees and stretched down over the stone lip, trying to catch his friend, but we were far too high and it was too dangerous. Shadwell New Basin was the only dock deep enough to take the metal hull of the *Gouden Kalf*. Now that big black boat was rising on the incoming tide, every second wave pushing her up against the slimy grey sides with a dismal clang.

'Khunni!'

The boy beside me yelled again and leaned further out. I caught the back of his belt to stop him from toppling over to join his friend.

There was a yell from the boat and a coil of rope landed

with a slap on the stones a dozen foot off. Lucca took it up and began to unravel it. If we could dandle it over the edge the boy could catch hold and we could pull him free. Houtman watched us, all the while jangling them bleedin' coins in his pocket.

Another wave rolled in and the *Gouden Kalf* rode higher, her riveted sides tolling against the quay like a cracked bell. I couldn't see the lad in the water, and now I couldn't hear him. I gripped the edge of the stones and leaned out further. There was something caught up in the paddle, something that wasn't weed. The boy beside me scrambled to his feet and made to pull off his shirt, but Lucca held him firmly by the shoulders. He shook his head.

Houtman shrugged and headed back to the gangway.

The lascar covered his face with his hands. He kept on repeating his friend's name like it might bring him back. I stared down at the paddle. I could see Khunni now. His body was trapped between the slats, his head below the level of the water.

God forgive me, I'd noted him earlier. He was wearing nothing on top except a loose patterned waistcoat. I can't deny I didn't take in the way the muscles moved under his smooth, dark skin. He had a tattoo that curled round his wrist. It was a snake, finely done, if you got close. And I did at one point when he stepped past me with one of the barrels stacked on his shoulder.

The *Gouden Kalf* groaned as a wave carried her away from the quay for a moment. The paddle wheel shifted with the movement and a horrible scraping sound echoed off the stones. As I watched, the lascar boy's broken body came free.

'Khunni!' I felt a hand on my arm. The other lad was staring wildly at me. His grip tightened, the fingers digging into my flesh.

'Khunni! Lady!'

I shook my head.

'It's no good. I'm sorry. He's gone.' I covered the boy's hand with mine. 'Khunni's gone.'

I don't know if he understood. He let go, backed away and then he span round and took off, running like the devil himself was on his tail. I stared down into the water. Now the yellow scum foaming against the quay stones was flecked with red.

The cab rocked to a halt at the end of the passage. It was just past six, but the day already felt as if it had lasted for a week. I stared down at the little cask Houtman had given me to 'mark our new arrangement'. It was unlucky. I didn't care if it was filled with liquid gold, I didn't want the bleedin' thing. As far as I was concerned, after this morning, an arrangement with Captain Houtman would always be stained with that poor lascar's blood.

It had been a bad business. Me and Lucca watched in silence as two of Houtman's men dragged the boy's body from the water with a hooked pole. He was broken, his face a mess of blood and bone, his arms unnaturally twisted. They fell limp from his shoulders as if they'd been pulled from the sockets. Part of the tattoo that wound round his wrist was missing where the flesh had been scraped from his body by the stones of the quay.

Lucca had covered the dead boy with a bit of sail cloth.

We hadn't said much in the cab on the way back from the basin. Lucca kept his face turned to the street, his forehead resting on the glass.

I pulled at his sleeve. 'Will you come back to The Palace with me?'

He shook his head. 'There are things I have to do.'

A rap came from above. The slat beneath the cabman's perch fell open.

'Two bob, as agreed.'

I tilted my head to see him through the gap. 'Give us a moment, will you?'

The cabman growled. 'Time's money, Lady.'

I bristled up. 'Well, I can't see anyone else out there looking for a ride at this hour, can you? There's thruppence more if you wait until we're done.'

He grunted by way of a reply and the slat slammed shut.

I reckoned Lucca had taken against Houtman quicker than I could down a gin rinser, but I wanted to hear it.

'What did you make of him, the captain?'

Lucca pushed his long hair back from his face. 'I didn't trust him or his boat, there was something ... a bad feeling, about it. The accident with the boy ...' He shook his head. 'There was nothing we could do, but all the same ...' He stared at the cask in my lap. 'No, I would not deal with Captain Houtman again, Fannella. It did not feel ... fortunate. You should ask Telferman where the trade came from.'

I nodded. 'I'll do that next time I see him. Which won't be long.' I hoped I was right about that.

The cab jerked as the horse fretted in the harness. Even

though it was early the air was already thick as a stew. I dabbed my throat with a 'kerchief soaked in lavender water. Grey soot stained the cotton. A blow fly fizzed about between us. I batted it away with the 'kerchief. There was something in Lucca's manner that wasn't natural. It wasn't just the dead boy. He'd been gloomy as a two bob mute since I woke in his rooms and I could tell he was stirring something round in his head just now. He didn't trust me not to go back to Nancy's – that was the meat of it, I was sure.

I wasn't going to give him the chance to hawk it up again.

'These things you have to do today, Lucca. Are you going to the workshops at The Carnival? I hear from Telferman that Fitzy and Jesmond are fighting like a pair of rats in a barrel.'

He scratched at some paint under his nails. 'You need to speak to them, Fannella. You have not been . . .' He faltered.

'Haven't been what? Go on.'

'You haven't been . . . present enough. You need to be seen.'

I folded the 'kerchief neatly and stuffed it into my sleeve. 'I've got quite a lot of things on my plate, or haven't you noticed?'

A muscle worked in Lucca's jaw as if he was about to say something, but he looked away.

'*Fa così caldo . . .*' He wiped the sweat from his neck with the flat of his hand. 'I never thought I'd say that about London. But then again there are a lot of things I never thought I'd have to say.'

I knew where this was going. I reached for the leather door strap, but Lucca caught my face between his fingers and turned it gently towards him. In the privacy of the carriage he'd loosened a button at the neck of his shirt and I could see the olive skin of his collar bone. On the right side the scars on his face spread in a mottled lattice down over his neck and shoulder.

'She chose you as her successor for a reason, Fannella. You are The Lady now, for good or ill.'

Here it came, another sermon. I shifted on the bench seat to stand up and the cab swayed on its springs.

'I'm going now. I'll pay him up top to take you to wherever it is you're off to at this hour.'

Of an instant, a thought caught me. 'You've got a fancy, haven't you, Lucca Fratelli? That's why you've been acting so odd.'

In the halls we didn't much look into people's arrangements. Like I said, I wasn't Lucca's type, but I'd be happy for him if he'd found a man who was. Christ knows he deserved it. Surely he knew that by now? The thought of him not feeling he could tell me cut deep. I reached for his hand.

'Don't you think I'd be pleased for you? Is that what you've been knotting yourself up about?'

He gripped tight. 'You need your wits about you, Kitty. Do not go to those places again. Promise me – keep yourself safe and your mind sharp. Paradise needs you; The Carnival needs you. Things are falling apart, there's talk.'

Falling apart.

I knew it myself. I'd let things slide, but I didn't want to hear it said aloud, especially not from Lucca. I tried to pull back, but he wouldn't let go. I flared up. 'You're worried that you'll be out on your ear – you and all the others in the workshops and the halls have been yapping behind my back, have

69

you? You reckon you'll be taking your paints to a new stage, if I don't straighten out, is that it, Lucca?'

He stared at me. That bleedin' fly started battering its fat body against the window.

'You need to be sharp. You need your wits about you. *Sì* – I do think you will need to – how did you say it? – "straighten out". And you will have to do it without me. It's what I've been trying to tell you, Fannella.'

Despite the heat pressing close in that tight space, I shivered. When Nanny Peck – the little round Irish hen I'd thought to be my true grandmother for all them years – had one of her presentiments she used to say a corpse tongue was licking her neck. I had the feel of it now.

'What do you mean "without" you?'

I watched a bead of sweat slip down the good side of Lucca's face.

'I have had word from my sister. Our mother is dying.'

Chapter Seven

I didn't actually believe it, not until he was standing there in the hallway of The Palace in a clean white shirt with a big scuffed leather bag slung over his shoulder. I couldn't ask Lucca not to go – it was his mother. All the same, it happened so fast. He'd rattled off back to his lodge house in that cab yesterday morning and now, a day later, he was saying good-bye.

I'd had a sleepless night to digest what it meant, but the truth hadn't sunk in until now. 'You'll write then – as soon as you get there?' I fiddled with the knot of the shawl I'd tied hastily round my shoulders when Tan Seng came to fetch me. It was so early I was still in my nightgown. My bare feet were sticky on the marble tiles.

Lucca nodded. 'Of course.'

'Only, I need to know you're . . .' I needed to know he was coming back as soon as possible, that's what I wanted to say, but it didn't seem quite decent under the circumstances.

I tried again. 'Do you know how long you . . . how long it might . . .?' That didn't come out right, neither. He shook his head and let the bag slump from his shoulder to the floor. 'Gia says it cannot be long. Our mother has been calling my name in her sleep.' He delved into the pocket of his breeches and took out a fold of paper.

'This is the letter.'

I opened it up. I couldn't make out a word of the close-packed script on account of it not being English, but I recognised the name at the end.

'Gia writes neat like you.' I handed it back. He folded it over and pushed it into his pocket again.

'No, Fannella. Gia cannot write. Someone must have written this for her. Perhaps the priest – that would be the way.'

'Gia's your sister?'

'*Sì* – the youngest of us. She still lives in the village with my mother.'

'And your father – what about him?'

'He is dead.' There was nothing in those words to let slip how he felt about that, although from what little I knew of Lucca's past back home there was no love there. I wondered about his mother. He took a step towards me.

'I have to go.'

'I know – the boat train leaves at eight.' I tried to smile, but my eyes began to glass up. I dipped my head to let him hold me close and smelt the familiar sharpness of turps and paint. Of an instant, I unhooked my fingers and wrapped my arms tight around him, burrowing my face into the folds of his shirt.

A great ball of sorrow was rolling itself around deep inside me and growing at every turn. In a moment it would come flooding out. I didn't want Lucca to go, but it wasn't right to stop him. I took a breath and caught the smell of his skin beneath the paint. It was clean and warm and it nearly set me off.

I swallowed hard. 'First Joey and now you. I'll say something for my brother, he's bleedin' good at disappearing.

I've a mind to take him on as an assistant to Swami Jonah – if he ever turns up again.' It came out feeble. Lucca knew. He stroked my hair and tried to speak light.

'Swami Jonah doesn't need an assistant. The only magic he needs to improve his act is someone to make the bottle disappear from his hands before he goes on each night. Listen to me, Fannella. Joey is always ... *astuta*.' He paused. 'I think you would say *resourceful*.'

I glanced up at something in his voice. He was staring over my shoulder.

He frowned. 'I never realised it before, but I was wrong about the painting you found in the rooms your grandmother closed away. I once said the boy had something of you in his face, but I was wrong. It is your brother he most resembles.'

I wiped my eyes, grateful for the distraction, and turned to look at the painting. The fine young gent I'd dusted off and hung in the hallway on account of the blue of his coat had fair hair and a pointed face. His large dark eyes were locked onto something beyond the frame and his left hand emerged from a flutter of lace to gesture, in a boneless sort of way, at a grand stone house set among trees painted a distance behind.

I turned back to Lucca. He was still staring at the picture – the furrow between his eyes pulling at the bad side of his forehead so an odd ridge rippled up to his hairline. He caught me looking and flicked a couple of dark strands forward. It was too late. Despite the scars, I'd seen something unexpected in his expression.

'What does ... what was it you said – *astuta* – really mean? You said I'd say Joey was resourceful, but what would *you* say?'

Lucca shook his head. 'Joseph can look after himself. He is ... cunning, Fannella, that's what I'd say. Never forget that, for all that he is your brother.'

I felt myself bridle up on Joey's behalf, even though I knew the truth of what Lucca was saying.

'I thought he was your friend from a long way back!'

'*Sì* – but he is ...' Lucca broke off as the faint chimes of the painted china clock in the upstairs parlour sounded six times.

'The cabman is waiting at the end of Salmon Lane. I have to leave, Fannella.' He pulled me into a hug. 'You must talk to her – to Peggy, I mean. She needs you. And besides, while I am away I do not want to think of you alone.'

'I won't be. I've got Tan Seng and Lok here at The Palace, and out there ...' My voice was muffled in cotton as I nodded towards the double doors. 'I've got the whole of Paradise to keep me occupied. I won't be wanting for company.'

'That's what I'm worried about, Fannella, some of the company you've been keeping ...'

I drew back, swiping roughly at my damp cheeks. 'You've made your point, Lucca. I won't go back to Nancy's place.'

Even though it was already bright outside, the hallway was dim. Lucca stared at me, his single eye dark as porter. I'd made a promise to him and I meant it, but that was before I knew he was abandoning me. A crooked chink in my mind showed a let out. The night my grandmother delivered me to the Barons she'd given me a bundle of opium sticks and, God forgive me, I'd used them, just like she knew I would. It was where I'd got a taste for the stuff. There were at least six black sticks left in the drawer of the desk in my office upstairs and, if needs be, there was always a place ...

'You must go to her, Fannella.'

Just for a moment I thought he meant Nancy. I blinked, guilty, as he carried on.

'Peggy, I mean. She needs you and you need her. Take her with you when you visit Edie Strong's mother.' He watched me for a moment. 'You will go, won't you? Every week someone threads white flowers into the wreckage of the doorway at The Gaudy. I believe a mother would do that for her lost child.'

I looked away. I knew he was right. I should have visited little Edie's mother, Brigid, weeks back to pay my respects to her girl and her grief.

Lucca carried on. 'You made a promise to everyone in the halls. You once called them your family, remember? You must go. Sometimes water is thicker than blood, Fannella.'

'That why you're leaving me, then?' I couldn't stop myself. The words rattled out hard and angry. He took my hand.

'I have to go. She is my mother – but you will be here.' He moved my hand to his heart and smiled. 'You are my sister, Fannella. Always remember that.'

I held tight. Lucca Fratelli was a true brother to me. Wherever Joey went he cast a deep shadow. I was relying on my grandmother to send some light into that darkness, but I was also relying on Lucca to be with me when it showed up whatever was hiding there.

'We won't be apart for long.' Lucca stroked the back of my hand. 'Gia says she ... our mother is very weak. I must be there when ...'

He stopped and I knew he couldn't follow that thought to the end. Instead he took a breath and changed tack.

'And there is Amit's brother too – you owe him that courtesy. Peggy will know what to say.'

I lit up again. 'Are you saying I won't?'

He sighed. 'Peggy is a gentle soul and just recently you ... something in you has ...' He faltered again and squeezed my hand.

'It is not good to be alone, Fannella. Do you not think I know this better than most? Go to Peggy. Promise me. You need a friend.'

I tried to give a clever answer, only nothing came out. I just blinked hard. Lucca bent down and untied the leather strap of his bag. He took out a small package wrapped in brilliant scarlet cloth and held it out to me.

'Here, I want you to have this, for my sake. I don't want to think of you ... unprotected.' I took it and was surprised at the weight of such a small thing. There was something hard rolled up in there.

'If you really thought that, you wouldn't leave me.' Again I couldn't stop myself. I tried to choke back a sob, but the tears came now.

He pulled me towards him once more and brushed the top of my head with a kiss. Then he reached down for his bag, swung it back over his shoulder, turned and walked to the wide double doors leading out to the street. Tan Seng, who'd appeared from below stairs as if I'd summoned him for the task, shuffled across the chequered floor, bowed and pulled one of the doors back. Sunlight cut across the hallway. Little specks of dust and soot quivered in the haze around Lucca's head and shoulders as he stepped outside. I heard the scrape of his shoes on stone and I darted across the marble tiles and out through the door.

He was already moving off down the passage. I didn't care that my feet were bare; that all I was wearing was a thin cotton nightgown and Nanny Peck's old shawl. I ran down the steps to the cobbles.

'You will come back, won't you? You promise me, Lucca!'

If he answered I didn't catch it, instead he raised a hand in a sort of backward salute. I watched until he turned the corner at the end and disappeared without looking back. I pulled the shawl tight, turned and looked up at the soot-stained walls of The Palace.

Four rows of tall, narrow windows glinted in the sharp morning sunlight. There were cracks in the brickwork and places where the black paint on the woodwork and the iron rail of the steps was buckled and peeling. I'd never seen it all so clear before. Tan Seng stood in the half-open door at the top of the broad stone steps. He bowed once and turned back into the shadowed hallway.

I'd never felt so alone.

Tan Seng brought the tray to the desk. I watched as he poured a thin golden stream from the pot into the cup, but shook my head when he took up the jug. I'd grown to like the odd smoked flavour of the tea the brothers served – just lately I'd found it was better, more refreshing you might say, without the milk. I took my cha like a lady now.

He bowed and stepped back, silent as a cat. His slippered feet never made a sound on the boards of The Palace. I still hadn't quite got used to the way he appeared in a room like a pantomime devil sprung up from a stage trap, only without the cracks and the sparks. I reckoned he could teach Swami Jonah a few lessons.

I reached for the cup. 'Have there been any messages for me? Something from Telferman?'

Tan Seng shook his head. Wherever my grandmother was hiding her cankered body, it clearly took a time to get a message to her and fetch one back again. It was three days now since I'd asked the Beetle to write. The tea scalded my tongue and I put the cup down sharp.

'It is not to your liking, Lady?'

'No. It's hot. The way I like it.' I tried to smile, but it didn't come natural. 'I'll be working here for the rest of the evening. Could you bring me something to eat later – nothing fancy, bread and cheese'll do.'

Tan Seng bowed again and turned to the door. A thin grey plait, the hair still dark at the bottom, emerged from the base of his black silk cap. It hung down the back of his tunic almost reaching his knees.

Of an instant, a thought came. What if Telferman wasn't the only one who knew where my grandmother had taken herself?

'Wait.' He turned back to me, his oval face a perfect blank. I couldn't put an age to him. Unlike his tiny, wiry brother Lok, Tan Seng's skin was smooth and unlined like he'd never tried an expression on for size. It was only the crimped skin of his hands that told he wasn't in the flush.

'Lady?'

I took a sip of the tea and wondered what to say. I wanted

78

to ask him how he knew where I was that night a week back when he'd told Lucca where to find me, but I wasn't sure how to put it without causing offence. Tan Seng and Lok had been good to me since I'd inherited my grandmother's house along with everything else, them included, but I wasn't sure how I felt about the fact he knew so much about my business. Of occasion I still wondered if the brothers served more than one mistress.

They are the most honourable men in Paradise. They are yours entirely and would give their lives for you. You will do well to remember this, always.

That's what Telferman had told me once when I asked him straight, but I had the feeling that *entirely* wasn't the right word.

'You wish something?' Tan Seng folded his hands into his loose grey sleeves and waited.

'I . . . It's just . . .' I put the china cup on the saucer and twisted it about so the handle wouldn't catch against the stack of ledgers to the side of the desk. I didn't look at him direct.

'How did you know where I was the other night – when Lucca, Mr Fratelli, came for me? I didn't think . . .'

'It is not safe.'

I looked up. Tan Seng's face was his customary mask, but his black eyes locked onto mine. 'The Lady should not visit such places, even if they belong to her.'

That last was true enough. The books told me that Nancy turned a shining sovereign and there was never any trouble. Most of her trade was skirted, which is partly why I chose to go to that dimly lit cellar under Shambles Passage. She paid her tithe on the quarter and it was a fair sum.

79

'But I only went twice.'

Tan Seng blinked.

'All right – it might have been three.'

He blinked again. 'Six times then, but I took care. How did you know?'

'Because it is my business to know. The Lady must be protected. It is my duty.'

The lace at the open window shifted, but the air outside was warm and cut with smoke like a sooty version of the tea steaming in the cup in front of me. My blonde springy hair was pinned high on my head to keep me cool, but I could feel it damp and heavy on my scalp.

'Are you spying on me?' There, I said it. 'Are you doing it for her, for my grandmother?'

Tan Seng shook his head. The tip of that plait flicked behind him.

'Listen. I don't mind if you are. Not really. I just want to know if you're . . . well, let's just say it's better if we all know where we stand. You worked for her for a long time before me. If you know where she is . . .'

'No!'

He came forward so he was standing at the edge of the desk across from me. I sat back in surprise. I'd never heard Tan Seng raise his voice before.

'I work only for The Lady.'

He freed his hands from his sleeves and placed his right palm flat on the desk so the long nail on his first finger arched over the wood and onto the leather worktop to point at me. He tapped three times, folded his hands away, bowed and turned for the door. As he stepped out into the hall he spoke again.

'Always for The Lady.'

But which one? I thought as the door closed.

I pulled a ledger from the top of the stack, opened it at the page where I'd left a marker for the *Gouden Kalf* and struck a line through the name. It would be the first and the last time I traded with Captain Houtman.

When they were tested, six of the twenty barrels he'd shipped over from Rotterdam were watered, the gin so faint you could feed it to a baby with no consequence. His special gift in that little cask had turned out to be brandy just about fit to scrape paint off a door. I hadn't taken to the man, but I suppose I'd expected there to be what you might call a faith between thieves.

I thought about Houtman standing on the quay counting the barrels off the boat, smirking like a clergy at a soup mission. He must have thought I was greener than an unfurled lily when he shook on the trade. I remembered the way he ran his eyes over me. I slammed the ledger shut and pushed it back into the pile.

I stood up and went over to the mantle. The girl who stared back at me from the mirror had dark circles beneath her eyes. I looked like the girl in Lucca's drawing. I traced the outline of my face and my finger left a smear like a ghost of one of his sketches.

He'd likely be in France by now. The train to Dover then the boat to Calais took the best of the day. I closed my eyes and rested my forehead against the edge of the marble mantle, but it wasn't cooling. The heat had started at the beginning of June and it hadn't broken. Every day came hotter than the last – the stench and the closeness clung to the skin and wormed its way inside. It was as if London was smothered beneath the piss-streaked skirts of an old fish wife.

I went back to the desk and took up the book for The Carnival. Tomorrow I had a meeting arranged with Fitzy and Jesmond. If there was talk about me, like Lucca said, I wanted to hear it from them.

I sat down and tried to concentrate on the rows of names and numbers but nothing came right.

Nothing had seemed right since Lucca left this morning. The thought of not having him around was something like losing a limb. Years back there was a night at The Lamb when me and Peggy had fallen into conversation with an old deck hand who'd lost a leg in an accident with the anchor chain. Thing was, he told us, he could still feel an itch on the sole of his missing foot and he said, of occasion, his phantom knee gave him gyp. I reckoned there must have been a sort of comfort in that; in thinking his leg was still there.

Lucca said I should visit Edie's mother with Peg. The thought made my belly curdle. How could I face the mother of Danny Tewson's unborn child, let alone go widow sitting with her? A pain shot up across the right side of my head.

He was right, of course. I'd left it too long on both counts. There was Ram too, Amit's brother. The pair of them shared lodgings at Bell Wharf Stairs. They were set down in my books, listed as chattels under 'D'. Well, one of them was.

I took another thick ledger from the pile and flicked my thumb along the side, feeling the chafing of the pages as Paradise and everything in it fluttered under my hand.

I searched for 'S' and ran my finger down the column. When I came to Edie I bit my lip, took up a pen and ran a line through her name. Her mother was just above.

Brigid Strong, 3 Palmer's Rents – laundress.

I noted the address.

I pulled at the sticky neck of my calico blouse. Another pain jabbed above my left eye and I cupped my forehead in my hands. When I looked up again the room was split in two by a jagged crack that flickered at the edges. It was like looking into a shattered mirror. The curved back of the unforgiving couch set against the wall by the door appeared to be broken.

Tell truth, the first time it happened I thought I was about to be celestially reacquainted with Ma and Nanny Peck, but now I knew it would pass. The sparking line would wander lazily across my line of vision creasing up everything it touched. The headache that followed on after would last for hours.

I shut the ledger. My eyes slid down to the left. Six of the opium sticks my grandmother had given me were wrapped in a scrap of patterned silk hidden under a sheaf of papers in the bottom drawer of my desk. Lucca's package was there too.

I hadn't opened it. I didn't need to. I knew from the weight and the feel that his dainty pistol with the ivory handle was wrapped in the scarlet cloth. I kept it hidden there with the opium sticks. The locket with Danny's hair was in there too.

That drawer was full of darkness.

I ran my tongue against the back of my teeth. Just one to set me right before the pain set in. I could sleep through it then. I reached down and began to pull the drawer open, but Lucca's voice went off in my head.

Promise me.

It was like I'd been scalded. I bit down so hard I caught the tip of my tongue and tasted metal. I straightened myself and took up the cup instead. The tea was cold now, stewed and bitter. A scratching sound came from the open window. A small, scruffy dun-coloured bird was watching me from the sill. The sparrow cocked its head to one side and took off sharp. It minded me of Edie Strong.

I tried to swallow the tea.

Tomorrow.

I'd talk to Peggy tomorrow. My throat burned and acid filled my mouth.

Chapter Eight

Aubrey Jesmond ran his finger around the top of the glass. After a moment it began to sing out loud, the odd, keen pitch of it setting my teeth on edge. It did the trick, though.

'Are you listening to me, Jessie?' Fitzy thumped the table so hard the glass jumped. Jesmond darted a look at me. I knew what he was doing, but I didn't give him the benefit of a face on it. The pair of them hated each other. The only time the men who ran my two remaining halls came willingly within an oar's length of each other was when I called them together to talk trade.

We were sitting in Jesmond's office at The Carnival. It was neat and sparse – the walls new painted a shade of green that Nanny Peck might have picked out as bilious. You couldn't call The Carnival fine. It was too small and too much of an old-style drinking hall for that. But Jesmond was making it pay, just about. From my quizzing of the books Aubrey Jesmond was a safe pair of hands when it came to money.

But now the money was coming from just one hall and takings were down.

The window behind the desk was open to let some air into the room and to let the fug of paint out. It didn't make much difference, mind. It was hot and stale as a cookshop in there, mainly on account of the stench rising up from Fitzy's unwashed chequer cloth. Jesus! That suit must have walked over to greet him of a morning.

Outside in the hall someone was jangling a piano.

Jesmond stopped rimming the glass and brought a small hand up to his shiny domed head to pat the unnatural black strands that clung on over his ears back into place. He pleated up his currant-bun eyes and smiled, revealing a row of suspiciously white even teeth.

'Of course I was listening, Paddy.' He was the only person who ever used Fitzy's first name and he made it sound like an insult. 'Fact of the matter is that I was concentrating so very hard on what you were saying, I didn't even realise I was doing it.' His voice was smooth and plush as a velvet couch. I reckoned there was some Welsh tucked away in there. He spoke in a sing-song way like the chapel preachers who came up from the valleys to stand on London street corners. Nanny Peck always held it was an affront to decent Limehouse folk to have to listen to their Methodising.

Jesmond pushed the glass away and sat back, folding his arms. 'Go on then. I'm sure Miss Peck is as eager as I am to hear you out.'

Fitzy sidled a look at me. His watery eyes were almost lost beneath the straggle of his fading ginger brows, but I could read him clear enough. Now The Gaudy was little more than a hole in the ground and The Comet was closed for the foreseeable he was making a pitch for The Carnival. He missed being at the centre of things and he wanted Jesmond's chair.

He pushed a folded newspaper across the table. 'Times are changing. He ...' Fitzy nodded his big head at Jesmond, 'doesn't have the experience. Not like I do, so he doesn't. He couldn't pick a turd from a jerry. If you look here ...' he tapped the newspaper, 'you'll see what the punters want. It's at the back – I've marked the page.'

Jesmond smiled again. 'I've made a success of this place. You can't deny it. The books don't lie, Paddy, so they don't.' He mimicked Fitzy's broad Irish.

'You've only been here two years, Jessie. I had the running of The Gaudy for twenty!' Fitzy stood up abrupt and gripped the edge of the desk. A vein the width of a thumb pulsed in his forehead. He leaned forward, his shoulders massing on either side of his neck like a mountain range. I knew there was a time, years back, when he was a bare knuckler. My grandmother had called on his muscle when he was young and sharp.

These days Patrick Fitzpatrick was winded like a pair of knackered Whitechapel bellows. The foundry workers patched and mended the great bags they used to fire up their furnaces, but eventually the leather fell apart at the seams.

'At a time like this experience is what counts . . . ma'am.'

The last word caught in his mouth. He still couldn't believe I was sitting there giving the orders when less than a year back it had been the other way round.

I stared up at him. 'At a time like what?'

Fitzy planted his hands flat on the desk top. 'People are confused about the way of things and I can't say as I blame them. There's been too much change. There's been talk.' He stopped and glanced at Jesmond who was absorbed in the turning of a ring on his smallest finger.

This was the meat I wanted. I sat back. 'What do you mean by "talk"?'

The yellowed tache beneath Fitzy's nose bristled.

'Say your piece, Fitzpatrick. I want to hear about this "talk" out there.' I nodded at the door.

Fitzy breathed deep. 'They're not happy. They don't feel settled and they don't see there's much of a future here. If you want my opinion . . .' He faltered, uncertain whether to give it.

I drummed my fingers on the desk. 'Go on. I'm listening.'

Fitzy cleared his throat. I noted that his broad face was pink as a fresh-sliced gammon now.

'You haven't . . . been taking an interest here for a while, ma'am, but it's like this; without three halls to service, the hands in the workshops come and go as they please. The girls in the chorus fight like cats backstage and sometimes on it. Jessie's lost three turns in the last fortnight. They've moved west, gone to better establishments – places where they don't get bitten.' He stared at Jesmond who was still interested in that ring of his.

Fitzy started up again. 'The sailor act is bringing them in, for the time being, the punters like a bit of skin, but most of the regulars we're holding onto wouldn't find another home.' He snorted. 'Look at McCarthy, he's soused as a herring three nights out of four these days.'

I didn't move, despite a sudden powerful waft of old cigar and tooth rot. 'If you're telling me Swami Jonah likes a drink, it's old news. A year back he sent me to The Lamb with a jug after the act most nights.'

Fitzy huffed. 'Well, now he likes to take a jugful before as well, so he does.' He shook his head. 'A magician needs a straight pair of hands. If I were in Jessie's place here at The

Carnival I'd tell McCarthy to give the Indian blades a rest. What we need is a bit of order – like the old days. And we need to give the punters something fresh to chew on. If I had the full running of this place I'd give Netta a solo. She's itching for it, and not just on account of the fleas.' Out of the corner of my eye, I saw Jesmond stop turning his ring. He flicked a look at Fitzy who was finally coming to his main point.

'As I see it, ma'am, Jessie here can count, but he can't keep control. Now, if I was to take on the overall running of The Carnival and The Comet, and Jessie reported direct to me . . .'

As Fitzy continued to lay out his stall I stared down at his stubby, yellow-stained fingers splayed out on the desk. I couldn't help thinking of the way he used to paw at Peggy. He wasn't gentle with it, neither. Many's the time I had to help her hide the bruises with paint from Mrs Conway's box. If her Danny had ever found—

'No!' It came out loud. I brought my fingers to my lips. I didn't want Danny Tewson in my head just then. Fitzy halted mid-sentence and then he sat down. The room was silent apart from the sound of his breathing – the air whistled as it fought through the thicket in his nostrils. Jesmond grinned. He thought he'd won.

I didn't like Fitzy, but he had his uses. He knew how to run a hall and how to keep the punters and the acts in line.

I nodded at the jug of water. 'Pour me a drink.'

Jesmond handed me a glass and lifted the jug. I wondered how he felt about taking orders from me. He was so silky and careful in his manner I reckoned I'd never really know. I took a sip of water.

'A bit of order – that's what you said, isn't it, Fitzpatrick?'

He grunted.

'I didn't quite catch that.'

He threw a filthy look at Jesmond, who was pretending to dab at some water spilled on the desk top with a spotted 'kerchief, and clenched his hands into fists the size of roofer's mallets. I knew he'd love to land one on him. I almost respected his restraint.

'You will repeat it, Fitzpatrick.'

He mumbled. 'Yes – order. That's what I said, right enough.'

I put the glass back on the desk. 'Then let me tell you something about order.' Jesmond was watching Fitzy like a cat watches a mouse hole. His face was perfectly still, but his little eyes were alight with expectation.

'You too, Jesmond. What I'm going to say goes for the pair of you.' I looked from one to the other.

'This shabby hall and the others too – The Comet and what's left of The Gaudy – are among the smallest of my concerns. If you think I'm going to waste my time listening to you two squabbling like a couple of fish wives fighting to trade the same street then you're very much mistaken. You both know what I am, don't you?'

Neither of them answered. It came to me then that what they needed was a bit of show. It was what they understood after all. I lashed out and swept the glass from the desk with such a force that it smashed against the wall. Fitzy stared dumbly at the water trickling down the new green paint.

'Don't you? Because if you don't I'll happily show you – and believe me you won't be left in any doubt on the matter.'

Jesmond moistened his lips. 'You're a ... a Baron, ma'am. Just like Lady Ginger before you.' He smiled, showing those odd little teeth. 'That's the way of it, ma'am, if I'm not mistaken?'

I nodded. 'That's the way of it all right, Jesmond, just like Lady Ginger. And if I'm not mistaken she had more to concern herself with than a couple of mangy halls at the scrag end of Paradise.' I stood up. 'If I can't trust you two to take care of my business here I might have to make alternative arrangements.'

I was gratified when Jesmond dropped his mole eyes to the boards. Fitzy clasped his big hands together so tight on the desk top in front of him I could see the whites of his knuckles through the freckled pink skin. The pair of them were sitting in front of me just now like a couple of schoolboys caught scrapping in the yard. I wanted to laugh out loud, but I managed to keep it in.

'Now, what I reckon is this.' They looked up. 'You, Fitzpatrick, will take on the role of Chairman here at The Carnival. I'm not your friend – and don't ever think I am – but I know the punters and the turns respect you. Wait.' I held up my hand as Jesmond tried to interrupt.

'You, Jesmond, will be in charge of the books – everything relating to the finances of The Carnival, and The Comet, when it opens again, will be run by you. You're slick with brass, I can see that. And from now on you'll be taking on responsibility for the repairs at The Comet and perhaps later on The Gaudy. I've been studying the books, there are some costs I'd like you to look into. Them Bermondsey plasterers Fitzpatrick took on have come up with a rare rate. We can do better.' I turned to Fitzy. 'You told me how important "order" was, didn't you?'

He nodded.

'Good. Then it will be like the old days. You'll be keeping order here every night – just like you used to at The Gaudy. You'll be in charge of the acts and the bill. I know you – you're a showman at heart, Fitzpatrick, whatever else you might be. I've only got one hall open at the moment, but I promise you this, there *will* be three again, just like it used to be.'

I took the newspaper from the desk.

'And I need you two *gentlemen* to work together to make that happen.'

⚓

I closed the door behind me leaving them to fight over the bones. I was surprised to see Michael McCarthy sitting at the piano in the shallow pit in front of the stage. It was him I'd heard earlier, picking at the keys. At the sound of the door he turned and stared at me.

Without his turban and broidered stage gear Swami Jonah was about as magical as a mug of jellied eels. He was tall and bald, the only singular thing about him being the scatter of moles on his face, which gave him a sinister cast in the lime-light.

When he wasn't putting on the foreign for punters he spoke broad Liverpool. Tell truth, I liked Swami Jonah, he'd always been good to me. Way back, before he came to London to work the halls, he'd been a dip boy on the streets, then a shipmate for a time. I knew he still had what you might call dealings round the docks. Like a lot of them Irish scousers he had a sentimental streak as wide as the Mersey, which came out in the long sad songs he sung for us at The Lamb. He had a good voice. After Ma died, I remember him telling me one evening, with tears in his eyes, how important it was for a girl like me to have a family.

'Mr McCarthy.' I nodded, but he swung round again and started to play a single note over and over. I watched his hunched shoulders as he jabbed at the same piano key. I was six foot away, but I could smell the gin.

'You all right, Jonah?'

He didn't turn, instead he carried on hammering. A high note this time, jarring like Jesmond and that bleedin' glass. I thought about saying more, but the set of his back against me made me button it; besides there was another difficult conversation running through my head.

I went through the stacks of chairs and sticky tables to the narrow red-curtained entrance hiding a flight of stairs at the back of the hall. I pulled back the greasy velvet and caught the rope that served as a rail. The stairs curved up to a passage running along the left side of The Carnival under the roof. It was all the place had in the way of a dressing room. As a rule someone would be working there of an afternoon, patching up the shredded netting and straightening out the costumes left strewn about the floor when the acts thought they might be about to miss last orders at The Lamb.

Less than a year ago that someone would have been me. And Peggy too. We took our sewing boxes between The Gaudy, The Carnival and The Comet, and even now I could tell my stitches – and Peggy's – in the silks. We were good at it. I daresay that even up close no one else could make out all the patches we'd sewn into the shabby bodices worn by the dancers.

Today the passage was empty apart from a costume rail pushed up against the wall. At night in the limelight the spangles and feathers gave the impression of something richly exotic, but in sunlight you could see them for what they were. Half the feathers looked like used mop heads and the sequins were tarnished with rust.

It was frowsy up here. Not as bad as Fitzy's suit, but enough to remind you that underneath all the paint and the glitter there were bodies at work. It wasn't what I wanted my punters to dwell upon. They came for magic, not sweat.

In summer, me and Peggy would spread the stage gear out across the cobbled yard in front of the workshops round the back of The Gaudy. It was an old trick, but the bright light burned away the smells caught in the fabric. I dragged the rail along to the window, unhooked the latch and opened up. It was so still and close out there that the feathers didn't even tremble.

I heard voices in the yard below. Cissie Watkins from the chorus was down there nestled up to a dark-haired lad twice her size. He had his back to me, but from the way they were huddled together I could tell they weren't rehearsing. It was clear they'd already had a lot of practice.

I watched them for a moment, envious of the easy way her hands ran up and down his back and the way he pulled her close, winding his fingers into her golden hair. I wondered if anyone would ever want me in that way. The only times

I'd allowed myself to think that someone might care I'd been badly mistaken.

I pushed the window open wider and the grate of the hinges made Cissie look up. She sprang back from her beau.

'Ki ... Ma'am! We just ... It's not ...' Cissie grabbed the boy's hand. 'It's just that it's quiet here in the afternoon and ...'

I leaned out. 'It's not up to me how you spend your free time or who you spend it with, Cissie. As long as you know your part, show up on time and put on a good show with the others every night, I'm happy.'

It was a chance to test out what I'd just heard. I shielded my eyes against the sun. 'Fitzpatrick says the sailor act's still bringing them in. According to him it's about the only turn that is.'

Cissie let go of her boy's hand and came to stand under the window. 'We've had a good run with it, ma'am, I won't deny it. But Netta says the sailor isn't going to get any fresher – every time we do it we're wearing it out. She says The Carnival's in urgent need of a new draw. She reckons it's stale as—' Cissie broke off as the dark lad nudged her with his elbow. He looked up, fearing she'd gone too far.

'Netta says all that, does she?' I flicked at a blow fly idling round my head.

Netta Swift was the leader of the chorus – she had a fine voice, neat ankles and comic timing you could set a fob by. Like Fitzy said, she was a rising star, and she knew it. In her place I'd be thinking about leaving Cissie and the others and branching out for myself. I decided to have a private word with Netta and come to a suitable arrangement. The

Carnival couldn't afford to lose her.

Tell truth, I had enough stored up to pay them all – the hands, the girls, the acts, the orchestra boys, Fitzy and Jesmond – five times over every week from here to a new century, but I wanted to prove to myself that I could make a proper go of it. I remembered what Lucca said the day he left.

You made a promise to everyone in the halls. You once called them your family, remember?

I cared about them three halls and the people who worked in them – most of them. It came to me as I looked down at Cissie and her handsome lad that if I could set The Carnival, The Comet and even The Gaudy back on track, then maybe the rest would follow. Paradise was a pit, but I could make it better, couldn't I? It was what I intended back at the start when my grandmother left it all in my hands, only I'd lost my way. For too long I'd been stumbling around in the dark.

My heart punched under the striped cotton of my frock. When I locked Danny under that ledgerstone I locked part of myself away there too. It came to me, with a clarity, it was what the Barons wanted.

'What do you think, then, about the act, ma'am?'

Cissie's voice came from below. I ducked my head and swiped at the bluebottle again, bleedin' thing was caught in my hair now.

'I think the sailor's got a bit of life in him yet. And don't worry about The Carnival – I've got plans for it. That goes for The Gaudy and The Comet too when they're open again.'

I thought about the newspaper in my bag. Later on I'd have a look at the pages Fitzy had marked for my attention. He generally had an eye for a novelty, I'll give him that. A bell started chiming – two, three, four strikes. I clenched my fist. There was something else I had to set right today, begin to set right, leastways.

I leaned out further. 'Listen, Cissie, I came here looking for Peg . . . Peggy Worrow. I thought she might be working up here this afternoon?'

She shook her head. 'You'll find her at home most like. She's not been too good, what with her Danny going off and the sickness from the baby. Terrible for her it is. I heard—'

I pulled the window towards me and it slammed shut with a sharpness I didn't intend.

'Peggy? You there?'

I stepped back and stared up at the shuttered windows. The narrow street was deserted apart from a small ginger tom blinking at me from a side alley. His fur stood out as unnaturally vivid against the grimy bricks. Something small and dead lay at his feet, a mouse most like, or maybe a bird. Without taking his green eyes off me, the tom dipped his head and caught the creature in his mouth, then he twisted back on himself and disappeared into the alley. I was alone out there now, but it didn't feel like it.

I scanned the silent street. I shouldn't have come to Risbies alone. It was a mistake. I should have waited until Tan Seng's new muscle boy was in place, but I wanted to get this over with. I knew I'd done wrong by Peggy and I didn't want anyone else around when I saw her again. Besides, I'd made a promise to Lucca.

I knocked again, just the once. The thud echoed in the hallway beyond. I waited for a moment and then I began to walk quickly away. I gripped the handle of my bag, uncomfortably aware that I was relieved Peggy wasn't at home. The stink from the open drain down the centre of the street was thickened by the heat. I could taste it.

There was a scraping noise from behind.

'Kitty!'

I froze. The tall brick houses of Risbies seemed to close together over my head, shutting out the light. My heart started bumping as Peggy's voice came again.

'Ain't you a sight for sore eyes.'

I turned slowly.

Blooming – that's the word you hear juggled about when a woman's carrying. Only Peggy wasn't blooming, if anything she'd grown thinner. Her eyes were sunk into dark pits above hollowed cheeks. Her lovely black hair was loose and dishevelled, falling in lank tails over her shoulders. There were stains on her dress. The girl I knew was neat as a haberdasher's ribbon tray and most particular about her looks. But this wasn't the girl I knew.

She leaned back against the door lintel. 'Cat bitten it off?'

I took a step towards her, but she folded her arms.

'No – you stay there and don't come an inch closer. You've been avoiding me and now I want you to see how it feels. You ignore me when we're within twenty foot of each other. You don't even look in my direction when I'm with the girls at The Carnival. You've told Tan Seng to turn me away. Seven times I've been to The Palace, Kit – seven – and every time the door was shut in my face. Even Lok – I ran into him on Pigott Street and he couldn't scuttle away quick enough. I thought he was my friend.'

She turned away. 'And I thought you was too.' Her voice came muffled. I knew she was trying not to cry.

'Peggy, don't!' I ran to her and caught her arm, pulling her round to face me. 'I'm sorry. I never meant . . . It's just . . .' My eyes scalded with salt. 'Things are different. It's hard—'

'Hard?' Peggy wrenched her arm free. 'Don't you think my life is hard now? With Dan and . . .' She flattened the palm of a hand against her belly. Through the thin material I could see the swell of it, despite her frailty.

'You know he's gone, Kit?'

I couldn't look her in the eye as she ran on.

'It was his gambling debts he was running from, not me. He wouldn't leave me.'

I cast around for something to say, but everything that came to mind was a lie. I looked up at Peggy's face. Her brown eyes were brimming with tears. It was unbearable. I stared at my toes poking out from under the hem of my striped blue calico. After a moment I managed to gather together a sort of answer and mangle it out.

'I know . . . and I'm sorry, Peg, so sorry.'

I knew too much, that was the trouble. As I concentrated on the dust, I remembered the way Danny had caught at the hem of my dress that night in the church, his fingers all bloody and torn. My belly rolled and my throat burned as the bitterness rose again. I struggled to swallow it back.

'You have to understand that things have changed for me too.'

She laughed harshly. 'Now you're a Baron, you mean? Just

like that evil old cow who was your grandmother. Oh yes – I know all about it. About you going off in the night in a mysterious coach and coming back a new woman.'

She must have dialled the look on my face because she went on. 'And how you stayed in your room for days afterwards going through your books and your ledgers putting a value to everything and everyone in Paradise. Lucca told me all about it. At least he still speaks to me. He comes to see me regular, in fact.'

She came down into the street so we were level. 'I know a lot about you now, Kitty Peck – and about him too for that matter.'

She lunged forward and slapped my face so hard I had to take a step back to right myself. I was so surprised I didn't even cry out. I just stood there smarting as she went on.

'You must have taken me for a poppet – letting me think the two of you were sweethearts when all along he'd prefer the company of . . . ' She shook her head. 'Not that it's any business of mine. He's a decent man, Lucca Fratelli. And he's truthful, which is more than I can say for you.'

She brushed the sleeve of her dress where I'd caught her like she was trying to wipe dirt away. 'Before I go in, Kit, there's something I'd like to know. How does it feel to be so high and mighty?'

I didn't have a chance to answer. Something whistled through the air. There was a metallic clang as it caught the wooden surround of Peggy's open door and clattered into the hall behind her. I span round, but the street was empty – the windows shuttered against the heat. I thought I caught a movement, a shadow, moving in the alley.

'Inside!' I pushed her roughly into the dingy hallway, slamming the door behind us and throwing the bolt across. Peggy bent to gather something up from the boards. She shook her head as she turned it about in her hands.

'Jesus!' Her hand trembled as she held the long-bladed silver knife out to me. In the gloom I saw the shaft was made from pale stuff, ivory or bone perhaps.

'And look at this, Kit.'

A coil of blonde hair, my hair, was between her fingers.

Chapter Nine

The knife lay on the corner table next to an empty china plate. If you didn't know better you might have thought it was the end of a dainty meal.

'It could have taken your ear off.' Peggy stared at the table and chewed her lip. 'Or mine.' She turned away sharp and bent over the hearth. There was a hollow clank and a splash as she busied herself. 'Did you see anyone out there, Kit?'

'No, I don't think so. You?'

She shook her head, but didn't turn to look at me.

'Maybe there was someone in the alley opposite,' I went on. 'I thought I saw something, but I wasn't going to stand around to find out, that's why I pushed you in. I'm sorry, I shouldn't have come here alone, Peg. Tan Seng always warns me not to go about without protection but nothing's ever happened until today.'

'Just my luck, then? Here. It'll calm your nerves – mine too.' Peggy handed me a fine tea cup filled from a kettle over the fire. Her hands were still shaking and I didn't blame her. As soon as we'd gone up the single flight of stairs to her rooms she'd locked the door, closed the window and half pulled the shutters across to shield us from the street. It was like a furnace in there. I put the cup down beside me. 'I'll let it cool.'

Peggy sat on the edge of the unmade bed. 'Old Mrs Stubbs downstairs says the fire keeps the air clear. She's had six kids and four are still breathing, so she must know what she's talking about. She reckons tea is good too – better than the water round here anyways.'

I looked at the door behind her. 'You still got the other room too – only you and Da . . .'

I faltered. I couldn't even say his name out straight. Peggy shrugged. 'I couldn't keep it on. Anyway, I'm saving every penny for this one.' She rested her hand over her belly.

I sat up straight. 'But you should have come to . . .' I stopped again. Peggy smiled, only it wasn't friendly.

'I did. But you didn't want to see me. Lucca's helped me out these past weeks. He's been a gent.'

I reached for the cup. Even though the tea burned my guilty tongue, I took another mouthful and let it punish me. I noted that my hand was shaking too – the thin brown liquid trembled at the fluted rim of the delicate china.

'He's worried about you, Kit.' Her eyes slid warily to the knife again. 'You look terrible, do you know that?'

'You don't look too clever yourself, Peg. You eating?'

She shook her head. 'I can't keep nothing down. Not just mornings neither. The sickness lasts all day. I can just about take tea, not much else. It can't go on much longer.'

I glanced at the empty cradle waiting in the corner. Danny had made it three months back for another child, and Lucca had painted it. A little red horse kicked his legs and tossed his mane at the head end, and a tabby cat, its painted tail curled around a knot in the wood, was asleep at the foot.

Peggy slipped from the bed. She padded across to the cradle and set it rocking.

'It'll come in useful round Christmas.'

The room fell silent except for the hum of the rockers on the boards. When it faded Peggy put her hand to it once more and the rhythm picked up again. I was grateful she still had her back to me when she spoke.

'Do you remember the last time I saw you, Kit? It was the night The Gaudy burned down.'

I took another sip of tea as she reached down to still the cradle. After a long pause she continued softly. 'That was the last night I saw Danny too. After I left you I went to meet him at The Lamb. He was in a black mood. He didn't want to talk to me – or anyone else. He took off about half an hour after I arrived – said he had to meet someone. I haven't heard from him since. Not a word.'

She looked at me, her eyes glittering with tears. 'But I know I will, when he sorts himself out and pays his debts. Then he can come back.'

There was a sharp snap. The cup in my hands smashed to pieces on the metal rail around the fire. Brown liquid soaked into the edge of the rag rug pulled up against the hearth. I'd gripped the china so hard I'd broken it. The handle was still caught between my thumb and first finger.

I stared down at the mess. 'Sorry, Peg. It slipped.'

She took a cloth from the table and dabbed around my feet. I knelt beside her and helped to gather up the fragments. Peggy stretched out her hand and I dropped the broken pieces into her open palm. It was almost like the old days when we worked at The Gaudy together, sewing side by side.

'That was the last good one.' She sighed. 'I had to pawn the set Danny bought me when we set up here. I'll never get it back from Uncle Fishman. And he knew it when he took it over the counter from me. You never used to be clumsy, Kit.'

'I'll get you a new one – a whole new set, if you like.'

She stiffened and the china fell through her fingers. 'That's your answer to everything now, isn't it? Money'll make it right. You going to buy me a new Danny, then?'

I stared at the dark stain left by the tea on the rug.

'I . . . I just . . . just wanted to . . .'

'You just wanted a bit of company, now that Lucca's gone to see his mother into her grave. I know all about it. He said he was going to ask you to come and see me, but I wasn't holding my breath. I don't have your quick tongue, Kitty, so I'd been practising that little speech I made on the doorstep just in case you bothered with me – and don't think I didn't mean a word of it. If you hadn't pushed me through the door, I wouldn't have let you in. The only reason you're sitting there now is because of that thing.'

She stood and flung the cloth onto the table to cover the knife.

'I think it's time you were off. If you're worried about stepping out alone I'll get Tom from two doors up to go to The Palace to fetch Tan Seng or Lok to walk you. Tom'll do it for a tanner. I'm sure you can spare that. Daresay I should be honoured to have a Baron sitting in my room taking tea with me, but I don't think we have much to say to each other these days.'

'That's not true!' I sprang up. 'I need you, Peg. You and Lucca are the best friends I've got.' I tried to find the right words. 'You're right. I should have come to see you. But I couldn't. When I became a Baron it wasn't what I thought. I had plans of making things right and dealing people fair . . .

and making everyone dote on me for it. But it's not going to be like that. It's not a game, Peg – it's not even like being up in the cage without a net to catch me. That was easy in comparison. You don't know what I've . . .'

What I've done was what I was going to say.

Peggy stared at me – her brown eyes crinkled with concern.

'Jesus, Kit – Lucca's right. You're whiter than a bedsheet and thinner than I've ever known. You can't afford to lose it, girl.'

'I can't afford to lose you.' I reached for her hand. 'Please, Peg, I'm sorry about . . . everything, truly I am. I'm not just here because Lucca's gone, not entirely. I missed you, but I didn't want to bring trouble. Everything gets . . . twisted because of me. Look at what happened today. You could have been hurt – killed maybe – and all because of me.'

Peggy sank slowly onto the bed and stared at the tea-stained cloth covering the knife.

'I don't know about that, Kit.'

She clasped her hands and looked down at the neat bulge caught in the fabric of her dress. 'I'm not sure that was meant for you. Fact is, since Dan's been . . . gone. I've not felt . . . I've not been . . .'

She looked at me direct. 'You might as well know, Kit. I've had things, horrible things, left on my step. Don't ask, because I won't tell you. I've had to sit up at night and go down there in the early morning to clean them away before anyone round here sees. One night someone scribbled the word *whore* across the door in shit. If Mrs Stubbs saw it she'd turn me out.

'Another time, when I was asleep with the window open, a dead cat was thrown into the room. It landed across me on the bed. Its stomach burst and there were maggots everywhere – in the sheets, on my skin. The stink of it . . .'

Peggy shuddered. 'I cleaned and scrubbed for days, but even now I can still catch it. And there's other things. Sometimes, when I'm out, I've been certain someone's following me. Up on the Commercial I've felt a hand on my shoulder a couple of times, but when I've turned there's just the crowd pushing around – all blank faces.' Peggy closed her eyes.

'Then, a fortnight back, someone caught me so hard by the hair, they ripped out a handful. There's a place here . . .' She dipped her head to show a patch as round as a sovereign where the scalp showed red and bald.

My heart pummelled away like a knuckle boy's fist. The locket Kite sent me: that was Peggy's hair curled up inside, not Danny's after all.

I assure you of my continued concern for those you hold dear and enclose a keepsake to remind you. Wear it and think of us.

I thought of the Barons now as Peggy ran on.

'I . . . I'm frightened, Kit. For me . . . and for this one.' She locked her hands tighter over the little mound that was Danny Tewson's child.

Christ! It was all a mess. I sat on the bed next to her and took her hand in mine again. 'Have you told anyone about this?'

Peggy shook her head. 'No. Lucca knows I'm not . . . not

right, but he thinks it's the sickness because of the baby.' She smiled proper for the first time. 'He made me some concoction with ginger and other bits and bobs floating about in it. It's what his mother took back home when she was carrying. It tasted like cat's pee, Kit. It made it worse. I had to throw it out, but I didn't want him to know. He's a kind man.'

I squeezed her hand. 'I know.'

She pulled away sharp.

'There was only one person I could think of who might be able to help, but she didn't want to see me. So, I haven't told a soul until today. Anyway, I thought I should keep it all quiet. Thing is, I think it's about Dan. Fact is, I'm sure of it. Someone's putting the fear on me to get to him. The more they make me suffer, the quicker my Dan'll be likely to find the money to buy himself out of his debts. If he knew what was happening to me he wouldn't stand for it. I know it.' Her voice came stronger as she straightened up on the bed. 'They could use it to put pressure on him, to sharpen him up, couldn't they? If he's gone to ground somewhere, the quickest way to flush him out would be to hurt us.'

Peggy rubbed a hand across her belly. 'Sometimes I think I can feel it move, Kit – and that's when I wish he was here with us.'

I dragged my eyes away and stared at the little heap of cloth covering the knife on the table. I couldn't see it clear through the tears. I stood and went to the window, moving the wooden shutter aside a little to look down into the dingy street below. If there was anyone watching down there my eyes were too glassy to make them out. My head was beginning to throb again. I pushed the damp ringlets away from my face, making sure they caught tight beneath the pins. There was something missing from what Peggy was telling me. I turned about, careful to stay in the shadow so she couldn't see my face.

'What makes you certain it's about Dan, Peg?'

'This.' She slipped from the bed and came towards me. When she was close she reached into the neck of her dress and pulled out a chain.

'Remember how you used to wear Joey's ring and his Christopher to keep him close?'

I nodded, moving deeper into the shadow.

'One morning, when I cleared a pile of shit and God knows what else from the step, I found this hidden among it. It's Dan's. I'd know it anywhere. It belonged to his grandfather. He never took it off.'

She held the chain forward and I caught the glint of gold – a ring.

Of an instant, I saw Dan kneeling in front of me again at Great Bartholomew's, his bloodied fingers, gripping the hem of my blue satin gown. They must have torn the ring from him.

'It's a message for me. I'm right, aren't I, Kit?'

I couldn't answer. I could feel a vein in my neck pulse with the blood rushing to my head. It was a message all right, but not for Peggy.

Her voice came again. 'What do you think?'

I folded my arms tight to stop her from seeing me tremble.

'I . . . I think you should come and live with me at The Palace, Peggy – for your sake and for the baby's.'

Chapter Ten

Lok let out a yelp of excitement when me and Peggy came through the door. He was in the hall, polishing the stair rails. He dropped his rag in surprise and then he scurried across the marble, clucking over Peggy like a hen with a fresh-hatched brood. He was tiny beside her. Considering he was the size of an underfed ten year old, skinny as a curtain pole and most likely older than Noah and the trees he built his Ark from, it was hard to imagine what use it might be when Tan Seng sent his brother out with me as a protection.

'Lok, could you make up the bed in the blue room, please? Peggy – Miss W ...' I glanced at Peggy. 'Mrs Tewson?' She nodded. 'Mrs Tewson will be staying with us.'

'Good. Very good, Lady. I go.'

'It's been a while, Lok.' Peggy flushed and folded her hands over her belly. The pair of them exchanged a look. Lok smiled so wide it almost broke his walnut-shell face in two. I knew that when she stayed with me before the pair of them had become close, but watching them together I realised just how much he'd missed having her around.

I had too, come to that.

We even caught Tan Seng by surprise. He slipped up from below when he heard the cooing in the hall. He bowed to me and then, satisfied with the order of things, he tucked his arms into his sleeves and turned to the stairs leading to the basement.

I called after him. 'Anything from Telferman yet?'

He paused on the top step. 'No, Lady.' He shook his head. 'Nothing has come from Pearl Street.'

I thought about the bone-handled knife in my bag. Peggy had wanted to leave it at Risbies, but I'd rolled it in a stocking and taken it with us. Tan Seng watched me. 'There is more, Lady?'

I nodded. 'I'll be needing that escort regular from now on. With Mr Fratelli away it's for the best.'

'It is arranged.' Tan Seng's face gave nothing away as he turned and padded down the stairs.

Peggy followed Lok up to her room and I stood in the hall-way alone. A golden crescent fell across the marble tiles from the fanlight over the door. The brightness of it thickened the shadows in the corners. There was a time when that window was blinded with soot and grime. Someone, Lok I reckoned, had arranged an armful of blousy red roses in a blue and white bowl on the hall table, but they'd drooped and fallen in the heat. The heavy smell rolling off them was almost putrid.

I bent to gather the crumpled petals. Straightening up I caught sight of the painting of the young gent in blue. Light rarely hit this part of the hall, but just now the sun showed it clear without shining up the oil paint.

I took a step back and half closed my eyes. The last time I saw Joey, it was here at The Palace. He'd looked a fancy bit of frock in his fine French gown with that blonde plait curled on his head.

Lucca was right, if you looked through the padding – the

lad in the painting clearly wasn't a stranger to a meat pudding – it was my brother up there. I was a fool not to have seen it before. The fine eyes, the wide, full lips, the fair hair divided at a widow's peak, they were all Joey's, along with the general air of lazy satisfaction.

'What have you done this time, Joey?'

As I spoke aloud, the chimes of my grandmother's clock in the parlour struck the quarter. The tripping tinkling sound reminded me of time running away.

The truth of it was that I was relying on her. It was all I had. If I didn't hear from Lady Ginger, and hear soon, I didn't know what I was going to do. And what then?

I stared up at the painting.

The more I knew about my brother the less I saw him clear. He was becoming a thing of smoke, not flesh and bone. There was a time before everything changed when me, Joey, Ma and Nanny Peck had lived in decent lodgings off Church Row. At night Ma and the old girl shared the bed in the room at the back and me and Joey slept in a low narrow space, more like a box, up a single flight of steps leading from what Ma called 'the parlour'. The little room was under the eaves facing north. It was raw up there in winter, even with our coats and paper packed on top of the bed.

Of occasion, when it was so bitter we could see our breath, we slept on a wooden truckle pulled out from under the couch and set in front of the hearth. I liked those times best. The heat warmed through the blankets and the soft light from the coals made the room and everything in it glow in a way it didn't during the day. There was even a comfort in the sound of Nanny Peck chugging away like a steam barge next door.

In Ma's room there was a deep cupboard set into the wall beside the window. It was where she and Nanny Peck kept their gear – dresses, blouses, linens and that. They didn't have much between them, and what little they owned had been washed and pressed a thousand times over so almost everything was a shade of grey.

I remember the way Nanny Peck's Sunday crinoline tried to bustle out through the cupboard door of its own accord. Once, when me and Joey was left alone and playing a game to pass the hour, he hid himself under the stiff black skirts. When I opened up he rustled them about and wailed like a banshee from one of the old girl's stories. I yelled and ran back to the front room. Then I raced down the stairs and out into the street. I kept going until I was lost in the crowd. I can't have been more than five years old at the time. When Joey finally found me, he made me promise not to tell Ma, or most especially Nanny Peck, where we'd been or what he'd done.

Thing is, we was forbidden to go delving about in that cupboard. At the back, hidden behind all the grey, there was a sky-blue dress belonging to Ma that we was never to touch. The bodice was sewn with seed pearls and the full skirts were fringed with silver lace that had tarnished to iron in the dark. I never thought to ask how she came by such a thing. It was just there – in the way that Nanny Peck was just there.

There was another time a few years later, though, when I came in from playing out on the street and I heard Ma crying. That wasn't so unusual – me and Joey was used to the way she slid from the light into the shade. Nanny Peck was sitting by the hearth with her back to the door. She had her sewing box out on the floor beside her and she was bent over something. She turned at the sound, shook her head and went to shut the door between the rooms so I couldn't hear Ma any more and she couldn't hear us.

Nanny Peck wagged a finger at me. 'Wicked, that's what you are, Kitty.'

I was confused. I stared at the door to the back room and then at Nanny Peck. I began to ask what I was supposed to have done, but she trotted over and placed her hand over my mouth. Her skin always smelt of cabbage and soap.

'Don't fib to me, now. It'll only make it worse. Ruined it is, and all because of you.' Her muddy eyes drooped with sadness. She breathed deep and went back to the stool beside the fire. 'You'll get nothing tonight and I hope you wake with the gripe tomorrow. That's what happens to them that spoils other people's things.'

I stared at her stocky grey back. 'But, I haven't done nothing.'

'No? What's this then, child?' She held up something blue. A scatter of tiny white beads fell from her lap to the floor. 'A visit from the little folk, was it?'

I looked at the seed pearls rolling on the boards and realised she was showing me Ma's good dress.

'Ripped at the hem. The bodice all torn. You didn't even have the grace to put it away after you'd finished with it. You just left it on the floor for her to find.' Nanny Peck nodded at the closed door. 'Look what you've done. She's taken bad – and all because of you. I know it's a pretty thing, but it wasn't yours to play with, child.'

'I didn't!' I went to sit beside her, but she shrugged me

away. 'Truly, it wasn't me. It's not fair. I never touched it. I'll swear it on that old black Bible of yours if you want.'

Nanny Peck huffed. 'The Lord hates a liar. If you speak to me again today I'll take you down to the yard and rinse your mouth out with carbolic soap.'

I knew better than to test her on that.

The next day it was all forgotten. The dress disappeared and Ma and Nanny Peck acted like nothing had happened. There was something else, mind. A month or so later I found a handful of tiny pearls and a scrap of tired silver lace in the little tin box where Joey kept his treasures. He hid it under a loose board beneath our bed in the box up top, but of occasion he showed me the pretty things he collected. He hadn't shown me the pearls and the lace.

Nanny Peck worshipped my brother. With his golden curls and wide blue eyes there was something of an angel about him. He was always a charmer – that was true of him as a child and as a grown man – and he could wind the old girl round his fingers like a card of wool. Don't mistake me; she loved us both fierce, but Joey, now, he was the special one.

I didn't mention the treasure box to Nanny Peck. She wouldn't have believed it of him, and besides, it was all over and forgotten. I didn't want to pick it open again and have them beads spill across the boards.

It was different now. I needed to open that box and bring Joey's secrets tumbling into the light.

Not a lucky man.

That's what Lucca had said about my brother.

I wished Lucca was here, although, in a way, he was. His voice was in my head right now, much like that old sailor's missing leg giving him gyp. I'd thought of him as an old woman when he told me to keep myself straight, but he was right. I needed to think clear. I needed to make sure my mind was never clouded up with smoke again.

Of an instant, it came to me that there was something I could do about that. Something of a practical nature.

I crushed the petals between my fingers and went upstairs to my office. I opened the window looking down onto the yard and then I knelt in front of the hearth to set a match to some old papers. Once a small fire was burning I went to the desk and opened the bottom drawer. I let the knife wrapped in the stocking tumble from my bag and then I took out the bundle of opium sticks. The locket filled with Peggy's hair was beneath it in the drawer.

I snatched it up too, went back to the fire and cast the sticks and the locket into the flames.

The pattern in the fabric caught first, the dye was incendiary most like. I watched as the Oriental loops and swirls fired bright giving the impression that the something wrapped inside was alive. After a moment the bundle became a golden ball. I poked it deeper into the hearth with an iron, pushed the locket into the ash and went to the door. As I turned the handle, the thick, sour-sweet smoke of the opium caught in my nose. I didn't trust myself to stay in that room a moment longer.

⚜

The fourth and final chime hung around like a stage door Johnnie. A purple crack running down the centre of the shutter told of a new day. Another morning was clambering up from the east, but as far as I was concerned yesterday hadn't even ended yet. I threw the book to the bedcover and wrapped my arms round my knees. The candle lamp on the nightstand flickered, sending shadows across the bed.

I hoped Peggy was sound asleep in the room across the hall. If she was, I reckoned it was the first real rest she'd allowed herself for a long time. My eyes stung with salt. All that time, she'd needed me and I'd kept her at a distance. The worst of it was that I'd been frightened for myself, not for her.

But someone out there had been thinking about her – and me.

Kite and the Barons were playing with me in the way a cat worries an injured bird. Taunting me by showing how close they were. What cut deepest was the fact they knew how much I cared about Peggy before I did. I swiped the back of a hand over my eyes.

The light creeping through the shutter was turning pink now. I wouldn't need the candle soon. I took up the book and ran my finger along the line again. I was teaching myself the code the news boys used to get their stories down quick as a man could talk. It helped pass the nights when sleep didn't come. Tonight I'd been doing it to prove to myself I could lock down a thought. There was something reassuring in the practicality of it. This, at least, was something I could do.

Of a rule, I made out the meaning of most of the dots, the curves and the dashes easy enough, but just occasionally I had to flick over to the proper text on the following page. The sense of it didn't come to me now. It was a passage from the Bible – I could tell that from the high dry tone – but every time I got to the second sentence the marks swam about on the page and I had to go back to the beginning.

I'd sent off for the course after Sam Collins showed me his notebook. He used shorthand to get down stories for his rag, *The London Pictorial News*. He thought very highly of himself and his flair for dashing words off smart and reading them back again. If I ever came across him again I wanted to show him he wasn't that special. I wanted to beat him at his own game. That was something like it.

Tonight I was losing. I kept thinking about that ring hidden in the shit on Peggy's step. She was in her bed across the landing now clutching it tight to her chest and dreaming of Danny. Christ! She thought it meant he was alive. I was the only person in Paradise who knew, for a certainty, that big Danny Tewson wasn't coming back. That ring was for my benefit, not hers.

And then there was the knife.

It was the Barons. Most likely, it was the work of Kite's man, Matthias. Tall and blond, he was, like an angel in one of Lucca's picture books, but he was a devil. I'd had dealings with him before. Of an instant, the leathery, spiced scent of the man's cologne came to me. It was almost like he was there. It was close in the room, but I shivered as I thought about the sharpened tip of his hawk-headed cane and how he used it.

Old Peter Ash, The Gaudy's gentle cornet player, he was another whose blood was on my hands. I'd gone to him when I needed the help of someone who could read Russian. And Matthias followed me. Two days later, when the orchestra boys pushed open the door to Peter's tidy little room in Pearmans Yard they thought it was hung about with crimson paper garlands. Just for a second or two, until they caught the smell.

Telferman said the red-headed woman dragged from the river had been mutilated. *Ripped apart* were his exact words. I twisted the plait hanging over my shoulder until it hurt. No. I wouldn't let Peggy go back to Risbies. She and the baby, when it came, could stay here with me until . . .

Until when, girl? The question went off in my head and repeated itself over and over. I couldn't see an end to any of this. Tell truth, I couldn't rightly work out a beginning, neither.

Joey – it kept coming back to him. The last time I saw my brother he was scared of something. And who could blame him?

Bartholomew waits.

That was the message our grandmother told me to give him when I found him in Paris. I didn't know what it meant back then, and Joey never let on, although I saw the way it drained the colour from his face. I understood it now – and so did poor Danny Tewson. The Barons punished those who displeased them by sealing them maimed, but alive, into a chamber beneath Great Bartholomew's Church. Joey must have known that.

When I'd squared up to my brother that last time, I'd asked him straight out to tell me what was going on, but he refused. I ran through his words again, remembering the way they came all smooth and cultured and the way they made me feel. See, Joseph Peck spoke like a toff when he chose to. And he chose to then to show up the difference between us.

It's not something new, Kitty, it's an old . . . complication. You don't need to know any more.

He was wrong. I did need to know.

An old complication?

At least he'd been telling the truth when he said that. Lady Ginger knew he was in trouble when she gave me that message. She was the only one who could help me make sense of things now.

If she was still alive.

Last time I saw my grandmother, my blood grandmother, not Nanny Peck, she was dying. Her parchment skin stretched so tight across her face, her cheekbones looked ready to slice through. I needed to see her before she took her secrets – and Joey's – into a lead-lined coffin.

I sat up straighter in the bed and rested the book on my knees. I'd always had a head for puzzles and such like, but it was easier to work my way through a page of Sir Isaac Pitman's Phonotypic Alphabet Work Book than to work out what was happening around me.

I traced the line again with my index finger, moving my lips as the words came true.

> Lay not up for yourselves treasures upon earth, where moth and rust doth corrupt, and where thieves break through and steal: But lay up for yourselves treasures in Heaven, where neither moth nor rust doth corrupt, and where thieves do not break through nor steal. For where your treasure is, there will your heart be also.

If I was a superstitious type, like Nanny Peck, I might have taken it for a message.

I wondered what Sam had made of these exercises, most

of them coming from the Bible. He didn't strike me as a church-going type. Beneath that straggling fringe of his and his genial bumbling manner of going about, he was sharp as a Smithfield boning knife. He wasn't always right, mind. The last time I saw him he good as called me a Tom.

There was a copy of his newspaper in my bag. It was the one Fitzy had given me. I shut the workbook and threw it down. Instead of lying here churning I could do something useful. The pink light around the window was tinged with gold now. I blew out the candle, slipped off the bed and went to release the shutters. The window was half open, but the air was still. Another day thick with dust and heat was swelling outside.

I turned away and went out to the landing. At this hour the house was silent. It was even too early for a miraculous turn from Tan Seng. I glanced at the door to the room where I hoped Peggy was soundly asleep and went down to the parlour. There was a flutter from the cloth-covered shape in the corner, then a metallic scratching sound as Jacobin, my grandmother's scraggy grey parrot, gnawed at the bars of his cage.

'*Pretty girl, Pretty Girl. Pretty Liza, Pretty Liza.*'

At some point she must have taught her moth-eaten pet to say that to her. See, my grandmother's real name was Elizabeth, although she would always be Lady Ginger to me.

I went to the cage to draw off the cloth. Jacobin cocked his head. Every time I looked into those black pupils rimmed with yellow I got the impression he was calculating something.

On this occasion he was. Of an instant, he twisted his neck and jabbed his curved beak at the bars. I moved my hand away just in time. Jacobin blinked, ruffled his feathers and hunched his back. After a moment he dipped his head and let out a string of profanities by way of a greeting. My grandmother had a colourful turn of phrase when it took her. The parrot was a good mimic, I'll allow him that. It was almost as if she was right there in the room with us. I thought about covering him with the cloth again, but it didn't seem right to leave him in the dark.

'Good morning to you too, you evil little sod.'

I swung back the shutters nearest the cage and loosed the catch on the window to let in some air. I turned to scan the room.

'*Little sod. Little sod.*' This time it was my voice.

My bag was on the table near the couch. I took out *The London Pictorial News*, knelt down and flattened it on the rug. Fitzy told me he'd marked it for my attention. I knew where he meant. There were generally two or three pages at the back where the latest turns were described for the benefit of punters. Close-packed columns described the acts in some detail and the halls where they could be found.

Of a rule, it wasn't unusual for a popular performer to fit in five or six stages a night. It was hard work, though – especially for a woman. Criss-crossing London in a cab with nothing more than a flask of gin to keep you lively took a toll. Mrs Conway reckoned she'd been in danger of losing her bloom until she came to work regular at Lady Ginger's halls.

Fact is, Lally Conway's bloom had crisped at the edges long before she set foot on the boards at The Gaudy. But there was a time when she and Fitzy had what you might call an understanding, so me, Peggy and the other girls kept up the pretence that she was fresh as a bunch of Devon violets. Poor old cow – we was so convincing, I reckon she actually began to believe us. Anyway, she was now in what you might call retirement, but in what I might call Ramsgate.

I flipped the paper over and started to turn from the back. I'd never had to jostle for space in *The London Pictorial*. I was news. Me and my cage had made the first pages, largely on account of Sam's colourful turn of phrase and a picture of me that shrunk my costume while expanding other more personal features to the point where I didn't recognise myself.

It was Sam who called me *The Limehouse Linnet*. The Barons used it when they came to give me a name. The fact I was Lady Linnet was his bleedin' fault.

I came to the first of the reports from the halls, but I couldn't see anything marked by Fitzy. I ran a finger down the column stopping if anything caught my eye. Over at The Bedford in Camden Town they had a veritable circus. Jugglers, acrobats, harlequins and a Signor Cardoni and his dancing lion. I hoped they were feeding it. The Carnival was a small hall, too small for a lion, even if it could dance like Salome herself. I didn't mind it when the turns got a mauling, but the punters, now, that was a different matter.

At The Alhambra up west, the equestrian ballet was still pulling in the crowd and Leybourne was working The Red Deer over Bethnal way. The Deer was a flea hole several rungs lower than The Carnival. It was a comedown – people were growing tired of him and his songs. Closer to home, Peggy Pryde, Jennie Hill's daughter, was at The Little Grasshopper in Mile End. They billed her as '*a flash of the vital spark*' as a reverence to her mother. I reckoned she was younger than me, perhaps sixteen at most.

Bessie Bellwood was at The Canterbury. Now, she was good. I'd seen her the one time she played The Gaudy. She had a ripe turn of phrase for hecklers and a salty line in material. I wondered that Fitzy hadn't marked her. Then again, he knew what he was doing – all the names of the acts listed on the page in front of me were familiar.

Stale was the word that came to mind. I thought back to my conversation with Cissie Watkins. Netta was right. The sailor act wasn't getting any fresher. The punters would be looking for something new. They always did. The sooner I had that talk with Netta Swift the better.

I flipped the page. Now I could see Fitzy's pen marks. I leaned closer for a better look.

MAN OF A MILLION BONES

Monsieur Auguste Torsade, master of anatomical impossibility, at The New Grecian Theatre for two nights only. Born with a physique of extraordinary flexibility, no chain can hold him, no bond detain him. No space can confound the contortions of his body. Secured in the watery darkness of a bolted metal chamber, snatching life itself from the jaws of mortality, he emerges triumphant. Decide for yourself if Monsieur Torsade is a man or a miracle.

I could see why he ringed it. The punters liked the physical acts, especially if there was an element of risk. I wondered if Monsieur worked alone or with a pretty girl who carried the keys in her mouth. A farewell kiss to a man in mortal danger was the easiest way to slip him the means of release. It was interesting, but nothing I hadn't heard about before. I went to the next one marked for my attention.

The Sisters of Scylla. A flesh act! I might have known. Fitzy's attention had been caught by three pretty girls prancing about in the state that nature intended and a steam pump wheezing modesty from the sides. Besides the sisters there was a counting pig, which I suppose was a novelty of sorts, although I wouldn't want to clean up after it of an evening, and a one-armed pianist.

There was nothing I considered to be fresh among them. I was disappointed in Fitzy.

I closed up *The London Pictorial* and tossed it onto the couch behind me. A couple of pages came loose and flapped across the boards, coming to a rest next to the base of Jacobin's cage. All things considered, it seemed like the best place for them. I stood and went to gather them together. As I pulled the last sheet to me I caught sight of an item run across two columns at the top of the page. My hand froze.

ESTABLISHMENT OF LONDON IMPERIAL AGENCY

On Tuesday last, the first meeting of Her Britannic Majesty's newly established London Imperial Agency was held at Windsor Castle in the presence of the Queen. These good men, under the guidance of General, Lord Denderholm, stand ready to guide and advise Her Majesty in all matters related to the Empire when their consequence is manifest at home.

It wasn't the words that stopped me. Tell truth, I didn't have a clue what they meant. No – it was the block print above it. Lord Denderholm's heavily whiskered face was set in a wreathed oval in the middle, slap on top of a map of the world, and a dozen or so other unnamed notables were arranged around him in smaller, less fancy circles. You could knit a scarf from all the mutton chops bristling on the page and still have leftovers for a sock.

Whoever had done the drawings was no artist, not like Lucca, but I reckoned he'd caught a fair likeness of every one of the 'good men' mentioned – most particularly the one at the bottom left. The face stood out because it was young and clean-shaven.

And it stood out because I knew him. I'd only seen him once, in the candlelight that night at Great Bartholomew's, but I'd marked him for the fact that he was so different to the rest.

The man on the page of Sam Collins's paper was Lord Vellum, one of the Barons of London. I'd stake my life on it.

Chapter Eleven

Lok thrust his hands into his baggy black sleeves and stared up at the narrow four-storey building in front of us. The lascar towered behind him. In his long white tunic and broidered waistcoat, Hari (that was his name, he told me, but he didn't say much else) cut a most unlikely figure in Holborn.

Tell truth, I hadn't given it a moment's thought back east. The world and his brother's dog shipped up on our steps in Limehouse, so the sight of dark skin and a pigtail wasn't exactly a novelty. You couldn't walk a hundred yards along the Ratcliffe without hearing tongues wearing out a dozen languages. But up west things was different.

When we climbed out of the cab and headed down Great Turnstile we caused quite a stir. A couple of junior legals gawped as we went past and a woman fanned herself most energetically before remarking, loudly, to her friend that she'd heard a blend of China and India could be most enlivening.

The new lascar muscle had been presented to me earlier by Tan Seng. As we stood in the hallway of The Palace it was like he was handing over the leash of a big guard dog, which, in a way, I suppose he was. Walking between Lok and Hari I realised how much I'd come to rely on Lucca. When we went about together the only time people cast an old-fashioned our way was if they caught a glimpse of his scars. To anyone that didn't know better we must have looked like a regular couple. It came to me then that I needed Lucca for more than his company.

After that business with the knife on Risbies, I knew I wasn't safe to go about alone, but as we turned left into Lincoln's Inn Fields it was clear I'd made a mistake going west with Lok and Hari. I hadn't minded being looked at when I was dandling up in the cage, but the attention I was getting now wasn't anywhere near as flattering.

We crossed to Remnant Street and a man – sleek and well dressed, I might add – paused and raised his hat. I took him for a toff who recognised me from the halls. I was ruffling up to acknowledge his greeting when he smiled and spat on the cobbles right in front of me.

'Whore.'

He bowed as if he'd just paid me the finest compliment and went on his way. Lok bristled like a stray sparring for a fish head. He whipped about and would have gone after him if I hadn't caught his arm.

'No! We're drawing too much attention as it is. We're nearly there.'

'Lady.' Lok bowed, but he didn't take his eyes off the man until he disappeared into the crowd.

Now we were standing in a shady passage outside Sam's office. I had his paper in my bag and I wanted some answers. The premises of *The London Pictorial News* seemed to have frayed at the edges since my last visit. Squeezed like an afterthought into a gap between two slightly finer buildings, the only sign of activity today came from the thick circular glass lights set into the cobbles next to the doorstep. I could see a glow down below and after a moment I could feel the faint rumble of machinery through my shoes.

The window was empty. Last time I stood out here and stared in through the grimy panes, a copy of *The London Pictorial* had been strung across on a wire and pegged open at a page showing a ripe drawing of me. Sam Collins had described the work of his block boys in the basement as 'artistic licence'; Nanny Peck would have described it as 'filth'.

The only thing in the window today was a mouse. A dead one. I recalled how Sam had hinted that times were hard in the news trade. He clearly hadn't been using artistic licence then. I loosened the ribbons of my straw bonnet and turned to Lok and the muscle.

'You can come inside with me or wait out here. I reckon I'll be half an hour, maybe an hour, at most.' I nodded at the door. 'It'll be close as a left-footer's 'fessional in there, so if you want to sit in the shade in the Fields for a while I won't mind.'

'Lady?' Lok frowned.

'You don't have to come inside. I wouldn't if I was you – it's too hot to be sealed up.'

The moment I said it, something black flapped its wings in my stomach.

I was haunted by Danny Tewson. Not by his ghost, you understand, I wasn't a credulous type and I wasn't what you might call a regular believer. If heaven and hell were waiting for us all, then I was pretty certain they kept their inmates occupied, rather than letting them out for a ramble.

No, I was haunted by what I'd done to him. It came upon me when I wasn't expecting it. A word, a gesture, a scene – anything could make him come alive in my mind when all the time he was rotting in that crypt. I pulled off my hat and leaned against the wall. I closed my eyes and gulped down a lungful of stale air.

'Lady?' Lok's voice came again. 'We come with you.' I opened my eyes. He bowed and sidled a glance at Hari. 'It is not safe alone. We come.'

I nodded. 'Actually, I reckon you'll be welcome inside, Lok. You can show Sam's clerk, old Mr Peters, how to make a decent pot of tea.'

The boy leaning on the wooden counter just inside the door was engrossed in a tatty pamphlet. He didn't look up as we entered. From the other side of the desk I watched his finger trace the lines beneath a drawing of a wild-haired man on a rearing horse. The boy's lips moved as he read.

'Shop!'

He started when I called out and swiped the pamphlet off the desk out of view. His eyes widened as he took us in. His gaze flicked from Lok's folded arms to the big lascar's patterned waistcoat and shaven head and then back to me in the middle.

'I've come to see Sam . . . Mr Collins. Is he in?'

The boy opened his mouth, but nothing came out. He was staring at Lok's plait now. It was longer than Tan Seng's. Of a rule he wound it up or tucked it down inside the neck of his tunic, but today it hung long and grey, almost touching the dusty boards.

'Cat got it, or can't you speak?'

The boy dragged his eyes away. 'He's not here.'

'Are you expecting him or is he out for the day?'

'I don't know, Miss.' He shrugged and stared up at Hari, who blocked most of the light creeping in from the window. It was obvious I wasn't going to get much more in the way of service from him.

'What about Mr Peters – he around?'

The boy nodded.

'And?'

'And what?' He sniffed and leaned over the desk to stare without an ounce of shame at Hari's sandalled feet.

'And can I see him?'

The boy tore his eyes from the lascar's toes.

'Now?'

I rolled my eyes. 'No, next Thursday. Of course I mean now! It's important. Here.' I dug in my pocket and handed him a thruppenny bit. 'Does that make it worth your while?'

'S'pose it won't do no harm.' He wiped his nose on his shirt cuff, took the coin and sloped to a door at the back of the office where I knew there were stairs leading to an untidy warren of rooms above.

We waited in silence for several minutes. Hari went to stand by the door leading out to the street. He folded his arms and planted his legs wide apart. Lok pretended to leaf through an old copy of *The London Pictorial* left out on the counter, but I knew he was watchful. I suppose I should have been grateful for their concern, but, tell truth, they were beginning to set me on edge.

The door at the back creaked open and Peters appeared. He paused in the frame when he saw Hari standing guard.

There was a wary look on his face, but it vanished as soon as he saw me at the counter.

'Miss Peck! What an unexpected supwise.'

I grinned. 'Hello Mr P. I've come to see Sam. Is he about?'

Peters frowned. 'Well now, he is and he isn't.'

'I don't follow you. He's either here or he's not. Which is it?'

'It's a vewy delicate matter, Miss. They took his desk away last week and most of the other furniture from the upper floors. We was wather expecting them to be back today. That's why the boy may have appeared to be a little . . . vague. He thought you might have been sent by them. Your . . . companion . . .' he glanced at Hari, 'certainly has the look of a bailiff's man.'

'Bailiffs?'

Peters nodded solemnly. '*The Pictowial* is cuwently expewiencing something of a cwisis. Our cweditors are circling. But Sam will think of something. He is most wesourceful. Isn't that wight, Billy?'

He turned as the door at the back creaked again. The boy who had been slouching at the counter when we arrived ambled over and retrieved his dog-eared pamphlet from a shelf under the wooden board.

'Isn't that wight?' Peters asked again. 'Sam will know what to do, eh lad?'

The boy shrugged. 'He'd better think bleedin' fast then. Pa says him and the lads are going to dismantle the machinery downstairs and sell the metal for scrap. They ain't been paid for three weeks now. Better they get the money than the bailiffs.'

I put my leather bag down on the boards, unpinned my bonnet and placed it on the counter between us. 'But Sam's not the editor, is he, Mr Peters? Surely it's not up to him.'

Peters rubbed the side of his nose and slipped a look at the boy. 'Between you, me and the bootscwaper, Miss Peck, I don't think our actual editor, Mr McPherson, has been quite himself for some time. His ...' Peters stared at the knotty grain of the counter, 'condition has made it wather difficult for us all, Sam especially. He's been carrying *The Pictowial* almost on his own. When our backers discovered Mr McPherson's ... affliction they withdrew their support.'

I thought back to my first meeting with Sam, here in this very office. I'd come with Lucca. I was all tricked out in my finest gear, but he'd seen through me. At first I took him for the editor, for all that he wasn't much older than us, but then he'd let something drop. I leaned across the counter. 'Mr McPherson's affliction, is it something he picked up at The Lion and Seven Stars?'

Peters nodded. 'He can't stop ... that is to say, it is vewy unlikely that he'll wecover.'

I pushed my hair away from my face. The bonnet had kept the sun off, but now my scalp prickled with sweat.

'Sam's hiding upstairs, then? Is that what you meant by "he is and he isn't"? I take it he's not here if the bailiff's boys come calling.'

Peters shook his head. 'Not at all. He was here earlier, but without a chair and desk it's difficult to work and it gets wather overheated on the upper floors on days like these.'

I thought about Sam's untidy cubby hole with its teetering stacks of papers threatening to topple at any moment. No wonder he didn't want to sit on the boards in the midst of all that. It would take a week to dig him free if they fell on him.

'He'll be in the Fields,' Billy piped up. 'Over to the right from the entrance, thirty yards down there's a bench under some old limes. He likes to sit there when he's thinking, but he'll be back soon.'

'And he'll be vewy happy to see you, Miss Peck. I know it.' Peters rubbed his hands together. 'But where are my manners! Perhaps some tea while you wait?'

That decided it. I took up my bonnet. 'Thank you for the offer, but I think I need a bit of air myself. I'll go and find him.'

'I'll be perfectly safe. He's over there, see?'

Lok squinted dubiously into the shade under a clump of lime trees twenty yards away. Lincoln's Inn Fields was a well-used pocket of green in the City, fringed about with lawyers' offices and good houses. Sam was sitting on a bench, just as Billy had said. He was hunched over some papers. I'd know him anywhere from that long brown fringe dangling over his face. His jacket hung untidily over the curved metal back of the bench and his shirt cuffs were rolled to his elbows.

'You two can watch me from here. There's only room on the bench for one more so you might as well sit on the grass and wait . . .'

'But The Lady must be safe. We must be near in case . . .' Lok stopped himself and fiddled with the end of his plait.

'In case of what?'

He didn't answer. Hari shuffled uncomfortably from foot to foot and stared across the close-mown grass at a boy and his sister arguing over a hoop. 'I'll tell Mother!' The boy snatched the hoop from his sister's hands and bolted across the lawn towards a gateway. The girl folded her arms. She stared after him for a moment, then she followed slowly.

'You'll have a clear view of me from here. I'm only going to talk to him, we're not planning on running away together.'

'But we must—'

'No!' I cut Lok off. 'Stay here and wait for me. Sit in the shade over there if you like. Point of fact, that's probably best, you'll be less notable.'

I didn't wait for a reply and I didn't turn to look back at the pair of them as I marched across the grass. I reckon they must have presented a comical sight, though, the tiny little Chinaman and his giant of a friend. They must have sembled something from a pantomime.

I paused in a patch of deeper shade before I reached Sam's bench. He was smoking, that's to say he would have been if he hadn't forgotten about the rolled-up stump caught between the fingers of the left hand. I watched as he jerked his fringe away from his eyes and shifted his grip to let a page fall to the muddle of papers strewn around his feet.

'I'd know your office anywhere, Sam Collins, from the mess.'

He twisted about and tried to clear that fringe from his view with the back of the hand holding the roll-up.

'Kitty!' He jumped up and more pages fell around him. 'What brings you here?'

'You do, as a matter of fact. Billy and Mr Peters told me

where you were, but I reckon I could've found you just as easy without their help by following the trail of papers you leave behind.'

He grinned, but it didn't quite reach his sharp eyes. Sam Collins never carried much meat, but he was rangier than I'd ever seen him. His rolled shirt sleeves were stained with dark spots I took for ink and as I got closer I saw stubble on his jaw.

'Peters offered you tea?'

I nodded. 'But I didn't take it. I've had it before, remember.'

'A wise choice.' He tossed the stubby roll-up to the earth and ground it with his foot. 'Peters will be disappointed. He's always had a soft spot for you.'

I swung my bonnet on its ribbons. 'Billy said you came here to think.'

Sam nodded. 'He's a good lad. His father works the presses in the basement.'

'Yes – he mentioned something about that.' I moved closer. 'You going to sit then, only I am. Budge up.' I plonked myself down and hung the bonnet from the curling metal bench end. 'Actually, they – Peters and Billy, that is – they told me about the bums – the bailiffs – and everything. It don't sound too good, Sam.'

He let out a short bitter laugh as he sat down again next to me. 'That's an understatement. If we ... if *I* don't find seven hundred pounds by the end of the week they'll take back the building. They've already taken nearly everything else.'

I set my bag down on some papers. 'Peters told me about your furniture ... I'm sorry.'

'Don't be. It was terrible stuff. If ... *when* we get *The Pic-*

torial up and running again the first thing I'll do is order myself a better desk and a decent chair. The last one was held together with string in the end. I doubt the bailiffs will get much for it.'

I stared down at the pages scattered around us. Most of them were covered in Sam's phonetic scrawl.

'What's all this then?'

'Old contacts, old notes. The last four years of my life are at your feet, Kitty. You're down there somewhere.'

'What are you doing with it all out here?'

'Research. There must be something I can use. A story that no one has told; a scandal everyone missed; a new lead on an old mystery. I'm looking for something that will give *The Illustrated* a run for its money. Our readers are dropping like red jackets at Isandlwana and the backers are scared. Of course they are – I would be too in their place. The market is flooded. Something calling itself *The London Evening News* launches any day now, have you heard about that?'

I shook my head.

Sam snorted. 'You will. It's to be printed on blue paper to make it stand out. Three of our former backers have invested in it. I've no doubt the others will follow their lead.'

He screwed up the paper in his hand. 'I need something to show them all that *The Pictorial* is worth their continued trust. I need to turn this dross to gold.' He kicked out and the papers at his feet flapped across the earth and grass round the bench.

I'd never seen Sam like this before.

I was quiet for a moment. 'Have you found it then, Rumpelstiltskin?'

He rubbed his chin and I heard the scrape of his stubble. As I waited for an answer I noted the line of his profile. Under all that hair Sam had a good, strong nose with a smatter of freckles across the bridge.

'Not yet.' He stacked the remaining papers beside him on the bench and turned to fumble in the shabby lining of the jacket hanging over the back. He found a battered silver case and flicked it open.

'Smoke?'

I shook my head. 'No thanks.'

'I don't blame you. They're bloody awful, but it's the only stuff I can afford. Helps me think.' He took a thin roll-up and a match from the little case. He struck on the side to light up, but he didn't take a drag. Instead he rested his forearms on his knees and turned to look at me straight, pushing his fringe aside to get a clear view of my face.

I got a clear view of him too. The skin around his eyes was shadowed making him look older than his years.

He flicked his roll-up at Lok and Hari who were lurking in the shade of a big oak tree.

'Interesting company you're keeping these days. Where's Mr Fratelli, Lucca?'

'His mother's sick. More than that, tell truth – she's near the end. Lucca's gone home to see her.'

'And home is . . .?'

'A long way from London. Naples or nearabouts – down south. Those two are . . .' I paused. I didn't want to tell him they were there to protect me. I turned to look at my guardians who were watching us close. 'They work for me.'

Sam grinned and a bit of his old sly spark struck up. 'So they're a double act?'

'Something like that.'

He took a quick draw on the roll-up. 'What happened to The Gaudy, Kitty?' He flicked some ash to the parched grey earth around the bench. 'I could make something of that.'

'It was an accident. The gas jets were faulty. Them old places catch quicker than a dockside tallow store.' The words rattled out like chandlery nails scooped into a brown paper bag. Even to my ear they sounded like tin.

Sam nodded. 'It was fortunate no one was hurt.'

'It . . . it was late. It happened after I closed up.'

He nodded again. 'That's what it said in *The Illustrated*. To be frank, I was surprised you didn't come to me first—'

'It's not like that. They came to me!'

Sam ignored my interruption and carried on. ' . . . so I made some enquiries.' He flicked back his straggly fringe and stared at me. There was a hard look in his brown eyes. I shifted on the bench and bent forward to pick up some of the papers. Sometimes Sam Collins unnerved me. It came to me then that he was as good a player as most of them in the halls. Under all the twitching and ink stains, he was sharp as a fox. Today he was a hungry one and that put me on my guard.

'And what did you find out?' I didn't look up as I reached for a page.

'This and that.' He paused. 'Amit Das and Edie Strong. I found out about them.'

The paper in my hand fell to the ground.

'You don't deny it then, Kitty – they both died in the fire?'

'Who did you hear that from?'

'You know I have contacts. I just asked the right people. Don't ask me who, because I won't tell you. It's a matter of professional confidence. We all have our secrets.'

He let that linger for a beat longer than was comfortable. I reached down for the papers again, gathering them into a neat pile on my lap. The page on top was covered in Sam's shorthand. As I tried to make out the meaning of the first line his voice came again.

'As a matter of fact I didn't use the information as a courtesy to you. For old time's sake, you might say.'

I faced him now. 'And what else *might* you say, Sam?'

He shrugged. The ashy tip of his unsmoked roll-up trembled and fell to the ground.

'It doesn't matter what I might say. *Pictorial* investors are hardly likely to trouble themselves with an Indian mute and a working girl. Besides, my . . . source was most anxious for me not to use the story. He's very loyal to you, Kitty. I found it rather touching .' He flicked some ash from the material of his breeches. 'And, if I may say so, perplexing.'

'What do you mean by that?'

'He kept calling you "The new Lady". He didn't refer to you by name, but he was most insistent that I shouldn't cause you any trouble. I would almost say he seemed . . . wary of you. But of course, as I know you, I can't have been right about that, can I?' He took a drag on his roll-up. The end glowed.

'Is there anything you'd like to tell me, Kitty? *Entre-nous?*'

'Entre-what?'

'It means between ourselves.' He tossed the roll-up away. 'Do you have a story that can save *The Pictorial*?'

Of an instant, I felt I was on shifting ground. There were a lot of things I could tell him that would make his investors and his readers sit up straighter than a Sunday Methodist with a hot coal rammed up his jacksy. I shouldn't have come here. I fanned myself with the page from the top of the pile and kicked out my cotton skirts so they billowed around my ankles. I pulled at the ruffled neck of my dress.

'I've never known a summer like this. I don't know how you men go about with all that rough stuff chafing at your skin. Watch it, you'll burn a hole.' I brushed some fallen ash from his woollen knee in what I hoped was a friendly way, but he took hold of my hand.

Out of the corner of my eye I saw Lok scramble to his feet. I turned and shook my head. He folded his arms and, after a long pause, sank cross-legged to the grass again.

Sam gripped tighter. 'Don't change the subject. I need your help, Kitty, please. There is something, isn't there? The Gaudy, the fire? It wasn't an accident. And there's more, I know it. I can see it in your face. You're a shadow of yourself. If you're in any sort of trouble—'

'No! It was an accident like I said.' I pulled my hand free. 'And that's all I'm going to say, so don't try your luck. As for me not looking my best, I've not been ...' I wasn't sure how to end that, so I didn't. I rubbed my wrist. 'You hurt me just now, clinging on so tight.'

He drew away sharp. 'I'm sorry. I didn't mean ... you're the very last person ...' Sam pushed his sleeves up over his elbows and leaned forward to rest his forehead in his hands. His dark hair stuck up at an odd angle over his fingers.

'Ignore me. I'm a tired and desperate man.' He tried to

laugh, but it didn't come out right. 'I take it you're not here because you heard about the straits we're in and wanted to help?'

I shook my head. 'I only heard just now from Peters and the boy.'

'Billy? He told you I came here to think, is that right?'

'I imagine it's better than sitting on the floor of your office.'

Sam nodded. 'On a day like this. Tell me, have you ever heard of Jack Ketch, Kitty?'

'You mean Mr Punch's hangman?'

'No, the real one.' Sam sat back and stared out over the grass. 'Years ago this was a place where the law took its dues. Jack Ketch was the King's executioner, but not a very talented one, it seems. There's a story about him and one of the unfortunate men he beheaded – or tried to. After the first stroke, apparently it took four in all to finish the job, the victim looked up and said to him: "You dog, did I give you ten guineas to use me so inhumanely?"'

He pitched forward and rested his head in his hands again. His shoulders started to shake and for a moment I thought he was sobbing, but then I realised he was laughing.

'I don't see what's funny about that.'

'Don't you? As a journalist I rather admire his bravura cynicism. I often think about him when I'm sitting here.'

I looked at Sam's bare arms and realised I'd been wrong. He wasn't so much skinny as wiry. Thing was, he was so spare that his clothes hung loose from his frame, giving the impression he was lost somewhere inside, but now, with his jacket hanging on the bench, I could make out muscles I hadn't expected to see on him.

'Listen.' I moved a bit closer. 'You'll find something. I know you will.'

'I appreciate your confidence in me, Kitty, but I fear it won't be enough. Seven hundred pounds is a great deal of money. Even if I had the powers of your Swami Jonah at my disposal, I doubt that I could produce it in time. You called me Rumpelstiltskin earlier – what I need is a miller's daughter in the basement weaving gold.'

He sat back. 'But you didn't come here to talk about fairy tales, did you?'

I shook my head. 'No, I wanted to ask you about something connected to *The Pictorial*. I was hoping—' I broke off. Of an instant, an idea had occurred to me.

'You may as well ask away, Kitty. Who knows how much longer I'll be in a position to answer?' Sam clearly thought I was minding his feelings – and in a way I was.

I snapped open my bag and fished out the newspaper Fitzy had given me. 'It's in here.'

'Not a bad edition, I thought, under the circumstances.' Sam took it from me. 'And probably the last.' Laying it out over his knees he began to flick through from the back, pausing when he reached the pages marked up by Fitzy.

'Is this it? The acts – you want to know what they're really like?' He shook his head and his fringe flopped back over his eyes. 'Don't waste your money, that's my advice. There's nothing new here. Torsade the contortionist works with an assistant. It's quite obvious how it's all done. The key to the shackles is in her mouth.' He ran an ink-stained finger down the page. 'And these others are all standard fare – tumblers, animals, plate spinners. The pianist can't hit one sound note in four, which is remarkable in itself, I suppose—'

I cut him off. 'It's not acts. I want to know about something at the front. There's a picture of some gents. Let me show you.' He handed the newspaper back to me and I turned to the page I wanted him to see. 'Here. This is the story.'

Sam nodded. 'Denderholm. He was in India for most of his life. Now he's returned and Her Majesty seems to be creating a post to keep him comfortable in retirement. It's nothing remarkable.'

'It's not him I'm interested in. It's this one, the youngest of them.' I pointed at the man I took to be Lord Vellum.

Sam raised an eyebrow. 'Interested?'

'I just want to know who he is.'

'Why?'

I stared at the page. It *was* him, I was certain of it.

'I reckon I know him from somewhere. I want to be sure.'

'Ah, so he's a punter, is he?' Sam grinned. 'Perhaps he's made a little too free with the chorus girls? Or has he done something else? Something extremely wicked and scandalous, I hope? Is there a story here for me, Kitty?'

'I doubt it. Not in the way you think at least. It's more a . . . business matter. I need to be sure of my facts before I take it any further. Do you know who he is?'

Sam shook his head. 'No, but I can try to find out for you.'

'From one of your contacts, is that it?'

'As I said earlier, a journalist never divulges his sources.' He stared at me direct, that hard look in his eyes again. 'Don't try your luck.' I noted he repeated my own words back to me as he took *The Pictorial* from my hands and read through the copy again.

'You intrigue me – as ever. There might well be something worth examining here.'

'Listen, I'm not interested in the London Imperial Agency, Sam. I just want to know who he is.'

He reached behind for his jacket and took out the silver case again. 'But reading this over, Kitty, it is actually rather interesting.'

'You wrote it, didn't you?'

'Not I.' He struck a match against the side and lit up another stringy roll-up. 'It came in from the Bureau. We use their stories to pad out the pages when we don't have enough copy of our own.' He raised the roll-up to his lips and pulled deep. 'Of late, I'll admit it to you, I've been having to rely more heavily on the Bureau to fill *The Pictorial*.'

'How does that work, then? What's the Bureau?'

'It's a source of general news. It supplies reports from criminal trials – which can be useful because the readers like them – but in the main it's dull stuff. Legal announcements, desiccated nuggets Mr Gladstone wants people to know. The only reason I've been able to use the Bureau is that a year ago I had the good sense to persuade McPherson to pay for a year's worth in advance. This story . . .' Sam tapped the page and a fresh tumble of ash began to burn a hole which he hurriedly batted away. 'Sorry – that's better. This story came with the block for the print.'

I looked at all the whiskered gents staring out at us. 'Why is it interesting?'

'Do you see the wording just here?' He read it aloud. '... *these good men, under the guidance of General, Lord*

Denderholm, stand ready to guide and advise Her Majesty in all matters related to the Empire when their consequence is manifest at home.'

I frowned. 'I don't follow your meaning.'

Sam took a drag. 'I'd like to know what "*their consequence is manifest at home*" actually means. It seems an odd phrase. What, precisely, does Her Majesty need advising on?' He turned to me. 'And why would it interest you, Kitty?'

'Like I said, I'm not interested in Lord Denderholm and the rest of them. I just want to know who that is.' I jabbed at the page. 'Him with the cheekbones and starchy white collar.'

Sam shot me a sly look from under his fringe. 'Would you describe him as handsome?'

The sound of a bell went off from somewhere over the other side of the Fields. I counted the chimes, and after the fifth I stood up abrupt. Twenty yards off, Lok and Hari rose too.

'It's late. I've got to go. I'd appreciate your help, Sam, but I can see you've other things taking up your time just now. I hope you find something among this lot. Truly I do.' I bent to retrieve some more fallen papers from the dust around the bench. 'Here.'

Of an instant, I couldn't resist showing him.

'Now, this one looks interesting. Ba ... Bardwell Street mer ... merder. *Murder!* Baf ... baffling dis ... discovery.'

I began to read Sam's coded scribble back to him. I glanced up as I paused for effect and was gratified to see the look on his face.

'You can't be! Give it to me, Kitty. Let me see that.' He dropped *The Pictorial* onto the bench and reached across to swipe the page from my hands, but I whipped it clear and carried on.

'Dis . . . dis member ed. *Dismembered* body discover . . . ed in wind . . . o. Ah! I see *window* less . . . at tic, *attic* room, is it? There's a dirty big thumb mark just there. L . . . locked from the ins . . . ide. Let's see, it actually reads: *Dismembered body discovered in windowless attic room locked from the inside.* You could make something of that one, I reckon! That's if no one's worked it out yet?'

I smiled and dipped a curtsey. Sam stood up now and snatched the page from me. I watched as his eyes ran over the lines. After a moment he nodded to himself.

'I don't understand . . . How did you work it out?'

'I've been teaching myself, that's how. I sent off for a Phonotypic Alphabet Work Book after you showed off to me that time. I thought it might be useful, for business and suchlike. It's not that hard once you get into the way of it. All them Biblical passages over and over – I dare say they're very improving to the mind, but it's dry as a nun's—' I stopped myself from committing a profanity. It didn't seem decent under the circumstances, given we was discussing religious affairs.

Sam raised an eyebrow. 'I believe the founder of the system was a most observant and God-fearing man, and besides, the language of the Bible is as good a test as any, especially for the more unusual forms.'

I quizzed at him.

'All those Xs and Zs? Zebedee, Zacharia, Zipporah, Zephania, Ezra, Ezekiel, Exodus, Xanthicus, and a very great deal of exaltation. I didn't pay attention at Sunday school, but

I daresay I know more about the Bible thanks to the phonetic alphabet than Archibald Campbell Tait. Repetition locks the more singular symbols into your memory.'

He pushed his fingers through his fringe. 'They say it's difficult to read another's hand, but you managed to read mine.'

I shrugged. 'You write clear. The stains make it hard in places, but I can still make it out.'

He stared at me and then his face broke into a smile that reached his brown eyes properly this time.

'You are remarkable, Kitty. You do realise that, don't you?'

I dipped my head and reached back to screw my springy hair into a tighter knot. I pushed the pins in hard and felt them nip the skin of my neck.

'I pick up most things quick.'

There was a long pause. 'Do you, really?'

I looked away and into the shade under the trees. Lok bowed and Hari took a step forward. I took up my bag and my bonnet. 'I'm due at The Carnival before seven. There's someone I need to see. Will you . . . Do you think you might be able to find out who that is?' I nodded at *The London Pictorial* open on the bench. 'I'd count it as a favour if you could, Sam.'

'I'll make some enquiries.' He sighed and grinned sadly. 'It will give me something to do; after all I'm likely to have rather a lot of time to fill in the near future.'

He held out his hand, formal like, and I took it.

'Something will come up, Sam. I know it will.'

Chapter Twelve

Netta Swift leaned back against the door, folded her arms and cocked her head to the side. Her dark eyes were so heavily lamped she looked like a 'gyptian from one of Lucca's books. The bold dabs of beet juice on her cheeks flared like bruises in the candlelight.

The halls turned everything round. If you went out on stage without the benefit of paint the limelight aged you by a hundred years, but away from the flares the effect was quite the opposite. In the soft glow of the oil lamp on Jesmond's desk, the cracked wax on Netta's face gave her the look of a woman of eighty.

I say, Jesmond's desk, but now he was in charge of the work over at The Comet and Fitzy had taken up permanent residence here at The Carnival. The smell of him fugged the air of the little office – and it wasn't his cologne. He didn't like it one bit when I asked him to leave Netta and me alone.

'Well, Kit?' I noted she didn't call me 'Miss' like most of them.

I didn't dislike Netta, but I didn't warm to her, neither. If I took it out and examined it up close, I suppose I might have said that I envied her. There were times when I was up there in that cage and half of London was gawping up my skirts that I'd actually found myself enjoying it – the attention, I mean.

I'd watched them run the sailor act twice through this

evening. Netta was a draw, there was no doubt about it. She knew how to weight a line, show an ankle and catch the limelight in just the spot to make her black eyes spark.

Now she was the one they all talked about while I was . . . I closed the lid on that. I didn't want to dwell on what I'd become.

Netta wasn't much older than me, but she was smart as a new whip. Peggy told me she'd made herself a favourite at The Lamb – singing for them all after-hours, entertaining them with her monologues. Watching her tonight, I could believe it, but for all her talent and her charm there was something cold about her. If she'd been a piano, one note in thirty would have played false. Most people wouldn't have noticed.

Tell truth, I had the distinct impression that Netta Swift would scramble over her mother's dead body, and anyone else's for that matter, to get what she wanted. I was relying on that. The Carnival couldn't afford to lose her.

'The punters were happy tonight, Netta. That makes me happy.' I nodded at the chair opposite. 'Sit down.'

Netta adjusted the bustle on her striped satin skirt, pulling it to one side so that she could fit on the seat. She loosened the blousy red ribbons holding the front of her bodice together, arched her neck and breathed out.

'That's better. There was a moment up there tonight when I thought we was going to melt. Marnie's not getting any younger – it's taking it out of her. Cissie looked fit to drop an' all. Dismal's been up to his usual. He was so far gone this evening I wasn't sure he'd find his way to the stage, let alone off it afterwards.'

'We both know that as long as there's a bottle waiting in the wings, he'll be there. He could sniff out a thimble of rum in a tannery.'

'And what about Swami Jonah?'

'What about him?'

'He's been at Dismal's game, only these days he can match him bottle for bottle and then take on a barrel more. He fell into the pit. Did you hear about that, Kit?'

I shook my head.

'Three of his pigeons got loose and the limelight licked the end of his sleeve so the sparks went off early. Incendiary he was. The Professor had to move his music stack. The punters thought it was all part of the act, but when he just lay there grunting like a pig, they knew what was what. The pigeons were so frightened they loosened up overhead. If you ask me, Mr McCarthy's become a liability.'

I moved the lamp so a little circle of light fell across Netta's side of the desk. 'I didn't ask you in here to talk about the acts.'

'I didn't think so.' Netta smoothed her skirts. 'But, if you want my opinion it's time to give the sailor a rest. Confine him to port, as it were. It's played well, but it's had its time. I hear they're running something similar over at Nixon's on The Strand. It's got less in the way of a tune and more in the way of a leg, if you get my meaning. Now, I don't reckon Cissie's boy would be happy for her to show her breakfast, and as for Marnie . . . don't take it wrong, but the punters wouldn't want to see much more there.' She paused and grinned slyly. 'Bella might be willing, mind. She's got a couple of assets she's always willing to share.'

'And what about you, Netta?'

'What about me?'

'I hear you've got some ideas. The sailor act isn't getting any fresher. Every time we do it we're wearing it out. We don't want to get stale, do we?' I repeated, very deliberately, what Cissie Watkins had told me. Netta's nostrils pinched together as she recognised her own words. She untied the ribbon on her sleeves and pushed the fabric up over her elbows.

'Scratches like a cat, this cheap stuff does. The skin of my back's raw from wearing this night after night.'

'What if I was to offer you something finer, Netta?'

'I'd be very pleased to take it.' She leaned forward and her eyes glittered in the lamplight, just as she knew they would. 'But tell me, Kit, what would you be expecting in return? I know about Lucca. He's not your fella, is he?'

She threw me there. I wasn't sure how to answer.

'He's a friend, that's all.'

'I thought as much. Actually, that's what he said too. So, he's set dressing, in a manner of speech?'

She parted her stained red lips and moistened them with the tip of her tongue. 'If you're looking for . . . let's call it company, then I'd be happy to be your friend. I always thought we might have something in common. We could make quite a team, you and me, Kit.'

I almost laughed out loud. Just like Sam, that time, Netta took me for a Tom.

I leaned back. 'Listen, what I'm offering you is—'

She cut me off. 'I think I know what you're offering. And I'm flattered. No, more than that. I'm pleased to be proved right. I always had a feeling about you and him; Lucca, I mean. I'm surprised we don't see you at The Wife.'

She was losing me now. And worse, I realised that she was interviewing me.

Netta raised a painted eyebrow. 'The World's Wife up Sabberton Street? You must know it?'

Of course I did. I bleedin' owned it. It was a place where women of a particular inclination could meet free. From the outside it had the look of a regular tavern. Tell truth, inside it didn't appear much different, until you was to take a close look at the customers, and even then you might not clock it.

Betsy Jordan – the proprietor – ran a good house and she paid her tithes regular. I'd met her twice after I took on Paradise, both times at The Gaudy, before it burned down. I remember she'd bowed to me, like she knew from the earliest what I'd become.

'Some of us go there for a night cap after we've been at The Lamb. You should join us.' Netta wriggled and pulled at the shoulders of her dress to show off more of her talents. I got a waft of ripe sweat and lavender water. It was so close in The Carnival's office that the stage paint was sliding off her face now. 'You don't come to The Lamb any more, Kit, not like you used to. So I was thinking that maybe you didn't find what you were looking for there?'

I stood up and went to the little window, pulling the shutters open. There was a scuffle outside, a rat most like. A scattering of stars showed clear in the ribbon of sky above the alley, but the air outside was cloying not sharp. I took a breath. It was like gulping meat broth on the turn.

'I'm not looking for company – not in the way you think, Netta.' I went to the wall cupboard and took out a bottle and a couple of glasses. 'I don't give a monkey's toss about where you find your friends and who they might be. We all need a bit of kindness in the world. But you're mistaken.'

'That a fact?' Netta leaned back and twirled the crimson laces from her bodice around her fingers. 'Only I got the impression that you might be a likely girl. And I'm not the only one. Them dirty pictures of you, Kit. No wonder you get them scrubbed off so fast.'

Now she'd lost me again. I came back to the desk and sat down, placing the bottle and the glasses between us. 'What do you mean – pictures?'

'Come on, don't play the innocent.' She stared at me. 'There's been three of them in the last two days. One in Gun Lane, one in Northey Street and one on the corner of St Ann Street, right opposite the church. I saw that one for myself. Anyone can see it's you because you're always facing out. A good likeness, I'd say. The other woman's just a back and a bare arse. So, I don't reckon I'm the only one who's mistaken.' She paused. 'If I am, that is?'

I pulled the stopper off the bottle. 'Gin?'

She nodded. As I filled the two glasses I noted that my hand was trembling. When I topped up the second glass the clear liquid flowed over the rim and trickled onto the desk top, staining the leather. The smell of it should have sweetened the air, but it made my belly fold on itself. I caught my hands tight together under the desk. I couldn't make sense of what she was saying.

'Listen, Netta, these pictures. I didn't scrub them off and I didn't ask anyone else to neither – what else do you know about them?'

She shrugged and took a sip. 'Nothing more than I've told you. They've appeared on the walls as if by magic. Always at night. Just lines – black and red. Crude – in every sense. No one knows who's doing it, if that's what you mean. But it's not so uncommon, is it? People are always daubing up profanities. Now you're . . .' She paused and took another swig of gin.

'Now I'm what? Go on, what were you going to say?'

She put the glass down and twisted the stem. There was a long silence between us. She pouted and twitched her mouth like she was trying words out for size. Eventually she came out with it.

'A Baron, that's what I was going to say. Now you're a Baron you're not going to be popular with everyone in Paradise. You're not the lovely little Limehouse Linnet these days. I reckon them filthy pictures is someone's way of showing you that. Someone who really knows you.' She smiled. 'Lady Ginger's gone and she's left it all to you. That's what Fitzy says.' Her dark eyes hardened. 'What did you have to do to get it all, Kit? Because I don't reckon Paradise come cheap.'

I reached for my glass and downed it in one, before filling myself another. I didn't offer the bottle to Netta.

'So everyone knows, then?'

'That you're a Tom?'

'No – that I'm a Baron.'

Netta shrugged. 'Those of us who take an interest and keep a clean ear to the wall. It's not exactly a secret, is it? There hasn't been an announcement as such, but word's getting round. I would have thought you'd be happy to crack the whip. I would in your place.' She looked around the office and wrinkled up her nose. 'To be honest with you, Kit, I'm surprised you bother with The Carnival and what happens here. You got more to think about now – a lot more. Lady Ginger now, she was always on her own and it told on her. But you don't have to be. I can help you, if you'll let me.'

Now I understood her. She was pitching far higher than a lead spot on the bill. I stared at the dark stain on the desk top where the gin was soaking into the leather as she carried on.

'Together we'd make quite a team. The truth isn't a weakness, Kit. You've got to be strong like she was. Make them respect you. I can help with that.' She leaned across the table and laid a hand over mine.

'What do you reckon?'

I pulled away sharp, reached down to the side of the desk and took up my bag.

'I reckon you're pissing up the wrong tree, Netta Swift. I'm not a Tom, whatever those pictures suggest. The reason I asked you to come and see me was this.'

I pulled a roll of paper from the bag and flattened it out between us.

'It's a contract. You've been right about one thing today at least. I am going to bring the sailor into port and I'm minded to make you a solo turn. No chorus, no others on stage backing you up, just you. You're good, Netta, and I don't want to lose you . . .'

I paused. 'I don't mean that in a romantic way, so don't take it wrong. I want you on my stage, not in my bed.'

Netta stared at the contract and then she laughed.

'I don't see what's so bleedin' funny.'

'Don't you?' She wiped her eyes leaving a smear of lampblack across the back of her hand.

'Pa always told me if you don't ask you don't get. I thought it was worth a try.'

I pushed the bottle towards her now and nodded at the empty glass. 'Go on, pour yourself another. I'm not in the market for a partner, Netta – business or otherwise. But what I need is an act that will bring in enough paying punters to help me rebuild The Gaudy and pay for the repairs at The Comet. Them plasterers and gilders don't come cheap.'

She frowned. 'But, surely, if you're a Baron, it don't matter. You could pay it all a hundred times over and still have enough change to buy a county.'

She was right, but it was a matter of honour, pride you might say, for me to see the halls and everyone who worked in them make good. The rest of Paradise was foul as a tanner's pit, but the theatres were ... I don't know exactly, but *clean* was the word that came to mind. Lady Ginger had called them a front, 'a painted facade', but to me, they were the heart of it all.

'That's not the point, Netta. I want to make a go of the halls. It's where I came from.' I took a swig of gin. 'You might say it's my family.'

'Funny sort of family, I call it. Was that why she left it to you?'

I gripped the stem of the glass. How could she know the truth? There was a stab of pain over my right eye as she went on.

'The cage, I mean, the bird act? Is that why you got it all? Anyone who could do that night after night without a net deserves respect. I don't think there's anyone else here, man or woman, who's got the balls for it.'

'Not even you, Netta?' The pain stopped quick as it had come.

'I'd do a lot of things, but . . .' A sly grin crept across her face, cracking the red wax on her lips. 'Was it the act, or did you do something else for her?'

I twisted the glass. 'It was nothing like that.'

She nodded. 'Would you go up again?'

I tipped back my head and finished off the gin. I was feeling more convivial towards her now.

'I doubt it. Anyway it's stale. The punters are looking for something new. They always are. Listen, you could be a name, Netta. You've got it in you. I've already asked Professor Ruben to sniff out some songs for you to try. Comic stuff, character – maybe a bit on the edge? I'll treble what you're getting now if you give it a try. And we'll talk again if it goes well. Will you sign?'

She eyed the contract. 'What's it say?'

'Here – read it for yourself.' I pushed it across the desk, but she didn't take it up. She folded her arms.

'I can't read, Kit.'

I wasn't surprised, half of Limehouse didn't have the benefit of letters. Of an instant I felt uncomfortable, though, like she'd caught me lording it over her.

'I promise you it's straight. Nothing to tangle you up or peg you out on a line. I'm offering two guineas a week, and more if you prove me right. There's an allowance for costumes as well. You need to look the part.'

'That sounds fair.' Netta pulled the contract towards her. 'As a matter of fact I've been working on something. I'm willing to try it if you are.'

'I thought you'd been trying it out already tonight?'

She held her head to one side and grinned. 'No. I mean an act. I've been working on something in private with ... with a friend. I'm ready – I reckon it'll go down like free beef dripping.'

'All right.' I nodded. 'Give it a go. Shall we say, two days' time, top of the bill? I'll let Fitzy know. How does that sound?'

'Perfect.'

'You sign here.' I pointed to the space at the bottom of the page I'd had Fitzy draw up. 'You can take it away tonight and ask someone to check it, if you like.'

Netta shook her head. 'No, I trust you. I'll sign it now if you have a pen. I know how to shape my name.'

I dipped into my bag and handed her a slim silver pen.

'Here, you say?' She pointed at the foot of the page. I nodded and watched her begin to write slowly. As the pen scratched across the paper she spoke again. 'Anyway, my fella don't speak much English, so it wouldn't have done a pile of good to show him.'

I raised an eyebrow. 'Only five minutes back you were making a play for me. I thought you said you wasn't partial to men?'

She passed the pen back over the desk. 'Of a general rule that's right. I do prefer the company of women. But I go with both when the fancy takes me. This one's been persistent. He don't say much, but he's a looker. Smells nice too – better than most men, anyways. He's a shipmate, so he won't be around long. I might as well make the most of him. We're meeting tonight.'

She stood up and steadied herself on the edge of the desk. 'That's strong stuff. Gone right to my head.' She held out her hand. 'So we have an agreement after all, then?'

I nodded as we shook on it.

'I'm sorry if I ... mistook you earlier, Kit.' Netta squeezed my hand a little too hard and swayed closer. She grinned and puckered her lips. I realised she was moving in to plant a kiss. I pushed my chair back from the desk, leaving her hanging across. Netta swayed back. She took a last swig from the glass and fumbled at her striped bodice to loosen more ribbons down the front.

'I can't go out in this. It stinks. He won't like it. I'll have to get changed.'

I folded my arms. 'Are you making another try for me? Because it won't work. I'm not interested.'

'Well, that's a pity, isn't it? No, I'm not trying to seduce you, Kit, not now, anyway. What's the time?'

'Past twelve, I reckon near to one.'

'Don't time fly?' Netta pulled at her sleeves. 'I just hope Cissie's still about somewhere to help me with the back. It's a pig to get off.'

'Turn round then.' I stood and went over to pull at the ribbons criss-crossing the back of Netta's costume until she could shrug herself free from the stiff ruffled shoulders.

As I untied the final bow at the base of her spine she laughed. 'I never thought I'd be this close to one of the Barons of London. Who'd have thought it? One minute you're up in the cage trilling and twirling and the next ...'

She turned, clutching the two sides of the bodice close. 'He saw you once. He must have done.'

160

'Who?'

'My sailor friend – he's a Baltic, I think. He comes from somewhere over the sea and north of Limehouse, anyway. I told him that I'd be late tonight because you and I had business to discuss and he let off a string of foreign. I don't think he was too happy.'

I handed Netta a red ribbon. 'If it was foreign, how do you know he saw me?'

She tucked the ribbon into her bodice, bobbed a sort of curtsey and went to the door. 'I took it as a reference to you and that cage. He must have seen you perform when he was here in the winter, matter of fact I'm sure of it.'

She twisted the handle and stepped out into the corridor, but her voice came back as she disappeared from view.

'When I told him he'd have to wait up late for me tonight he spat on the floor and said, quite clearly, "Fuck Lady Linnet."'

Chapter Thirteen

Tan Seng took the letter and bowed. If he thought it was odd that I was standing there barefoot in my night shift and Nanny Peck's plaid shawl he didn't show it.

I'd gone to my office and scribbled it all down as soon as it was light. It wasn't a fancy note, but the meaning was clear. There was ink under my nails now that made me think of Sam. I stared at the letter as Tan Seng folded it into his sleeve. I'd added a heavily underlined postscript reminding the Beetle about my grandmother.

'I want Telferman to deal with the business as soon as possible – make the necessary arrangements today if he can. It can't be later than tomorrow.'

Tan Seng bowed again. 'I will send to Pearl Street immediately.' He turned to the stairs.

'Wait! Please.'

He shuffled about on the black and white hall tiles. A shaft of sunlight from the fanlight over the door caught his face.

'Lady?' He stepped into the jagged shadow of the staircase to avoid the brightness.

'Do you know anything about pictures of me?' I nodded at The Palace's doors. 'Pictures on walls out in the streets?'

He shook his head. The plait flicked from side to side behind him. 'They are gone, Lady. It is not right for such things to be seen.' He stared at his feet.

'It was you, then? You made arrangements for them to be ... removed.'

He didn't look up. 'Bad things. We made sure they were scrubbed away.'

I moved closer. The tiles were warm and sticky beneath my feet. 'You mean you and Lok went out and did it?'

Tan Seng shook his head again. 'In Paradise The Lady has many eyes, many hands.'

Of an instant, I was minded of a saying put around about my grandmother. People reckoned that every cobble in Limehouse was one of Lady Ginger's eyes. I realised there was a truth in that. Only now it seemed all them 'eyes' belonged to me.

I looped a stray coil of hair behind an ear. 'Why didn't you tell me about them, Tan Seng? If anyone's daubing the walls of Paradise with pictures of me, I reckon I have a right to know about it.'

'These were not seemly, Lady.' Mouse-black eyes scanned my face. He cleared his throat. 'We made sure they were not seen.'

'Well, someone saw them, otherwise I wouldn't know about them. Netta from The Carnival told me about the one at St Ann Street. She made a special trip to get an eyeful. And if she saw it, a hundred others did too.'

Tan Seng dipped his head. 'I am sorry, Lady. We must act with more speed.'

I frowned as I took in what he meant. 'Are you saying there will be more?'

He fumbled in his sleeves and didn't answer.

'Has this happened before?'

'I must make sure that this is delivered to Pearl Street, Lady. Please.' He bowed and tried to slip past me to the stairs down to the basement where he and Lok had their quarters.

'Stop!' I caught his shoulder. When he turned there was surprise in his eyes as well as something else, something that looked like the beginnings of tears. He glanced away and stared at my ink-stained hand still resting on the grey silk of his gown. I realised I'd never touched him before. I felt as if I'd committed an intrusion and pulled away.

'I'm sorry. I . . . Tan Seng, you just said you must act with more speed. You made it sound as if you're expecting it to happen again.'

The high-buttoned collar twitched as he swallowed.

'This *has* happened before, hasn't it? Was it pictures of *her*, my grandmother?'

He shook his head and started to back away from me towards the stairs. 'The Lady has many friends, but there are others who wish her harm. We will always stand against them.'

My feet slapped on the marble as I crossed the tiles towards him, but he was already on his way down. I caught the carved wooden post at the top of the flight and watched him slip into the shadows below.

'Answer me, please, Tan Seng,' I called to his retreating back. 'Did someone leave drawings of her around Paradise, and if they did, do you know who it was?'

Before he disappeared completely I heard him muttering something I couldn't catch, and then he added more distinct, 'Long time.'

I pulled Nanny Peck's shawl around my shoulders. The

poor thing was patched and threadbare now, but it was all I had of her. There was a time when it smelt of her too. Just after I lost Ma I used to burrow my face in the few things they left to bring them back. Ma's stuff smelt of Lily of the Valley and Nanny Peck's stuff smelt of soap.

The shawl still smelt of carbolic, but I'd washed it so many times I'd rinsed the old girl away. It made me sad that I couldn't catch a trace of her in the coarse fabric now. We might not have shared the same blood, but we shared something more important. As I stood on the tiles there was something I got all right, though – the sound of her tight little voice, scandalised at the sight of them pictures.

Filth! That's what it is, my girl. Pure and simple.

Nanny Peck was no connoisseur, not like Lucca, but she would have been right on one count there. As to the other two . . .

I crossed the hall to the stairs leading up the parlour on the first floor. As I passed the table I looked up at the painting. I had half a mind to call Tan Seng back and ask him if he knew who it was – after all, my grandmother had hidden it away. But something told me this was an occasion when he wouldn't hear on purpose, just in case I carried on quizzing him where I left off.

The young gent in the painting pointed at a white stone house over to the right, the columns along the front half hidden by trees. Joey was hiding somewhere. I badly needed to know where, but most of all I needed to know why. If I didn't hear from Telferman today I'd go to his office and turn out every drawer and cabinet until I found what I needed.

'And another thing about that bird; when it's not swearing, it starts singing and most of the songs it knows aren't fit for the docks, let alone the halls. Then there's the other stuff you can't make head nor tail of. I wish you'd get rid of it.' Peggy stared at Jacobin's cage.

The parrot fluttered up from the grainy floor, grasped the bars in his ridged grey claws and fixed her with yellow-rimmed eyes. He opened his nut cracker beak and wriggled his tongue. Peggy shuddered and shifted further down the couch.

'It knows when you talk about it. Look at it now, watching us.'

'Telferman reckons Jacobin's at least sixty years old.' I looked up from the lists sent over by the customs boys. The mariner smiths had nearly completed their repairs to the *Gouden Kalf.* Houtman's black paddle ship would be leaving Shadwell New Basin in five days' time. I wouldn't deal with him again. I fanned my face with a sheet of paper.

'Jacobin can't last much longer, Peg.'

'One more day is too long so far as I'm concerned. It's not natural, the way it looks at you like it's thinking something. And it stinks.'

'I've got used to him.' I stood and went over to the cage. 'The heat makes it worse. I'll ask Lok to give him a good clean out, he's fond of him. He told me that parrots are clever. They pick up everything they hear. Fact of the matter, Jacobin probably *is* thinking something when he looks at you.'

'Well, I'd rather it didn't.' Peggy stretched and moved a

bolster round to sit in the small of her back. She'd begun to look more like herself. Her black hair was clean with a sheen to it and her skin had a bloom again. While I went through the papers Peggy sewed. I didn't ask what she was making, I didn't need to. Tell truth, every time I caught sight of that bundle of soft white cotton rolled neatly on top of her needlebox it was a shroud that came to mind, not a christening gown.

'Dan didn't go much on it neither ...' She paused and corrected herself. 'Don't go much on it. He reckons they're vermin. He says he wouldn't have one in the house. And I reckon you should put a chain round his foot to keep him from flying up at you. A big chain.'

'*Chain, chain, chain.*' Jacobin stretched his wings as far as he could in the confines of the cage and rolled his head on his scraggy neck. I was almost grateful to him. If Peggy noticed that I turned the subject every time she mentioned Dan, she hadn't let on, but she had a way of bringing him into regular conversation that suggested he'd just stepped out to see a man about a dog and was expected back at any moment.

'*House of Chains.*' Jacobin hopped up to the bars so he was level with me. He repeated the words again. '*House of Chains.*'

'What's that then?' I heard the snap of the needlebox lid behind me as Peggy retrieved something. I shrugged. 'Something he's picked out from what you just said.' Jacobin cocked his head to one side. I got the distinctive impression he was taking the measure of me. It was cruel to keep a creature like that in a cage, but he wouldn't survive if I let him free.

Nanny Peck once took me and Joey to a shop on Mile End Road where, outside, a hundred little birds in wooden cages were singing fit to bust their hearts. The cages were strung from rope in rows three deep all the way from the second storey to the ground. I remember the sound of them all – the yellow canaries and the dull brown linnets – and the sight of the cobbles beneath them coated with shit and seed.

I wanted to let them all loose, or at least buy one for tuppence to give it freedom, but Nanny Peck told us songbirds never thrive if you let them fend for themselves.

'They lose the knack of living,' she said.

Something that Netta said kept coming back at me. No one, except Telferman and the other Barons, knew me as Lady Linnet. I hadn't even told Lucca until he found that note.

Fuck Lady Linnet. That was what he said to her. How did Netta's sailor boy know me by that name?

Jacobin went off again. '*House of Chains. House of Chains . . .*'

I ran a finger down one of the bars. 'Perhaps he means his cage, Peg?'

There was a crisp snipping sound as she trimmed the cotton in her lap. 'I don't like that bird, but it seems a cruelty. It's wrong to trap a living thing in a small space. No wonder it's bad tempered. At night, when you pull the cloth over – if it's clever like you say – that parrot must wonder if it's ever going to see the light of day again.'

Jacobin swung his head around so he was looking me straight in the eyes.

'*Light of day, light of day . . .*'

Christ! It was like he knew about Danny. I stepped back as he made a lunge for the bars, his razor beak just missing my finger. The papers in my hand fell to the rug. I turned warily from the cage and bent to collect the scattered pages. There was a metallic scrabbling from above as Jacobin threw himself at the bars.

'There, I've finished. I can't do no more.' The couch springs squeaked as Peggy reached down to place the cotton gown on top of the needlebox.

I straightened up. 'You feeling all right?'

She nodded. 'I get an ache sometimes, that's all. It helps if I move around.'

'Can you take something for it? I could get Lok to brew you up one of his teas.' I placed the papers on a folded card table set against the wall next to the cage. 'They taste like river mud, but they work, sometimes.'

'Is that what you've been taking at night to help you sleep? I've heard you walking about, Kit.' Peggy scanned my face. 'And them rings under your eyes don't lie.'

I went to sit next to her. 'Lok's concoctions don't work for me. Nothing does.'

She took my hand and I stared at the simple gold ring on her wedding finger. Danny's ring. I tried to block the roaring sound in my head as her voice came from somewhere far away. ' . . . must be hard for you. I don't know anything about the Barons, other than that they're to be feared. If you ever want to talk about it, Kit, you can trust me.'

She squeezed my hand. 'Whatever I hear, it will stay with me, I promise. Besides, even if you are a Baron, I don't reckon you're like her – your grandmother, I mean. You're one of us. Underneath it all you're still the same girl – the girl who rescued me from that warehouse and from that . . .

that . . .' Her voice faltered. 'Listen, I'll never forget it – and neither will my Danny. We'll always be on your side, always, whatever.'

I pulled away and went to the mantle, pretending to fix my hair in the big gilt mirror above it. I couldn't see my face clear through the mottling of spots and crackles in the old glass, but I could see Peggy watching me. I wondered she couldn't hear my heart clanging like St Dunstan's bells.

I swallowed. 'You can't help me, Peg. No one can. But you mustn't worry, neither – you've got your own . . .' I stopped myself. How was I going to finish that? I caught sight of my eyes in the glass. Peggy was right about the shadows. Tell truth, I'd always been proud of my eyes – it was a vanity, you might say. Until now I'd flattered myself that their blue had a touch of Devon violet to it. Now they seemed hard and colourless.

I span round. I didn't want to look at that lying face.

'What I mean is you've got the baby to think of, Peg.'

'But I want to help. You have to let these things out or they eat you up from the inside. I know how close you and Lucca are, and with him away I just thought you might need to talk to an old friend. We've always been tight, you and me. You can trust me.'

I shook my head. 'It's not as simple as that. I only wish it was. Don't ask and don't fret about me. I'll deal with it.'

'*Deal with it, deal with it . . .*'

Jacobin went off again. I flinched as I recognised Lady Ginger's clipped, girlish voice. Peggy twisted about on the couch and threw the scrap of cloth she'd snipped from the hem of the gown she was making at the cage. The parrot caught at it through the bars and started to shred it with his claws and beak.

'At least that made it shut its ugly trap. If you want my opinion that thing's evil, just like them dice she left you, along with her ...' Peggy paused. She glanced at the roll of cotton on her needlebox. 'Maybe you could ... that's to say you *can* tell fortunes from them, can't you? It's why she left them to you?'

I nodded, relieved she'd changed the subject. 'She said it was a rare gift. I can't tell fortunes, mind. I just see pictures and even then not every time.'

'Could you throw the dice to see about the baby?'

I felt a cool whisper on the back of my neck. The first time Lady Ginger had spoken to me direct she'd asked me to read the dice for her. I went along because I thought it was a game. Now I wasn't so sure.

'I don't think that's a good idea, Peg. Anyway, why? You're well, aren't you? You're looking better every day.'

'It's nothing like that. I ... I just want to know if it's a boy or a girl. Try it once and I'll never ask again. I swear.'

'Listen, Peg. Sometimes it's best not to delve too much. Some things aren't meant to be told. It's not right.'

She laid the flat of her hand on her belly. 'Dan reckons ...'

'I'll get them.' I turned away abrupt. I didn't want to know what Danny Tewson had said about his unborn child.

'Lady.'

Tan Seng and Lok were standing by the door. I hadn't heard them enter the room. Tan Seng bowed. 'There is another, Lady. You asked that when a bad picture is made, you should be told. Word has been sent.' He glanced at his brother, who nodded. In his old dark gown embroidered over with tiny silk flowers that caught the light from the window behind Jacobin's cage, Lok looked like a threadbare starling.

'We have arranged for the picture to be cleaned away.' Tan Seng bowed again and disappeared through the door. Lok smiled at Peggy, bowed to me and then he followed his brother. I ran across the room and caught them on the landing.

'Where is it this time?'

The brothers exchanged a look. It was somewhere between a warning and resignation. Tan Seng cleared his throat.

'The Lady does not need to trouble herself. It will be dealt with.'

'Where is it?'

Lok tugged at Tan Seng's sleeve and the brothers let loose a tumble of words I couldn't understand. I took a step closer and raised my hands for them to stop.

'I want to know where this picture is and I want to see it for myself.'

Lok stared at his feet and his brother fixed his gaze at a point about a foot above my head. Neither of them answered.

'What's going on?' Peggy was standing behind me now, framed in the door to the parlour. 'What did Tan Seng mean about pictures, Kit?'

'I'm not entirely sure, but I'm going to find out.' I folded my arms, 'Well, where is it this time?'

Chapter Fourteen

Bell Wharf Stairs led direct to the river from a narrow passage off Cock Hill. It was around midway between Limehouse Basin and Shadwell New Basin, and it wasn't somewhere a person would go alone.

I'll admit it wasn't a part of Paradise I'd spent much time in or given much thought to. There was a warehouse on Love Lane, where, according to Telferman's papers, I had an interest, but, truly, this was a low place. The greasy passage was the width of a man's shoulders, narrowing in some places so you had to turn yourself to the side to slip through. The walls were caked with soot and slime. I held the 'kerchief to my nose and tried to concentrate on the lavender water I'd doused it with, rather than the stench of human shit.

I didn't reckon on being able to use lavender water after this, it would never mean flowers again. Buildings rose up several storeys on either side. Even though the day was bright, when I glanced up at the chink of sky above it looked grey, not blue. Colour was a luxury here.

It was the first time I'd felt cool in weeks. I actually wished I had Nanny Peck's old plaid wrapped around my shoulders.

Hari was a couple of paces ahead and Lok and Peggy were just behind. I didn't want Peggy to come, but she insisted and I couldn't change her mind. She reckoned the walk would do her good, but now we were here she clearly wasn't so sure.

She hadn't said a word since we turned off Cock Hill. I didn't blame her; I wouldn't want to open my mouth here either for fear of what I was taking in.

Water, or something like it, tumbled through a channel between my feet. Eventually it would spew out into the Thames. I stepped over a pile of something I didn't like to give a name and felt a tug on my sleeve. A stringy naked arm extended from a cat-thin gap between two of the houses.

'Spare us a penny, love.'

The hand released my sleeve, forming itself into a cup of flesh and bone that barred the way. Lok stepped up so he was level. I shook my head to stop him as the muffled voice came again. 'A penny'll do. I don't ask more and I won't take more. I got me pride to think of.'

I peered into the crevice between the walls, trying to catch sight of the woman speaking. There was a ripple in the shadow as the woman pulled back from the thin light.

I reached into the pocket of my dress and closed my fingers round a coin. 'Why don't you come out? I won't hurt you. Here . . .'

I held out the coin. Now I looked I saw it was a shilling.

'Careful, Kit.' Peggy's voice came from behind. 'If they see that here there'll be a mob around us.'

Of an instant, the hand shot out again to snatch at the coin. At the same moment Lok darted forward and hauled the woman into the passage. I wished he hadn't.

She wasn't wearing clothes in the way you might recognise. Instead, her bunched and oddly twisted body was wrapped in a multitude of rags. The only part visible was the naked arm and the dirt-crusted hand that tried to take the coin. I had to step back at the smell that rolled off her.

'Sweet Jesus!' I heard Peggy swallow a mutter of shock and disgust.

'Don't.' The woman cowered against the wall, tugging the material round her head to hide her face. 'Don't take it back. It's not fair to trick a person.' Her voice came thick through the rags, the words not quite formed like she was speaking through a mouthful of suet.

There was an odd bulge beneath the cloth on her right side. She shifted the lump and swung about. Immediately Lok sprang between us and yanked hard at the rags. I had it in mind that he thought she had a weapon tucked away – and she did, in a manner of speaking.

The wrappings fell apart to reveal the woman's arm cradling a greying bundle against her naked breasts. Beneath the bundle two wrinkled yellow sacks mottled with watery blisters fell to the material knotted around her waist. There was a shuffle as Hari folded his arms and turned his back on the wretched sight.

'He don't like the light.' The woman scrabbled to cover herself, but as she clutched the fabric to her body, the covering over her head slipped back. Weeping sores the size of pennies showed clear across her scalp beneath thinning hair. She lowered her head, twitched a bony shoulder and tried to keep hold of her dignity and the bundle while trying to shrug the trail of grubby material back into place. It didn't work; instead, the cloth fell to the cobbles beside the open drain.

I heard her swear under her breath. She leaned forward but she couldn't bend low enough to retrieve it.

Poor sod, I couldn't bear to see her shame.

'Here, let me.' I glared at Lok and snatched up the covering. I held it out, but my hand froze as I caught a clear sight of her. She didn't have a nose. Two dark holes ate into the centre of her face pulling her upper lip into a red wound that revealed the two upper teeth that remained in her ulcerated jaw. A mass of angry crusted lumps spread from the side of what was left of her mouth obliterating her cheek and her right eye. Her right ear was just a knob of gristle.

I caught my breath, but held her good eye. It was blue. I'll always remember that. She blinked as I thrust the strip of rag at her. I heard Peggy stifle a gasp as she took in the woman's face.

'Cover yourself. And take this too.' I made myself take her hand and I pressed the shilling into her palm. I didn't want her to see how I felt about touching her.

'I'm sorry. My . . . My friend Mr Lok here was mistaken. He thought you wanted to hurt me.'

The woman closed blistered fingers around the coin and pushed it into the folds of what passed for a skirt. Then she draped the sodden rag over her head again, tucking the ends into the scraps gathered round her shoulders, careful that it shouldn't slip again. Clutching the bundle tight to her breast, she turned and stumbled towards the crevice between the buildings.

'Wait! Please.' She halted at my call, but didn't turn.

'What's your name?'

After a moment she mumbled a reply through her broken lips.

'Dora – it was Dora.'

There was something wrong there, but I carried on. I can't say why, but it was important to me to find out more. I wanted to see her as a person not a monster.

'How old are you, Dora?'

'Twenty, or thereabouts. What's it to you?'

Christ! She was little older than me. I wouldn't have known from the look of her. Then again, I wouldn't have thought it possible for a being to live under such an affliction. I knew what it was all right, the French Gout, but I'd never seen a dose gone so far.

'Where do you live, Dora?'

She twitched her head at the shadowed gap in front of her.

'You got a room down there?'

She didn't move and she didn't answer.

'You mean, you . . . you live in the alley?'

She kept her back to me and nodded. 'When you go down a way, the houses meet above. It's dry.'

There was defiance there. I reached into my pocket again.

'Dora, I want you to take this too. For the little one.'

I stepped forward and rested my hand lightly on her shoulder. She didn't turn.

Years back, Nanny Peck had rescued a sparrow from a cat in the yard behind Church Street. She'd brought it up to our rooms thinking it might gather itself together. She let me hold it and I remembered the feel of all them tiny little bones and feathers trembling in the cup of my hands. I desperately wanted to show that sparrow I didn't mean it no harm, I wanted to protect it until it was well enough to go free. That's what came to mind now. I caught Dora's free hand and forced the sovereign between her fingers.

She didn't even look at the coin as she slipped silently back into the darkness.

Of an instant, I felt sick to the pit of my belly. A sovereign wouldn't cure her. It wouldn't make everything turn up roses in her world. Nothing would. And she was just one among so many. In every dark corner of Paradise there was another Dora hiding her face and her shame from the light. What was I supposed to do? And then there was the men, the boys, the widows, the orphans, the maimed, the broken, the cankered. I was a fool to have accepted Lady Ginger's offer. This wasn't a game or a test any more, it was my world, my responsibility, and I was failing at every turn.

I stared at the narrow gap. Dora was gone now.

'It won't do no good, Kit.' I turned at Peggy's voice. In the gloom I could see tears glittering in her eyes. 'That baby she was holding, did you see its face?'

I shook my head.

'Its skin was like paper, Kit. Old, dry, wrinkled paper. It must have been dead for months.'

Dora – it was Dora.

I realised then what was odd about that answer. That poor child's mother had already buried herself along with her boy. If I started to cry now the tears wouldn't stop. I pulled Nanny Peck's shawl up over my head and took a lungful of putrid air.

'Let's see this picture. Lok, you lead the way. Hari, you stay close to Peggy.'

I watched Lok's spare little body move away from me up the passage. His long grey plait was caught up in a loop on his back to keep it from trailing in God knows what. I brought the 'kerchief to my face and swiped roughly at the dampness on my cheeks.

That sparrow Nanny Peck brought in had died too.

'It's disgusting.'

'I can see that for myself, Peg.'

I stepped back and stared up at the red and black image daubed on the wall. It was me all right. Tell truth, it was a good likeness if you looked beyond the exaggerated curves and hollows. Something about the ripe abundance of it minded me of the drawing of me up in the cage that had appeared months back in Sam's newspaper.

But this was more than titillation. My hair was a loose scribble of curls fanning out across the whitewashed brick like a peacock's tail. My face was straight on, full red lips parted to show the tip of a tongue. My eyes were open and fixed on the viewer like a challenge. I was naked and another naked figure, a man this time, knelt in front of me, his face buried in another scribble of hair lower down. My hands were on his shoulders, painted to look like I was gripping him hard, the nails digging into the skin of his back.

Standing there at the top of the steps with Peggy, I was almost grateful it was a man this time.

It was past midday now and the sun was sending little ripples of light off the river. They danced in the puddles on the steep stone steps and shivered across the wall, giving the eerie impression that the painting was moving.

I scanned it from the bottom to the top. Tell truth, I don't know what I was looking for, but I thought there might be something. Halfway up the wall, the looping ends of my hair curled together to form a profanity in perfect copperplate. I was crowned with the word *WHORE*.

'What's it mean?' Peggy piped up again.

'I think that's very clear.'

'I don't mean that – I can see for myself what he's . . . what's there. No. I mean, why would someone do this?'

I shook my head. 'Tan Seng said it's happened before.'

'I know. On the way over Lok told me they've had them cleaned away sharp before people could see them.' Peggy looked back at the lascars standing with Lok and Hari at the end of the passage.

'Them two were sent along first thing to bar the way down here. Lok says they've been here almost since word went out. Tan Seng arranged it straight off.'

'Then I'll thank him and them for sparing my dignity. It's a dirty sight, isn't it?'

She nodded. 'But this passage don't go nowhere 'cept down to the river. There's not many folk who'll have seen it.'

'Lok says that too, does he?' I made a face at her and stepped closer to touch the wall. The hot, sticky weather meant it wasn't quite dry. Red and black paint stained the balls of my fingers.

Peggy's voice came again. 'There's no need to suck a lemon. I mean, why is it here where no one will see it?'

I rolled the paint between my fingers. She was right.

'Thing is, I don't reckon Tan Seng meant *this* time, Peg. He said something about it happening a long time ago – mucky pictures, I mean. I think it upset him. He didn't want to talk about it and he didn't want me to see it.'

I glanced to the end of the passage. Hari and Lok were deep in conversation with the two lascars sent to fend off gawpers. I was grateful for that too. The thought of all of us standing there taking an eyeful of me arrayed in something less than all my glory was more than uncomfortable.

'What do you want to do now, Kit?'

'Get it scrubbed off smart, I suppose. Although now I've seen it I'm none the wiser.'

I leaned back on the wall opposite the painting and stared up at it. The pointed chin was mine and the arch of the brows. No one who knew me could be mistaken. In a dark passage a couple of blocks back Dora was holding a dead child to her breast. This filthy scrawl was nothing in comparison and yet . . .

What did it mean? Who would do something like this, and why?

I slid a look at Peggy. She was staring up at the painted version of me too. I took in the curve of her belly under the rose-sprigged cotton. As I watched, she pushed a strand of black hair back from her face and Danny's ring glinted in the light coming off the river.

There was a message for me in that ring and there was a message for me on the wall – and it wasn't a gilt-edged calling card dipped in jasmine. I lifted the damp coil of hair at the nape of my neck and moved the pins about to position it higher. Perhaps I *should* get the dice out again?

'I've seen enough. I'll get them to clean it off now.'

My heels echoed from the walls as I started off down the passage. The houses lining the river front here were a little finer than the alleyways and passages we'd passed on the way. Most of them had belonged to old-time merchant captains who liked to keep an eye on the profit when their ships came in. These days it was a warren of lodging houses and rooms.

Why here at Bell Wharf Stairs of all places? Of an instant, a membrance came to me – a duty and Lucca's advice. I turned back to Peggy, who was still frowning up at the picture. At least there was one decent thing I could do today.

'You up for a visit, Peg?'

I rapped again and waited. I was sure this was the right landing. The number six was on the door and beneath the faded red paint there was another mark, something like a cross, with the arms bent about.

Peggy turned from the narrow latticed window to the left of the door and wrinkled her nose. 'It's got a funny smell this place, sweet like flowers but smoky with it. I've a mind to open this out and let some air in.'

'Well, seeing as that would come straight up from the river, I can't see how that would improve things.' I tried once more, harder this time.

'Maybe he's deaf, Kit? His brother was a mute. I wouldn't be surprised if there's a weakness there.'

Perhaps she was right? The only thing I knew of a certainty about Amit Das's brother was his place of lodging and the fact I paid him regular. Tell truth, when I went through the books I was surprised at the amount I paid him, but seeing as how I was responsible for the death of his nearest, I didn't like to question the matter with the Beetle.

The building was better inside than I expected. The tall dusty entrance gave way to a wide hall with a broad wooden staircase marching up from the middle. Numbered doors led off to the left and right on every landing.

I'd asked Lok and Hari to wait for us below. I reckoned it was better that way seeing as I wasn't entirely sure what I was going to say to Ram. An apology didn't seem to cover it exactly. Lucca was right that I needed to see him, but it didn't seem fitting to barge in on him mob-handed, not if he was grieving.

I'd felt Lok watching me as I went up the first set of stairs. I'm not one for the reading of minds, but he seemed almost pleased – no, more than that, *satisfied* – that we were here.

I knocked again, harder this time. Peggy was right about the smell. It wasn't natural for Limehouse, fact is it put me in mind of a gentler version of Nanking Nancy's pit. As soon as that thought came I pushed it away.

'Open the window, Peg. You're right about the air up here, after all. It's making me feel noxious.'

The door in front of me opened.

'Sandalwood, clove and patchouli are considered to purify. I must apologise, Miss Peck, if the scent of my home offends you.' The tall man in the doorway bowed. I was so surprised I couldn't say a word. Out the corner of my eye I caught the flutter of Peggy's hand from the window latch to her bodice.

'Enter please, both of you.'

The man stood to the side to let us pass.

Chapter Fifteen

I hadn't expected Amit's brother to be anything like the man sitting at the neatly ordered desk in front of me. Ramesh Das (to give him his full name, seeing as that's how he introduced himself) was at least twenty years older than his brother and elegant in the way of a long-limbed sighthound. His large dark eyes were kind, but watchful. As I sat there on a small upright chair made from wood that gave off a smell like a crow's medical chest, I knew he was making a judgement. I didn't feel uneasy, not entirely, but I was confused.

I reached for the painted glass set on a low brass table between me and Peggy. I noted that she did the same, taking her cues from me. She hadn't said a word since we'd been ushered into the long high-ceilinged room overlooking the river. Instead, her eyes darted about taking in the extraordinary things arranged about us.

Ramesh Das was clearly something of a collector. Beyond his desk there was a wall of books – some of them shelved so high he needed a ladder to reach them. The room was filled with objects too: statues, paintings, maps, rugs and cushions. Over in the corner near the ladder there was a captain's globe the size of a barrel.

The tea brought to us by a barefoot boy in a loose white tunic was like nothing I'd tasted before. Ramesh smiled as I took a sip, allowing the spiced taste of it to fill my mouth.

'Is it to your liking?'

I nodded. 'It's very good. Thank you.'

He lifted his own glass. 'It is chai, masala chai. I have lived in London for nearly forty years, but I must confess I cannot abide the tea you English drink.'

Not only did he look nothing like I expected, he didn't sound like it, neither. If you wasn't looking at his skin and his long dark robe – something like a nightgown but broidered about at the neck and sleeves – you might have thought you were taking afternoon tea with a duke.

He turned to Peggy. 'What do you say, Mrs Tewson?' (That's how I introduced her.)

She looked warily at the glass in her hand. 'It's . . . it's very pleasant.' She sounded surprised. She tried a second mouthful and I knew she was taken by the rich sweetness of it.

Ramesh nodded. 'Forgive the indelicacy, but I believe chai is considered to be most beneficial to ladies in your condition. I will have some sent to The Palace.'

Peggy's cheeks flushed as she took another sip.

I set my glass down on the table. 'When you opened the door, you called me Miss Peck, straight off. But I've never met you before.'

Ramesh leaned back in his chair. 'I have been expecting you. To be frank, I was beginning to wonder if you would come at all. It is many weeks now since Amit died in your service.'

It was my turn to blush.

'I . . . I didn't . . . That's to say . . .'

When the words didn't come right I took up the glass again. As the sweetness went down, I felt the failing slip to my belly with it and curdle. There was Edie Strong's mother too. I still hadn't paid proper respects there, neither.

I put the glass down carefully.

'You're right, Mr Das. I should have come sooner. It's been too long and I won't insult you with an excuse. I'm very sorry about what happened to Amit. The fire at The Gaudy was ...'

There was so much to say there, but I couldn't. I looked down at my hands, aware that Ramesh was watching me close as I finished off.

'Your brother was a good man.'

'Amit was many things, but he was not my brother.'

My head shot up.

'But he ...?'

As I took in the long features, angular cheekbones and high forehead I couldn't see a ghost of poor Amit. Of course, it was obvious now; the man sitting in the ebony chair opposite me had as much in the way of blood ties with the big, broad-chested mute who had given his life for me as I'd had with Nanny Peck.

'Then who ...?' I shook my head. 'I'm sorry, but he's listed ...' I paused again. It sounded cold to talk about a dead man like an item on an inventory.

Ramesh opened his hands and spread his fingers wide. 'Amit was a foundling, abandoned by the poor wretch who gave birth to him here in London. One supposes that when his ... silence became apparent his unfortunate parent could not see a future for him. Some thirty years ago he came to live with us here. In a way, I suppose, you could call us brothers, for that is how we lived. My wife loved him very much.'

'Your wife?'

'She too is gone, Miss Peck. It was our greatest regret that we were not blessed with children of our own. In some ways, Amit was my child as well as my brother.'

'I am sorry for your loss, Mr Das. That's what I came here to say.'

He blinked. 'They are not lost to me. I have no doubt that I will meet them again.'

I didn't mark him down for a Bible type, but his words suggested the opposite. I stared at the rug, tracing a way through the woven pattern. Perhaps I should say something in the way of a comfort?

'In heaven, you mean?'

Ramesh smiled. 'Our souls travel many paths, Miss Peck. When I come to the end of this journey, I will begin another. During my new wanderings I will meet Siya and Amit again – next time she might be my mother, my sister or perhaps my child and Amit may, truly, be born as my brother. All will be revealed in time. For now, I do not question. I simply accept.'

I sidled at Peggy. She was staring down at the greenish liquid in her glass. We were neither of us what you might call devotional, but even so I knew this wasn't something they dished out with milk and bread at a regular Sunday school. I cleared my throat.

'You're saying that you'll come across them all again – here in Limehouse?'

Now Ramesh laughed, but not to make a mockery. There was a warmth to the sound. He flattened his palms together as if to offer up a prayer and grinned wide. Of an instant he seemed to lose about forty years and I saw him as he must have been when he and his Siya were new together. He would have been a looker. 'It is a possibility I had not imagined, but you may be right, Miss Peck. Forgive me, I did not mean to confuse you.' He tilted his head. 'Do you know of reincarnation?'

I shook my head. The only carnation I knew was a market flower.

'Then I shall explain. It is our belief that death is merely a beginning. When a person sheds their mortal form, their soul will be reborn. We all live many lives and learn many lessons until we are ready.'

'Ready for what?'

'Peace.'

He settled back in the black chair and regarded me for a long moment. 'Do you think your grandmother will find peace, Miss Peck?'

The question caught me. Before I could answer he turned to Peggy.

'May I ask an indulgence of you, Mrs Tewson? Would you mind leaving us alone for a short while? I will ask Jani to prepare a package for you. Herbs and spices to bring ease, and also chai. I believe it was to your taste? I will have him bring it down to you while you wait with your companions.'

Peggy darted an anxious look at me as Ramesh continued, 'If you wish to reassure yourself, the brothers will vouch for me.'

'You mean Lok and Tan Seng?' I shifted on the upright seat and a patterned silk cushion wedged behind fell to the rug. This wasn't the dainty sympathy visit I'd imagined. I wasn't in control of the way things were going. It was like that time with Netta over again.

It's an odd thing, but I didn't feel threatened sitting there with a stranger in that room overlooking the river, instead I felt lost. When we was small, Joey had an Oriental puzzle box made of forty squares of wood that locked together to form a pattern. It was a battered thing given him by an old rope maker who lived three houses down from our rooms in Church Row. There was only one way to move the strips around to open that box and only one way to shut it up again. Once I learned the trick of it, it was easy enough to remember the order. It took a while to work it out, mind. Joey was annoyed I did it quicker than him.

A membrance of that box came to me now. I felt as if I was moving the squares around to find the entrance, but what did it lead to? Tell truth, right then I wished Lucca was here with me instead of Peggy. She was a heart, but he was a mind.

Ramesh bent to retrieve the cushion. 'We have known each other for many years. Mr Lok, his brother and I. He will have no fears for your safety.' He handed the bolster back to me. 'I will not detain you for long, Miss Peck. Here, please make yourself comfortable. Jani!'

At the call, the door at the end of the room opened and the dark-skinned boy who'd brought the tea earlier joined us once more. Ramesh rattled out a stream of words in foreign and then he turned to Peggy. 'Jani will escort you now.'

He stood up from the desk, pressed the fingers of his right hand to the centre of his forehead and bowed. Peggy didn't move.

'Is that what you want me to do, Kit? Only I . . .'

I reached across and squeezed her hand.

'It's fine, Peg. Leave us, please.'

Chapter Sixteen

The door closed. We sat in silence until the tapping of Peggy's heels and the creaking of the wooden boards faded. Ramesh Das folded his hands into his sleeves.

'The picture on the steps was crude, but the likeness could not be mistaken. It was the real reason for your visit today, I think?'

There didn't seem to be much point in denying it. I shielded my eyes against the light streaming through the tall window next to the desk.

'Tan Seng told me about it. I wanted to see it for myself before it was cleaned off. But, truly, when I stood there I had a membrance of Amit and where he lived. I put off coming for so long, but as I was here it seemed the right thing to do.'

Ramesh nodded. 'If the time is not right, a man cannot die even when seized by the jaws of a tiger, but when the proper time arrives he will be felled by a blade of grass.'

'What's that supposed to mean?'

'We believe that an hour is appointed for every action. When Amit died it was his time, as it was the proper time for your visit today. I assure you, the picture will be scrubbed away or painted over, swiftly.' He paused. 'Tell me, did you learn anything from it?'

'Only that there's someone out there who's taken against me. Someone with a dirty mind and two pots of paint, one red and one black. Tan Seng said it happened before, a long time ago.' I dipped my head into the shadow to get a better view of his face.

Ramesh freed his right hand from the sleeve. There was a thick gold ring on his middle finger. I saw a flash of blue as the stone caught the sunlight.

'In the city of my birth images were often daubed on walls as a protest or as a challenge. Which do you think it to be?'

I stared at the ring and thought about the one on Peggy's finger. The one sent from the Barons.

'It's a challenge.'

Ramesh nodded. 'The picture at the steps – and any others that may occur – will be removed. There is no more to say.'

He stood and went to the window.

'The sunlight troubles you, forgive me. The brilliance is reflected from the river. It reminds me of home.'

He spoke with his back to me as he adjusted one of the red-painted shutters. As he moved it, a shaft of light fell across his desk bringing everything up sharp. There was a square of paper pinned to the wood above one of the arched pigeon holes across the top row. I hadn't noted it before when he was sitting there. It was familiar. I shifted for a better look and recognised the whiskered head of Lord Denderholm at the centre of the neat-cut scrap from *The London Pictorial*.

It was most definitely the same piece. On the left just be-neath the elaborate wreath around old walrus face there was Lord Vellum, notably fresh among the company he was keep-ing on the page.

'What's that?' I pointed at the scrap of print as Ramesh sat down. He followed my gaze and unpinned the paper, folding it carefully into a square before sliding it into one of the open wooden compartments on the second row of the desk.

It was clear as a blazing boil on Fitzy's nose that it wasn't something he wanted to jaw over, but I carried on. 'It's from *The London Pictorial News*, isn't it? Why've you cut it?'

He brushed at something on the sleeve of his gown and reached for his glass. 'It was of interest.'

'Interesting in what way, exactly?'

He glanced at the edge of the folded paper poking from the compartment and took a mouthful of chai. 'One of the men is known to me. I had not seen him for many years. I was ... curious, that is all.'

'Can you show me which one ... please?'

'Why do you ask me to do that?'

'Because I know one of them too, that's why.'

Ramesh set down the glass and pulled the paper out again. He unfolded it and handed it to me. 'Which of them?'

I pointed at Lord Vellum. 'This one with the high collar and a face like a fifty guinea racehorse. That who you mean?'

'No. This is the man I knew.' He pointed at Lord Denderholm. I noted his fingers were long and slender like Professor Ruben's, the nails white against the dark like clean white moons.

'How come?'

When he didn't answer I looked up. He was staring at the paper in my hand.

Now, Swami Jonah did a mental act with a furled sheet of newspaper. He'd choose a likely punter and get him (it was always a him on account of the incendiary nature of skirts) to stand at one side of the stage holding it out while he stood over the other side and concentrated. After a couple of seconds, the paper burst into purple flames started by a faint dusting of lyco and a tiny Lucifer hidden inside the roll. It was a matter of timing, distraction and the years Swami Jonah had spent as a Liverpool pocket dipper. Only then he went by his real name.

Mostly the punter wouldn't get hurt.

The thought came to me now because of the way Ramesh Das was looking at the paper. If there was ever such a thing as proper magic, as opposed to the stage variety, he could have burned that scrap to a cinder without striking a light.

I tried again. 'How come you know him?'

'It is an old . . . acquaintance. I met him many years ago, before I came to London.'

I remembered then what Sam said about the old mutton chops.

He was in India for most of his life. Now he's returned and Her Majesty seems to be creating a post to keep him comfortable in retirement.

'So you knew him in India?'

'As I said – it was many years ago.'

Ramesh didn't offer up anything more on the matter. He settled back into the shade and I got the distinctive impression he didn't want me to see his face clear.

'May I ask how you know that man?' He pointed at Lord Vellum on the scrap of newsprint. I wasn't sure how to answer that.

'It's . . . You might call it a business matter. That's all.'

As I cast about for more in the way of a likely reply, Ramesh plucked the paper from my hand, folded it up neat and slotted it back into its place on the desk, pushing it in as deep as it would go.

'It is a most . . . interesting coincidence. Now, let us return to my first question, *Lady*.'

The floor beneath me seemed to roll like the deck of a ship. I took a breath and sat up straight.

'It's Kitty, please call me Kitty.'

He studied me for moment.

'My question, Lady?'

'Which one?'

He leaned into the light slanting through the half-shuttered window between us. Of an instant, it was like he was marked on stage by a limelight flare. I saw the lines of age around his mouth and on his cheeks, and the amber flecks in his soft brown eyes. I thought I caught a sadness there before he bowed his head.

'The only one that matters to us all, in the end.'

'Do you mean the question about my grandmother? Is that why you asked Peggy to leave us?'

He nodded. 'Do you believe Lady Ginger will find peace?'

'In this world or the next?'

He didn't answer, so I did. 'If you want my opinion, peace is for those with an untroubled conscience. If you know my grandmother, then I reckon you don't need me to set you straight.'

'She is a remarkable woman.'

'That's not the word I'd use.'

'Then what would you say of her?'

I looked out through the sliver of window. A tall-masted ship was being towed along the river by a steam barge. After a couple of seconds it was gone.

'You worked for her, didn't you? Amit too. That's why you're down in the books. I pay you, don't I?'

Ramesh nodded. 'The payment is made through Marcus Telferman. You are correct, however. I worked for your grandmother and now I work for you.'

I stared at my lap, noticing that my own nails were bitten to the quick. Black ink was grained into the swirls on the ball of my right thumb. I forced my hands into the thin cotton sleeves of my dress.

'What is it that I pay you for, exactly? Only you don't come cheap.'

He moved his chair aside at the desk so I could clearly see the piles of papers and ledger books stacked neatly in the open compartments. He gestured at the papers. 'I am your eyes, your ears and your tongue, Lady. There are many here who think and speak only the language of their birth. The riches on which Paradise is built come from far across the sea. My role is to ensure that nothing is lost, nothing mislaid, nothing misunderstood . . .'

Lady Ginger's voice came unbidden into my mind. It was the night when she took me to Great Bartholomew's in her coach.

Have you never wondered how Paradise found its name? It is the land of plenty – a land of spices, silks, jewels, exotic creatures of bestial and human kind. We have fallen, but the wonders and riches of the world are crammed into the warehouses that huddle beside the Thames.

I'd fallen all right. The word repeated itself in my head as Ramesh finished up.

' . . . I look into the hearts and the minds of the far-born who carry out your bidding in the docks, on your ships and in your warehouses.'

'You're a spy, then?'

He took up a tiny metal statue of a man with the head of an elephant from the top of the desk. 'That is too crude. My purpose is to communicate your wishes and to ensure that they are understood.'

'And you did that for her?'

He held the statue towards me. I took it, surprised by the weight of such a little thing.

'It is Ganesha, Lady. He is the remover of obstacles – and sometimes he places them in the path of those who deserve to be hindered. Many years ago your grandmother did me a great service and I will always be grateful to her. Now I serve you – I do so for her sake.'

I turned the statue about in my fingers. The little elephant had a wily, knowing look like it was keeping a secret, or laughing. I handed it back.

'But you don't even know me. Fact is, if it hadn't been for Amit I wouldn't be here now.'

Ramesh tilted his head. Now he had a face on him like a city matron measuring up a bolt of cloth for quality and price. After a moment he smiled.

'I knew you would come in good time, Lady. Our paths would have crossed eventually. I trusted that you would seek me for the sake of my brother. From what I knew of you, I thought it would be your way. Tan Seng advised this also.'

I was about to cut in with a question there, but he went on.

'Besides, at first I did not like to add to your burdens. It cannot have been easy at the beginning and I am certain it is not easy now. To be a Baron is a heavy thing. I understand, from a friend, that you have made several visits to a . . . a place of recreation in Shambles Passage.'

He meant Nancy's pit. I reached for my glass. The chai was cold, but I took a sip anyway.

'Would that friend be one of the brothers, Mr Das?'

He stared at me. 'It would not. Would you like some more chai? I will call Jani.'

I shook my head. 'This is still good.'

'I fear you are right about your grandmother. She walked in shadow.'

He touched the little figure to his head then his lips and murmured something.

'You said that you serve me for *her* sake. What did she do for you?'

'She set me free.' Ramesh placed the statue back on the desk top and turned away to rifle through the papers until he found what he was looking for. He drew out a battered leather-bound notebook.

'You questioned the amount paid to me. It is not only me you pay. There are many in Paradise who work for me, on your behalf. Please do not look so alarmed. You will find healers here and *dhatri* here as well as those who take a more . . . muscular interest in the proper running of your affairs.'

'*Dhatri?*'

'Midwives. There are poor women in Paradise who owe their lives and the lives of their children to your grandmother – women a white, English physician would never stoop to serve.'

I stared at the book. 'She never ... I mean, she was ...' A familiar pain started up over my right eye as I took in the unfamiliar thought of Lady Ginger as lady do-good.

'She was a cow, to be frank with you, Mr Das. An evil old cow and we was all terrified of her.'

A look of distaste flickered across his face. He touched his forehead again with the tip of his thumb.

'It is disrespectful. Your grandmother is alive still, as far as I am aware.'

I grasped at something there. 'You know where she is, then?'

He shook his head. 'I do not. Telferman will tell me when your grandmother reaches the end of her present journey.'

The silence in the room was broken by a metallic clatter as I put the empty glass back on the brass table.

'Listen, I'm sorry if I offended, but that's been the way of it. She's never treated me with kindness. Tell truth, I didn't even know we was related until ... ' I stopped as another thought came to me. 'If you've known her, worked for her for years, like you say, then you must have come across my brother, Joey – Joseph Peck?'

Ramesh blinked. 'I met him only twice, when he was with your grandmother. He is a most ... charming and persuasive young man.' Something in his tone told the lie of that.

'You didn't like him much, then?' Sunlight was falling full on my face again now through the gap between the shutters. I stood and shifted the chair a foot or so to the right while Ramesh pondered the question. He stared out at the river through the milky panes and twisted the ring as he thought.

'I did not dislike him, but I did not think he was a suitable choice as a successor. I told your grandmother this. I knew too much about your brother to trust him or rely on him.'

'What does that mean?' I sat down heavily. 'What did you know?'

'I think you understand already, Lady.' Ramesh shook his head. 'I do not judge. In my own land there are men known as *hijra*, they are welcome – in their gowns and paint – at celebrations and ceremonies. They are thought to bring luck.'

'And what did you think of Joey?'

'I did not think him lucky.'

I started. Wasn't that what Lucca said too, almost word for word?

Ramesh offered me the book. 'Mr Telferman admires your acuity.'

'My what?'

'Your perception. He says you have a sharp mind. Perhaps you are more like your grandmother than you know?'

He let that linger before going on. 'You are most welcome to take this ledger to familiarise yourself with the affairs I manage on your behalf. You will find nothing wanting. Everything is accounted for. My network – *your* network . . .' he bowed his head, 'is thorough.'

I stared at the thicket of grey hair on his bowed head. Most men of his age would be spare on top by now, but Ramesh Das was thatched like a country cottage. Perhaps he needed all that hair to keep his secrets from flying out?

My secrets. I reached over and tapped his arm.

'Do you know where he is – Joey? If you're keeping a look out for my affairs, like you say, you must have heard something. I need to know. He was in London at the back end of April, but then he went to ground when . . .'

I broke off, unsure how much more to say.

'When Lord Kite's man, Matthias, tried to find him?' Ramesh finished the sentence for me. He rose to draw the shutter further across the window. Now his face was in shadow.

'Listen to me, Lady. I do not know where your brother Joseph is, or what he has done, but I do know this: Matthias Schalk was searching for him. He killed a man, a musician, from one of your theatres thinking him to have information.'

'Old Peter, Peter Ash, that was his name. And I led Matthias to him.' I thought about the old cornet player's neat little room with its cushions and paintings. I remembered again what Lucca had told me about that room when they found him.

His stomach ripped open, his organs draped around the room like a bloody Christmas garland.

I turned the glass. 'It was my fault.'

Ramesh shook his head. 'It was his time. There is a devil in Matthias Schalk. He has been Kite's man for two years now and he is greatly feared. Here in Paradise and beyond. We watch for him. He is known to us.'

'How . . . how do you know all this?'

'Because I worked for your grandmother and now I work for you, Lady. It is my business to know. If Schalk is searching for your brother, I pray for his sake that he never finds him. The man is . . .' Ramesh muttered something under his breath. I saw him make the sign of the eye with his thumb and forefinger. Nanny Peck used to do that too – when she came across an unfortunate with a deformity. I didn't have to understand the words to get a feeling for his meaning. Matthias Schalk was unnatural. I'd felt it too.

'He takes pleasure in his work.' Ramesh paused. 'A woman's body was taken from the river. The marks upon it were . . . unmistakable. It was him.'

'You're talking about the redhead, unusually tall? I heard that she . . .' My guts swam as I remembered what the Beetle said had been done to her. Of course it was Matthias's handiwork, who else?

'Poor creature.' Ramesh touched his forehead. 'We must pray to the gods that there will be kindness in her new life. Your grandmother called him Ogen. It means "eyes" in Schalk's mother tongue. You must know already that Kite is blind.'

I nodded. 'And him, Kite – what do you know about him?'

'He is a Baron, Lady.'

'Is that it? Don't you think I know that for myself?'

Ramesh didn't answer. He held the book towards me.

'There are many in Paradise who are loyal to you. The men and women who work for you through me are here.'

As he moved, his broidered sleeve shifted to reveal the fine bones of his wrist and the skin of his arm. There was a mark among the dark hairs on the back of his forearm. I saw it was a snake, just like the one on the lascar boy crushed by Houtman's boat. The pointed head, something like a spade from a deck of flats, crept around his arm inches above his wrist.

'What's that – there on your arm?' It came out abrupt, but I carried on. 'I've seen it before, or something like it.'

Ramesh pulled up his sleeve to show it clear. It wasn't a tattoo as such. It was more like a scar or maybe a burn. Although it had healed a long time back, the damaged skin was crimped like the edge of a cookshop pie and paler than the rest of him.

'What is it?'

'Originally it was intended as a punishment, Lady. I have borne this mark for many years and now I use it as a sign. Those who work for you do not always speak the same language. The *naga* shows they are among those who can be trusted. It is a symbol of brotherhood among those I use to do your business. Where did you see it?'

'There were two lascar boys at the docks. It was a new trade. They came to help with the unloading. I thought Tan Seng had sent them . . .'

I paused, understanding now that it was most likely the man sitting in front of me.

'One of them had a tattoo like the mark on your arm. There was an accident – he fell into the water and was crushed between the boat and the stones of the quay. I don't reckon there was a bone in his body that wasn't broken by it. I was there. I . . . I couldn't do a thing to help him.'

'You are referring to Houtman's shipment? The *Gouden Kalf* is due to leave in . . .' Ramesh took up a sheet of paper from the side of the desk and ran a finger down the lines of close-packed writing. He held it up close to his eyes to see it clear. 'Five days' time.' He glanced at me over the top of the sheet. 'I understand Houtman is not a man to be trusted.'

I nodded. 'I know that well enough.'

He put the sheet back on the desk. 'Yes, the dead boy was in your pay, as was his brother, Mehal, who was also there. I arranged it. Mehal was maddened with grief by what he saw.'

I thought about the way the lascar boy clutched at my arm.

No wonder he looked so wild, it was his brother down there caught up in the paddle wheel.

'It was a terrible thing to see.'

'Indeed.' Ramesh closed his eyes like he was imagining the scene. 'His mother says he has run away.'

I pulled at a loose cotton thread in my sleeve. 'She's lost two sons, then? I'm sorry for her, truly. I didn't know they was brothers, but I know he – Mehal, you said? – took it bad. He knelt on the edge staring into the water and he kept calling his brother's name, Khunni, over and over.'

'Khunni?' Those amber-flecked eyes flicked open again. There was sharpness to them now. 'That cannot be right.'

'I remember it clear. I'm not mistaken. He took my arm and he kept saying it – Khunni.'

Ramesh stood up and his shadow fell across me.

'Khunni is not a name, Lady. You are mistaken in that. It is a word. In our tongue it is the word for *murderer*.'

Chapter Seventeen

We walked back to Salmon Lane in silence. I could tell Peggy was burning herself to cinder to know what we'd spoken about in a private way after Jani had shown her out, but I wasn't going to tell her. Point of the matter was that I didn't understand the half of it myself.

'Lok says Mr Das worked for her, for Lady Ginger, for a long while.' Peggy's voice came from behind me. She tried again. 'Is that what he wanted to talk to you about? You were in there a good while, Kit. Longer than I expected.'

I stopped and fiddled with the coil of hair pinned at my neck. It felt like an old sponge rubbing at the skin. 'Not now, Peg. I need to think, and anyway it's too hot and dusty to speak out here. It catches in the throat.' Before I turned back to carry on I caught her exchanging a meaningful eye with Lok.

We made our way up through the warren near the river and then we pushed along the Commercial. I thought about taking a ride, but there were four of us and as a generality the growlers stayed west of Limehouse.

The street was packed tight as a pilchard press.

Lucca told me once that back in his village they take a rest of an afternoon in the summer months on account of the heat. It was the sensible thing to do, he said. Even the field workers took themselves home, closed the shutters and had a kip until it was cool enough to go outside again. I'd always thought that was peculiar. Until now.

Looking about, it was very clear to me that Londoners weren't sensible. If there was the slightest chance of making coin they'd be willing to stand on the edge of hell's deepest, fieriest pit till their pockets was full. The air was so thick on the Commercial I held a 'kerchief to my mouth and nose. The carts and buses made it worse. Every time one went past scorched dirt swirled up from the cobbles and settled on our clothes and skin.

Clouds of flies mobbed about the piles of horse shit in the road. I had to keep batting them away from my face as we walked – and worse, I felt their bodies catch in my damp hair. Just ahead of me I saw Hari stir the air with paddle-like hands as a swarm gathered around the patterned material of his waistcoat. The cotton of my dress was soaked through. When I moved, it pulled the flesh of my armpits so tight I knew I'd find raw marks there later. When I wasn't taking down a lungful of horse shit, the stench of the soap-shy bodies passing by came on strong.

We were an odd sight, the four of us. Of occasion I caught someone staring at me, but they'd look away sharp if I noted them. Halfway down the Commercial a woman dragged her child into a doorway as we went by. After we passed I felt her eyes on my back. Further down, a tall, lean-faced man with a draping of limp ringlets – he wasn't one for a rasher of bacon, if you get my meaning – paused and lifted his black hat to me.

It came to me then that people were coming to know who I was. *What* I was. I was beginning to understand now why my grandmother never went anywhere alone. I'd taken all that hoopla with the lascars and the Chinamen for show. But now I knew better.

I'd always thought that a Baron was powerful, a person to be feared, but now I saw quite plain that I was in a sort of prison. Lady Ginger knew what she was doing when she sent me up in that cage. I wasn't scared of anything back then – not really, but now . . .

The stabbing pain was going off over my eye again as we turned left into Belgrave Street. My head tumbled with pictures I didn't want to see: that poor type in the alley, Dora, with half her face gnawed away; that ripe daub of me on the wall; and the lascar boy crushed at the dock. (His real name was Dalip, Ramesh told me.)

Murderer. That's what his brother had called out that day as he gripped my arm. He meant me, I was sure of that. Dalip had died working for me, just like Amit and Edie. No wonder Mehal had run off. I was the angel of death as far as he was concerned.

Then there was that woman they found in the river.

Ramesh was right about Matthias Schalk. My brother had a devil on his tail.

Christ knows, I had enough to keep me busy from now until Doomsday, but everything, *everything*, came back to Joey in the end.

When we swung into the passage off Salmon Lane I called out. 'You can get off now, Hari.' The big man turned to face me. He shot a glance at Lok and I felt, rather than saw, the quick nod.

I reached into my bag. 'Here, you must take this for your trouble.'

'No!' Lok sprang between us. 'The Lady does not pay. It is not the way.'

I clutched my bag tight. Of an instant I felt like a child caught in a wrongdoing. There was a sound ahead as the double doors to The Palace swung open. Tan Seng shuffled out onto the step and bowed.

'A message has come for you, Lady.'

Hope brought me up sharp. Lord knows, there was nothing natural about my relationship with my grandmother, but, all the same, Lady Ginger was the only one who might have an answer to the questions wrestling for space in my head.

I started forward. 'Is it from Telferman?'

He shook his head.

The Comet was the last place I wanted to be right now.

The carpenters, the plasterers and the gilders had gone home for the day and the place was silent. Most of the furniture – tables, chairs and that – was mounded under sheets. Light came from the two broad fans set high at the back of the stage. Usually they were covered by red drapes, but the workmen needed as much light as they could get to fix the ceiling.

I looked up at the wooden boards zigzagging across the space high above our heads. It was Lucca who'd saved me that day when my cage came down, bringing half the ceiling with it. The thought of him was almost like that stabbing pain over my eye. Every day I wanted to hear that he was on his way back, but I knew it was wrong to wish him home on account of his mother.

I bent down to scrape together some thin gold flakes off the boards. I rolled them between my fingers and held my hand out towards Aubrey Jesmond.

'This stuff don't grow on trees. I reckon there's more sprinkled about down here than there is up there.'

Every so often a patter of sawdust trickled down through the gaps in the boards above us. Hari brushed the shoulder of his waistcoat as he peered up at the ceiling. I spread my fingers wide and let the fine gold flecks fall to the floor.

'You're here to keep things regular, Mr Jesmond. You're good with money – I don't want it wasted. You know that once we get this place back in order I've a mind to install you on a permanent footing. But you need to make it pay, and that begins with the work going on now. To my understanding this stuff is real gold. What's it doing lying about down there?'

'Indeed it is, ma'am. I'll see that the men are more careful in future.' The smooth voice had the distinctive ring of a valley pulpit today. I noted it came out stronger when Jesmond was anxious. His small dark eyes twitched to a blink. It was a habit of his. Lucca had called him a fox, but Jesmond always put me in mind of a mole, a fat one.

'I . . . I believe there have been some laxities, ma'am, under Paddy, Mr Fitzpatrick that is, but now I'm in charge those days are over.' He fiddled with the rim of the felt bowler between his hands.

So that's what this was about. I almost laughed out loud. I was standing in the half dark listening to the petty wrangles of a couple of old theatricals waiting for me to turn their little lives to gold, when it seemed very clear to me that everything I touched turned to shit.

I gripped the handle of my bag. 'I think you know very well, Mr Jesmond, that I've got more things to be worrying about than the halls these days. If you reckon Fitzy's been wasting my money then I'm grateful you brought it to my attention, but if it was a mug of winkles I wanted I'd send someone else out to chase the barrow. If you've got tales to tell in future I trust you and Telferman to deal direct. Is that clear?'

He nodded and slid a look at the boards above us. The air in here was as bad as outside, worse maybe. Something sharp with a tang of old piss made my eyes smart. Hari caught it too, he kept swiping his eyes with the back of his hand.

'And what's that stink, Mr Jesmond? The punters won't pay through the nose if they can't breathe through it.'

Jesmond passed the bowler from hand to hand. 'It's ... mostly the fresh plaster, ma'am. They started up on a new section over to the right there yesterday.' He tipped the hat upward in the direction he meant, but I couldn't see through the boards.

'By the time it's dry it won't be a trouble. I really do think you should see the ... work. The ladder runs from the second gallery. You needn't worry, it's quite firm up there. The boards will take the weight of the three of us if you want this ... er ...'

'Hari – his name is Hari, and yes, if we go up he'll come too.'

I leaned back on the lap of the stage and watched a bead of sweat trickle down the side of Jesmond's pouched face. Of an instant I had what Nanny Peck would have called a clarity. 'But I don't think you asked me here to take a tour of the workmanship, did you?'

Jesmond stroked some dust from the felt. 'Not entirely, ma'am. No.'

He turned the hat around by the rim and cleared his throat.

'I . . . I really think you ought to see the work.' He didn't look direct at me now. 'There's something up there, ma'am. Something vile.'

Chapter Eighteen

Jesmond held the Lucifer to the candle lantern. In a moment the glass glowed bright sending shadows scuttling over the curved walls. It was late in the day now and almost dark outside. Then again, it was always shady up in the galleries. The light from the fans behind the stage would never make much of a mark up here.

He held the lantern between us. I saw the beads of sweat at his temples run grey down the sides of his cheeks and catch in the stubble of his jaw. His black hair – what was left of it – was mostly boot shine. Now we was close I recognised the waxy smell of the lampblack coming off him.

'It . . . it's rather . . .' Jesmond blinked and swallowed. His eyes slid over my shoulder and up to the left. 'I feel I should warn you that it's quite . . . er. Quite . . .'

He didn't finish his sentence. He handed me the lantern and bent to fiddle with another. His hands shook as he tried to strike a second Lucifer against the side of his match box. It took four tries to get a flame.

I held my lantern up. Tools, brushes, buckets, pots and strips of timber were stacked around us on the wooden benches of the second gallery. The ripe smell was sharper up here on account of the plaster drying out twenty foot above. I could almost reach up to touch the workmen's boards overhead.

'It's just over there.' He turned now to let the light of his own lantern show the way. At the centre of the gallery's back wall a sturdy metal ladder rose from behind the second row of benches and disappeared into a black gap in the boards over-head.

'As I said, it's quite safe to go up. Some days there's been nearly a dozen of them working up top. A couple of them are big lads – have to be, look you, for that kind of work. It will bear our weight – all of us.'

He held the lantern higher to take in Hari, who was lean-ing over the edge of the gallery rail and staring down at the stage. 'I'll light another for your . . . for Mr Hari, shall I?'

I shook my head. 'I'd feel . . . better if he was down here.'

I hadn't wanted Hari and Lok standing next to me at Bell Wharf Stairs earlier when I looked at that filthy picture and I didn't want him up there with me now. Point of fact, I didn't much want Jesmond holding my hand neither, but he'd already seen it – whatever it was – so the damage was done.

Anyway, he knew exactly where it was.

'Just a moment.' I set the lantern down on a pile of timbers and bent to hitch up my cotton frock to stop the material from catching around my legs as we climbed. I tucked the ends into my waistband.

'Let's get it over with then. You go first and I'll follow.'

⚱

The air trapped beneath The Comet's roof was hot and thick with the stench of the plaster, but that wasn't what made my belly clench tight as a knuckle boy's fist.

It was worse than the other one, far worse.

Jesmond set the lantern down below the panel and then he stepped back into the shadows like he couldn't bear to look at me – the real me, that is, not the one rolling her eyes and arching her back on the wall. The flickering light gave the thing a horrible liveliness; it was almost as if all that flesh up there was moving of its own accord. The brown lines on the plaster shivered with the movement of the candle flame.

Something sweet, but sour with it, came burning into my mouth. It was the chai Ramesh Das had served up earlier, but now I wanted to spit it out onto the boards.

There were three figures this time, all naked and coiled around each other. Tell truth, I wasn't sure it was actually possible to bend a body – or a tongue come to that – in the directions they was taking, not unless you happened to be a contortionist like Fitzy's Man of a Million Bones. According to the picture sprawling across a newly plastered panel of The Comet's ceiling I had a rare talent.

I recognised myself in the midst of it all and I recognised the two men with me. That was what punched me in the gut; it was Lucca and Jocy.

The artist, if that's what you could call whoever had done this, had caught all three of us very finely. There was no mistaking who it was making free up there. Lucca stared straight out over my shoulder, the leering expression of the good half of his face pulled the scarred side into a mockery of a smile. His hands slipped around the bodies so that . . .

Well, one was on a part of me and one was on a part of Joey.

Caught between the two of them, I was painted to face my

brother. Our profiles – tongues twisted together – matched almost exactly. Someone was making a point to show the likeness off. One of Joey's hands pawed an over-ripe breast, while the other, sliding lower, held Lucca tight.

Jesmond cleared his throat. 'It will be gone by daybreak tomorrow, ma'am. I promise. I'll have it removed.'

I didn't turn to look at him. I didn't want him to see my face. I could feel my cheeks burning with shame.

'Who found it?'

There was a pause.

'It was there this morning when I came to unlock for the works. It appeared overnight.'

'But why did you come all the way up here first off? What made you look for it?'

I heard Jesmond shuffle on the boards behind me. I turned around now.

'Well?'

He stepped into the circle of light and bent to retrieve his lantern. Of an instant the image seemed to move again.

'It was the smell. With everything closed up and the heat . . .' He blinked. 'See, it's not entirely the plaster – the stench, I mean. When I came this morning I thought something had got in and died up here – an old tom cat maybe. But then when I saw it up close, I realised what it was.'

I turned to look up at the plaster panel again as Jesmond carried on.

'It's the shit. Whoever did this used shit, not paint. And I don't think it's animal, if you understand me. Question is: how did they get in? There's only two sets of keys and I've got them both.'

I took in the sweeping greasy lines and fought down another bitter mouthful.

'How many of the men have seen it, Mr Jesmond?'

'None of the men, just ... just me, ma'am. I turned them all away this morning, gave them a story about the plaster not being dry enough to work on. I thought it was the proper thing to do under the circumstances. I was going to cover it over myself, but then I thought you should probably ...' He stared up at the picture. 'I thought you should see it. To my mind there's something ... vicious about it – and I don't just mean the ... flesh of it. It's more than that – it cuts deeper. I'm no artist, but I can see it has a quality. Whoever came up here and did this, they knew you and Mr Fratelli and ...' He paused for a moment, picking over the bones of his next words.

'I'll be honest with you. I didn't much like your brother, Joseph, but to blacken the memory of a dead man ...'

'Dead!' I whipped about, almost dropping the lantern to the boards. 'What do you mean by that? What have you heard?'

Jesmond stared at me like I was a Bedlam. He blinked and took a step back. 'He ... he's been dead for nearly three years now.'

I wiped a sticky hand across my forehead. Sweat was streaking down between my shoulder blades. I'd changed gear back at The Palace before setting out again, but now I felt rank as a herring girl. I glanced at Jesmond, who was watching me close. No wonder he thought me mad. As far as he was concerned, Joseph Peck – the bones of him – was most likely wrapped in a bit of old oilskin and resting at the bottom of the river with his pockets full of stones. Most of them in Paradise thought Joey had been dead a long while.

As if he read me, Jesmond went on. 'That accident at the docks – it was a bad business, ma'am. And his body never came to light so you couldn't even bury him. I won't pretend your brother was a friend of mine, but I wouldn't wish it on a man. And I wouldn't wish this …' he raised his lantern to the picture again, 'on anyone. I called it vicious, but my old father, see, he would have another word for it – *drwg*. It means evil – this painting is evil, that's what it is.'

I stared up at the plaster panel. He was right. It was more than an insult. There was something dark and unnatural about those clever curling lines. It was evil all right. I remembered how Ramesh Das had made the sign of the eye when he talked about Matthias Schalk and I shivered, even though you could crisp a meat pie up there under the roof.

I set the candle lantern down and rolled my sleeves up as far as they would go.

'What are you doing?' Jesmond frowned. His black eyes almost disappeared into his head.

'I'm getting myself ready. You might want to do the same if you want to keep that shirt clean. Is there white paint in any of the pots lying about downstairs?'

He nodded. 'Thirty pots of the stuff – all accounted and paid for.'

'Good!' I took up the lantern again and started towards the top of the ladder. 'Because we're going to need it. You and me are going to paint this over before we leave here tonight, and I don't care if it takes every one of those thirty pots to clean this shit away.'

We washed layer after layer of paint over that picture until there was nothing left to see. Just the filthy stench of it remained and I'm not entirely sure if – at the end – I was really taking it in or imagining it. When I was done it felt like my arms had been pulled clear of the sockets.

It was light again when we stepped outside. Not full day – everything was coated in the milky grey that washes up just before dawn. Hari, who had stayed below while we worked, went to stand a little way from us, turning to take in both ends of the street. I didn't want him to see that painting, but now it was covered over I was grateful to have him there. As I watched him scan the cobbles I saw plaster dust in his beard.

Jesmond turned his bowler about in his hands. I watched him pick at some white spots caught on the brim, but he only made it worse. I put a hand out to stop him.

'I'll buy you another. You worked hard tonight.'

'Thank you, ma'am.' He scraped again at the felt. 'It was the right thing to do, showing you, I mean? Only it . . .'

' . . . wasn't something fit for a lady to see?' I finished off for him.

He nodded. Even though it was early it was already warm. The metallic tang of London soot scraped the back of my nose, but I was glad to be on the street. The air out here was a thousand times sweeter than the fug under the dome of The Comet.

'I don't want word of this going round – not to the workmen, not to Fitzy, not to no one. Is that understood?'

'Completely, ma'am.' Jesmond blinked.

'I mean *no one*,' I went on. 'If I hear a word about this, I'll know where it's come from.'

His lips twitched as he fixed on his shoes. The conker-brown leather was spotted with paint like his hat. Of a rule, Aubrey Jesmond was a sleek one. I had no doubt he was weighing up the price of a new pair. That wasn't what I wanted him to think about just now.

'That's an order.' My voice came sharp. Hari turned to look at us. He started back towards me, but I shook my head.

Jesmond looked up and his fat little fingers fluttered to his lips. 'Well now, the thing is that – ah – this puts me in rather a delicate position, ma'am, seeing as how ... well, I wasn't actually the one who ...'

His voice petered out. He didn't sound like a silky chapel preacher now.

I planted my hands on my hips. 'What are you saying?'

'I ... I wasn't the one who ... found it, not exactly.' He mumbled the reply.

'Who did, then?'

Jesmond coughed. 'Netta.'

'Netta found it?'

'Indeed she did. And she came straight back to my lodgings to tell me.'

I didn't catch on at first.

'But you told me that when you came here to unlock yesterday morning it was you who went up there to the roof.'

Jesmond swallowed. I actually heard the gulping sound of it. 'That ... now, that wasn't entirely true, see. Netta and I had made ... what you might call a night of it before. It's her first turn at The Carnival tomorrow – *today* as it happens now – as a solo. Paddy thinks she's ready. He doesn't know, but I've been giving her some … advice. Helping her with her performance. Coming from a chapel background, I'm not usually one for strong liquor but she …'

'You had a skinful with her, is that it?'

Jesmond nodded. 'I'm not used to it you see, ma'am.'

I saw it all now. No wonder he was blacking his hair. If he was trying it on with Netta Swift, he'd want her to think him at least twenty years younger than he really was. Mind you, I wondered if he realised she was trying it on with him.

I've been working on something in private with a friend. That's what she told me when she signed that contract. I knew who she meant now. I took a step forward. 'And you were too far gone yesterday morning to unlock for the work-men, so she came over here and did it for you?'

Jesmond nodded. 'That's about the sum of it. I took it as a kindness. What with Paddy watching for a slip. He doesn't like me being here.' He blinked. 'When Netta couldn't rouse me, she took the keys and came here. Then she came straight back and told me what she'd seen. Shocked she was.'

I bet she was.

I folded my arms. 'And I took you for a shrewd man. I'm not saying I thought I could trust you, not entirely, but I reckoned you could do the job well enough on account of wanting to look after yourself. Well, as it turns out you've been doing that all right. Now I see it quite clear – you're no better than old Fitzy, and Christ knows he's as low as a rat's arse. I've a mind to be rid of the pair of you. Come on, Hari.'

I started off up the street, my heels drumming on the cobbles.

'What ... what will you do, ma'am?' Jesmond's plaintive voice came from behind.

'I'll have a word with your fancy piece, that's what I'll do. You and Netta! That's a rare joke. You're catching the wind in a sieve there, Aubrey Jesmond. If you think you've been helping her you're most probably right, but not in the way you think.'

Hari loped along next to me. His shadow almost reached the end of the street as the sun came up full behind us. I didn't look back as I called out.

'You stay away from me. I don't want to see your face at The Carnival tonight mooning after Netta Swift. Meanwhile, you better look sharp. I want The Comet ready to open again by October. If you want to keep your place, Jessie, you'll make sure that happens. October the first, not a day later.'

I stopped now and swung round. 'And you can buy your own bleedin' hat.'

Chapter Nineteen

Hari walked me back to The Palace. At the end of Salmon Lane I told him to push off and get some kip. I watched his broad back as he strode away. If he wondered what me and Jesmond had been doing up there under the roof of The Comet for the best part of the night, he didn't ask. Then again, I'd noticed he wasn't one for the convivials.

The Palace door swung open as usual, only it was Lok who greeted me this time. He frowned as he took in the spatters of paint on my dress. He sidled up at my hair and I knew there was whitewash in it. I asked him to fill a bath in my room, but I didn't say anything more. Boiling the kettles and shifting the copper kept him occupied for the next quarter while I sat on the bed and waited.

'It is ready, Lady.' Lok poured the last steaming jug of water into the tub. He turned, bowed and slipped from the room. I peeled off the stained gear and kicked it into a corner. I'd never wear that dress again, even if every speck of white was scrubbed away. It had been tainted by the picture on the wall.

I lay there in the water for almost an hour, but I didn't feel clean. I kept thinking about Netta Swift and her sailor friend – the one who knew the name the Barons had given me. It seemed a mighty coincidence that Netta had found that painting in The Comet. Then again perhaps it wasn't a coincidence at all. Perhaps she'd been there when someone daubed it on the wall?

We needed to talk. And this time I wasn't in a mood to offer her gin or a contract.

I took a breath, dipped my head beneath the water and stared up through the glassy surface. The world became a shifting, clouded place. It was a test of sorts. Lying there locked up tight under the water I knew what I was dealing with, I knew the limits.

I counted to seventy and then, when my lungs felt like lead in my chest and everything started to go dark, I pulled upright splashing a great wave of water over the boards.

I reached for the wrapper crumpled up on the rug next to the copper, draped it round me and went to the far side of the room, leaving a trail of wet footmarks. On the top of the wardrobe there was a box I hadn't opened. Something I'd ordered back at the beginning of all this when I was a novelty to myself. Christ, there was actually a time – and not too long ago – when I thought I was playing a sort of game.

I climbed on a chair to take the box down. The smell of violets came strong as I shook the dress from its tissue wrapping. I hooked it on the wardrobe to drop the creases and then I sat on the bed and stared at it. It was a costume.

I closed my eyes, thinking to rest for just a moment, but it was past six when Peggy came in to wake me. I heard the chimes ringing out from the china clock on the mantle in the parlour as she patted my hand.

'Wake up, Kit. It's getting late. You don't want to miss it. Netta's first night.'

The Carnival had a most distinctive smell to it. Smoke, wax and spilled gin mingled with dust and old damp. Tell truth, it was looking something better than it had in a long while. For a start, the tables were set out in tidy rows instead of strewn around like a fight had gone off, but it was a knackered coal horse in comparison to The Comet and The Gaudy, and always had been.

The candles set in tarnished branches around the walls made it look worse, not better, which struck me as odd seeing as how the softness usually covered the truth. And the truth was The Carnival needed pulling down and starting over again.

'I haven't seen her yet, ma'am.' Fitzy leaned back against the painted boards. On the stage behind him the flares were glowing low in the cups. There was no point wasting the limelight.

'It's Netta's big night tonight, so it is. You'll remember what it's like? Perhaps she wanted some time to herself. Gather her juices. Tell you what . . .' Fitzy grinned and the faded red hairs poking out from his nostrils knitted into his tache. 'She's got a rare pair of lungs on her. We'll take a packet. The song's ripe as a Stilton and the costume . . .' He whistled and creased an eye in a proximation of a wink. 'Begging your dainties, ma'am, but you wouldn't need a thruppenny spyglass like they do at the Garden to take in her talents.'

He turned to Professor Ruben, who was flicking through sheets of music down in the shallow pit that ran along the front of The Carnival's peeling bow-front stage.

'What do you say, Prof?'

Professor Ruben adjusted the flame of the lamp on the up-right piano and flattened out a crumpled sheet. As he looked up at me, I caught a wariness as he took in my new bottle-green satin with the pin tucks, high neck and black French lace trim at the sleeves. I looked a proper lady tonight.

He nodded, a brief jerk of the head that was almost a bow. 'I hardly recognise the girl I knew a few months ago.' He paused and stared over my shoulder at Lok, who was standing in the shadows under The Carnival's only tier. In his long black gown he was almost invisible except for the glow of his face where the candles caught his skin.

Professor Ruben looked at me again. 'Have you heard from Lucca?'

I shook my head. 'Not yet, but then it's not been so long.'

'We miss him here. As you must.'

I wasn't sure what to make of that. Surely he didn't take us for a couple?

'He'll be back when his mother's . . .' I broke off as a flounce of chorus girls burst through The Carnival's side door. The over-bright colours, the paint and the feathers marked them out as a rare species on the streets of Lime-house.

They squawked like a flock of parrots too. When they caught sight of me standing with Fitzy and the Professor in front of the stage they settled into a silence that didn't come natural. There was a time when they would have called me over, but now they kept a distance. Of an instant, I was keenly aware that I stood out from them like a temprance in a taproom. The sober dress I was wearing now likely cost a hundred times more than all their froth and fancies piled on a ragger's barrow, but I didn't think one of them would swap their rig for mine.

I saw a couple of them nudge each other as they went to the curtained opening leading up to the passage over the stage. Netta Swift wasn't among them. I wondered if Peggy had had any luck. She'd gone upstairs to the corridor the girls used as a dressing space.

'To lose a mother is a terrible thing. You know that yourself, ma'am?' I turned back at Professor Ruben's question. Like the rest of the orchestra boys – not one of them under forty, mind – his face had a natural sadness to it even when he was smiling.

He smiled now. 'I understand he hasn't seen his mother for many years, but when her time comes it will be a comfort that he is with her.'

'To her, you mean?'

Professor Ruben shook his head. 'To him.'

I thought of Ma. I never got a proper chance to say my farewells there. Then again, her mind had gone a long time before the rest of her caught up. Me and Joey had sat with her the night before the funeral. He held my hand as I stared at the pale body laid out on the bed in the back room. Someone, Joey perhaps, had tricked her out in her best gear – the dress we was forbidden to touch. I remember the moonlight catching on the little pearls sewn onto the bodice. Looking back, it's an odd thing, but neither of us cried that night. We just clung to each other, a couple of kids sitting in the dark.

Fitzy fiddled in his jacket pocket. As he moved the smell of tobacco and sweat fetched up with the cigar between his fat fingers. 'I wasn't asking about Lucca. Netta – what do you reckon to her, Prof?'

Professor Ruben slid a sheet of music onto the piano, flapped out his tails and sat down. 'She'll be a tonic for The Carnival. The punters are ready for something new. You were right to try her as a solo, ma'am. But she's not as good as you were.' He nodded at the stage. 'Old Peter – a blessing on his name – said you were the best he'd ever played for.'

I clasped my hands tight in front of me. 'He was a good man.'

Fitzy struck a Lucifer against the peeling wooden board behind him before speaking. 'To be frank, ma'am, I'm surprised you're bothering yourself with our Netta, tonight. This shabby hall and the others too – The Comet and what's left of The Gaudy – being among the smallest of your concerns.'

He deliberately repeated the words I'd used to him and to Jesmond a week or so back. He lit the cigar and took a draw before he finished off. 'Not now with you being in the way of a lady of business, as it were.'

I ignored his tone. I wasn't in a mood for a spat with Fitzy tonight.

'Do you know when she's due in?' I leaned over the rail. 'Are you doing a run-through with her before we open tonight, Professor?'

He shook his head. 'She didn't ask for one. Besides . . .' he studied Fitzy's chequered back, 'I hear she's been . . . practising.'

'I heard that too, or something like it.' I undid the jet buttons at my cuffs and pushed up the dark lace sleeves. Tonight The Carnival was clammy as a workhouse laundry.

Professor Ruben called out a greeting and waved. I turned to see Isaac and Tommy – the other orchestra boys – come in through the side. When they saw me their eyes fell to the boards. I was becoming familiar with the stab of that now.

Behind the patched red stage curtain people were moving about. There was a scraping noise and a bump as something heavy was shifted into place. The boards shuddered and the limelight flares along the lip jumped in their cups. Of an instant I wasn't looking at the stage of The Carnival – it was The Gaudy that came to mind, that last night before it burned itself to a pit.

Workmen had been picking over the site for weeks now and they still hadn't found little Edie's body. I thought about her mother and that promise I made to Lucca. Palmer's Rents, that was where she lived, wasn't it? No wonder Lucca kept going on about mothers, before he went. It was his own he was thinking of.

I flapped a hand in front of my face to ward off Fitzy's smoke.

'I want to see Netta before she goes on. She can't be long now. I've a mind to go up top to wait for her to come in. She'll need to change out of her street gear. There's something we need to discuss.'

Fitzy pulled on the cigar and the end glowed up red. 'She signed the contract in front of you. You don't need to persuade her to stay on. She can't go anywhere without buying herself out, so she can't.'

'It's not that. I want to—'

'To wish her well? Is that it now, ma'am?' He ground a

boot heel over the little pile of smouldering ash that had fallen to the floor between us. His eyes tightened up under the ginger straggle sprouting across his forehead.

'You can see her in my office later, if it's a piece of privacy you're after. Netta's been telling the girls how ... let's just say how *fond* you are of her.'

Jesus! That bleedin' woman was slippery as a tray of monger's eels.

'Tell you what, ma'am.' Fitzy moved close. I stepped back as he breathed a warm fug of smoke, gin and tooth rot into my face. 'Why don't you take Lady Ginger's box? No one's had the use of it since she's ... been gone. It would be fitting. It's about time, you might say. Let the dogs see the rabbit.' He waved his cigar at the gilded cup-shaped box set to the left of the stage on the tier above us. The velvet curtains were drawn close.

'You're dressed the part tonight.'

I felt the hairs on the back of my neck stir as his voice came again.

'Watch Netta from up there – make sure you're getting your money's worth. I'll tell her you want to see her afterwards and send her up to you.'

The slatted door opened and Peggy stepped into the box.

'Why are you two sitting here in the dark?' She opened the door to let the light from the narrow passage outside show up the space. 'There's a bracket on the wall. I'll fetch something.'

She disappeared and came back a minute later with a

lighted candle. She forced it into the metal ring and wrinkled her nose.

'Smells like something died in here, Kit. I reckon it's under the boards.'

I hadn't drawn back the curtains yet. I'd sat there in the gloom with Lok tucked close behind and listened to the sound of the punters filling the hall below. They were in the mood for fresh meat. You could catch it in your nose as strong as the stink of old mouse. Peggy sat down next to me and reached for the curtain.

'Let the dog see the rabbit, then.'

'No!' I stopped her, unsettled to hear her repeat Fitzy's words. There was something wrong there – as far as I knew, once the dog saw the rabbit it ripped it apart.

'Why not? It's about to start up.'

'Wait a moment, please, Peg. What's it like out there to-night?'

'Lively. Fitzy's prowling around like he owns the place. He's got a face on him like a cat that's swallowed a dairy. Listen, there's no point being here if you can't see anything.'

She reached out again, but I caught her hand sharp.

'Not yet.'

Peggy stared at me. I let go and fiddled with the lace on my sleeve. Once that curtain went back they'd all look up and see me in Lady Ginger's place. If nothing else it was a most theatrical way of making an entrance. If any of them had a doubt about it, they wouldn't after tonight. There was a roar beyond the curtain as Professor Ruben and the orchestra started up. I could hear the punters stamping, thumping on the tables and catcalling the hall. It was like the times I went up in the cage.

Fresh meat.

I turned to Peggy. 'Did you hear anything from the girls just now – anything about Netta, I mean? Was she there?'

Peggy shook her head. 'No, not yet. But I had a word with Marnie Trinder. She says Cissie and the girls aren't too happy. They didn't reckon on Netta abandoning them so sudden. They thought she was going to take a solo and carry on with the sailor act. Marnie don't care too much, but then she's older. There's not so much riding on it for her, but the others . . .' She paused as the sound of Fitzy's voice came strong. The hall hushed up as he took the chair. For all his faults he was a good showman.

'Listen, Kit – can we open up now?' Peggy turned to Lok. 'What do you say?'

'It is for The Lady to decide.' He bowed at me.

'There was one thing.' Peggy sighed and smoothed her skirts. 'Marnie says a box come for Netta – a big one done up with ribbons and that. She said . . .' Peggy glanced warily at me. 'Marnie said she had the idea it might have come from you – as a gift.'

'Who gave her that idea?' I shifted forward on the little padded seat and a cloud of dust and moth went up around me. 'Don't tell me – Netta?'

Peggy nodded. 'She's been giving it out among the girls that you two are . . .' She paused and looked away. That decided it. I wasn't about to sit up here in the box letting all them think I was here to see my fancy piece perform. There were a lot of things me and Netta were going to have a little chat about later.

'Let's have a look at her, then.' I twitched the curtains back at the side nearest the stage, just enough for us to see if we sat quite snug, but not enough for anyone out there to know who was up here.

Fitzy was standing in the middle of the boards. The lime-light threw his shadow across the drapes behind him. From up here his big red head looked like it might burst. He held his arms out wide, a cigar clamped between the finger and thumb of his right hand.

'The Carnival presents to you an evening of vivacious variety, a plethora of pleasures, a cornucopia of contentment. From the mystic East . . .'

'That Dagenham, then?' someone called out from the hall.

Fitzy paused, amiably, while the audience enjoyed the droll interruption. He glanced up at the box, his watery eyes catching the gleam off the flares. He gave the smallest nod that might have been a bow, but then he carried on with his chaunt. As he went through the acts lined up for the evening – the *titillation* he called it – the punters didn't hold back on expressing their lively opinions.

'Ain't that pissed old faker disappeared up his own arse yet?'

If I'd been Swami Jonah standing in the wings I might have had second thoughts about going on after that. Credit where it's due, Fitzy could handle them. He took whatever they said and threw it back. He shielded his eyes and peered in the direction of that last call.

'Not his own arse, as far as I'm aware, but then maybe he's been up yours recently, sir?'

The punters stamped their feet. Taking a fob from his top pocket Fitzy squinted at the dial.

'And at exactly nine of the clock, not a minute sooner and not a minute later – so make sure you've charged your glasses – we'll be presenting a novelty, so we will.'

More catcalls and thumps on the tables. Fitzy tipped himself back and stared theatrically into the slips on the left. Then he came to the front again and gave a conspiratorial wink.

'The best of the bunch, plucked from the Garden of England, the fresh Rose of Kent, Miss Netta Swift will bloom here on The Carnival's stage.' He stuck two fat fingers into the ginger fuzz around his lips and let off a whistle.

'And let me tell you, she's hot for it, gents, positively boiling herself to a stew of anticipation.'

I reckoned that somewhere out in the slips Netta was watching him too. She must have thought herself tastier than a steak and kidney pudding as he finished up and the hall went off like a firecracker on Guy Fawkes.

Chapter Twenty

Something was wrong. The moment she appeared on the stage I felt it, but I couldn't rightly put a name to it. Netta stood half in shadow at the back, turning her head to the left and the right careful to let the light catch them big black eyes of hers.

There was a chorus of cheers – and worse – but when Netta smiled, fluttered her hands to her breast and dipped her head in a proximation of modesty, they all hushed up. She came forward to stand full in the limelight in the centre of the stage. The rustling silver lace of her skirts caught the lights and the little pearls sewn into her low-cut blue bodice shone up.

The skin of my back crawled like a nest of ants was running about under the satin. As I watched, I caught one of the little jet buttons of my sleeve so tight it came off in my hand, taking a shred of lace with it.

I recognised that dress – it was the one hidden away in that cupboard in the back room at Church Street. The one me and Joey was forbidden to touch.

Netta Swift was wearing Ma's one good dress, a copy of it, anyway.

'She can't!' The words came too loud. Peggy, who was craning to get a view through the crack in the curtain, patted my arm.

'Shhh – it's too late now, Kit. You can't pull her off. A person might think you was jealous.'

'It's not that – it's the dress.'

Peggy turned. 'What's wrong with it? It's a sight more proper than some of the other gear she wears. Almost old-fashioned. I reckon she looks a picture.'

Down on The Carnival's stage Netta moved closer to Professor Ruben and the orchestra boys. I watched her dip down low to give the time, three little strikes of her first finger on the naked skin of her forearm – although I knew she was after giving the punters an eyeful of flesh elsewhere – then she straightened up. Swirling the silver lace of her skirts about, she turned and went back to the centre of the stage where the limelight showed her clear.

As the first notes of her song played out Netta kept her back to the hall, then she span around, flung her arms out to the sides and threw back her head to show her long pale throat and rounded breasts nestled up to best advantage. She took a deep breath, which filled out her front even more, and began to sing in that low husky voice of hers.

> I've got a little secret, shall I let you have a go
> At guessing what is hiding snug beneath my furbelow?
> It's really very simple, to find out what it is,
> But just to keep things interesting, I thought we'd have a
>   quiz.

A murmur of amazement went through the hall, some of the punters stood up for a clearer view, but it wasn't Netta's singing they were locked on. It was the line of sparking crimson rippling around the hem of her dress. A grey mist bloomed about her pretty ankles. If you didn't know better you might have thought it to be a theatrical effect, a heavenly cloud come to carry her up and away.

But I did know better. As I watched from the box, the crimson glow spread quickly, too quickly, up into the band of silver lace over the lower folds of the skirt. The delicate pattern flared bright against the blue of the material beneath before it turned black and melted into flames.

That was when Netta's song turned into a scream.

She doubled over and thrashed wildly at the fire that was eating the bottom half of her dress. It didn't matter how hard she beat at the material, the flames kept coming back, spurting out like faulty jets. The tips had an odd greenish tinge to them like they'd taken up the colour of the silk.

Falling to her knees Netta started to tear at the pearly bodice where black scorch marks were beginning to spread up and across the blue like sweat stains. It was as if the fire was burning up inside the dress, trying to gnaw its way out.

The punters were silent now, but I knew they were entertained in the worst possible way. Professor Ruben scrambled out from the shallow pit along the stage and tried to smother her with his jacket, but he couldn't get close enough. Even up in the box I could feel the heat coming off her.

There was a shout. A boy ran from the slips with a bucket of water. He went as near as he dared and flung it over Netta's head, only it didn't do no good; the flames guttered and spat for a second before rising again, stronger than before. In less than ten seconds every part of that dress was burning, the blazing fabric clinging so tight to her body you could see the shape of her clear through the smoke. Kneeling there with her blistering arms flailing about she looked like a fiery angel from a Bible picture.

The boy backed away, his hands still clamped round the empty bucket, his mouth opening and closing. I could smell something like roasted meat and dripping. I brought my hand to my mouth as Netta's screams became a wail of agony. Her black hair was alight now.

'Jesus Christ!' Peggy stood and went to the back of the box so she couldn't see any more, but I couldn't drag my eyes away.

'Sand!'

Fitzy scrambled up the stairs to the left of The Carnival's stage, hauling a huge metal bucket in each hand. He hurled the contents of the first pail over Netta and she fell back. The flames seemed to die down as she sprawled across the boards. Lumbering forward, he emptied the contents of the second bucket across her as someone else, Dismal Jimmy I think it was, came from the side with another bucket of water and a rug.

Once he'd thrown the water over the smoking sandy mess on the stage, Jimmy flung the rug over it. It did the trick – the flames didn't start up again. The mound beneath the rug twitched and moved for a few seconds and then it was still.

From beginning to end, Netta's first and only solo on The Carnival's stage had lasted less than two minutes. I prayed to God that she was dead – for her sake.

'It was the last thing we needed, so it was.' Fitzy thumped his fist down on the desk in front of me. We were in The Carnival's office and it was late.

'We could have made something of her, but now . . .' He swiped at the bottle between us, filling his mug to the brim. I watched him empty it in two gulps.

'You're all heart, Fitzpatrick, so you are.'

I didn't like her, but she didn't deserve to die like that. Netta's body, what was left of it, had been rolled in the rug and taken back to her lodgings. When they scraped her up from the stage, I saw the pattern of the lace scorched into the boards. Poor bitch.

The worst of it was that a little part of my mind was winding itself up like the insides of a fob. Netta had died for me, in a manner of speaking. I was the only person in the hall who could have recognised that dress for what it was.

I went out to the street to pay the carter who carried her back to her lodgings in Brook Street. As I walked through the hall to the door following the men carrying her body I heard them all muttering. The girls and the hands were clustered together in sour little bunches like grapes that haven't seen the sun. They were still out there now waiting for me. I'd asked Fitzy to gather them together.

Limelight accidents were a common thing in the halls. Everyone who didn't know the truth of it thought that was how Lucca came by his face. I was clear that no one watching this evening would have seen what happened as anything other than a misfortune. Point of fact, I reckon the half of them thought they'd had a ripe entertainment and had gone home to tell their nearest it was a shilling well spent.

But I knew different. Why was Netta wearing that dress? Where had it come from?

Then there was the fire itself.

I had a clear view of the stage from the box. Netta had never come near enough to the cups along the front to catch a spark. Even when she dipped down low to show off her assets, she was careful to leave a space. Nine times out of ten Netta Swift knew what she was doing.

It was that tenth time that worried me. Someone intended her to die out there tonight – and I reckoned it was the same someone responsible for them pictures of me.

I glanced at Peggy, who was grey as a boiled herring. She was slumped forward in the chair set against the wall of Fitzy's office staring at the frayed edge of a rag rug. She needed her bed. Lok caught me looking at her and tilted his head in her direction in a meaningful way.

'Has Netta got family?' I stared at Fitzy's freckled paw wrapped around the mug and thought how strong he was still to have carried them sand pails to the stage like that, much good it did.

'Not in London.' He shook his head. 'No, her people are from somewhere near Canterbury, that's all I know. I thought you were in a position to . . .?'

I stood up abrupt. 'Listen, I want to make it quite plain that whatever you've heard, from Netta, God rest her, or from anyone else, she and I were never anything to each other. She worked for me and that's the sum of it. I'm sorry for her – it was a terrible thing to see – but that doesn't mean I've changed the way I think about her. I didn't much like her when she was alive and, if you want the truth, it would be cant if I said any different now she's dead. She told me she had a friend, a sailor. Do you know anything about him?'

Fitzy shrugged. 'From what I hear she had a lot of friends. Popular girl, so she was.'

Wasn't she just? I wondered if he knew about Jesmond. I was on the point of telling him, but then I thought about that picture up in the gallery at The Comet and realised it would open the lid on another box of apples turned to rot. I was glad I'd ordered Jesmond to stay away tonight. Netta had used him, but she'd turned his head. Turned it boot black, anyhow.

'We need to ask some questions to that lot out there then.' I jerked my head at the door. 'Stay here, Peg. You sit with her, Lok. This won't take long.'

As I stepped out of the office the noise in the hall died. Everyone who was working at The Carnival tonight was gathered there – the Brothers Cherubimo (a tumbling duo from Birmingham), Professor Ruben and the orchestra, Dismal Jimmy the Glasgow droll, Swami Jonah, the girls from the chorus, Barney Knuckle the Lancashire clogman, Signor Marcelli and his dancing marionettes (bleedin' sinister things they was), Mr Chibbles and his performing dogs, and the hands from out back.

They all stopped murmuring and stared at me. I didn't see much warmth there. Normally, Lucca would have been here with me and that would have been a comfort.

'Jonah.'

The word came distinct. It was low, almost a whisper, but they all heard it. I took in their faces, all arranged into a wary blankness, and I didn't know which one of them said it. Fitzy had called me the very same that night when he'd stood outside The Palace, weeping for his girl, The Gaudy.

And it was true. Nothing had gone right in the halls since the day my grandmother left them to me. Tonight it was Netta. Before that there was The Gaudy taking Amit and little Edie with it into the dark. And then there was Old Peter and Danny – there was always Danny.

But it wasn't just the halls. Outside in Paradise things weren't straight. The big redheaded woman who delivered Joey's note to Telferman, the drowned boy, Dalip, even Dora in that alley. I knew I wasn't responsible for her, but I felt as if I was.

I *was* a Jonah. I'd brought nothing but misfortune, and all the while the Barons were circling Paradise like dogs stalking a lame horse. Right on cue, one of Mr Chibbles's mutts started to whine.

I folded my arms tight across me to stop them from seeing me shiver, even though it was close as a tanner's pit in there. A woman's voice came from the shadows at the side.

'Are you going to let us off home, then? Some of us have beds to go to – even though we won't sleep tonight. Not after seeing that.'

I peered into the gloom. Most of the candles set along the walls had burned out, but a score or so were still guttering in their brackets. Some of the company were sitting at the tables, but most of them were standing, itching to be on their way. I couldn't blame them.

'That you, Marnie?' I thought it was, but when she didn't answer I carried on. 'Listen. What happened to Netta tonight was a terrible thing and I'm sorry for her, truly I am.'

There was some muttering and shuffling about. I heard a couple of the hands snigger. I thought about putting them all straight once and for all, but there didn't seem much point to it now she was gone. Instead, I moved forward.

'I'll stand her a funeral – a proper one. It's only right. And you'll all be there, every last one of you, to show your respects. That understood?'

'Is that an order?' The Liverpool accent was unmistakable.

I nodded. 'You can take it like that, Mr McCarthy, but I would have thought you'd want to be there as a mark of respect.'

'I think we know how to take it.' He sat heavily on one of the spindly little chairs ranged around the edge of the hall. 'A matter of respect, is it? Now that you're . . . in a position to give it out, Kitty, ma'am, I suppose we have to obey you.' His voice was slurred, the words slip sliding into each other like wet fish on a coster's marble.

There was more mumbling. I didn't have time to argue the toss with Swami Jonah over what I was. He was too drunk to listen anyway. I wanted to get out of there as much as the rest of them. The smell of cooked meat – and something else too – was still fugging the air. If I thought about it, my stomach heaved itself into my throat.

I swallowed. 'Tonight has been—'

'A fucking disaster.' Fitzy's voice came from behind. I was tempted to take up the empty bottle lying on the table in front of me and break it over his fat greasy head. Instead, I didn't look at him.

'I don't think I needed you in the chair for that, Fitzpatrick.'

I moved forward. 'Tonight has been a shock for us all. To die up there like that, it's ...' I shook my head, the proper words to describe it didn't come. I moved on. 'Netta's death casts a shadow on us all, but we have to go on, keep working. I made a promise to you all when I took on the running of the halls – and took on more besides ...'

I paused. They were still as cats at a mouse hole now.

'You all know what I am – what I've become. Christ knows tongues around these parts are looser than a dollop's arse ...'

Some of them laughed at that. It gave me a lift.

'And out there in Paradise, people are beginning to know too. I have ... responsibilities that go far deeper than what you see here. But I never forget that I made you a promise when I became the proprietor of these halls – all three of them, The Carnival, The Comet and The Gaudy when we build it again. That promise stands, whatever else I am. You work hard for me and I'll work hard for you. Tonight won't have done us any favours. I need you to be loyal and I need you to believe in me. I won't tell a lie, things haven't been good. We've had more than our share of bad luck ...'

Tell truth, I knew it was something more than that, but I wasn't going to burden them with the workings of it.

'But I can make it right. *We* can make it right. We need to stick together – all of us. This is where I came from. We are a family ...'

I caught myself using Lady Ginger's words and balled my hand to a fist as I finished up. 'Never think I've abandoned you, because I won't – no matter what comes.'

You could have heard a roach fart in the silence. It wasn't like that last time, when they cheered and hollered and when

Peggy's Dan took my hand. I blinked hard as the tears started up in my eyes. Jesus, this was a mess – all of it.

I was grateful when Professor Ruben spoke up.

'On behalf of the orchestra, I thank you, ma'am.' He stood up from the table where the boys were gathered around a couple of empty bottles and gave a slight bow. 'But it has been a hard night for us all. Perhaps what we need now – all of us – is to go to our beds and to our loved ones and be grateful for what we have.'

'Thank you, Professor.' I nodded. 'You're right, as usual. Get off, all of you. And if you say your prayers, say one for poor Netta tonight.'

There was a deal of rustling, grumbling and scraping of chairs as they readied themselves to leave. There was still something else I needed.

'Wait!'

They all turned to me.

'Before you go, I hear a box came for her – for Netta – all wrapped up fine with ribbons and that. Do any of you know what was in it and where it came from? Marnie – I hear you had plenty to say about it.'

'You hear that from Peggy?' Marnie Trinder stepped out from the knot of women standing at the side. 'You saw what was in it, ma'am. We all did. It was that dress with the lace and the little pearls. Netta's face was a picture when she took it out.'

Just behind me, Fitzy thumped the rail around the orchestra pit and swore again. I turned to look at him. He took a swig from the mug in his hands. 'I wondered why she wasn't wearing the costume she practised in yesterday. It was a mistake and I would have told her so if she hadn't gone up like a Roman Candle. For a start, the other one was cut off here.' He made a chopping motion below his knee. 'So you could see more of her legs. The punters like a neat ankle. Those long skirts killed her, so they did, catching the cups like that.'

Fitzy thought it was an accident, then? I let that lie as Marnie piped up again.

'She couldn't wait to put it on. I helped her with the fastenings – all them little pearly buttons down the back. Never had anything so fine, she said.'

I stepped forward. 'And from what I hear, she said something more – about where it came from. That right, Marnie?'

She looked down and rubbed her hands together. 'Well, I thought . . . that's to say we all thought it was a gift, from . . . a good friend, ma'am.'

The sniggering started up again. That was it. I was going to lay it out for them.

'That *friend* wasn't me. And seeing as how you're all thinking it I want to make it plain, here and now so none of you forget it. I don't care who any of you lay yourselves down with. As long as everyone's happy with their choices, that's their business and none of mine, but Netta Swift was nothing more to me than someone I paid – for her work here on the stage, not in my bed.'

The hall was silent for a moment and then there was some more scuffling about. Whether they believed me or not I couldn't tell, but there was nothing else I could say.

Marnie cleared her throat and spoke again. 'There . . .

there was something, Kitty . . . ma'am. There was a note in the box under all the paper and that. It's still up there if you want to take a look at it.'

I opened the window in the long narrow room to let in some air. It didn't work, mind, that meaty smell was up here too, mixing with the frowse of the bodies and the costumes.

Marnie went to the far end and came back with a long pale box wrapped about with fat ribbons. I held up a candle lantern as she set the box down on the floor between us and started to untie the tangle of silk.

'Did you see who delivered it?'

Marnie shook her head. 'It came to the back – one of the men brought it up to her.'

As she lifted the lid a rich leathery, spiced scent rose from the tissue. I covered my nose and mouth and stepped back.

Marnie quizzed at me. 'As soon as she opened it Netta said she knew who it was from.'

And I did too now. I'd recognise that scent anywhere. It was the cologne worn by Lord Kite's man. Something Netta said that day when she came to me in the office went off in my mind.

He don't say much, but he's a looker. Smells nice too – better than most men, anyways.

Netta Swift's fancy man was Matthias Schalk. I'd lay my life on it. I caught the smell of him in the dark that time at The Gaudy, before it burned down. I'd never forget that cologne or the way it made me feel.

245

Marnie started to rustle through the tissue in the box. She winced as she folded back a layer of paper and drew out her hands. She blew on her right palm and rubbed it again like she was scratching an itch.

'I don't know where this rash has come from, Ki . . . ma'am. I've never had anything like it before. Maybe it's the heat?'

'Show me.' I reached out and took her hand in mine, turning it over to see clear in the lamplight. There were blisters bubbling across the skin. The tips of her fingers were raw and peeling too. A year or so back I remember Lucca telling me that one of the hands in the workshop had to leave because every time he touched the size they used on the flats his hands swelled up. In the end he took a night job at a bakery up Bethnal.

I frowned. 'You helped her with the dress tonight, didn't you, Marnie? You said you did up the buttons at the back.'

She nodded. 'There must have been near on thirty of them. And then I helped her with the underskirts and that, frothing them out under all the silver lace. They all smelt lovely – like the paper in the box. Whoever sent that dress to her must have doused it first.' She looked at me.

I stared down at the tissue. Marnie was right – someone had most definitely soaked that dress, and the box it came in, with scent. I bent forward and breathed deep. There was another smell there, underneath the spice I caught something like . . .

Like the dirty mustiness from the back of an old wall cupboard where fleshy mushrooms bloom in the rotten wood. There was something familiar about it, but I couldn't pin it down. It was powerful noxious. I realised that along with

246

roasted meat, the hall downstairs reeked of grave earth.

Marnie bent forward. 'The note's at the bottom under all the tissue. Netta hid it away when she saw it. She said she was going to get her friend to read it to her later. She's like me – neither us have our letters.'

I reached out and caught her arm. 'Don't.'

I took a cloth from a side table and wrapped it round my hand. I knelt down and batted the paper back until I found the envelope, face down, at the bottom. I tipped it out of the box and it landed right side up. There was nothing written on the front and it was still sealed. I opened it and took out the note. As I stared in confusion at the angular sloping writing that stabbing pain went off over my eye. I glanced at Marnie, who was busy scratching the skin on her palm.

The letter that came with Netta's dress was for me.

Chapter Twenty-one

The note was brief as the black writing was jagged.

> *Lady Linnet*
> *I trust you will forgive the theatrical excess of this evening's entertainment. I merely wished to capture your attention.*
> *The Temple Church, tomorrow evening at nine o'clock. You will not be harmed, I give you my word.*
> *Kite*

I propped the card against the brass inkstand on my desk and stared at it hoping if I looked long enough I might see something more. Of course, that was a fancy. There was a fluttering sound from the open window. I looked over and saw that little dun-coloured sparrow again, the one that put me in mind of Edie Strong. It cocked its head, fluffed itself out and took off again.

I took a gulp of warm air and rested my forehead on my hands. Sleep hadn't come, but it was what I needed. Proper rest, I mean, the sort that shuts you down and lets your mind pick itself over until everything's sorted into place. I reckoned I could sleep for a century and nothing would come right.

I heard the tinny chime of the clock in the parlour across

the hall. I counted nine strikes. Twelve hours to go. What did the old bastard want?

I likely knew the answer to that, but if Kite thought I knew where Joey was he was fishing for salmon in the Thames. I considered the note again. I didn't have to go, did I? He didn't own me.

I give you my word.

I almost laughed aloud – almost – at the thought of Lord Kite's *word* being worth any more than a sheet of Bromo.

There was a tap and the door opened. Tan Seng bowed. 'A visitor asks to see you, Lady. He says it is most urgent. He refuses to leave.'

I stood up sharp.

'Is it the Beetle . . . Telferman?'

Tan Seng shook his head and bowed again. 'He says you know him well, Lady. It is a Mr Collins.'

Sam looked a good deal better than he had in the Fields. His cuffs were clean for a start and he'd shaved the reddish stubble from his chin. His hair still needed a good trim, though. He flicked it back and stared at me.

'Still not sleeping, Kitty?'

I didn't answer that. I sat up straighter in the chair as those clever brown eyes took in the room. He nodded at the door. 'This is a very . . . fine house. Very fine indeed, once you're through the door. Part of your recent inheritance, I understand?'

I didn't answer that neither, but it didn't put him off.

'And how pleasant to meet Mr Lok again. We passed on the stairs. May I sit down?'

Tell truth, I was minded to point him at the stiff couch Fitzy always grumbled about, but Sam pulled the chair out from the opposite side of the desk, sat down smart and pulled a notebook and pencil from his pocket.

I took a breath. No one would need a fire in this heat, but the taste of smoke and metal hit the back of my throat. Limehouse air – it was always the same whatever the season. I swallowed. 'What brings you here so early in the day, Sam?'

'I would say it's a *who*, rather than a *what*.' He tapped the tip of his pencil on the desk top.

'Netta Swift – that's who.' He let her name swing there for a moment and placed his black notebook on the table between us.

'There. I'm not going to write anything down. I just want to hear about it from you.'

Christ! Netta's charred body had been fugging up her lodgings for less than nine hours, and Sam already knew about it. I pushed Kite's note under my skirt on the seat of the chair to make sure it was hidden and shifted back.

'What have you heard?'

He shrugged. 'As much as anyone might pick up on the streets. It's a tragedy, I suppose. Netta was poised on the edge of a new career, perhaps an exceptional one, and then . . .' he snapped his fingers between us, 'gone in a ball of flame. That's what I heard, anyway. They say it was the flares catching her skirts.' He sat forward. 'But I'd like to hear what you say. It's quite a coincidence.' He tapped the pencil again. 'Trouble follows you like a dog chasing a butcher's cart.'

Jonah.

The word stole into my mind as I stared across the desk at Sam. He looked something like a dog himself just now; the wiry, excitable sort they send down rat holes. I twisted the plait at the back of my neck and pushed away a stray loop of hair. It caught on the black jet earring dangling from my ear. I tugged at it, but it didn't come free.

'Here, let me.' He stood and reached across. 'I can see where it's tangled up.' As he loosened the hair I smelt tobacco and soap on his hands. His fingers brushed my cheek as he worked at the knot.

'There.' He sat back and smiled. 'You didn't answer my question.'

'I didn't think you'd asked one.' I folded my arms. 'You've changed since we last met, Sam Collins. Business picked up, has it?'

He reached into the pocket of his jacket and took out the silver case I'd seen in the Fields.

'May I?'

I nodded. He flicked open the lid and offered the case to me.

I took one. 'These look better than the ones you had last time. As I recall, them things you were dragging on were thinner than a maggot.' Tell truth, the only reason I took one of Sam's smokes was for the sake of something to do with my hands.

He struck a Lucifer on the side of the case and reached across to light it for me. 'Quite the Bohemian, aren't we Kitty? Then again, I imagine you're many things these days?'

I glanced up at him. 'And what's that supposed to mean?'

He flicked his shaggy fringe out of his eyes. 'Two days after I saw you in the Fields, someone paid *The Pictorial*'s debts. In fact the generous soul has put so much into the coffers that we can continue for another three years at least. Our benefactor is now *The Pictorial*'s principal investor. You could call them the owner.'

'What do you call them?'

He laid the pencil on the table and glanced over at a rustling noise from the window. The sparrow was back again. I reckon it had a nest nearby. It held its head to the side and watched us through the lace.

Sam nodded at the sill. 'A plucky little bird.' He raised the cigarette. In the sunlight I noticed the firm line of his lips and the jut of his chin. There were grooves at the corners of his mouth worn there through smiling, not temper. He took a pull and I pushed a little brass pen tray between us to catch the ash.

'Thank you. Now, the thing is, Kitty, I'd like to show ... our benefactor how grateful I am – how grateful we all are – Peters, Billy and his father, the basement boys, even old McPherson. Do you know, he cried like a child when he heard the happy news.'

As the smoke went down it tasted good, not as good as the opium, mind, but something about it calmed me down and sharpened me up at the same time.

'I take it that was before he took himself off to The Lion and Seven Stars to celebrate?'

Sam laughed. 'Indeed it was. How well you know us all.' He paused and waved his cigarette about in a way that threatened the rug. 'One might even say it's as if you were one of us.'

I pushed the tray even closer to him.

'We're not out in the Fields now. You haven't come here to talk about me, Sam. And if you have you're going to be disappointed. I'm not one for a 'fessional – not like Lucca. So if you think I'm going to sit here jawing about what I might or might not have done you'll go away with an empty book.'

Sam frowned. He was clearly about to make a point, but I cut in quick.

'Listen, The Carnival needs all the help it can get after what happened last night. There's nothing the punters love more than a bit of drama, 'specially if it involves a pretty girl and a bit of flesh. But what happened to Netta was a horror, not something to relish in the normal way of things. Once they've had their fill of it, they'll start thinking about what they saw – what they really saw on that stage. A woman suffering and dying in the most public and pitiful way – that's not the way to get a reputation. Not the one I want for my halls anyways. I was there last night and I saw it all.'

I ground my own cigarette in the tray and the smoke rose between us.

'You asked me about Netta when you came in here. I'll tell you about what happened to her . . .' I paused, 'from a bird's eye view – and you can write it all down for your readers.'

'Read that last bit back to me.'

Sam pushed away that fringe of his and ran his finger down

the margin of the notebook. '"Beautiful, but deadly, the dress was the gift of Miss Swift's intended. We can only imagine the wretched plight of that unfortunate now as he contemplates the tragic consequence of his gift of love."'

He looked up and grinned. 'Yes! They'll swallow that. I might embroider it a bit too. It's always good to hit them here.' He tapped his chest and the pencil left a black mark on his shirt. 'You have an ear for this, Kitty.'

I shook my head. 'Nanny Peck, my grandmother, she's the one you should thank. She used to read aloud to us from the newspapers. She had a rare taste for the sentimental.'

'It never goes out of fashion.' Sam turned to delve into the pocket of his jacket, which was now hanging over the back of the chair. He retrieved the silver case, flicked it open and offered it to me again.

I shook my head. 'No, thank you.'

He struck a light. 'You said us?' The question came out casual, but I knew it wasn't. If a mouse shed a whisker Sam Collins would know where it fell. I smoothed my skirts and eased my feet out of my shoes under the desk so I could wrap my toes round the spindle strut of the chair.

'I ... I had ...' I gripped the wood with my stockinged toes. 'There were two of us. Me and my brother Joseph – Joey. That's what we called him – me, Ma and Nanny Peck.'

'Older or younger than you?' Sam busied himself with the cigarette, drawing until the tip flared red.

'Older – by three years.' I stared at the leather desk top, not wanting to catch Sam's eye.

'And where is he now?'

'He's ... gone away.' I changed the subject. 'What about

you, Sam? Do you have family – brothers, sisters and that?'

He shook his head. 'I'm an only. My mother died when I was sixteen and my father followed soon after. He died of grief, I think.'

'I'm sorry.'

'Don't be. My parents were so wrapped up in each other they didn't have much time for me. They were good and kind, but I think I always knew I wasn't the centre of their world. They left me enough to get by. The rest . . .' he snorted, 'such as it is, I've done for myself. This errant brother of yours, where is he now?'

Now, wasn't that a question? Sam's brown eyes locked on mine and once again I was minded of a terrier.

'Look out for the ash, will you? It's on the rug again.'

I pushed the brass tray towards him. 'Can you read me that bit about the funeral again?'

He nodded and flicked back a couple of pages. He jerked his hair clear of his eyes and grinned.

'I've got a better idea. Why don't you read it to me? I don't mind telling you I was impressed that day in the Fields when you translated my scrawl. Let's see if you're keeping up your studies.' He handed the notebook to me and tapped his pencil halfway down the page. 'I think it's there.'

I flattened the book in front of me and scanned the dashes and squiggles. I read through the lines to myself and once I was sure I had the meaning I began. '"The proprietor of The Carnival, Miss Kitty Peck, latterly The Limehouse Linnet – no stranger to the danger that may befall a performer she – has promised that Miss Swift will be buried with full honour, solemnity and delicacy in a manner most befitting. Miss Peck has offered to pay the full funerary costs as a mark of respect to a fellow performer, declaring Miss Swift 'A star in the ascendant, cruelly deprived of her chance to shine.'"

I looked at Sam. 'Does that sound fair?'

He took a pull and nodded. 'You misread delicacy for dignity, but otherwise it's very good. And by the time I've finished with it, you'll be the heroine of the piece. I think I'll have you running on with the rug instead of the Scotsman. What do you think?'

'I think that's a step too far, Sam, even for you.'

'Well, as you know, I am always at your service, ma'am.' He made a mock salute and the cigarette lodged between his fingers tumbled to the floor. 'Sorry. I am also a clumsy oaf.' He dipped beneath the desk to retrieve it.

'No harm done.' He leaned across to tap the cigarette end against the tray. I took in the ink smuts across his knuckles and his long fingers. I sat back in the chair and brought a hand to my face. The skin was hot to the touch. I opened the drawer to the left and took out a cotton 'kerchief scented with lavender water. I dabbed it to my forehead as Sam rifled through his notebook.

'Speaking of being at your service – that day in the Fields, Kitty, do you remember you asked me a question about a picture in *The Pictorial*?'

'Lord Denderholm and the others, you mean. I asked you to find out who the youngest one of them was.'

Sam nodded. 'You made me think there might be something more there.'

Of an instant, I was alert. 'And was there?'

'I think there is, yes. I think there most definitely is. It was all a mistake, you see.'

I frowned. 'No, I don't see.'

Sam rubbed his hands together. 'Sorry, I'll start at the beginning. Do you remember I told you about the Bureau?'

'You said it was a source of generalities. Legal items from the courts that people like and boring tidbits from Mr Gladstone that people don't care so much for.'

'Exactly – you have it in one. I have a ... let's call him a friend who works for the Bureau. He owes me a couple of favours so I stood him a drink and asked him to find out some more about the London Imperial Agency. It was as if I'd asked him to murder his mother.

'I practically had to catch him by the scruff of the neck to keep him in The Mitre. He was so agitated by the merest mention of the Agency. I had to buy another three or four tankards before he was ... calm enough to tell me anything. And that wasn't much, to be frank. But it was interesting.'

I scrunched the 'kerchief into a ball. 'What did he say? It must have been something. I assume you got him drunk enough to loosen his tongue?'

Sam nodded. 'Of course. It always works, but it's a fearfully expensive way to land a fish. What he told me was that the piece about Lord Denderholm and his colleagues should never have appeared in *The Pictorial* or anywhere else. There was a royal rumpus about it when it did. Apparently there was some mix-up at a very senior level. Wrong report ended up on the wrong desk at the wrong time – that sort of thing.'

I rubbed the 'kerchief over my wrist. 'Well, it can't have been that much of a mistake. Someone took the trouble to make likenesses of them all. That's why I was interested. I saw Lor . . . him . . . that face in *The Pictorial*.'

Sam blinked. I knew he was storing that away, but he didn't follow it up.

'Wrong time, Kitty. The information is intended for release eventually, but not now. My friend was told that it's too early. But too early for what? That's what I want to know. The other thing he said – and I quote – was: "Thank goodness it only appeared in your rag, Sam, otherwise heads would roll."'

'That was quite unnecessary, don't you think? Anyway, the good news is that I might be able to gather together a little more information. His superior at the Bureau keeps more sensitive items in a locked cabinet. My friend believes there's more on the matter hidden there.'

'But he's scared already. How can you convince him to break into the cabinet, Sam?'

He grinned. 'Because I have this.'

He reached into the lining of his jacket and produced a small metal ring strung with keys.

'One of these fits the main door. Once inside I'll find that cabinet for myself. My friend was really quite . . . distracted that evening. Your magician, Swami Jonah, is it?' I nodded. 'Well, he's not the only master of sleight of hand.' He jangled the keys.

'You want to be careful, Sam, you'll get yourself arrested. I don't want another . . .' I was about to say another misfortune on my conscience, but I buttoned it. 'I don't want you getting into trouble on my account, that's all.'

'On the contrary, Kitty. I'll be doing this for me – or

for *The Pictorial*, which is much the same thing. I scent something interesting here. Don't worry. I'm always careful. I've done this sort of thing before.'

I'll bet he had. I circled the tip of a finger over a knot hole in the wooden edge of the desk.

'Did you find out who they were, all the other men in the picture?'

'They are mostly connected to outposts of the Empire, either through the great trading companies, through the army or through the service. Four of them appear to be aristocrats of the most idle variety. I know the names of them all now. Except one, who appears to be a total mystery.'

He slammed the black notebook shut. 'I think you know already which one that is. Tell me, how do you know him?'

I stood and went to stand in front of the mirror.

'Who is he, Kitty? What is he to you?'

The stabbing was firing off over my eye like someone was poking a knife into my head.

'Nothing. It's a business matter, like I said. He's nothing.'

'And what about Lord Kite – is he nothing too?'

I swung about. Sam was staring at the rug near his feet.

I darted across the room and snatched up the card poking out from under the edge of the desk near his foot. I'd forgotten I was sitting on it. It must have fallen when I went to the mirror. As I took it in my hands I was certain that Sam had only seen the name scrawled at the end, nothing more. Most of the note was hidden.

He tapped the quivering cone of ash from the tip of his cigarette into the tray. 'I must say, Kitty, you seem to be moving in exalted circles. Tell me, is his lordship an admirer?'

I opened a drawer, placed the note face down inside, slammed it shut and locked it.

'He saw you up in your cage.' Sam went on. 'You made his heart beat like a gong and now he bombards you with love notes. Perhaps the pair of you have an . . . understanding?'

I sat down and pushed the drawer key into my skirt pocket. 'It's nothing like that, Sam Collins, so don't you go speculating on the matter.'

'Perhaps you already know the identity of the handsome young man in that drawing, Kitty? Perhaps his name also begins with a "K"?'

He leaned back, took a drag and blew a smoke ring. We watched the perfect oval float down and dissolve between us over the desk top.

After a moment, he started up again. 'It's not unusual for an aristocrat to marry low. I believe it's good for the bloodline. Keeps it vigorous. They do the same with their horses, you know.'

I stared at him.

'Ah! There's a wife. Is that the problem? Now, that would be a story for *The Pictorial*. A society scandal, the songbird tussling with a swan.'

I'd had enough of this.

'Listen, I'll tell you who he is, Sam.' He straightened up, his brown eyes expectant. 'He's none of your business, that's what. And I'd appreciate it if you kept your filthy sinuations to yourself. It's not three months since you good as accused me of being a Tom. Now I'm a Johnny's dollop, am I?'

I stood up abrupt, went to the door and opened up into

the hall. Tan Seng was on the stairs carrying a loaded tea tray obviously intended for us. He bowed.

'We won't be needing two cups. Mr Collins is leaving now.' I held the door wider. 'I've got things to see to, Sam, so if you don't mind I won't be offering refreshment this morning.'

Sam ground the remains of his cigarette into the tray and stood up. As he swung his jacket from the back of the chair, I caught a draught of soap and tobacco again.

'Of course. It's time I was on my way. *Carpe diem* and all that.'

'I haven't got time to talk about the price of fish, if that's what you're saying.' I stepped aside to let Tan Seng slip into the room. Sam brought a bony hand to his face and rubbed his chin. I got the impression he was muffling a smirk.

'Seize the day, Kitty, seize the day. That's what *carpe diem* means. I expect your fine . . . friend can tell you all about that. They all have the benefit of a classical education.'

He sauntered past me to the door and I watched him lope down the stairs. He paused at the landing just below, flicked back his fringe and looked up. 'If I find anything in that cabinet, I'll let you know, ma'am.' He grinned and saluted again, before disappearing down the next flight to the hall.

When I heard The Palace door slam I went back into my office and unlocked the drawer. I took out Lord Kite's note. I saw that my hands were trembling. Only it wasn't fear, it was fury.

How dare Sam Collins call me 'low'? After all I'd done for him and his bleedin' stinking rag.

Chapter Twenty-two

The cabman rapped on the roof and opened the trap. He peered down at the three of us and sniffed. There was a world of meaning in the sound of it: suspicion of the foreigners jammed together in his hack; disgust that a woman should keep such company; and an urgent desire for us to tumble out so he could move on and take the money of a more respectable type.

'Two shillings.' He stuck his hand down, palm open.

'You said one.' I jagged my head to the side so I could see his face through the slat overhead.

The fingers waggled just over the feather trim of my bonnet. 'It's two now – on account of them. A decent Christian wouldn't want to sit in there if they had an idea who'd been there before them. If I'd known I wouldn't have taken you. That's why you sent the boy, isn't it?'

I unhooked the half door in front of us and motioned for Tan Seng and Hari to climb out. I'd asked Lok to stay at The Palace with Peggy. I knew she liked his company. When I wasn't around I suspected the pair of them made themselves cosy as Darby and Joan. Peggy didn't ask where I was going, but she must have sensed something coming off me as we stood in the hall waiting for the boy we'd sent to bring the cab to the end of the passage.

'You're thin as a mop handle, Kit.' She held a hand to

my cheek. 'And them shadows under your eyes are turning purple. You want to take more care of yourself.'

'It's not me you should be fretting for.' I looked down at her rounded belly. 'You're coming on a treat.' That little mound was fast becoming something more than a suggestion.

She looked down and smiled. 'I swear I can feel him sometimes, but Lok says it's wind.'

I reckoned she and Lok had plenty to talk about now.

The carriage jerked and squeaked as Hari followed Tan Seng down onto the street. I dipped my head to look out. It was almost dusk. Somewhere nearby a bell struck the quarter.

'I said Temple Church. Where is it?'

'You're close enough.' The cabman pointed at a dark archway between a jumble of old-style houses, all wood and dirty plaster, the storeys almost tumbling over each other.

'I can't take you any nearer. You'll find it through there, three passages down, across a courtyard and then first right. You won't miss it. It's the lawyers' church, right in the middle of their nest.'

The hand jabbed down again, knocking the brim of my straw.

'I said two shillings.'

I grabbed that grimy hand and yanked hard so the man almost toppled from his perch. Then I bit down hard on his smallest finger and was gratified to hear him yelp – more in surprise than pain. I scrambled out of the cab and flicked a shilling up at him. It clattered across the roof of the hack and he made a swipe for it.

'That's all you're getting. These gentlemen work for me. If I want them to accompany me I'll pay a fair rate for the journey. I won't be insulted and I won't have them listening to your cant.'

The cabman smiled, lips curling back on a row of stumps. He shifted the reins into his right hand and reached behind his back with his left.

'And I won't let a bitch like you get the better of me.'

Of an instant he lunged forward.

Tell truth, I'm still not entirely straight what came next. It happened so fast. One second I was staring up at the cabman, next there was a blur and a mighty crash. The horse whickered and then it bolted – dragging the empty cab behind it. I heard a woman squeal as it clattered to a halt thirty yards or so away.

The cabman was sprawled in the gutter now and Tan Seng was standing over him. He had his slippered foot on the man's chest and he was gripping the leather flail of a whip. The stick was still in the man's hand. It didn't seem possible that the old boy had caught it and pulled him down, but the evidence was groaning in a pile of steaming horse shit right in front of me.

'Lady.'

Tan Seng bowed and dropped the whip. Then he bent forward and collected something shiny from the cobbles. He knelt and pressed the shilling into the cabman's hand and stood up. He nodded at the archway.

'We go now?'

⚓

Credit where it's due; I had something to thank that mangy cabman for. I'm not sure we would have found Temple Church without his instructions. Beyond the archway it was a warren. A lawyers' nest he'd called it and something about that made me think of Lord Kite stirring his black feathers and turning his pebble-blind eyes towards me.

We crossed a wide paved courtyard and took the passage on the right. At the end we came out into the open again. The church was ahead surrounded by railings. I'd never seen one like it before. It looked like two different buildings butted up against each other. One was round and fat with a steepled turret sprouting from the middle and one was a long, hall-like affair.

I paused. Perhaps it *was* two buildings? The long one with the door in the side looked most likely, but the windows were dark. I could see a faint glow in the panes of the turret on the round one and I caught the sound of singing – a choir.

I pushed at some hairs working their way from under my bonnet. One of the blue feathers sewn to the brim hung limp in front of my face. I reached up, snapped it off and threw it to the dust.

For some reason Madame Celeste's voice went off in my head. I'd spent all them days in her cat-piss attic learning how to twirl on a bar thirty foot up, but since my last time up in the cage I hadn't given her a thought. Her best advice came to me now and I was grateful.

If you ever allow yourself to think you might fall, you will. It's simple as that, girl.

'Come on then.' I straightened my shoulders and stepped forward. My heels echoed on the stones.

'Lady Linnet.'

The voice slid from somewhere behind. Even before I turned, I knew who it was. I could smell him. My heart battered against my ribs like it was trying to fly out.

Matthias Schalk was leaning against the wall. His blond hair caught the last rays of the evening sun giving him the look of something Lucca might have admired in one of his books. Only there was nothing celestial about Matthias Schalk. He was built like a brewer's stack.

Hari took a step forward so he was standing between us. Tan Seng moved soundlessly to join him. Schalk shook his head. 'I thought the message was clear, Lady Linnet. You do not need protection. My master will not harm you. He has given his word. The word of one Baron to another cannot be broken. It is the law.'

His accent was hard and angular. I'd heard enough ship-mates in the halls who'd put in for a duration to know he came from somewhere a long way north and east of Limehouse. Ogen – that's what Lady Ginger called him. Ramesh Das told me it meant 'eyes' in Schalk's own tongue. He smiled, but it was sour as a lemon. It came to me that he minded me of someone, but it wasn't the moment to go tracking it down. I watched him, careful to keep a distance from that hawk-head cane.

'Perhaps your predecessor, the great Lady Ginger, did not have time to explain the rules to you before she ... left.' Schalk moved forward. The scent of him came stronger – leather and spice and all things noxious. I thought about Peter Ash, and I thought about that woman they dragged from the river, Joey's messenger, that poor redhead whose body had been diced to a profanity.

An eel thrashed in my belly.

He caught me looking at the cane and brushed a hand over the curved silver head. 'A gift from my master. He is waiting for you, Lady Linnet. He does not like to wait.'

Schalk nodded towards the doorway in the long building across the yard. 'I will remain here with your companions. You may regard it as a surety between us. As long as you observe the law, these men will not be harmed. And I trust that my safety is also assured.'

A bell began to measure the hour.

I glanced at Tan Seng. He blinked and bowed his head.

⚱

The door whispered to a close. Temple Church smelt of polish and fresh paint. The sound of singing was clear now – a dozen voices, all men, all chanting praises to the Lord. It was gloomy, but to the right, where that dreary racket was coming from, there was light.

The voices stopped and I heard rustling and shuffling. Moments later a line of men dressed in long dark gowns trooped down the aisle towards me, each one of them clutching a flat red book to his chest. They didn't even flick a look at me as they filed past and went out through the door. It was silent then, the sort of silence you could stir with a spoon.

I bit my lip. This part of the church was dim, within a quarter of the hour it would be dark. As far as I could tell the rows of old boxed-up pews were empty. But there was still a glow over to the left where the choir had come from.

The word of one Baron to another cannot be broken. It is the law.

I kept that in mind as I went to the light. It was just one building after all. The central aisle led into a wide circular space lit by single candles set in sconces on just two of the pillars. It's an odd thing, but it seemed a lot bigger now I was inside than it had from across the yard – and more like I imagined a castle might be than a church. When we was kids Joey had a story book: the tales of King Arthur and his knights. It came to mind now as I took the place in. You could fit a bleedin' big table in here.

'Music is a balm to the soul. It is the finest art form. Do you not agree, Lady Linnet?'

Lord Kite's drawl seemed to hover in the air.

I turned in the direction of the voice. At first I couldn't make him out in the shadows, but I heard the sound of his footsteps. A moment later he came through an arch and into the centre of the circle.

The rounded walls about me disappeared. I was back at old Bartholomew's. Danny Tewson's ragged fingers scrabbled at my skirts and somewhere behind him a ledger-stone stood open and ready. The vision was so real that the stink of that place, centuries of incense, dust and mouse, stoppered my nose. Something clambered into my throat. Hot tears streamed down my face. That brought me back. Even though Kite was blind I wasn't going to weep in front of him.

I didn't move and I didn't make another sound. I let the tears slide down my cheeks to work their way beneath the stiffened collar of my dress.

Everything about Kite's person was bleached to a ghost of itself. Moon-white hair curled to his ears from the sharp widow's peak that divided his high forehead. A long narrow nose shadowed bloodless lips. It was his eyes that caught, though, sealed by a milky film they gleamed in the candlelight. Even though I knew he couldn't see me, those eyes were watchful.

Like before he was tricked out in black except for his shirt. Fine gear it was, I could tell by the sheen of the cloth. He was wearing that silver bird-head ring with the ruby eyes and something winked in the folds of silk at his collar. I took it for a jewelled stud. It glinted in the candlelight like his glazed eyes.

He stood for a moment, listening. Then he turned direct to me and bowed.

'They tell me great paintings can move a man to tears. Have you wept before such things, Lady Linnet? If so, I confess I cannot share your appreciation, although on occasion I have experienced pleasure when a picture ... or a drawing has been described to me.'

I understood what he meant straight off – them filthy pictures. He waited for me to speak but I didn't give him what he wanted.

'Did you enjoy this evening's practice?'

Still I didn't answer.

'Perhaps the sacred music was not to your taste? No doubt you are more familiar with the profane?' Kite smiled. 'Hopkins, the choir master, is a great asset to the Round. I come here often to listen to them rehearse. I am the only person permitted to do so. You should be grateful, Lady Linnet.'

'Grateful!' I couldn't help myself. That choked out word bounced off the walls.

'I have allowed you to share my pleasure. Is not that a reason for gratitude?'

Oh yes – Danny Tewson, Peter Ash and Netta Swift. I had a lot to pay him back for.

'Why am I here, Lord Kite?'

He walked straight towards me, but I held my ground. At the last he veered past and carried on until he came to a rail ten foot behind. He stopped, as if he knew exactly where it was.

'Come, stand beside me.'

When I didn't move he turned and stared straight at me. 'You have nothing to fear this evening. I gave you my promise. I merely wish to show you something.'

'Is that why your ... creature made certain that Netta Swift burned to a cinder – just because you wanted to show me something?'

Lord Kite grinned. 'Vanity and greed are a most ... incendiary combination. Poor Miss Swift, she was very willing to help Matthias – for a price.' He spread his hands. 'And she has paid. Her death is not a loss. She was a disloyal servant to you. But I think you already knew that? Tell me, did you shed a tear at her passing?'

When I didn't answer he turned away.

'Come closer. Look upon the effigy of William Marshall.'

I walked slowly across the circular floor, my steps echoing from the curved walls. When I was a yard or so distant I stopped. The fluttering candle flame on a column nearby picked out the shape of a man lying on the ground behind the rail. A man made of stone.

Joey's book of King Arthur came to me again. The man wore armour like the knights in the pictures. He lay there behind the rail with his sword and his shield. His blank grey face with its shuttered eyes put me in mind of Lord Kite. Now I looked there were others too, knights scattered about the floor like monstrous toys from a nursery box.

Kite spoke again. 'There is no heaven for people like William, Lady Linnet, and there is no hell. There is the comfort of oblivion. If I may offer you a little advice, at the beginning of your tenure, it is to remember that. It will make your decisions easier to bear.'

He seemed to stare into the soaring space above us.

'People sing in places like this to fill the void. They cannot endure the silence. Imagine seven centuries of song to a God that does not exist.'

Tell truth, not being the Sunday school type, it wasn't something I'd given much thought to. But Nanny Peck had been a believer – of occasion she used to read to us from her big black Bible – and Lucca was a regular kneeler too. Even though I couldn't remember when I last said my prayers of an evening, I reckoned Kite was taking a liberty.

'I thought you said music was a balm to the soul.'

'It was a figure of speech.' He turned them pale eyes on me. 'I have not called you here to speak of philosophy or to give you a history lesson, my lady, there is something else you must learn.'

The blow came fast and accurate, his ring scratching my jaw. I didn't even have time to yelp. I just clapped my hand to my skin where the nick of the bird's curved beak had drawn blood. I looked at the red smeared across the tips of my fingers.

'You gave a promise – one Baron to another.'

Lord Kite brushed his fingers as if he wanted to rid himself of the touch of me. 'You are not harmed, merely humiliated. If you wish to strike back, do so now. Indeed, you could kill me here in the Round, after all I am blind and defenceless, but I do not think you will. You are free to go whenever you wish, but I imagine you do not wish to leave yet, do you?'

He was playing with me, taunting me like a cat with a fallen nestling. I wanted to lash out at him then, scratch that dead white skin off his face until his skull showed through tatters of bloody red flesh, but he was right. I wanted answers. I balled my fists up tight to stop myself from going for him.

'I won't harm you. I give my word. That's the law, isn't it?'

He nodded. '*Pacta sunt servanda.*'

I let that pass, whatever it was.

'You said I had something to learn. Let's start with that dress, shall we? The one Matthias got Netta to wear.'

'Ah – a delicate thing. And so very dangerous. A woman would have to take great care when wearing such a garment near naked flames.'

Netta *had* taken care. She'd hadn't gone near enough to the limelight flares to catch.

'But you are not concerned about Netta, are you?' Kite looked direct at me, his corpse eyes shone in the candlelight.

'Did you appreciate the cut and the style, my lady? You, and your brother ...' he almost spat the word, 'were very much in my mind when I instructed the seamstress.'

The church was silent for a moment. I didn't have anything to lose by asking him straight.

'I . . . I recognised it, if that's what you're driving at. It was hers, my mother's, I mean. It was the one good dress she had. She kept it all them years because it meant something. It must have been special to her because . . .'

Kite's face flushed. His features twisted up with a fury he could hardly master. He knew it and he turned from me. I watched him clench up his right hand as if he was trying to hold a mastiff on a leash. A spark leapt inside. This was something important. I went closer and was gratified to see him move away. It made me bold.

'We was never allowed to touch that dress with the lace and the little pearls. It never came out of the closet in her room, so how did you know about it?'

He turned to face me, but now his face was still as the knight at our feet.

'Because I gave it to her.'

'No!' I stepped back and my skirt caught on the rail guarding the figure. 'You can't have . . . she wouldn't . . .' A thought jabbed itself into my mind. That stabbing went off again as I considered the possibility.

'That can't be.' The words came loud enough to catch the echo of the space. '*Can't be*' repeated itself for a couple of seconds before fading to silence that hung heavy as a bell.

Kite smiled. 'Believe me, Lady Linnet, the knowledge that I did not father you or that degenerate brother of yours is a constant source of solace.' It was like he read my mind. He took a fob watch from his pocket, flicked the golden case open and traced a long finger over the dial.

'So late already. I have a dinner at the Inn. Where is he, Lady Linnet?' He spoke that last bit casual, as if he didn't really care about an answer.

It wasn't Joey I wanted to talk about, just then. 'What about the dress? Aren't you going to say any more about it? If you gave it to her then you must have—'

He cut in. 'It was a caprice. I merely wished to see if . . . if you recognised it. That is all. It was a most effective lure. You came here today despite yourself, because you were curious. Admit it. Ask yourself.'

He paused to let me take that in. 'I also wished to demonstrate the extent of our reach into your estate. Can you be sure of anyone in Paradise, Lady Linnet? Think about that later, when you are alone. You are often alone now, aren't you?'

The hem of my skirt ripped on the rail as I stepped forward to slap that beaky face of his so hard my fingers left red stripes on his skin.

'That's for Netta. I'd give you another for Danny and for Old Peter if it wasn't for the fact that I couldn't trust myself to stop. But we've given our word to each other, haven't we – *pacta sunt servanda*?'

Kite didn't move. 'A strike for a strike. We are equal, in that if little else. Now let us return to my question. Where is your brother?'

'I don't know and even if I did, do you think I'd tell you? The last time I saw him was before The Gaudy burned down.'

Those blind eyes narrowed. 'So he was here in London in April?'

Shit! I'd given him something.

'Don't distress yourself for his sake, my lady. You merely confirm what I already knew.'

It was as if Kite read my mind again. In other circumstances, I might have offered him a job at The Carnival. He was a rare talent. I stared at the silver pin twitching at his throat as he went on.

'Joseph Peck is not in Paris. We ascertained that from his houseman. A strange fellow – I believe you might know him? The Monseigneur.'

I almost spat on the stones. 'I knew he wasn't to be trusted. Evil little git.'

Kite laughed. 'On the contrary, he was very loyal – right up to the end.'

I reached out to steady myself on the rail. I knew the Monseigneur – or Monsieur Chartrand, to give him his proper name – had worked as my grandmother's spy in Joey's house – but then Joey knew that too and it didn't seem to bother him. Of an instant, I regretted what I'd said.

Right up to the end.

What had they done to him? My chest wound itself tight as a rope maker's hitch.

'Let us go back to my question, Lady Linnet. Joseph did not return to Paris. Someone here must know where he is, someone here must be helping him. I know, for a certainty, that person would not be Lady Ginger ... which leaves me with you. I called you here this evening to remind you of your duty. The Aestas session draws near. If you disappoint us there will be others like Netta, many others.'

Kite smiled. 'It is a simple choice. Give us your brother or we will take Paradise.'

'I don't know where he is. How many times and how many ways can I tell you that?' I heard the rising pitch in my voice and struggled to master it. 'I almost wish I did so this could be finished with. Don't you think I might have a few things I want to discuss with him?'

I took a sharp breath. 'It don't matter how much you threaten or how many people you set your dog on with that wicked cane of his. It won't make no difference. I don't know where my brother is – or even if he's alive. I can't give you what I don't have. I can't magic him out of my pocket.'

A muscle twitched beside Kite's thin lips. I wondered if something I said had got through.

'Listen, if you're in the mood for a quiz I've got a question for you – why do you want him so bad? What's he to you?'

Kite's left hand shot forward to catch my chin in a grip so tight I would have cried out if I could open my mouth.

'That question is not as straightforward as you might imagine, dear Lady Linnet. You might want to consult your grandmother about it. Her culpability in this is almost as great as his.'

His right hand slid up my bodice and followed the line of my neck to my cheek. The tips of his fingers brushed across my cheeks, my nose, my lips and my eyes. The touch was dainty, almost feminine, like he was brushing the dust from a piece of fine china.

'Remarkable.' The word slipped out as a whisper. I felt a shudder go through him as he released me and stepped away.

'They told me, but I didn't believe them until now.'

'Who? Who told you what?'

'The other Barons. Lord Fetch, for one – you remember

him, surely? The ripeness of him. And Lord Mitre, Lord Silver, Lord Oak, the Lords Janus. They all remarked on the likeness.'

Somewhere nearby a bell clanged for the half.

Kite bowed. 'I do not enjoy cold mutton, Lady Linnet. You will forgive me, but I must draw this supernumerary meeting to a close. We will meet again very soon at the Aestas session. I trust your parable will be ready. In addition, know this, we are watching. If your brother contacts you, we will know. If you do not offer Joseph to us, others close to you will suffer.'

He turned and walked into the darkness beneath the archway leading to the angular part of the church. He didn't need a candle to show the way.

As his steps echoed from the stones his voice came again.

'I have one last question. Ask yourself this too. Who is your father, Lady Linnet? Who do you think he might be? Who did your whore of a mother lie with? I think the answer will surprise you.'

Chapter Twenty-three

As I shifted about on the slippery cushions the contents of my head seemed to move slower than the rest of me, like a stew that someone had stirred in a vigorous manner and left to spin about in the pan. For a moment I wasn't sure where I was. I stared up at the low brick arches overhead, trying to make sense of the space and the gloom of it. It was the smell that told me.

I sat upright on the bunk, but my brains lingered on the stained pillow. Of an instant, everything blurred and doubled itself. There were two little flames in the lantern beside me, two greasy feathers, two long pipes lying on the floor. After a moment the pipes rippled and merged themselves into one.

The woman on the low bunk over the way turned over and hacked so loud you'd almost expect to see a lung lying there on the stones next to her own pipe. There was an itching at my temples. I reached up and felt the band of a cap digging tight into the skin. I looked down at the breeches on my legs and felt a rush of shame.

Nanking Nancy's was quiet. So far as I could make out from the lamps only four of her bunks was occupied. I swung my legs over the side and rested my forehead in my hands. My mouth was dry as the Billingsgate salt house.

It all came back.

The candles had burned to stumps before I finally went back down that black aisle and out into the yard where Tan Seng and Hari were waiting. Matthias Schalk was there still too. A single gas lamp half hidden by a scraggy tree cast a slick of yellow across the stones.

Schalk bowed. 'My master told me to wait. It was the bond. Now that your servants can see you are unharmed, I will leave.'

He started off across the yard towards the arch where we'd come in earlier. I watched the roll of his broad shoulders and the swagger in his stride and took in an oddity. For all his bulk, he was silent as a cat.

I yelled after him, I couldn't help myself. 'How can you do such things, Matthias Schalk? How can you wake in the morning and haul that carcass out of the sheets knowing what it's done?'

He turned and bowed again.

'I am most flattered that Lady Linnet has taken the trouble to learn my name.'

'It wasn't from Netta. You lied to her and then you murdered her, making a spectacle of her death, poor cow.' I thought of the big redhead dragged from the river. 'And then there's all them others. Tell me, when you look at yourself in a shaving mirror of a morning, don't you ever feel like slitting your own throat in shame?'

Schalk scraped the tip of his cane on the cobbles as if he was writing a word or drawing a picture. The silver hawk head caught the lamplight. 'What can I say, Lady Linnet?' He grinned. 'You know my work. I am an artist.'

He flipped up the cane, caught it and bowed.

'*Proost*, Lady Linnet. I bid you good evening and good health.'

He sauntered to the arch.

The three of us sat in silence in the cab all the way back to Limehouse. Tan Seng crouched forward to scan the streets. It was quiet now, past eleven. Hari made a snuffling sound beside me. His big head dipped lower and lower until it was resting on my shoulder. I didn't have the heart to wake him. The cabman up top clearly didn't care who he took on board. I heard him whistling as we clattered along.

Kite's final words kept winding around my head.

Who did your whore of a mother lie with? I think the answer will surprise you.

Tell truth, I didn't remember ever having a father – Joey didn't, neither. And it didn't matter. Ma and Nanny Peck might have been an ill-assorted pair – not that we noted it, mind – but they were tight as the halves of a walnut packed in a shell, and they loved us fierce. Besides, plenty of kids in Limehouse didn't have the benefit of a father's name they could go by.

But looking back, there were things we never spoke about when Ma was alive. Both of them – Nanny Peck most especially – had the knack of carefully changing the matter if we was to introduce a subject that might take a personal turn.

They were storytellers, the pair of them, and the talent for invention served them well when me and Joey strayed into places where we weren't welcome. I didn't have the smallest suspicion that Nanny Peck wasn't my real grandmother until Lady Ginger told me the truth of it that day in the cemetery when the mist rose around us, fugging up the past, hers most especially.

There were a lot of things kept hidden away from us like that bleedin' dress in Ma's closet. Joey had taken it out and given it an airing, hadn't he? And it hurt her bad when he spoiled it. It was like he'd stirred something up that shouldn't have come to light.

I saw one thing very plain now – my brother had always had a knack of stirring things.

I plucked at the folds of my skirt. Kite said he gave Ma that dress, but when? When did she know him? Why would he give her something like that and why would she keep it all them years?

Then again maybe it wasn't true at all. Perhaps he was lying?

I knew straight off, that wasn't right. The way the old goat's face twisted up when I told him about the way she'd kept it, like it was something precious, told the truth. He was careful to keep a rein on himself, but just for a moment he couldn't hide the way he felt.

Questions – that was the heart of it. I never got any answers from anyone. It was all lies and secrets tangled together, breeding with each other like lice in an old mattress.

My head was a writhe of thoughts that couldn't find a home. It could burst open and spray a thousand trailing ends into the carriage and I'd never be able to pack them away again. That pain went off on the right side and crawled to the top of my scalp.

As I sat there in the dark of the carriage I knew a way to make it stop. I tried to push the smoke from my mind, but this time I didn't have the strength to shut the door after it. As we rattled along I worked out how to slip out from The

Palace again without anyone knowing I'd gone. I was good at secrets too.

'Come awake, have we?' Nancy peered down at me; the glass in her spectacles fetched the lamplight blanking her eyes. For a moment I took her for Kite standing there.

'Haven't seen you here in a while ... Mr Riley. That'll be a guinea. You took Persian again – two pipes.' She glanced around the dim-arched room and knelt beside my bunk.

'Someone's come for you, ma'am.' She spoke so quiet only I could hear. 'It's not safe to go about like this – to get yourself into this state.'

She pulled her loose black sleeve up a little way to show her wrist. A faintly marked snake coiled on her skin, beneath an ivory bracelet. 'Like I said before, I make it a point to know my customers. My eyes aren't the best, I grant you, but I know who you are, Lady. And I take it you know what this means?' She moved the bracelet to show the tattoo more clear. The spade-like head of the snake curled onto her palm to the base of her thumb.

'You're among friends – but you shouldn't have come, not alone again.'

She stood up and scanned the bunks. Someone coughed over near the back wall.

'On your way, are you, young man? I've heard it's another lovely day up top. You wouldn't want to waste it.'

She offered me her hand and pulled me up. The room span, the lamps blurring to smears of orange that didn't stop moving when I closed my eyes.

'This way.' We walked through the rows of bunks to the curtain at the entrance. I wasn't sure who I'd see there and on account of the opium I didn't have it in me to care. Nancy held back the drape to let me go through first. She followed and shifted the curtain behind her so we were standing private in a narrow space in front of the stone steps leading up to the street.

The Chinaman sitting at the little table in the doorway turned to nod at Lok, who was standing just behind him.

'Lady.' He stared at my breeches and bowed curtly. His plait flicked.

'I'm sorry.' I mumbled the apology. I wasn't sure if it was to Lok, to Nancy or most particularly to Lucca.

I fumbled in a pocket.

Nancy shook her head. 'You don't pay me, Lady. I pay you. Very lucral it is – with women being a speciality, but it's a dirty thing the opium. I wouldn't touch it and if you want my opinion . . .'

She stopped as I hawked up a gobbet of black slime.

Nancy's spectacles twitched. 'A person could lose their soul in the stuff.' She jerked her head at the low, brick arched room behind her. 'They're all wandering here – the regulars. If you need it – and I'm not advising it – send someone to collect. I did the same for her – for Lady Ginger – for medicinal purposes, you understand.'

She pushed the spectacles up her nose with the tip of that single long nail of hers. In the glow from the lamp hanging from the arched ceiling I could see her clear. Her skin was brown and wrinkled like a pair of old leather bellows. She caught me staring. 'Yes – I'm smoked as a kipper, my gir . . . my Lady, and I don't even use it. Just being in the environs takes a toll. If you want to keep that pretty face of yours fresh, steer clear of the trade. Take your cut of the earnings, but not the goods, that's my advice.'

She tucked her arms into her black sleeves. 'It's the strangest thing you coming here these last few times dressed as a gent, when for all those years you came as you were – really were, I mean, a woman. Then again, it's no business of mine how you go about. I suppose it's by way of a disguise, now you've taken her place . . .'

I shook my head. Nancy wasn't making sense. I'd never come here without breeches scratching my legs. I leaned back against the brick wall as she carried on. Her painted lips twisted and wriggled. I wanted to laugh.

'Soon as you came in here this evening I sent word to The Palace, like your friend with the scar asked that last time when he came to find you. She was good to me, Lady Ginger, and if she chose you to take her place she must have known what she was doing.'

I was coming back to myself now. I straightened up. 'When . . . when was Joey here?'

Nancy frowned. 'Joey?'

I coughed again and wiped sticky black from my mouth with the back of my hand. I needed to be clear but my head was thick with the opium. I took a deep breath and thought about what I wanted to say.

'When . . . When was I last here dressed as a girl? When did you last see me in a dress?' The words came out slow and deliberate.

'I would have thought you'd know that.' She stared at me. 'Then again, maybe it's not so surprising. To my collection you were far gone that time as well. I wouldn't have let you leave in that state if I'd known the truth of it.'

She chopped out a stream of words to the man at the table. He opened the lid of a black lacquer box set in front of him and took out a book. Then he flicked from the back, running a long nail down column after column of squiggles and dashes.

Nancy sniffed. 'He'll find you. We give all our customers a name to recognise them by and we make a remark on their particulars. It's good to keep track of the trade. As a matter of fact I'm very certain we made a note of it when you came back. It was quite a surprise seeing you after all that time. I never forget a pretty face. Of course, we didn't know then that you were about to . . .'

She stopped as the man jabbed at a mark halfway down a page.

Nancy turned to me. 'May – the very beginning of May. That was the last time we saw you here dressed in a frock . . . ma'am.'

Chapter Twenty-four

I carried the fug of Nancy's cellar in my head all the way back to The Palace, that and the silence of Lòk. As we came in through the door, Tan Seng held out a note. He didn't say a word as I took in Telferman's scrawl. The pair of them made me feel like a child sent to Coventry.

That note was like a bucket of cold water tipped over my head. It sharpened me up and cleared out the opium. I washed and changed, and then I went straight to Pearl Street. Lok came out with me again, but he still didn't speak. Instead he walked three paces behind, herding me down Narrow Street like a bleedin' sheepdog. All the way there I felt his eyes on my back. I didn't have to turn round to see the look in them. He was waiting for me now in Telferman's hall. The bench was so high his feet didn't touch the floor.

'Lady.' Telferman stood up from his desk.

'You've heard from her, then?'

'No. I have not.' He fiddled with the loop of shiny black ribbon round his neck.

My heart dropped like a stone down a well. 'Then why call me here?'

'Because I have heard from Dr Pardieu.'

The Beetle started to count along the silver keys threaded on the ribbon. He stopped when he found the one he was looking for.

'Your grandmother is near the end, Lady Linnet. Pardieu informs me the remainder of her life can be measured in days, not weeks. Perhaps hours.'

'Pardieu's with her? She kept that old crow on even when she left Paradise?'

Telferman nodded and bent to unlock a drawer in his desk. 'Like me, he has served Lady Ginger for many years. Your grandmother valued, *values*, his discretion. She would not allow anyone else to attend her. Most especially so now her time is near.'

I knew my grandmother was wearing out her mortality, but now it came to it I couldn't imagine the light going out of those black bead eyes. Last time I saw her in that coach I got the impression she was gripping onto life tight as a miser with a sovereign in his fist.

'How long have you known?'

'Since Pardieu's message arrived early this morning. Here.'

He took a fold of paper from the drawer and pushed it across the desk to me.

'Forgive me, Lady, but you do not look entirely . . .'

I snatched the note. 'Thank you, Mr Telferman. I am quite myself.'

The only person I knew who could answer those questions turning me about until I couldn't see a straight way was likely to be laid out cold before I could speak to her. The paper in my hand trembled. Telferman stared at me. His face dialled something between sorrow and concern. He seemed to be about to make another remark of a personal nature, but then he thought better of it.

'I will make arrangements immediately, Lady. The

Brighton train would be best. It is the fastest and most direct route. We will need to change at Tunbridge Wells for Hastings, where we will be met.'

'We? You're coming along to hold my hand?'

He took his fob watch from a greasy pocket. 'There are papers that must be signed. I am to take them to her. The evening train departs at five. There is still time to send word ahead.'

'She's not going to have me drugged and carted to her this time like a piece of furniture?'

He packed his fob away again and scratched the side of his nose in consideration. 'It will not be necessary. Not now that the Abbey is to pass into your hands.'

He pointed at the note. 'Read.'

I slammed it on the desk top. 'It's answers I want from her, Mr Telferman, not more bleedin' property. That's why I came here today. You promised to write and make it clear that I needed to see her.'

'And I sent word as instructed, Lady Linnet. You may recall that I said it would be judicious to do so after what happened to the woman.'

'The one they fished from the river, the one who delivered Joey's note? Ramesh Das knew about that too.' I stared down at my hand on the letter. There were still black smuts on my fingers. I balled it to a fist to hide the guilty stains. 'It was him, wasn't it? *He* told you what had happened to her. He gave you all the ... details.'

Telferman nodded. 'I understand that you have now met Mr Das. I trust that you are satisfied? We work in harmony to conduct different ... strands of your affairs in Paradise.'

'He runs the muscle and you run the books – something close to that anyway. Yes, I was satisfied. As a matter of fact, I trusted him straight off. What I can't understand is why you didn't introduce us back at the beginning. If he's working for me like you do, that would have been the natural way of it.'

Telferman's brows arched over the frame of his spectacles. 'My colleague is somewhat eccentric. You've met him now, so I imagine you have an understanding of that. He believed that you would come to him when the time was right to do so and if the meeting was destined to occur. To be frank, I was beginning to wonder if that time would ever come but when that paint ... ah ...'

He stopped himself and patted some dust from a stack of papers to the right of the desk.

'You were going to say when that painting appeared on his doorstep, weren't you?'

Telferman nodded, but didn't look at me. 'Those vile images – all of them – were the crudest insults. They have been removed. These are early days. It is clear to me that someone is trying to undermine your authority, Lady Linnet.'

I nodded. 'I know that all right. And I know who did them now – Lord Kite's man, that's who. He practically told me so himself.'

The Beetle frowned. The grey hairs of his spindly brows shot out and upwards giving another truth to my private name for him. 'The Barons of London circle each other, but it has always been my understanding, from your grandmother, that they respect each other's jurisdiction.'

'I have the idea that respect is the last thing Lord Kite feels when it comes to me ... or my brother. But I don't have an idea of much else. I'm sick of secrets, Mr Telferman. Sometimes my head's so full of winding passages and stairs that lead nowhere I get lost in there.'

I took up the note. 'Now, let's see what old Pardieu has to say.'

There must have been a time when that big black carriage was a fine thing, but that was before the moths had taken a liking to it. The tassels on the red curtains at the window hung in shreds and the fabric of the seat was torn, with great tufts of horsehair poking out like Sam Collins's fringe. The smell of old leather and naphtha came strong. I couldn't tell if the last was from the Beetle sitting opposite or from balls tucked around us. Nanny Peck had had a stock of them in Church Row. Much good it did. The only thing them moths didn't have a taste for was her Sunday crinoline. Joey always said it proved they had an eye for female fashion.

Joey said a lot of things I should have paid more attention to.

I flattened my cheek against the window. It was dark now, but the moon was nearly full. It made the fields and the trees outside look like they was licked over with frost, but it was hot as a tanner's pit inside that carriage, with a ripe smell to match.

As we bounced over a rut in the lane the Beetle's hands tightened over the leather bag perched on his knees. He didn't open his eyes. I knew he was awake, but it suited him not to have to talk. He'd played the same game in the train.

'Lady?' Tan Seng reached into his sleeve and took out something long and grey. For a moment I couldn't make out what it was. There was a sharp crack as he flicked his wrist and the ivory fan clattered open.

'Thank you.' I took it from him, grateful for the coolness even though the air I wafted about was stale as a spinster's trousseau.

Pardieu's note was brief and to the point. His feathery scrawl sloped downward on the page like it didn't have the vigour to keep itself straight.

There is little more I can do. The Lady knows this and understands that time is short. She asks that her grand-daughter should be brought to her immediately. I urge you to make the necessary arrangements as quickly as possible. I cannot guarantee that she will be in a state to receive. I must warn you, her behaviour is erratic.
   AP.

When I'd gone back to The Palace there'd been a long conversation – in Chinese so me and Peggy couldn't follow – about who was going to come with me to the station and then on to . . . wherever it was we was all going now.

I say conversation, but it was more in the way of an argument – the first time I'd ever seen the brothers disagree. Lok got quite animated at one point, tapping his chest and flinging his hand in my direction in a manner that indicated that he thought he should be the one to accompany me. I thought I caught my grandmother's name three times in the jumble of words. Tan Seng listened to his brother, his face completely blank, and then he bowed to me.

'The Lady will decide.'

Lok turned and I saw the appeal in his eyes. I felt Tan Seng watching me too.

I wasn't sure what to say. If it was my protection they were arguing over, it was a judgement of Solomon they were asking for, that being one of Nanny Peck's most favoured tales for a rainy Sunday afternoon.

I couldn't rightly put an age to either of them. Despite his tiny stature, I knew Lok was stronger than dock boys twice his size and likely a third of his age. And then there was Tan Seng. Tell truth, even though I was there I still couldn't make sense of that business with the cabman. It happened in the space of a blink.

Point of fact I trusted them both when it came to matters of safety, but just then I got the distinct impression they were arguing about something else.

I looked at Peggy. She was standing at the foot of the stairs. The light from the fanlight over the doors caught her hair, burnishing up the chestnut running through the brown. She looked better every day – lush like a garden in May. I'd done right bringing her to live with me; it didn't change what I'd done to Danny, mind, but it was something at least.

'Can't they both go with you, Kit?' She stepped down onto the marble tiles of the hall and I saw the tips of her bare toes under the hem of her skirt. This was her home now.

'I'm not leaving you here on your own, not overnight.' I turned to Lok. 'I'd like you to stay with her, please. If I knew you were here at The Palace with Peggy tonight I'd feel happy.'

I knew it would make Peggy happy too.

When Lok saw us off in the hall later that day he didn't look happy. Just before we left, he spoke rapidly to his brother and handed him a small black box, flat it was, like something Lucca might use for his paint. Tan Seng took the box, nodded and placed his free hand on his brother's arm. Now, that surprised me again – the pair of them never showed much in the way of affection to each other when I was around. Of a rule they bustled about at a careful distance like a couple of waiters carrying trays at a fancy hotel.

Lok looked down at Tan Seng's hand and then he spoke softly – I heard my grandmother's name again twice. He stepped away from his brother, bowed to me and went to the stairs leading down to the basement. It might have been the heat of the day, but as he disappeared I saw him swipe at a dampness on his cheeks.

⟊

The wheels caught another rut and I gripped the leather strap beneath the window to steady myself. We lurched to the left and the rusty seat springs grated and wheezed. The carriage had been waiting for us at the station, just as the Beetle had said.

As we stepped down from the train onto the platform the air came different – there was sea in the smoke now. I say the carriage was at the station, but actually it was at the end of an unlit tree-lined road two streets distant. Telferman led the way and I knew of a certainty he'd made this trip before.

There were two big greys harnessed at the front, the pair of them nodding their heads and kicking at the dust, impatient to be off. Even when we were close I couldn't make out who was up on the box, on account of the hat rammed tight on his head and the shadow.

It was late now and the road was deserted. I scanned the crescent of tall white buildings screened by neat clipped hedges. I couldn't see a light in any of the windows. Respectable Hastings folk obviously didn't keep late hours. They kept roses, though; the sweet, fat scent of them caught me immediate as we turned the corner.

Tan Seng was silent and the Beetle moved with a surprising lightness. Apart from the tapping of my heels on the cobbles, the only sound was the miserable racket made by a single gull keening overhead. It put me in mind of the last time I'd been summoned by my grandmother. When I woke in that locked room, the only sounds had been the ticking of the clock and the yowling of the birds outside.

Telferman called up to the driver and stood aside to let me go first. As he opened the carriage door I saw that the scrolling letters 'EWR' painted in gold on the lacquer were peeling away. It must have been her name, my grandmother's real name, I mean.

All those years I'd thought my mother's name was Eliza Peck. But Lady Ginger had told me the truth of it that winter day when we stood together in front of Ma's grave.

My grandmother had arrived at the cemetery on a carved wooden chair carried by four of her Chinamen – looking back, a couple of them must have been Tan Seng and Lok – and then she'd asked me to walk with her down the row of cypress trees and overgrown stones to the plot where I knew we'd left Ma.

But it was wrong that day, all wrong.

We couldn't afford a headstone when we buried her. Back then Joey and me didn't even have a Lucifer to spark a fire, but now there was a fine-carved marble memorial on her grave – a memorial we hadn't paid for with a name I didn't recognise.

ELIZABETH REDMAYNE

1836–1875

BELOVED DAUGHTER AND MOTHER

SHE TOOK LITTLE BUT WAS OWED MUCH

I was furious, thinking that some family had taken a liberty, even if it was a bleedin' expensive one, but Lady Ginger told me I was wrong. She'd paid for the stone herself, she said, because Ma was her daughter.

When she was born I gave her my own name, because, at the time, it was all I had left.

Of an instant, I was standing in the cemetery again trying to make sense of it all. The east wind snatched at the hem of my skirt and my grandmother's doll-black eyes watered at the sharpness of the air.

The carriage rocked again, jolting me back to the fusty interior. I pressed my forehead to the glass and flapped the fan. There was so much I didn't understand. Fingers from the past were still stirring the pot in the present, every so often a bit of gristle would rise to the surface and then disappear before I could fish it out and take a good look at it.

I knew one thing, though. If I wanted answers I'd have to keep sharp. My grandmother liked games; even if she was raising death's door knocker with her withered hand she'd still have the strength to play me.

There were two questions in particular – and I wasn't going to leave until I had the meat off them.

One: What had Joey done to make Lord Kite and – as far as I could make out – all the other Barons want him so badly?

And two: Who was our father?

It seemed to me that if I had them facts straight in my head, then I might have a key to everything else.

Once we'd gone through the town we were out in the country. At first I reckoned we were going east, but the narrow lanes twisted about so much that we could have been heading back to Hastings for all the sense I could make of it now. The carriage swung so violent to the left that I had to catch the strap again to stop myself from slipping from the squeaking seat. Telferman opened his eyes.

'I believe we are nearly at our destination.'

'How can you tell that?' I peered out of the window. 'It's all the same out there. Just trees and fields and then more trees.'

'It is the sound.' He raised a finger as if he was about to conduct a piece of music. 'First running water and now . . .' he nodded, 'we are crossing the bridge at the perimeter of your grandmother's estate.'

I shifted for a clear view through the grimy pane. The Beetle was right. A gleaming ribbon of water was visible beyond a low brick wall and there was a hollow drumming echo as the carriage rolled over a series of arches. Moments later wheels and hooves crunched on gravel. One of the horses whinnied, no doubt he had the tang of fresh hay and home in his nose.

'Where are we, Mr Telferman? I think you can tell me now.'

He pulled at the scraggy curtain of his own window.

Telferman bent his head to take in the view. 'We are in the wood. In a moment you will see it. Fraines Abbey has been part of her . . . *your* family's estate for many years. She always valued its privacy.'

The carriage jagged hard to the right and we came out of the trees. I saw it now.

Fraines Abbey stood on a low ridge at the end of a drive lined by vast hedges clipped into peculiar shapes. Moonlight fell across rows of balls, pyramids and hump-backed masses that cast shadows across the silvered grass. At the end of the drive that divided the hedges into two mounded armies, a long turreted building sprawled across the gently rising land. As the carriage circled the ring of gravel in front of the house I looked up at the blind windows. A wide arched door opened and a pool of light splashed down the steps.

One of my grandmother's Chinamen came out.

He watched the carriage shudder to a halt and then turned back to the doorway where a dark shape moved behind him. It was a moment before I realised it was Dr Pardieu standing there with a lantern.

Telferman patted his bag. 'It too will be yours . . . soon. I have the documents here.'

Chapter Twenty-five

'There is little point now in carrying her to the bed chamber.' Dr Pardieu shook his head. He sucked on the large front teeth jutting out over his lower lip as he considered his words. 'She will die in the room beyond that door.'

Even in the lamplight I could see the layer of white scurf scattered across his black shoulders. Like the Beetle, he smelt of old moth and old man, with an undertow of something medicinal.

We were in an echoing hallway, seated either side of a marble fireplace twice my height. Fat-bodied fruits and flowers clambered up towards a distant ceiling and on the way they draped themselves round a painting set in a panel over the hearth. It was too dim to see the painting clear – my grandmother wasn't one to spend her fortune on light – but I got the impression it was a man of wealth. All I could really make out was a hand poking out from a buttoned cuff at the bottom edge of the picture, long fingers scrabbling at some coins and papers spread across a desk. The flicker from the lantern the doctor had set down on the stones of the hearth between us gave the impression that the spidery fingers were moving.

Apart from the stiff-backed chairs by the fire and the painting, the only other thing in that dark hallway was a long wooden table with a china bowl set in the middle.

I heard something crack as Pardieu rested his forehead

in his hands. His limp grey hair fell forward to cover his face. 'She has not slept for three days now and I have not had the opportunity to seek respite either. My wife will be most anxious. I have been here a week waiting for ...' He straightened up and tried to arrange his face into an expression that conveyed sympathy and servility. Instead, he looked like he was gripping on a fart.

'I ... that is I mean to say, I do not wish your grandmother to ...'

'I understand, Dr Pardieu.' Tell truth, the most surprising thing I took in from what he'd just said was that he had a wife waiting at home. That was harder to digest than the thought that he might be watching the clock at a deathbed. He shook his head and more dry white stuff fell onto his jacket.

'I must confess it has come to the point where I cannot tell whether it is night or day.'

'It's night, Dr Pardieu – or very early morning, which is much the same thing. It will be light soon enough.' I stood and went across the hallway to the window intending to pull back the heavy curtain.

'This place needs some air.'

'No!'

He sprang up as the word sang out around us. 'You must not – it is not permitted.' He reached out towards me, his fingers waggling like he was Swami Jonah trying to charm me to the spot.

'No light is permitted here – no natural light. She is most specific on the matter. Please do not touch the curtain.'

I glanced at the tapestry covering the door to the room where my grandmother was currently holding court with

Telferman and wondered what I'd see when it was my turn in there.

The Chinaman who'd let us in had guided the Beetle to the far corner of the hallway and the pair of them had muttered together. A moment later, they came back to the doorway where they'd left me standing in a puddle of light with Pardieu and his lantern. The Chinaman bowed to me and then he sidled close to Tan Seng to rattle out something that sounded part way between an order and a question. Tan Seng nodded and then the three of them took off again, disappearing into the shadow over to the left. I heard a door creak open and then an echoing thud as it closed.

After they'd gone Dr Pardieu stood there in front of me shuffling and sucking his teeth, and then he tried a couple of remarks about 'difficult days' before scurrying across the hall. I didn't have much option but to follow seeing as how his lantern was the only light in the place. We must've been sitting there in the gloom for the best part of an hour.

Pardieu caught me looking at the tapestry covering the door. 'Since yesterday she has refused all forms of relief. In some ways that is good, her head is clearer now, but the cost . . .' He shook his head. 'She will not take her . . . medicine again until she has seen you. She made that very clear to me.'

I walked back to the hearth and tried to make out the painting. It was for the sake of something to do rather than an interest. If Lucca was here with me – and I wished he was – no doubt he'd have something of an educational nature to say about it.

As I looked up I felt a twist of hair work loose. I reached to push a pin into the plait coiled high on my head. The back of my neck crept with a dampness that made the collar of my muslin blouse stick to my skin. I fumbled to loosen it, but my fingers were sticky and clumsy with heat.

I rested my hands on the marble lip of the mantle thinking the feel of the stone might cool my skin. I stared up at the painting and of an instant the thought came to me that somewhere over the sea in another country, likely as hot as it was here, Lucca was sitting at his mother's deathbed. It was an odd sort of coincidence, wasn't it? Although, when I took it out and looked at it up close I couldn't rightly tell you how I felt about my grandmother.

I didn't feel love and I didn't feel grief neither – not like Lucca – that much I knew. I wasn't here to pat her pillows, dab at my eyes and play the dutiful. I was here for business.

I moved back from the hearth and looked up. I still couldn't see much in the picture. It was a sallow gaunt-faced gent in a long dark coat. The light from Pardieu's lantern slicked up the varnish making it difficult to make him out proper.

I turned to Pardieu. 'How long does she have?'

'She is stealing time now.' He made that wet sucking noise again. 'She is, however, remarkable. Most people whose condition is so far advanced would not be . . .'

He stared at the flagstones. His fingernails scraped at the dark material of his breeches as if he might scratch up an answer.

'She is . . . she is . . .'

There was a creaking noise. Of an instant, the air in the hall thickened. I span about to see the Beetle standing in the open doorway to my grandmother's chamber. He shifted the tapestry to the side to allow Tan Seng to shuffle past him. I'd never seen the old boy look so grim. The shadowed grooves round his mouth gave him the look of one of Signor Marcelli's dancing marionettes. He was clutching that narrow black box Lok had given him tight to his chest.

'She is ready to see you now, Lady Linnet.'

The Beetle didn't follow me back into the room. Instead he bowed his head as I passed. He closed the door behind me and I heard the tapestry slump back into place. I caught the murmur of voices and listened for a moment, thinking I might hear something useful, but nothing came clear. The muttering grew faint then it stopped altogether as the men moved away from the door. I turned to face the room. The darkness ahead was so thick I could snatch it up and wrap it around my shoulders like Nanny Peck's plaid.

At first I thought there wasn't a light in there at all, but after a moment I caught a glow that seemed to be a long way off. I waited, hoping my eyes would grow accustomed, but it didn't do much good. The candle, or whatever it was, was too feeble to show anything more than itself.

The air was stale. It was oddly sweet too, but not in a pleasant way. I stretched out my hands and went forward, conscious that the tap of my heels on the stone was the only sound in the room.

I came to what felt like the edge of a table. I guided myself along it, running the tips of my fingers against the cold surface. I could feel something like a pattern there – the top was made from little pieces of stone, not wood. When the edge ran out, I went deeper into the room, confused that the light didn't seem to be any bolder or any closer. The sweet smell came stronger now. It wasn't opium and it wasn't flowers – it was more like the medical hum of Dr Pardieu, laced with bacon on the turn.

Of an instant, I knew it. The last time I saw my grand-mother was the night when she took me in her carriage to my first meeting of the Barons. She didn't want me to unfasten the curtains so we'd sat in darkness, but I remembered that final glimpse of her face as I opened the door – the canker sores lit up by the torches outside old Bartholomew's.

The air in that carriage was much like the closeness in the room, but now the proximity of death gave it a horrible ripe-ness.

She is stealing time.

Stealing time from the grave, that was what Pardieu meant.

I peered at the light ahead. It wasn't a lamp and it wasn't a flame. It was a flicker that seemed to be suspended in mid-air in the dark. I moved forward again, my steps muffled now by a carpet or a Turkey rug underfoot. At last, as I drew closer to the light, the room, a shadow of it, began to form around me. Cabinets lined the walls and ill-assorted chairs sat at angles beside small tables cluttered with objects.

And now I realised why it came so faint. There was something like a wall ahead – the dull yellow glow from a candle or lamp beyond fluttered along the top. When I was less than ten foot away I saw it was a screen.

There was a rustle from beyond the painted panels.

'There is a chair set ready for you.'

Lady Ginger's voice was shattered. Each word came in jagged fragments like she was dredging them up from the depths of her throat and hawking them out. I was near enough now to make the screen out clear. It was painted with an Oriental design. Pretty birds and golden flowers masked the ugly business of dying.

It was as if she read my mind.

'Death I can bear, but not indignity. The chair is to your left.'

My grandmother started to cough. There was a wetness in the sound like she was drowning in her own spittle. I stared at the screen wondering if I should ignore her and . . .

And what exactly? Hold her hand? Smooth her brow? Read her a consoling passage from the Bible? The coughing became a rasp that petered into a gulping noise. I looked to the left. Just as she said, there was a single chair set well away from the light, I could just make out the curve of the polished arms in the flickering from behind the screen.

I went to it. Before I sat, I turned towards the light.

And there she was, the great Lady Ginger.

What was left of her.

Twelve foot off, my grandmother sat on an old black chair. I knew straight off it was the one carved over with dragons, the one her Chinaman had always carted her around Paradise in. It had something of a throne about it, but the wretched creature strapped into it now couldn't even rule the tremors of her body.

In the half light I saw her bird-skull head jerk from side to side. She was almost bald. Penny black patches spread like mould across her bone-white scalp. There must have been hair growing from somewhere because a grey plait, the tatty remains of one, drooped over one shoulder and fell into the folds of material in her lap. There was a wide band of black at her waist – a strip of leather or some other strong stuff to keep her in place and keep her upright.

Twig-like hands poking out from the ends of her sleeves had a horrible restless liveliness. They clenched and twitched, and occasionally – in a violent spasm – they gripped the arms of the chair so tight that the candlelight made the knuckles shine out in the gloom like a row of moony pearls. It came to me that she was holding on fast for fear of letting her soul fly away.

My grandmother was lost in a high-necked scarlet gown that spread out in a puddle around the feet of the chair. The silk was streaked with dark stains; some of them glinted in the light from the single candle burning on the low table beside her.

Them black eyes were the same, though. They caught the flame and glittered in the hollows of her shrunken face. Her head trembled as she leaned forward a little way. She opened and closed her mouth as if to speak. Instead, something dark dribbled to her gown. She stared down at the mess and her right hand knotted into a fist. Of an instant, she found her voice.

'Sit!'

It came out with a surprising force.

Lady Ginger wriggled about like the seat beneath her was hot as a griddle and then she spoke again.

'This is a draughty house. My bones ache with the chill of it. That is why I have made myself a nest. The screen shields me from the cold. I am so very cold.'

Cold? The room was like a furnace. I took a step towards her, but she bunched herself together.

'Do not approach me, Katharine. I would not wish to add to your nightmares. I imagine you have enough of them to keep you awake?' Her face twisted into something like a smile. 'Sit where I can see you and you can see . . . enough of my condition.'

She'd mastered herself enough to get her words out now. Lady Ginger had a fluting, girlish way of speaking. Don't imagine it for a weakness or a sign of feminine charm – that peculiar voice cut to the bone. There was always glass in her mouth, only now it was broken.

I stared at her and she stared at me. Her head quivered as she took me in. We was never in the way of passing family compliments or making dainty talk. Anyway, under the circumstances enquiring about her health would have made us both look foolish.

'What big teeth you have, grandma.'

God forgive me, it wasn't a decent thing to say to a dying woman. It was a line from a story Nanny Peck used to tell me and Joey when we was little. Back then, neither of us knew that our grandmother – the real one, that is – was more savage than a wolf in a fairy tale.

Lady Ginger started to cough. Her body jerked about on the chair, but the strap kept her in place. After a moment I realised the coughing was laughter. She huddled herself together and tried to sit up straight. Then, very slowly, she clapped her clawed hands together. I caught the flash of the big ruby ring on her thumb.

I had to admire the old cow – riddled with canker and

noxious with the pain of it, she could still put on a performance.

'Your impertinence is most enlivening, Katharine. I have
grown tired of the long faces about me. Now sit and listen.'

I did the first of them and craned to see her clear in that
gloomy little tomb she'd built around herself.

'Where is he? I know Joey sent a message to you. Telferman told me.'

Lady Ginger blinked. 'You will listen. I have not taken my
. . . medicine for three days now because I wanted to be certain that when we met, for this last time, my head would be
clear.'

'Like your conscience, grandmother?'

I saw another shudder go through her. That hit home, girl,
I thought. It made me bold and it made me carry on.

'Because, let me tell you, I could soak my conscience in a
tub of Reckitt's Blue, scrub it a hundred times over and hang
it out to dry in a daisy field and it would still be dirty grey.'

My grandmother wiped her lips with the edge of a sleeve
and nodded. 'The Barons' test. The man who . . . died was
someone close to you?'

'He was a bleedin' sight closer to my friend. She's carrying
his child. And it's not just Danny – it's everything. Listen,
you said? Well, you're going to listen to me for once. You
gave me a lie that day when you passed Paradise on. Build
your own empire – that was what you wrote in that letter
when you took off to lick your wounds like an old cat. Well,
I haven't exactly made a success of it, have I? It's all turning to
shit. Good people have died because of me. I see their faces
every time I close my eyes so Christ knows it's no wonder you

don't want to die, grandmother. Every time you blink you must see an army lined up in the dark.'

I thought Lady Ginger smiled at that – and it made me want to twist the knife.

'Don't! Don't for a moment think I pity you now sitting there like a sack of butcher's remnants. If you can feel anything at all – which I doubt – you deserve it. You and me, we might be flesh and blood in the regular way, but you're nothing to me. I hate you and I hate what you've made me.'

Lady Ginger closed her eyes. 'Then I have succeeded, Katharine. That is precisely why I chose you. Joseph would not do what I am about to ask of you. He would have been so easily corrupted, but you . . .' She coughed, spat something black into her hand and wiped the diseased spittle on her dress. '*You* can make it stop.'

Her head trembled as she opened up again. The diamonds glinting at her ears matched something like tears welling up in her eyes. She looked away.

'I have waited so long for the right time and the right person to avenge her. And it is you, Katharine. And you will not be alone.'

She was rambling now. I knew if I wanted answers to my questions I'd have to tip them out smart.

'I reckon I've waited a long time too. Where is he? Where's Joey?'

The question hung there for a long moment.

'He is safe, for now.'

I stood up. 'No! I want more than that. How do I know it for a certainty if I don't know where he is? Lord Kite's looking for him. He threatened me. Did you hear that? I imagine you did seeing as how everyone who works for me seems to work for you.'

I didn't let her come back, but clipped straight on.

'That stone-eyed bastard hates Joey, that's one thing I'm sure of, but he wants him too.' I had a clarity. 'It's more than that, isn't it? He *needs* him. Why?'

Lady Ginger closed her eyes again. Her shrivelled body tightened into a knot of pain as a great spasm shot through her. After a moment she sighed. It came out as a long rattling wheeze.

'Because of what he can do, what he knows and what he can do with that knowledge.'

Those black eyes flicked open. The terrible life I saw burning there was unnatural given the state of the rest of her. She raised a hand. The rings on her fingers hung loose as bracelets on a wrist. They clattered together as she moved.

'On the floor just behind you there is a sheet of paper. Take it up and look at it.'

I turned. Something pale and square lay there on the stones, just like she said. I darted over, snatched it up and shook it open. The cracked voice came again as I peered at the page. 'You will need a light to read it by. There is a lantern and a strike box on the table to your left.'

I fiddled with the Lucifers. As I reached inside the lantern to light the dusty stub of candle my fingers broke the strands of a spider web strung across the metal. It stuck to my damp skin. When the waxy knub had taken the flame I wiped my hand on the cotton of my dress, but I could still feel the web caught around my fingers.

My grandmother coughed. 'You will oblige me by keeping

your distance with the light. Read it.'

I looked at the page and frowned. If I'd thought I was about to receive an answer I was disappointed. The sheet was covered in numbers and symbols, a dozen lines in all. No sense, no order and no point.

'Read it to the end, Katharine – to the very last line. Read it in silence.'

'Why? It's nonsense. Another one of your games, is it?'

'In a way. Read it again – every single line.'

'You can't bleedin' resist it, can you?' I scrunched the paper into a ball and threw it down in disgust. 'I reckon you'd climb out of your grave if there was a chance to play me. Well, it might amuse you to see me puzzling over scraps, but I'm not going to give you the pleasure. You've wasted your time – what little of it you've got left – and mine.'

I started off up the room again, blundering towards the place where I thought I'd come in. Tears burned in my eyes, but I fought them back. I didn't want to give her the glory of besting me again. I was a stupid little fool to think she might actually offer me something I needed. I thought I remembered where the little tables and cabinets were, but the darkness ahead was a wall.

Lady Ginger called out.

'If you want to save your brother . . . and Paradise, Katharine, you will read that paper.'

I stopped and her voice came again. 'Pick it up and read it again, every line.'

I turned. All I could see was the screen.

I heard her try to smother a cough. 'Would you deny the request of a dying woman?'

Tell truth, I didn't much care about her, but she'd hooked me. I walked slowly back to the chair, bent down and reached underneath for the ball of paper. I pulled it open. Just as she asked I read it again, every line and every symbol, much good it did. It was a meaningless jumble. I looked up.

The clot of my grandmother stirred on that carved black throne.

'Now burn it!'

'I've only just read the bleedin' thing.'

Lady Ginger hunched forward. There was an eagerness in her eyes now, and something else she snatched away with a blink. Fear.

'Trust me, child.'

The fringe of red sparks caught along the edge of the paper. As I watched them eat into the page, Netta Swift came to mind. I turned to Lady Ginger. Her head was slumped forward, but her right hand was twitching at the arm of her chair. I could hear the rattle of her nails on the wood. Her left hand was curled in her lap.

I looked at the brass dish. The paper was curling now, in a moment it would be a smoking heap of cinders. The top half of the sheet rolled back upon itself, green-tinged flames licking the edge. I saw the first two lines of letters and numbers again before the page blackened and collapsed on itself.

'I've done what you asked.'

Lady Ginger opened her eyes and shifted herself in the chair. 'Is it gone?'

I nodded.

She looked down into her lap. 'You will oblige me by taking your seat again.'

I did as she said. Tell truth, for all that her theatricals made me want to wring my grandmother's stringy neck until she choked out what I wanted to hear, a part of me was curious. I waited, only she didn't say nothing.

'Well?'

She didn't look up. 'A moment more, Katharine.'

I'm not sure how long we sat there. It seemed like an hour, but I reckon it was only a couple of minutes. Lady Ginger's head trembled as she stared down at the hand curled in the stained red folds of her lap. The room was silent apart from the sound of her breathing. It sounded like there was a pouch of marbles in her throat.

There was a metallic click, a whirring noise and a jingle of musical notes. It was a tune I recognised – an old song about nymphs and shepherds. The jaunty tone of it struck me as ridiculous. It belonged to another place and another time.

My grandmother looked up. I saw a flash of gold as she pushed a small fob watch into the scarlet folds of her sleeve.

'Repeat it to me, Katharine.'

I thought I knew what she wanted, but two of us could play at parlour games.

'That song? You want me to sing it, grandmother?' I made sure the words came out sweet as a violet pastille, the sort a child might choke on. 'I only know the chorus.'

Her black eyes burned. 'You have a pretty voice. Remember, I heard you sing when you went up in the cage.' She gasped as she folded her hands around the band at her waist.

'That was also a trial. Repeat what you saw on the note before you burned it, every line. I will know if you make a mistake.'

There! It was another bleedin' mind game after all – nothing more. I slammed my fist on the arm of my chair. 'I'm not Swami Jonah, in case you hadn't noticed. Why don't you just tell me where Joey is and we can finish this? You can get on with dying and I can . . .'

Lady Ginger blinked. 'You can do what, Katharine?'

I glanced at the tray of ash. It was just numbers, letters and symbols – much like Sam's coded scribble. What did she mean? I bit my lip as an uncomfortable thought wormed its way into my head. What if my grandmother's mind was as sick as her body? What if she was already rambling too far in the valley of the shadow to show me the way out?

Her voice came again. 'Are you saying you cannot repeat the sequence, Katharine?'

'I can repeat it all right.' I shook my head. 'What I can't understand is why you want me to perform for you like I was a turn at The Gaudy, when there's so much more I need to know.'

'You talk of need, child. I *need* to know if you can remember the sequence. If you can, I will tell you where your brother is. If you cannot, it is better that you never know. This is not a game – it is a promise.'

I rattled off the sequence until I reached the final row in my mind's eye.

'F E Q 56 23 then an arrow pointing left.' I counted the

letters and numbers out on my fingers, tapped the ball of my thumb on that last symbol and folded my arms. 'And that's the end.'

It was easy enough, although when I came to a couple of the symbols I had to describe them because I didn't have a proper word or a name. For an instance, there was something that looked like an 'h' with a hooked tail hanging off the end; I had to have a couple of goes at that before she tipped me the nod and flicked a hand for me to continue.

I'd always been able to remember things. As soon as my grandmother asked me to read that paper twice I had an idea what she wanted. I knew she'd already heard from Telferman that I had what you might call an affinity for bookwork. Of a rule I only had to run an eye down a ledger page once to lock all the facts into place in my head. It unsettled the Beetle, who clearly thought it unnatural rather than something to admire.

I waited for her to speak. I wasn't expecting a compliment or a round of applause, but I knew I'd done what she wanted.

Beyond the shiver of her head, Lady Ginger didn't stir. She was slumped to the side in the chair now, the fabric of her gown bunched around the strap keeping her straight. She was watching me, though. Her black eyes never once left my face as I worked through the rows in my head, counting down on my fingers as I went, and they didn't blink now.

'Well?' I reached up as a sudden and familiar pain bloomed above my right eye. My forehead was sticky with sweat.

She cleared her throat and tried to wipe her mouth with her sleeve. The movement defeated her. Her arm fell limp into her lap, the hand twisting oddly back on itself, jerking uncontrollably into a knot of gristle and bone. She struggled to tame it and then she squirmed in the chair to place her other hand over it.

'You will have to try harder next time, Katharine. There was an error.'

She must have dialled the look on my face. 'The last arrow points to the right. You must be careful that your confidence does not lead you to make mistakes.' She took a deep breath and nodded. 'Otherwise I am satisfied. You are truly a Redmayne, however you might feel about the name.'

I stood up abrupt and the chair fell to the floor. 'You needed to test me with a page of numbers just for that! That was all it was for – a bleedin' memory trick to prove we was related?'

I took a step towards her. I wanted to see her face clear, but she shrank into the shadow.

'You will stay where you are, Katharine. The ability you have demonstrated is uncommon, but seems to be a feature of our . . . heritage. Our . . . blood.'

'You mean Joey?' It was coming clear now. 'He can do it too, I know he can. We used to test each other when we was small – word games and that.'

Lady Ginger nodded. 'And *that*, precisely as you say, has signed his death warrant. Your brother is the only person alive who can complete the sequence to open the Vinculum – the vault where the Barons of London have stored their wealth and, more pertinently, their secrets for centuries. Joseph stole it.'

Chapter Twenty-six

My grandmother stopped wriggling and jerking. There wasn't even a twitch in her fingers curled over the carved black arms of the chair.

'Retrieve it from him, Katharine.' Her voice snapped like a whip. Of an instant she didn't look like a dying woman. It wouldn't have surprised me if she'd stood up and caught me across the face with one of them sharp-stoned rings of hers to make sure I was paying proper attention.

I was doing that, all right, only nothing was making sense.

'Where ... where is he, then? And where's the sequence?'

Lady Ginger stared at me. 'That is a dullard's question. Think, child – it is what I have trained you to do.' Even now, she was enjoying the game. I knew it as she watched me. 'Surely it is obvious?'

'It's ... it's here.' I tapped my head. 'Joey's got it all locked away in here – and Lord Kite wants it?'

'Bravo! Not so difficult, was it?' She huddled forward. 'The trick will be taking it from him. Truly, I do not know what you will find.'

I raised my hands. 'Stop. No more riddles. Where is—' I broke off as that jangling tune went off again – muffled this time by the folds of her sleeves.

Lady Ginger scrabbled into the red gown and took out the

golden fob again. She flicked open the case and held it away to make out the dial.

'Already?' The word came as a whisper, but I caught it. Her bony fist tightened over the watch and the jingling stopped. She nodded and her blackened lips curved into a sort of smile.

'I have chosen my hour and it approaches. Even now, Dr Pardieu will be preparing my . . . medicine. We will not meet again, not in this life. An old friend of mine believes that we are born again and again. An endless cycle of death and life. I wonder if he is right?'

'You mean Ramesh Das. I know him – he works for you.'

Lady Ginger shook her head. 'He works for *you*, Katharine. After today, they *all* work for you. And you will need them.' She started to cough, but struggled to swallow it.

'Telferman has something of importance – I gave it to him today. When the time is right he will pass it to you. Read it, child, and understand what I have done. You will leave me now.'

'That's it, is it? You're sending me off like a package. I want more.' I moved closer. 'My mother – your daughter. There's so much I need to know before you . . .' I paused. 'Before I leave. Joey and me, our father, who is . . .'

She raised a hand to ward me away. 'Stop . . . please.'

I halted, more in surprise than obedience. It was the first time she'd ever used a politeness to me. Now I was just a couple of yards from my grandmother I could see her plain. The wet canker sores on her head were dark and puckered at the edges like a fat-fingered seamstress had stitched them to her skull.

Someone had tried to disguise the wreckage, it was almost pitiful to see that. Fine black lines were painted around her eyes and there was a thick layer of chalky powder on her head and on her cheeks. I thought I knew who that someone was. The black lacquer box Lok had given to Tan Seng had been full of paint, of sorts, after all.

As Lady Ginger quivered in the chair like a half-formed nestling, the powder rose around her in the candlelight as a fine cloud. Of an instant, the words read out by the clergy at Ma's burial came into my head.

Earth to earth, ashes to ashes, dust to dust.

I was standing at a graveside now. The smell of death scraped into my nose and clawed the back of my throat. I don't know how long she'd been sitting in that chair waiting for me, but the stench in the room wasn't just disease. It was piss and shit.

My grandmother's eggshell head trembled like an autumn leaf in a gust of wind as she stared at me. 'I know what you want, child. But you won't hear it from these lips. I could not bear to see the look in your eyes. Ask your brother – ask Joseph. He despises me – and rightly so. If he can remember the sequence, he will remember so very much more. Family, Katharine, it is always a simple matter of family. Remember that.'

She closed her eyes and arched her back as pain knifed through her. She knotted herself into a ball until it had passed and then she stared up at me. It was unnatural the way her black eyes burned in a face creased up by proximity of death.

'Do you hate them?'

'The Barons?'

'Who else?'

'They disgust me – the whole bleedin' lot of them. Just thinking about them now makes me feel dirty – and yet you made me one of them, grandmother.'

She began to laugh, but the sound drowned in another choking fit. She struggled to take in a lungful of air and it bubbled in her throat. Her hands clawed at the arms of the chair and she twisted from side to side as she tried to force it down. Once she mastered herself again she sat there watching me, still as a dog waiting for table scraps. I noted that the trembling had stopped.

'The contents of the Vinculum can destroy them, Katharine. You can end centuries of injustice if you can take the key from your brother.'

'Then where is he?'

She closed her eyes. 'You will find him in Bethlem.'

'Christ!'

'Not exactly, but I believe we both know that. Your brother is in Bedlam.'

I waited for more, but it didn't come. I thought for a moment she might have died right there in front of me. It was only when I saw a shudder ripple through the spoiled silk of her gown that I knew she was still there and still listening.

'Is that it, then? Is that all you've got for me? Joey's in Bedlam – now off you go and have a little chat with him? That's not what I came here for. It's not enough!'

'It is all I am prepared to offer.' She turned her face to the blank wall of the screen. 'You will go now.'

I thought about dashing over and tipping her out of that chair onto the floor, but what good would it do? I knew her too well to imagine she might give a direct answer to a question. Even now, with the last grains of sand running to the bottom of the glass, she was still shuffling her chess pieces around the board.

There was a long silence.

'I'm still here, you know.' It sounded pathetic, but I called out anyway. She raised a fluttering hand as if to stop me and her eyes snapped open.

'Ah, Dr Pardieu – you are welcome.'

It was like she'd conjured him up. Right on cue he stepped from the darkness and into the puddle of light. He went about quiet as a woodlouse. I hadn't heard a step of his approach. Lady Ginger's eyes flicked to the small black leather bag in his hands. I saw something like hunger there, or maybe it was greed.

She nodded at him. 'You have my medicine?'

He glanced warily at me and his hands tightened on the bag handle. 'Everything you need is prepared, Lady.'

She smiled. 'Good. I am so very tired.'

My grandmother tried to pull herself upright in the chair, but the effort brought on another bout of choking, heaving coughs. More black stuff spattered onto the front of her gown.

When the fit passed she spoke again.

'Leave us, Katharine.'

I tried to get closer but Pardieu came between. He shook his head and the light shone up his buck teeth. 'The Lady needs to rest now.'

'But there's something *I* need ...' I tried to dodge round him. It was too late to think about minding her dignity. Old rabbit face gripped my arm and forced me back. Tell truth, I was surprised by the strength in him. He pushed me gently but firmly away from my grandmother and the stink of disease was muffled for a moment by the naphtha in his cloth. I was almost grateful for it.

'She wishes for peace.'

'And she always gets what she wants, don't she?' I tried to throw him off but he held tight. I thought about biting his hand, but I didn't want to taste his medicinals. I glared at him.

'What about me – what about what I want?'

'Release her.' My grandmother's voice was steady.

Pardieu turned and nodded once. He stepped aside so I could see her clear. Now, she was sitting up straight as Britannia on a penny. Tan Seng was at her side.

'You will leave me now, Katharine, and you will take your destiny into your own hands. Tan Seng will escort you from the room. I have nothing more for you today except this . . .' Her black eyes moved to Pardieu as she weighed her final words to me.

'Joseph is 214. Deal with it, Lady Linnet.'

Chapter Twenty-seven

Pardieu didn't give me a choice. At a single nod from her, he sloped across with his little black bag, closed the screens around my grandmother and folded the sight of her away. The room was completely silent, but the shadows fluttering on the ceiling above the gilded box showed there was movement.

Whatever was going on behind them painted birds and flowers, it was clearly no business of mine. Tan Seng bowed and shuffled past. He picked up the candle lantern and started off up the room. After a moment I went after him, following the light. As we made our way to the door I saw that we were in something like a long, wide corridor with a jumble of paintings and furniture stacked at the sides. On the right, tall windows were shrouded by curtains.

Just before we reached the door there was a sharp clicking sound. A clock somewhere in the clutter drew breath and started to strike the hour, and then another joined in and a third took up the chimes. In a moment it was like a hundred clocks were jangling away in there. Some of them played a tune, some of them merely rang out a single note. The performance went on for a minute. When the last one faded, Tan Seng went to the window. He set the lantern down and hauled a curtain aside. I had to shield my eyes against the rush of light. The candle in the lantern giddied about and then it snuffed out. I reckoned it must have been the movement of the curtain.

He turned to me and bowed. 'She is gone, Lady.'

My grandmother's shrivelled heart stopped at five in the morning – or thereabouts.

The journey back to London was a dismal wake on a train. Telferman clutched his bag of papers and pretended to sleep, and Tan Seng stared at the box in his hands. I didn't grieve her passing. *Cold and hard as diamond* – that's what she said I should be, and I was when it came to her. No, as that first train of the day grumbled back to London I thought about Joey.

When the station hack delivered Tan Seng and me back to The Palace I didn't go to my bed. Instead I went to my office and sat at the desk staring at the knots in the wood and the dents and nicks in the leather top. If Joey was in Bedlam, like she said, I had to go to him, but I couldn't just clip up the steps and ask for him by name, could I?

Something Lord Kite said in the Temple Church came back to me most forceful.

We are watching. If your brother contacts you, we will know. If you do not offer Joseph to us, others close to you will suffer.

If they really were watching me, like he said, then I'd lead them straight to him.

I went to the window and pushed it open to let some air into the room. I leaned out and stared down into the yard below. Lady Ginger hadn't been much of a gardener. The square patches behind all my houses in the passage off Salmon Lane were rambling with summer greenery. A thicket of ivy clambered along the walls and over to the left it was choking the life out of something that might have been an apple tree.

After the country, the air was clogged. It was why my grandmother had gone there in the end. When her tarry lungs, what was left of them, couldn't suck any more life out of London, she'd taken them to Fraines Abbey and worked them like a pair of knackered bellows until Pardieu made them stop.

According to the Beetle, Fraines Abbey was mine now.

There was a fluttering and a scratching sound to the right of the window. I looked over and saw the head of that bold little sparrow poking out from the edge of a broken gutter. That must have been where its nest was. It wouldn't have been troubled by rain, that was certain. The bird winked its bright black eyes at me and then it took off across the yards, fading to a brown speck of nothing. Considering that most of the birds in London were dull as a curate's cassock it was a wonder the girls at The Carnival could lay their hands on enough feathers to make parrots of themselves.

Of an instant, I realised how I could get myself out of Limehouse and into Bedlam without anyone knowing where I'd gone.

⚓

As I stepped off the omnibus I heard two men sitting in the slat seat inside pass a comment – not one I'd repeat. I didn't blame them, I looked like a dollop putting out for a penny. I could see the bright green feather on my hat bobbing about through the veil, and the hem of my violet skirt didn't quite cover enough of my ankles to make a lady of me.

If Nanny Peck could see me now she would have had plenty to say – and none of it complimentary. Lucca too – he would have rolled his eyes, pursed his lips and trotted out something in his lingo. I would have understood him, mind.

Tell truth, it took a deal of effort on my part to look this cheap. There was a time, not so long ago, when the girl I was would have given her eye teeth to go about dressed as a carnival, but she was as dead as Lady Ginger.

The conductor twanged the wire and the omnibus juddered before the horses dragged it away up Garden Row. Now it was moving again, one of the men who'd remarked on my gear felt bold enough to stand up and poke his head round the stair pole. He called after me.

'I'd tumble you, girl. Even if you sembled old Gladstone himself under that bloomin' veil you could keep your hat on and I'd be happy to pay.'

The feather on my hat quivered between my eyes. The man was leaning out of the bus now and making a gesture with his hands. His mate was pressed up against the window, a sly smile plastered across his greasy chops.

'Not more than thruppence, mind, on account of the stink.'

I folded my arms and yelled after them. 'Why don't you shove your coins where Queen Victoria won't see sunshine!'

The moment it came out, I regretted it. What if someone had followed me from The Carnival, someone who recognised my voice?

I'd taken trouble with my gear. Well, Peggy had. She'd chosen a low-cut dress in an unnaturally lively shade, added a flounce of yellow petticoats and topped it off with more feathers than you could pluck from a peacock's arse – big ferny ones. The costume, because that's what it was, came from the tiring room above the stage at The Carnival.

I'd decked myself out as a chorus girl.

If I was in a mood to take a pleasure from it, I might have said there was a richness to the fact that in order to go about unremarked, I'd dressed in a manner designed to make a show of myself.

I'd arrived at The Carnival's main door with Peggy and Lok. It was early afternoon and the hall was quiet except for Professor Ruben sitting at the piano. I watched him dab a cloth along the keys, fussing like a housemaid. He was very particular about his instrument. Despite the heat he had a long dark coat on. The tail flapped over the stool. I was surprised to see him, but I knew he was working out a new arrangement for one of the chorus songs. Most likely the girls would be here within the hour to run it through with him.

If he thought it unusual to see the three of us go up to the tiring room, he didn't show it. I was grateful when he called out my name and flapped a sheet of music at me, in the way of a greeting I thought. I waved back.

It was hot as a kipper house up there. Mingled with the general frowse there was a strong smell of paint that minded me of Lucca's old workshop at The Gaudy. Peggy had to open the window because it made her feel noxious. As she worked the catch she remarked that standards had slipped since we was in charge of the rails. She was right. I reckon if I'd stood there long enough, one of them sweat-stained dresses would have walked over of its own accord and tried me on for size.

As it was Peggy picked out a regular eye-poker. Tight and bright, and different as possible to the neat grey cotton I'd worn on the way over.

Lok turned away as she laced me into the violet bodice and adjusted the sleeves.

'You're sure you'll be safe in this rig, Kit?'

I planted my hands on my hips and sucked in my waist to let her pull the strings. 'The rest of them go about like it and they don't seem to come to no harm.'

'It comes natural to that lot. The girls in the chorus like to make a show of themselves.' She wrinkled her nose at the smell rising off the fabric. 'There's some rose water on the trunk by the window. You'll need more than a dab of that. There – you're done.' She span me round. Her eyes filled with concern as she took me in.

'I'll ask one more time, where are you going?'

I shook my head. 'I can't tell you, Peg. It's better that way, believe me.'

Lok made a clucking sound. His face was crumpled with disapproval.

'Not good, Lady. It is not good.'

I looked down at the purple billowing around me. 'Not good to go out like this?'

He clicked his tongue again and glanced at Peggy who had gone to fetch the cologne. 'Not good to go out alone, Lady.'

'Kit, have a look at this.' Peggy was staring down at a long black case lying open at her feet. From the looks of it, and on account of the cage and the gilded table propped up against the wall nearby, it was one of Swami Jonah's stage properties.

'There's one missing. You can see where it fits in the silk.'

She bent forward, but I swung round at the sound of voices from the hall below. Someone cackled and there was a clatter on the stairs.

I snatched up the feathered hat Peggy had chosen for me, forced it on my head and pulled down the veil.

'Will I do?'

Peggy straightened up and nodded. 'They won't recognise you. No one would, not even Lucca.' She frowned. 'Especially not Lucca.'

Three of The Carnival's dancers joined us in the room. I noted that for once they were dressed in what you might call sober gear. I pushed past them to the stairs, uncomfortably aware that I stood out like a canary in a flock of sparrows. One of them tutted, which was rich, considering.

Peggy was right about Lucca, he wouldn't recognise me.

Now, as I stood there in the Row watching the omnibus move off I wished he was with me. I folded my fingers tight around the handle of my bag. Lucca wasn't with me, but his little pistol was. Before I left for The Carnival I'd rolled it out from the red silk 'kerchief he'd wrapped it in and stared at it. It was a delicate thing with a pattern traced into the ivory of the handle. Tell truth, I wondered why a person might take the trouble to make a beauty of such an ugly intention.

I brushed my skirts, noting that the fingertips of my white mesh gloves were already black. The wheels and the horses had thrown up a cloud of dust. Somehow it had come through the veil and was in my mouth and in my eyes. That man had been right about one thing: in this rig I was rank as the floor of Jacobin's cage.

I stared at the end of the street and then checked the way

behind. Bedlam was hidden behind a wall topped with iron railings off Lambeth Road. I'd deliberately got off the bus two streets distant to make sure no one had followed. There was a number of people scurrying about, but no one who struck me as trouble.

The big black gates to the Bethlem Hospital were closed. I tried to pull them open, but they was locked. I stared across the clipped lawn at the massive, red brick, three-storey building spread out beyond the rails. In the centre a row of pillars covered what I took for the entrance. Sitting above there was a great dome like the one on top of St Paul's. Tell truth, it didn't look fearsome, it looked bland. I don't know what I was expecting – not having been here before – but it wasn't this.

I scanned the windows – there were scores of them – and wondered if somewhere up there Joey was looking out.

There was a noise over to the left and a man in blue work gear and a cap came out from behind a row of shrubs. He was pushing a wooden barrow stacked with grass and weeds. The wheels squeaked as he turned to shunt it along a gravel path leading towards the pillars.

'Excuse me.' I gripped a gate rail and called through to him. He didn't stop.

'Wait, please!' I tried again. 'I want to see someone. How do I get in?'

He paused now, turned and shook his head. 'Not the day.'

The man stared at me. Of an instant, on account of a

certain blankness in his expression, I knew he wasn't a regular paid gardener. I couldn't tell you his age, it was as if his face had never been troubled by a thought that left a crease. His wide blue eyes moved to my hat and he grinned. 'Pretty.'

I nodded and the tip of one of them green feathers dandled in front of me. The man started forward – one hand outstretched as if to catch hold. He moved like a small child who hadn't quite got the measure of his limbs.

'Feather.' He grinned wider. 'They're pretty, like flowers.'

'Can I come in? Is there a way through?' I repeated the question, although, tell truth, I wasn't sure he'd understand. He glanced at the feather again and then his eyes slid off to the right. He moved his hand to point in the same direction, but then he balled it to a fist and shook his head with a violence that made his cap go askew.

'No way in, not today.' He chewed his lips. I noted the way he looked over to the right again.

'Listen.' I hooked my bag over my arm and reached up to my hat to snap off one of the bobbing peacock feathers. I pushed my hand through the rails and held it out to him. 'If you tell me how to get in, I'll let you have this.' I waggled the feather about. The green and blue eye winked in the sunlight.

The gardener reached out, but I pulled back sharp.

'Only if you tell me.'

'Not allowed.' His eyes never left the feather in my hand. He wiped his nose. 'Not today.'

'But I can only come here today. If I go now you'll never have this pretty feather. In fact you'll never see it again.' It was like teasing a kitten with a string end. I didn't feel decent about it, but it was a chance and I had to take it.

The man turned to look back at the pillars. I knew he was checking to see if we was being watched. After a moment he shuffled round on the gravel. 'Delivery gate – you might come in through there, if Mr Marstin's willing.'

'Where's that then, the delivery gate?'

He took off his hat. 'I'm trusted.'

'Please.' I wiggled the feather.

As it shimmered in the light, one of Nanny Peck's tales came back. She used to make fishing hooks for her brothers. She tied bright feathers to the hook to semble dragonflies and such like, so the fish would think it was getting a meal instead of becoming one. Her brothers always said she made the best flies in County Wicklow. But it was dangerous too. If they'd been caught, them boys would have ended up in front of a justice quicker than you could swallow a sprat.

As I stood there, the feather dancing about in my gloved fingers, it came to me that I was fishing for Joey – and it was dangerous.

The man stopped fiddling with the little cap and stepped closer. 'You have to follow the wall. All the way.' He nodded to the right. 'Then there's a green door.'

'And that's where I'll find this Mr Marstin, is it?'

He nodded. 'But don't ... don't ... d ... d ...'

His eyes grew round with fear and his words collapsed on themselves, but I understood what he was trying to say.

'I won't tell him I spoke to you. I promise. Here.'

I thrust the feather through the bars and the man caught hold. He smiled and held it close to his chest like it was the most precious thing in the world. Then he turned around in a circle on the spot in the gravel, all the while swaying gently.

'Enter.'

I pushed the door open and the smell of cigarette smoke came wafting out.

Mr Marstin – if that's who it was sitting there – didn't bother to look up from the newspaper spread out in front of him on the desk top.

'Laundry to the left, vittals to the right.' He nodded at another door opposite the one where I came in and flicked the page. A blow fly bumped up against the grimy arched window behind him and buzzed in fury. The window was barred.

'I'm neither. I've . . . I've come here to see someone.'

He looked up now. A grin squirmed around beneath his whiskers as he took me in.

He leaned back and took a pull on his scrawny smoke. 'Well, well, what have we here?'

I stepped forward. 'Like I said. I've come to see someone.'

'Not today you ain't. It's not a visiting day. Can't you read?' He jerked his shiny balding head at a tin sign nailed to the grey-painted brick wall.

I ignored him. 'I've come a fair way to see my . . . friend.'

Marstin stubbed out his smoke. 'Then you'll have to go a fair way back again, won't you?'

The air in the room was rank. If Marstin's armpits were on nodding terms with a soap bar they was standing on opposite sides of the street. The cheap tobacco didn't help matters, neither. Whatever he had rolled up in that skinny Rizla, he must have scraped it up from the floorboards.

Then again, standing there in that narrow brick-lined

room, I was painfully aware that I wasn't exactly a bunch of Jersey roses myself. The cologne Peggy had splashed over the bodice had faded to a musty tang and now when I moved someone else's body sweated for me. Like Marstin, that someone was a stranger to a washstand, but they clearly had a liking for cheap scent – of a sort that turns to vinegar.

I held the handle of the bag so tight my knuckles cracked. 'Please let me in, just for an hour. That's all I need.'

Marstin shook his head. 'If you was to ask me to let you in for a single minute my answer would still be the same, and that answer would be "no". You'll have to come back on the proper day.' He eyed my rig. 'And even then, I can't say as you'd be acceptable. I know your sort.'

Given I was tricked out like a tuppenny bangtail, it was almost a fair comment but, I wasn't going to take it – not from a man like him. I knew what he was soon as I clapped eyes on him, and I was pleased.

I went closer. 'And what "sort" is that exactly?'

He closed the newspaper. 'I think you know what I mean, Miss Pert. Our regular visiting ladies are most particular who they mix with. We get quite the high type coming here doing good works and handing out their broidery squares. Let's just say you don't strike me as a person they'd want to take tea and a slice of caraway cake with.'

He drummed his fingers on the table top. There was enough dirt caught under his nails to sow a row of carrots. 'Oh yes – we get them in here now. Simpering ninnies, the lot of them. I blame old Hood and his new regime, that's who.' He stared out of the barred window as if he was seeing someone through the glass. 'Course, he's been gone for years now, but some of his lily ways have lingered. We still got the chair in the basement, though. And some of us old-timers know how to use it.'

I didn't have a clue what he was on about. All I knew was that somewhere beyond this stinking office, I might find Joey.

I folded back my veil so he could see my face. 'Please let me see him. I'd count it a favour.'

Marstin stared at me and snorted. 'A *him*, is it? So, you got a fancy fella in here? Turned his head soft, did you?' His eyes left from my face and crawled down my body. He moistened his lips. I heard the wet smack of them beneath the whiskers. 'Just out of interest – what sort of favour are we talking about?'

'This sort.' I snapped open my bag, took out a pouch and tossed it onto the desk in front of him. There was a heavy clanking sound as it fell open spewing out a stream of coins.

Marstin looked at it for a long moment. Then he stood, went to the door leading out to the yard, opened up and called a name. He turned to me.

'An hour – no more. Jeffries will take you up. Who is it?'

'I . . . I . . .' Tell truth, I wasn't sure. I thought about Lady Ginger's last words to me. '214.'

Marstin started to laugh. He moved back to the table and swiped up the coins and the pouch in one swift lunge.

'I reckon you've just wasted your money and your time, missy. If you can get anything out of that Mary Ann, then I'm the Prince of bleedin' Wales.'

334

Jeffries' moustache reared up like a bristle-coated caterpillar as I stepped out from Marstin's office, but he didn't pass a comment as he led me across a closed-in yard surrounded by high windowless walls. He took out a ring of keys and fiddled through until he found the one he needed to open the battered black door at the top of a flight of steps in front of us.

Once we was inside he led the way in silence through a warren of dismal grey-painted corridors that smelt of bleach and piss. We was evidently somewhere deep in the Bethlem – somewhere we'd be unlikely to be noted. Every so often Jefferies paused to listen. When he was satisfied there was no one about, he carried on. He didn't turn to see if I was following. Fact is he never looked at me at all.

So this was new Bedlam? It was a word we used often enough to describe a person who'd lost his way, but I'd never given a thought to what it might mean. The place had a grim reputation in Limehouse, that much I could tell you, but now I was here it didn't seem cruel so much as sad. As we hurried down another bare corridor, I caught the occasional sound behind the rows of closed doors. Sometimes it was laughter, occasionally the mutter of conversation – although it seemed only one person was speaking to herself – but most often I heard sobbing.

There were slats in all the doors where I supposed a person could look through, but even if I'd had the chance I wouldn't have wanted to. The thought of spying on another's misery struck me as a low thing to do.

Jeffries stopped by a wide metal door at the end of the corridor. He reached into his pocket again and took out the keys.

335

'This leads through to the men's side.' He still didn't look at me as he knelt to fit a key in a lock at the bottom of the door. '214, is it?'

'Yes – that's right.' I hoped so anyway.

Jeffries stood again and reached to a lock at the top of the door. 'Not said a word since he came in, he hasn't. The only reason he's still here is that recently someone paid the balance on his keep.'

He turned to me now. He had a face on him like he'd swallowed a bluebottle. His upper lip curled again. 'Would that be you?'

I shook my head. I had an idea who it *had* been, though. She was dead.

He twisted the key in the lock. 'We're keeping them all tight at the moment. The heat makes them lively. What makes you think you might know him, then?'

'I ... I had a message, from a mutual acquaintance. She thought ... that's to say she knew he was here. She gave me a number, nothing more.'

'That's all he is to us, a number. What's his name?'

When I didn't answer straight off Jeffries jangled the keys.

'Come on now. You must know his name if you've come all this way to see him.'

'J ... Jimmy. His name is Jimmy Riley.'

'And what's Jimmy Riley to you?'

'He ...' I tightened my fingers round the bag handle. It was a fine question, wasn't it? What was Joey to me?

'He's someone I've known a long while. I promised his ... his old mother I'd see him.'

Jeffries snorted. Talk his language, girl, I thought.

336

'Besides, he owes me.'

Now he grinned. 'You won't get any sense from him and you won't get anything else. He's lost up here.' He tapped the side of his head. 'They all are – don't you know what this place is?'

'Course I do. I just need to make sure J . . . Jimmy's here. It's what you might call a business matter.'

'I can believe that.' Jeffries sniffed. 'Worked as a team, did you? It's bad enough for a woman to sell herself, but a man. I read my Bible every Sunday. It's all there in Genesis Chapter Nineteen. The Lord punishes his kind.'

I knew straight off what he was talking about. Nanny Peck had a particular liking for the story that came next about Lot and his wife. Tell truth, I can't be sure I wouldn't have turned round out of curiosity myself. I stared up at him. 'And there came two angels to Sodom at even?' Jeffries blinked in surprise. 'I know my Bible, thank you. I don't need a lecture. I just need to see him.'

There was a grating whine as Jeffries swung the door open. Ahead of us there was another long grey corridor, much like the one we'd just come along. He locked up behind once we were through and started off again without a word. His polished boots echoed off the walls.

Halfway down he stopped in front of a door. He flicked the slat open and peered inside. He nodded to himself and turned to me.

'When he came in the dress was stuck to his body.' He smiled. 'It was the blood.'

Sweat slithered down my back. 'What do you mean, "blood"?'

Jeffries' moustache wriggled. He was enjoying himself now. 'From the wound on his head. They thought he was a woman when they found him on the street, see, but then the doctor examined him and found ... found out what he was, so they sent him here. It was a kindness, seeing as how his wits was gone. He could have gone to Newgate. To my mind that's where he deserves to be. Now, before I let you in to see him...'

He held out his hand.

I snapped open the clasp of my bag and fished inside. I'd come prepared – Joey always cost me dear.

Chapter Twenty-eight

The door closed behind me and a key twisted in the lock.

'One hour. No more.' The slat fell back into place and I heard the echo of boots as Jeffries walked away.

It was hot as a glassblower's arse in there. A blind was pulled down over the window, but sunlight came strong through the dull material so I could see the striped shadow of the bars. The narrow room was sparsely furnished. All I could see was a low rumpled bed over to the left and a table beneath the window. A wooden chair lay on its side across the bare tiled floor. There was a jerry under the table.

'Joey?' I whispered his name. There was a rustle from the bed. What I took for a mound of grey blankets moved. I went closer. Someone was curled into a ball under there.

'Joey? Is that you? It's me, Kitty.' I reached down to pull the sheets aside.

A hand shot out and caught my wrist. The colourless bundle gathered itself together and the person holding fast to my arm shifted to pull themselves upright. I winced as the grip tightened.

'I'm alone – it's just me.'

The bundle unravelled itself. An angular, close-cropped head appeared. My brother blinked, released my wrist and leaned back against the wall.

'Who else would she trust?' He stared at me, but didn't

move. The sheets were still wrapped around his scrawny frame like a bandage. Of an instant, a painting in one of Lucca's books came to me, Lazarus rising from the dead – the tomb windings knotted round his shoulders.

'You took your time, little sister.'

The words came out like he was chewing on a mouthful of autumn leaves. Joey's eyes moved slowly from my forehead to my chin.

'Tell me, am I still a beauty?'

I didn't know how to answer that. Even though the blind was pulled I could see the scar running up his forehead and into his stubbly fair hair. It cut into his right eyebrow pulling it upward into an exaggerated arch that gave his lean face a quizzical expression. And that wasn't all.

The left side of his mouth was torn. A wound slashed up across his face. The flesh of his cheek had been ripped apart almost to the level of his ear. It had healed over, but it would never go unnoticed on account of the matchstick marks left behind after someone had tried to sew him together again. But I'll say this, there was still something about him – Joey still had the look of an angel, even if it was frayed at the edges. Despite the patching, he was still a looker.

'They won't let us have mirrors.' He freed a hand from the sheets and ran the fingers over the scar on his brow. 'Is it bad?'

'You'll pass.' I dropped my bag, sat down on the bed and reached for his hand. I curled my fingers round his. 'Joey, I . . .'

Of an instant, he pulled me down, folding me tight in his arms. His skin smelt of carbolic, but under that there was something else. I huddled close and took in the comfort of family. After a minute or so he let me go. He bent his head to whisper in my ear.

'You stink of the whorehouse, little sister – and your clothes are a disgrace.'

Christ! After everything, that was all he could find to say. I shook him off.

'Don't you dare—'

'Shhh.' He placed the tips of his fingers over my lips and whispered again. 'Not too loud. They mustn't even know I recognise you.' He glanced at the slat in the door. 'They watch.'

I turned. The slat was closed. The sheets fell as Joey twisted about and stared over my shoulder at the door. He was wearing a loose grey shirt and faded breeches. It was as if all the colour had been scrubbed from the room. I felt his eyes rake over my dress.

'You look like an explosion in a paint factory. Do you know, you're the only person I've spoken to in nearly three months? I thought I was beginning to lose the knack.' He touched his lips again and his fingers fluttered along to the scar on his cheek. He frowned and moved them away.

'We'll make a good pair now, Lucca and I. Where is he? I imagine he's mooning about nearby. He usually is.'

I shook my head. 'He's not here. He's been gone a while. A last visit back to his home. His mother's at death's door – she might even be through it by now.'

Joey ran a thumbnail over his lip and a warmth shot through me. I knew that gesture of old. My brother always did that when he was thinking.

'Which one brought you, Kitty?'

'I told you, I came alone.'

'I mean the orderlies. Which one brought you to me?'

'Jeffries. Someone called Marstin let me in at the delivery gate. I paid them both.'

'That's useful to know.' He nodded, more to himself than to me. 'You're here to get me out?'

I shook my head. 'Not today. I didn't even know for a certainty it was you here until a minute ago. I've only got an hour.' I scrambled onto the bed and tucked my feet beneath the violet skirts. My brother stared dubiously at my hat. I ripped the bleedin' thing off and shook my hair free. He reached forward and brushed a strand of it away from my face.

'Where did you get that hat?' Half his face grinned. 'From a coster's drab?'

Steps echoed from the corridor outside. We both froze, but whoever it was moved on past.

Joey nodded at the upturned chair. 'It would be better if you took that. If they look in and see you sitting like that . . .'

I slipped off the bed, righted the chair and pulled it close. Joey shuffled across the mattress and rested the torn side of his face against the brick wall so we were less than a head apart.

'I don't want them to know I can speak or think. It's safer that way.' He spoke clear now, but low.

'At first I couldn't do either – it was a blow to the head. But after a week or so I came back to myself.'

'What happened, Joey?'

'I can't recall it clearly. I'd arranged to meet—' He broke off sudden so I carried on for him.

'Della. I know all about that. You arranged to meet Della

Lennox and her kid at The Gaudy, but you never came. If you're interested, which I doubt, they're safe and far away now. Where were you that night?'

He avoided my eyes. 'I went to a . . . an establishment in one of the lanes off Broad Street. I'd been there before and it was as good a place as any to lie low. Nancy has always been good to me, but I was a fool and I was scared. Once I started, the relief of it . . .' He twisted the sheet. 'I took too much. It was a mistake. I lost track of everything. By the time I left I'd been there for a day, maybe even two. It was night again when I went back up to the street and I knew it was too late to help them. I was . . . ashamed, but more than that, I was thirsty. Opium does that. I went to a gin shop on Cock Hill and I . . .'

He shook his head. 'It all gets muddled. I think I spoke to someone there. When I left I was followed.' He touched the gash in his cheek. 'There was a knife – I know that much. I saw it fall in the gutter. A silver knife with a bone handle. But that's all. The next thing I recall is waking up here. When they found me lying in the street I had nothing – no money and nothing that could identify me. They thought I was a wo—'

He paused. 'You know this, Kitty, I was dressed as a woman, but then when I was examined . . . It's why they sent me here. It was the best thing that could happen. When I realised where I was, I knew I was safe as long as I was lost. This is as good a place as any to hide – better than most.' He stared at me. 'But now here you are. Telferman passed on my message.'

'You sent word to Lady Ginger, not to me.'

Joey glanced at the slat again. 'It was too obvious. I

343

thought our grandmother might deal with it. She always does.'

'She's dead, Joey.'

He opened his mouth to say something but nothing came out. Something like disbelief crossed his face.

'It's just me and you now . . . and Bartholomew's pit.'

Of an instant, his blue eyes darkened, the pupils spreading like ink through paper.

'I don't know what you mean.'

'Yes you do. Don't try to lead me up a path. Why did you come back knowing what they . . . what the Barons might do to you?'

He stared up at the ceiling where another of them lazy, summer flies had started to buzz and bump against the plaster.

I caught his hand. 'Why, Joey? I don't understand.'

'I don't expect you to, Kitty. As a matter of fact, I'm not sure I do myself.'

He tilted his head and stripes of sunlight coming through the barred and blinded window fell across his face.

'In Paris life was good, wonderful even, sometimes, but I missed London. I missed the thrill of it, the game of it. It made me feel so very . . . *alive*. Even when . . .' He paused and sorted his thoughts. 'Even during the most difficult times it was exhilarating. When I felt my heart beat so wildly in my chest that it might burst through my ribs I was glad of the pain. If you want the truth, such as it is, I was bored. In Paris I felt like a bird in a pretty cage. When I saw you again and saw how alike we could be I thought I might be mistaken for you. There was a safety in that in Limehouse and beyond, I thought . . .'

I threw his hand down. 'That's just it, Joey Peck, you never think, do you? Not about others, that's for sure. It's not a bleedin' dress-up box we're playing with now, it's people's lives. I don't have time to feel bored, but I tell you what, I'm scared. Remember Danny Tewson, Peggy's boy?'

He shrugged and closed his eyes.

'He's under the church stones in Bartholomew's pit now and I can't get him out of my mind – the sound of him. They used him to threaten me on the night I took our grandmother's place.'

Those dark blue eyes snapped open. 'So, you've become one of them, little sister? You really are a Baron.'

I nodded. 'And I wish to God I wasn't.'

Joey was silent for a moment. Then he slipped off the bed, pushed past me to the table and pulled the jerry out from beneath. He turned his back to me and pulled at his breeches. I heard the stream of his piss spatter into the tin. I looked away, embarrassed. It was like he wanted to humiliate me. As the metallic rattle of his flow came to an end he spoke again.

'It was meant to be me. All along she told me it was me.' I felt my brother's hand tighten on my shoulder as he scrambled past me and back onto the bed again. He folded his arms. 'And I believed her. It was my birthright, Kitty, not yours.'

I balled my hands into fists so tight I could feel the nails digging though the soiled lace into my palms. I wanted to lash out and knock that sulky pout from his lips. Even now, there was a fullness to them that told a tale. I saw then that Lady Ginger had been right. If she'd left Paradise in his hands, my golden brother would have tarnished up quicker than a

345

candlestick left in a cupboard. I felt a wetness on my cheeks and tried to brush away the beads of sweat with the tips of those cheap mesh gloves.

'No need for tears. You've made it worse. Here ...' Joey reached forward and ran his long fingers over my face. 'Tell me, how did she die? I hope the bitch suffered.'

'She'd been ill for a long time. You knew that?'

He nodded.

'She held on longer than was natural. In the end Pardieu fixed it for her to go when she chose.'

Joey snorted. 'Is that old crow still picking over her carcass?'

'He was, until five o'clock yesterday morning. Telferman took me to Fraines Abbey. It's mine too now.' I couldn't resist that. I paused to satisfy myself that he'd taken it in. Joey held my eyes and plucked at a stray thread on his sleeve. He gave it a vicious tug and ripped it free. He rolled it between his fingers as I went on.

'There were papers to sign – at least that's what Telferman said. Tell truth, I think she wanted to see me for a last time. No, that's not right. It was like she *needed* to see me. Even at the end she was still setting bait for her traps, but she told me where to find you, in a manner of speaking.'

A thought came to me. 'How did you get that message out, Joey?'

He balled the scrap of thread between the pads of his thumb and first finger and flicked it at me. 'Elsa, one of the women. She's a deaf mute. I ... persuaded her.'

I quizzed at him.

'Oh, I was quite charming.' He smiled and ran his thumb

across his lower lip again. I got an inkling of the sort of charm he meant.

'It wasn't so difficult. Poor Elsa, she's a large odd-looking creature, but pliant. On Sundays, after the dreary business of chapel, they let us out into the grounds – men and women together. The air is supposed to be beneficial. They keep watch, but there are places where, for a short time, a couple can be private. Elsa was very enthusiastic. We came to an arrangement. I have discovered that I possess a talent for mime.'

My brother adjusted the gaping neck of his shirt and sat straight on the bed. He was warming up now and his voice was finding its rhythm. I noted that his injury had done nothing to interfere with his fancy accent. As he went on, I knew he was enjoying telling me about his clever scheme. Joey Peck loved an audience almost as much as he loved himself.

'I have made a study of this place, Kitty, it leaks like a sieve. We are not always confined – the Bethlem is not a prison, exactly. It was easy to take a sheet of paper and a pencil without anyone noticing. And, of course, they don't expect us to think, which gives an advantage.'

'But if she – this Elsa – is in here with you then how did you send word?'

'It was simple. Her twin sister smuggled it out. The packet was marked for Telferman's attention, but there was another message within for our grandmother. The sister is a deaf mute also, but unlike poor Elsa her mind is intact.'

I saw it now. 'She's a redhead, this Elsa? Tall?'

Joey nodded. 'And her sister is her double. She works in Lambeth in a laundry, I believe.'

'She's dead too, Joey – you good as killed her.'

He shook his head. 'She's still here. I had to avoid her in the grounds last week.'

'Not Elsa – her sister! She was fished out of the Thames after delivering that letter to Telferman's door. She was ... tortured before she died.'

His eyes widened. 'Thank Christ she was a mute. Do you think she gave—'

I cut him off. 'Think of your own skin first, Joey, that's always your way, isn't it? That poor cow died because of what you asked her to do.'

I was gratified to see his eyes sidle off. 'And no, I don't think she gave you away. You'd be lying on that bed turned inside out if Matthias Schalk knew where to find you.'

A muscle twitched his jaw. I carried on.

'Yes – I know him now, and I know Lord Kite as well. I know the whole bleedin' tribe of them. I'm a Baron, remember. I'm what our grandmother made me.'

I stopped at the scuffle of footsteps directly outside. Joey lay back and pulled the sheet up over his head. I snatched up the hat, plonked it down in my lap, scraped back the chair and sat up straight. The slat in the door clattered open.

'So, is he who you thought – this Jimmy Riley you mentioned on the way up?' It was Jeffries again. I held my head to one side in a fectation of sorrow and sighed.

'It's Jimmy all right, but he don't know me.'

Jeffries laughed. 'I told you that. You should have saved yourself the trouble and the coin – not that you're getting anything back, mind. You coming out, then? No point in staying. Like I said, his mind's far gone.'

I turned to the slat and shook my head. 'You said an hour.

It's been nowhere near yet. It's his poor old mother I feel for. I couldn't face her if I didn't spend a decent hour with him, even if he don't know me from Adam.'

'His poor old mother should be ashamed of herself for bringing an abomination into the world.' I heard the sound of rattling keys. 'Half an hour.'

The slat fell back into place and we sat quiet until Jeffries' steps faded along the corridor.

Joey sat up again and I moved back closer to the bed. He stared at the door.

'There's talk about him and Marstin – the pair of them have worked here for years. Most of the orderlies are fair enough, but those two . . . They say there's a spinning chair in the cellars left over from the old days. The pair of them use it, late at night when the fancy takes them.'

Of an instant he gripped my wrist again.

'I have to get out, Kitty. I've had enough of safety. This place will *make* a madman of me.'

I stared at his hand.

'I need something from you too, Joey.' I moved his hand and looked him in the eye. 'More than just one thing; the Vinculum, the sequence key, Kite, our mother and our father. Lady Ginger said that if your mind was still in place you'd re-member it all. And there was another thing – she said you despised her for it.'

Joey's blue eyes burned cold. 'Get me out of here and I'll tell you everything, little sister.'

'No. That's not how it works this time.' I shook my head. 'We're not sitting in the parlour at Church Row playing at forfeits. I want it now, before I leave. I promise I *will* find a way to get you out, but before that I need answers.'

He pouted and turned to the wall. Of an instant, I was minded that my beautiful brother's power to charm whatever he wanted had never truly been tested. Joseph Peck was spoiled as a saucer of milk left out overnight in a blowsy summer.

'What if I'm not prepared to tell you, Kitty?'

I reached for his pointed chin and turned his face to me.

'Then you won't get out. It's simple as that.'

Chapter Twenty-nine

There were beads of sweat in the stubble of Joey's hairline. He glanced at the window. 'You can't open them. I've thought about breaking the glass to let in some air, but it's thick as a plank. Bethlem's not a prison, as such, but for me it might as well be.'

'I made a promise to you, Joey. I won't let you down. We're running out of time.'

'I don't know where to start.' He ran his fingertips over the scar on his cheek, lingering over the two crude marks left by the stitches.

'The beginning is as good as anywhere.' I pushed a hand through my hair. My scalp was sticky with grease from that bleedin' hat.

'You don't understand, Kitty, there are so many beginnings. It's . . . it's complicated.' He brought his thumb to his lip.

'What about Ma?'

'No!' The word came too loud and he clapped his hand over his mouth.

'Why?'

'Because . . .' He swiped the back of his hand over his eyes and shook his head. 'Not there.'

I took a breath. 'All right, start with the sequence and the Vinculum.'

'How do you know about it?' Joey stared at me.

'Because she told me. Our grandmother tested me. The last time I saw her she was more interested in finding out if I had a mind like yours than saying a fond farewell. It wasn't what you'd call a sentimental parting of the ways. Do you remember those games we used to play when we was kids – memorising things, making up codes, playing with letters and that?'

He nodded.

'Well, it turns out we had something of a rare talent – both of us.'

Joey's Adam's apple rose in his throat. 'I have a rare talent for trouble, little sister, that's true.' He leaned back against the wall and closed his eyes. The only sound in the room was the buzz of that fly.

'She used me, Kitty, I know that now. Lady Ginger played me – she used me as a messenger when she wished to communicate with the Barons. I was a . . . person Lord Wren would find amenable and that was useful to her. It was also a sort of game. You know what she was like? By the time I met her, Kitty, I believe she may have been partly mad.'

Wren? The name wasn't familiar. I went through the men I'd seen that night and the names I'd heard: Mitre, Oak, Fetch, Janus, Iron . . .Vellum. 'Wren' wasn't among them. But I didn't question it – Joey had started and I didn't want him to stop. As he spoke the light through the blind caught the fine golden bristles on his cheeks and upper lip.

'She sent me to meet him with documents, bills and papers, but all along I was the package. She knew that. Wren and I recognised that we . . . shared an interest. We could . . .

deal with each other. I knew he was a Baron. It was . . . intoxicating to be near such power. The rich lead such charming lives. It was all so very different to our narrow little world in Church Row. I was already developing a taste for something finer . . .' He opened his eyes. 'You already know all this, don't you?'

I nodded. Joey picked at a nail. 'Lucca Fratelli gossips like an old woman. Really, he is quite a bore. I wonder you keep him so close.' He pulled his legs up against his chest and looped his arms around them as he continued.

'This went beyond anything I'd known. Wren was the greatest of the Barons and beyond their company he moved in the highest circles. He was at court, Kitty – close to the Queen herself, but I never quite understood what he did. I suppose the name was a clue. Their names always are.' He paused and stared at me, expectantly.

'Wren? But it's nothing – the smallest of birds.'

'And you said you passed her memory test. I'm disappointed. Think again, little sister.'

I frowned. He was right, there was something – one of Nanny Peck's old stories. All the birds gathered to choose a king, but they couldn't find a way to settle the matter. Then, the tiny wren suggested that the crown should go to the one among them who could fly highest and they all agreed that it was a fair test. It was the eagle that went highest of all, soaring into the sky above a mountain top. Then, just as his great wide wings grew heavy, the wren, who had been hiding in the feathers of his back, took off and went higher still. After all that effort, the eagle was too weary to match him. And so the wren was crowned king of the birds.

Nanny Peck said that back home, wrens were regarded as an ill omen. They were wise, but they were cunning with it. They'd won their title and their rank through trickery and they wasn't to be trusted. It was why, at Christmas, rowdy gangs of 'wren boys' went out hunting in the fields and lanes, determined to beat that clever little bird back into its place.

I never much liked that story. It always struck me as cruel.

'The king of the birds, Joey. Is that it?'

He nodded. 'Lord Wren rode on the Queen's back. He hid himself in the black of her mourning. There was nothing he didn't know – nothing he didn't influence.'

'You said "was". I don't know a Lord Wren. He wasn't there at Great Bartholomew's. What happened?'

'I killed him.'

Joey locked his eyes on mine. 'I didn't mean to, it was a sort of accident. It was our grandmother who told me about the Vinculum and its key. She wanted it for herself. She told me about it and she told me where I might find it. Looking back, it's so easy to see how she used me, tempted me, but I'll give her this, she was right. For all that Wren was a brilliant man, he was a fool when it came to . . .'

Joey shrugged. 'He didn't understand that a pretty young man from Limehouse could aspire to be his equal. When I knew what the Vinculum contained, I knew I could use it too. Why be a rich man's thing when I could be so much more? I went often to his house in Lowndes Square. His servants knew what we were at – they knew me.' Joey smiled, but it was a sour look. 'Some of them feared me, for what I knew of them. Knowledge is power, Kitty.

'I arrived early that last evening. Wren wasn't due until the

early hours – some business at Windsor. As usual I was allowed to wait in his rooms where I knew there was a hidden
safe. It was easy to find and the code was almost too easy to
guess. Wren was a cold man, but as a child he idolised his
older brother who went to serve in India and died there –
fever. There was a painting of him in full military uniform
in Wren's room. It was something like a shrine. I think that
brother, Rufus, was the only person Wren ever truly loved.
The code for the safe was 93631. It was too easy.'

'He used the alphabet and gave a number to each letter?'

Joey nodded. 'Very good, little sister. Just like the games we
used to play at Church Row. I opened the safe and I found the
key to the Vinculum. Two pages of it in code. It's still here.'
He tapped his head. 'I was going to bide my time and use it.
If everything had gone as I planned Wren would never have
known.'

He stared at the window. 'Unfortunately, things didn't go
to plan. Wren came home early and found me. The last thing
he expected when he opened the door to his room was to find
the portrait of his dearly departed brother swinging from the
wall, the door of the safe gaping open and his catamite sitting
by the fire with a glass of whisky and a sheaf of old papers on
his lap.'

Of an instant, I saw the scene clear as a picture in one of
Lucca's books. The glow of the fire, Joey settled back in a big
leather chair, the amber of the liquor in the glass and the glint
of gold buttons on the swaying painting.

Joey shifted on the mattress. 'There was a struggle. I tried
to leave the room, but he caught me round the neck and
forced me against the wall next to the fire. I still had the glass

in my hand and I smashed it against the mantle. I cut him with it, but he was too strong. He twisted it from my hand. He wasn't delicate, Kitty, for all that he went under the name of Wren. I thought I was going to die as his hands tightened round my throat. As I scratched against the wall my fingers brushed the tip of an iron resting against the fireguard.'

Joey paused. 'You cannot imagine how much blood and meat a man's skull contains. I beat him with that iron until his wet grey brains were smeared on my face, on my hands and on the sleeves of my shirt.'

More footsteps sounded from the corridor outside, but they carried on past. Joey waited until they were gone before he continued.

'You must see I didn't mean to kill him. It was a mistake, a terrible mistake. I knew the Barons would hunt me to the gates of hell and beyond for what I'd done. But I also knew I had a valuable weapon.'

'You mean the sequence?'

Joey nodded. 'I burned those precious papers. I made sure they were a heap of ash before I climbed out of his window and fled to our grandmother. She made me disappear and I took the sequence with me.'

I twisted my hands together in my lap.

Joey was a murderer.

All along Lady Ginger had told me the truth. Right from that first meeting in her room at The Palace with the parrot calling out from its cage in the corner. Her clipped little voice went off in my head.

Miss a murderer? What a loyal little sister you are, Kitty Peck.

'Kitty?'

His voice brought me back. I pulled the sticky, pointless gloves from my fingers, careful not to look my brother in the face. 'Surely there were other copies of the sequence? Something as vital as that can't have been left with one man?'

'There is always one keeper, Kitty, for the sake of security. One keeps the sequence and one guards the location. For hundreds of years the greatest secret of the Barons of London has been entrusted to just two among their number. And I killed one of them.'

'And that's why Kite wants you so bad?'

Joey nodded again. 'Kite is the guardian of the Vinculum, but he cannot open it without the sequence. Wren was his brother.'

That made a horrible sense of everything. No wonder Kite needed Joey and no wonder that need was spiteful as vinegar dashed on an open wound.

A thought struck me. 'Did you know who Wren was – who he really was, I mean?'

Joey nodded. 'Carstone. That's the family name and it made them untouchable. The late Edmund Carstone was the state and his brother Anthony still is the law. Kite is a judge – a very highly placed judge.'

Of course! It's why he called me to meet him at that church in the heart of the legals' nest.

A picture was coming together, but pieces of the puzzle were still bumping around in the box without a place to fit.

'But that's not all, is it, Joey? If you took off like that with him, Wren, lying there, how did Kite know what you'd done?'

Joey lunged forward and clapped his hands together. He

moved so quick and the sound came so loud I flinched. The bluebottle lay on the floor beside my chair now, wings crushed, legs twitching. I watched it struggle to right itself.

'She told them, Kitty. Our grandmother told Kite she had . . . *obtained* the sequence and he knew, immediately, how she came by it. She was playing him.'

I looked up. 'You gave it to her, then?'

Joey wiped his hands on the sheet. 'Of course I didn't. Not after what she . . .' He faltered.

'Go on. Not after what?'

He scanned my face. Now his blue eyes didn't look sharp or hard.

'You asked me to start at the beginning, little sister.' He swallowed. 'It all begins with a brother and sister and from there it tangles upon itself until it's almost impossible to unravel.'

I twisted up my hair tighter and higher to feel the air on my skin. 'Don't give me riddles. You're as bad as her. Just tell me straight, Joey. We don't have much longer. Tell me what I need to know.'

'Need or want?'

'Both.'

He ran his thumbnail over his lip. 'I'll give you the barest of facts. Trust me, it's for the best. I won't start at the very beginning. I'll leave that for someone else, Marcus Telferman perhaps. Christ knows, his long nose was always so far up our grandmother's skirts it's a wonder it didn't get wedged between the cheeks of her arse.' Joey laughed. In other circumstances I would have joined in with him, but just then nothing seemed amusing.

'When she came to London she gave her child away, Lady Ginger, I mean. She gave our mother away. Not *away* exactly, but into the care of a woman who had come with her from Ireland.'

'You mean Nanny Peck?'

Joey nodded. 'Nanny Peck was her own servant – a maid of the house. They were of an age.'

'Why did she come to London?'

'She was unwed and with child. That's all you need to know. She was clever and hard. She made her fortune in Limehouse and as her wealth grew so did her power. But Lady Ginger kept watch on her daughter and as she prospered she made sure that child was cared for. Our mother grew to be a beauty, Kitty – you know that?'

I nodded, but didn't interrupt him.

'Lady Ginger was proud of her. Our mother was her weakness. Just before she became a Baron she took up with her only child again. She couldn't resist showing her off. She treated her like a pet, like a silky lap dog, taking her round Paradise in that old black carriage of hers and flaunting her like a pretty trinket. Nanny Peck was a rare old bird, but she hadn't shown our mother the life that Lady Ginger laid out. It was a temptation. But it was also a mistake. All along, Lady Ginger didn't realise that our mother might have a mind of her own. Secrets she might be keeping.'

I cut in now. I couldn't hold myself. 'Did Ma know ... I mean, how ...?'

Joey held up his hands. 'This is the short version. It's what you need to take out of here today. That was how Lord Kite first saw her, our mother, I mean. She was in Lady Ginger's box. The one at The Gaudy, I think it was.'

'But he's blind!'

'Not back then he wasn't, this is years back, before you were born, Kitty. And he wasn't a Baron then either, although his older brother was.'

'Wren?'

Joey nodded. 'Kite developed a passion for our mother. He followed her everywhere, he bombarded her with flowers and gifts. Mostly she returned them, but some she kept. Jacobin was one of his more imaginative offerings.'

'That mangy old bird? I wouldn't call him a gift, more like a curse.'

Joey shrugged. 'She was young – I think she enjoyed the attention, all of it. She encouraged Kite, but she didn't love him. She led him on a dance and it went on too long. When he found out the truth he was humiliated. And that was one of the beginnings. Kite and his brother were cruel, Kitty. What they did next is . . .' He faltered and stared at the door. There was a scraping noise. I was so lost in the story that I didn't hear the steps outside. I sprang up and darted over as the slat moved.

'It can't be time yet. It's not been an hour.' I leaned close and blocked any possible view of the room. I heard a metallic rattle as Jeffries went through the keys.

'It's been an hour dead. Collect your gear together. We don't encourage visitors to leave anything behind.'

'Please, I haven't . . . it's not . . .' I peered through the slat. 'Give me a little time more with him, please.'

'Out.'

I turned to see Joey smothered beneath the sheet again.

My bag was on the boards next to the bed. I stepped back as the door opened and Jeffries loomed in the arch.

'Two guineas for ten minutes, please.' I bit down on my lip so hard I could taste blood.

That moustache under Jefferies' nose curled. 'And where would you get that kind of money – someone like you?'

I snatched up my bag, took out my purse and fished out two shiny coins. I held them out in the palm of my hand. Jefferies stared at them for a moment and then he glanced at the mound on the bed. He nodded and took the guineas off me.

'Ten minutes – that's all. I won't take more so don't try it again. A man's got to have principles.'

When I couldn't hear his tread any more I whipped around. Joey was sitting upright again. He reached into the bed sheets.

'You can make it stop, Kitty. God knows it's time.' He drew out a small dark book. 'Every room has a Bible. Methodists are very persistent. I've hidden the sequence in here. When I first came to my mind again I wasn't sure if I could remember it, so I tested myself. Look through the pages and you'll see. You must take it when you leave today. Learn it and then destroy it. I've told you what you need. Now you must get me out of here.'

I wasn't interested in the bleedin' sequence now. It was Ma I wanted to hear about.

'Never mind that. Kite and his brother, what did they do? Get it out quick.'

My brother stared at me. 'When you became a Baron did they test you?'

I nodded. 'It was Danny Tewson, I told you. They watched me seal him into that black pit. Why do you ask that?'

Joey swallowed so hard I heard it.

'When ... when they tested our grandmother, they took her daughter. They ... *had* our mother – in front of her. It was a punishment for both of them. Wren and Kite watched as every one of them took his turn. She was so heavily drugged that afterwards Pardieu thought she might never come back to herself. And in a way, she never did. I think we both know that, Kitty.'

Of an instant, the floor rolled beneath me. I thought of them, the Barons of London – all the grey-faced men I'd met that long night in Great Bartholomew's.

'No.' The word caught in the back of my throat. Bile came flooding into my mouth and I couldn't swallow it back. My stomach kicked and I bent forward to let a rush of sour liquid splatter to the boards. My legs gave way and I sank into a heap of gaudy, stinking fabric.

'It's not true.' I could hardly get the words out.

Joey slipped off the bed and crouched in front of me. He reached out to stroke my hair.

'I heard it from our own grandmother's lips, Kitty.' He laughed bitterly. 'I think she thought it would bind us together. But from that day on I hated her. She wanted the sequence key to the Vinculum so that she could work some revenge on them all. She saw it as a way of putting things right again. But I wouldn't give it to her. And that was my revenge for what she did to our mother, for what she allowed to happen.'

I gripped his hand. 'But why her, Ma, I mean? What had she done to them?'

'It wasn't what she'd done to *them*, it was what she'd done to Kite. He couldn't have her because she was already married. When he found out he said she had made a fool of him. The worst of it was that the gown she wore to the ceremony was one he had given her.'

I saw it clear. Joey was talking about the beaded blue dress hidden away in the cupboard at Church Row. The one he'd taken and spoiled. Netta had been wearing a perfect copy of that dress the night she died on stage at The Carnival. It was Ma's wedding gown.

Kite's hatred of us both went deep as a stinking well.

'I don't understand. Who did she marry? Who is our father?'

Joey slumped down beside me. He circled an arm round my shoulders and I rested my head against him. Broad stripes of light fell direct through the blinded window now, almost, but not quite reaching us where we huddled together.

'It didn't end there, Kitty.' He whispered into my hair and stroked my cheek. 'A few weeks later pictures started to appear on the walls of Paradise in places where they couldn't be missed. Vile pictures, obscene – the work of a madman.'

'Pictures of Lady Ginger?' I turned to look at him.

He shook his head. 'They were pictures of Ma. In every one of them she was naked and ... And she was swollen here.' He placed his hand gently on my belly. 'Lady Ginger sent her away, into the country with Nanny Peck. But ... the pictures were right about one thing. There was a child growing inside her.'

'Oh Joey.' I kissed his hand. 'That was you?'

When he didn't answer, I turned to look at him. There were tears streaming down his face. His arm tightened round my shoulders.

'I was fortunate, Kitty. I always am.'

I couldn't bear to think of it. The Barons had taken Ma when she was with child. My brother was lucky to be alive. Outside there were heavy footsteps and the jangling of keys. Joey didn't say another word. He sprang up from the floor and dived to the bed, pulling the sheet up over himself again. I wasn't far behind. There was just time to snatch up the Bible and push it into my bag before the key sounded in the lock.

'I'll get you out,' I whispered, as loud as I dared, and hoped he heard me.

Jeffries took me back through the Bethlem the same way we came in. He never said a word, he just fiddled with his bleedin' keys. After a while I realised he was doing it deliberately. Of occasion, when we passed a door, the poor soul locked inside would start beating and calling out. It made him rattle them keys even louder. I'd pulled the veil of my hat down to hide the tears that didn't stop coming. Through the lace I could see that from the look on his face he was enjoying the power of it.

When we got to Marstin's office he knocked once and turned back the way we'd come. Marstin opened up and thrust his hand out.

'I said an hour. You've had extra and that costs.' I didn't

have the fight in me to argue back.

After he let me out I headed back to The Carnival. It was the last place I wanted to go, but in this gear I was too notable. If anyone was watching Salmon Lane, it wouldn't be too hard for them to trace where a girl done out like a parrot had been. Better to change back into my own plain gear and send word to Tan Seng to send someone to walk with me.

I took a couple of street buses part of the way, but the jerking of the carriage and the jolting of the horses made the pain shooting through my temples dig so deep I almost fainted. On the second bus I sat up top on one of the garden seats thinking the air might help. It didn't – that stinking hat trapped the rising heat so it was like breathing down soup on the turn.

My head was so full of questions they were smothering each other. Every time I tried to work something through it was jostled out of place. My scalp crawled under the lemon straw crown, but it wasn't the heat.

I kept seeing Ma. No matter what I did, that scene ran through my mind again and again. I tried to concentrate on her face or the sound of her singing or telling us a story, anything to block the thought of her with the Barons, only nothing worked. Every time I tried to unravel what Joey had told me it came slithering back to her with them – and Lady Ginger, her own mother, looking on.

No wonder she left it to Joey to tell me. If I'd been in his shoes I wouldn't have given her what she wanted, neither. The old cow's words rustled in my head like dry leaves.

He despises me – and rightly so. If he can remember the sequence, he will remember so very much more.

He remembered all right. And now I knew it was something I'd never forget.

Or forgive.

I'd make those grey men remember what they'd done to Ma, and then I'd make them pay.

I stared down at the people pressing about on the streets, all of them puffing and sweating about their daily business. There wasn't one among them I wouldn't swap places with. Christ knows, even poor Dora creeping along that alleyway with a corpse pressed to her breast knew what she was about.

'It can't last. It has to break soon.' An old woman's voice came from behind. 'We've not seen the like since 'fifty-eight.'

'I well remember it,' her friend, from the sound of her voice a woman of a similar vintage, agreed. 'The stink! And nothing would shift it. If you opened the windows it was bad enough, but if you shut 'em up it stewed itself strong in the house like tea left too long in the pot. It was in the cupboards, in the linens, in the larder even. You could taste it in your bacon of a morning.'

The first woman spoke again. 'The storms at the end! Most powerful they were. I thought Coady Street was likely to be washed down into the river. My George reckons we're due for a deluge any day now. "Better build ourselves an Ark, Sarah" – that's what he says.'

I opened my bag and took out Joey's Bible. I started to flick through the pages, looking for the sequence. Tell truth, I wasn't entirely sure what he meant when he gave it to me, but at least it was something real and in my hands. It was something I could do.

The papers were thin as Rizlas. The cramped black print

was packed so tight I had to bend close to see it through the veil. As I flicked through, scanning each page, the chatter of the women behind moved on. Apparently George was impressed by a new daily publication although he felt it was a 'trifle too lively' for his wife. He'd taken to reading it alone in the parlour after she'd served up their evening chops.

I stopped skimming the pages when Sarah said, 'And it's blue, *The London Evening News* is printed on blue paper, every page, like a soap wrapper.' It was the newspaper Sam had told me about. The rival to the one I owned. I wondered if Sam had found out any more about Lord Vellum and his cronies. That was another bit of puzzle without a home to go to.

The Bible pages rustled as I carried on searching. I stopped and peered at the page open in my lap. The clear space at the top, at the bottom and running up the margin was covered in pencil marks – tiny letters, symbols. In all there were four pages like it.

It was the sequence to open the Vinculum.

Learn it and then destroy it.

I scanned the marks. I could remember it easy enough. It was shorter than Lady Ginger's test. I ran a finger across the top of the page. The sequence was hidden in the Book of Daniel, around the text of Chapter Five.

3 Then they brought the golden vessels that were taken out of the temple of the house of God which *was* at Jerusalem; and the king, and his princes, his wives, and his concubines, drank in them.

4 They drank wine, and praised the gods of gold, and

of silver, of brass, of iron, of wood, and of stone.

5 In the same hour came forth fingers of a man's hand, and wrote over against the candlestick upon the plaister of the wall of the king's palace: and the king saw the part of the hand that wrote.

I knew the story. Point of fact, it was one of Nanny Peck's favoured Sunday readings. It was a lesson on pride, she said. King Belshazzar gathered all his great lords together intending to impress them with his riches and then, just when they were all about to get started on the feasting, writing appeared from nowhere on the wall, only no one could read it. Belshazzar ordered that Daniel, who was reckoned to be a mind, should be brought to the room and he told them all what it meant. Not that it did Belshazzar a favour.

I turned the page and read to the end.

25 And this *is* the writing that was written, MENE, MENE, TEKEL, UPHARSIN.

26 This *is* the interpretation of the thing: MENE; God hath numbered thy kingdom, and finished it.

27 TEKEL; Thou art weighed in the balances, and art found wanting.

28 PERES; Thy kingdom is divided. . .

I knew it was deliberate. Joey had made a most careful choice when he hid the sequence from the Barons.

Chapter Thirty

The omnibus jolted over a rut and the pain stabbed so deep into my head that the page in front of me split into a thousand pieces. All the little black letters seemed to throw themselves up into the air like smuts of soot from a chimney. When they stopped moving and floating around it was hard to make sense of them. I closed up the Bible and pushed it back into my bag.

When we came to the Commercial I climbed down and walked the rest of the way. The sky was a peculiar shade of dusty yellow. It felt as if it was pressing down so low you could reach up and scrape it with your nails. The old biddies were right, the heat had risen throughout the afternoon to such a pitch that a storm was stirring the air. Under the veil, my hair, which had been lank for days, was curling.

The thought of peeling off the cheap stinking gear I'd taken from The Carnival quickened my pace. When I got back to The Palace, in my own clothes again, I was going to have a long conversation with Tan Seng and Lok. It was time to dig up the past, no matter how difficult or painful it was to uncover the bones.

As I turned the corner I was surprised to see a crowd jostling on The Carnival's crooked stone steps and queuing in the street. When I went closer, of an instant, I recognised them all – everyone who worked in my halls was there – all of them dressed in the drab of mourning.

Christ! I remembered now. On account of everything else it had gone out of my mind.

Netta's funeral had taken place earlier this afternoon. I'd closed The Carnival for one night as a mark of respect. I'd paid for a fine hearse, a quality coffin and a decent plot at Bow cemetery, and I'd sent a packet to the clergy at St Ann's to make sure she got a good sendoff, but I hadn't been there. And I'd forgotten about the wake back at the hall, which I'd paid for as well.

I tried to dodge down the side alley to the door at the back, but it was too late. One of the girls had seen me.

'Look at her.' Forty pairs of eyes turned in my direction.

The girl, Bella Cundell it was, carried on. 'It's not respectful. She was here earlier. I saw her up top all done out like a dog's dinner while decent folk is in mourning.'

'Who is it, then?' Another voice, male this time, joined in. 'If you saw her she must be one of us. Show your face.'

I turned, but there was another group of sober sides coming up behind me now.

'Never mind her. I want to get in to send Netta on her way. There are thirty jugs set ready in there and a tray of cold meat pies. Open up, Fitzy – this is a wake not a Temperance meeting.'

I span back, grateful to whoever had spoken. There were cries of agreement. The people at the top of The Carnival's steps started beating on the peeling doors. A general chant started.

'Open up, open up, open up.'

But Bella Cundell didn't join in. She linked arms with

370

Cissie Watkins and they came towards me. They looked like a couple of starlings in their shiny black crêpe with cheap glass stones glittering in the skirts.

When they were level, Bella caught my arm. 'Afraid to show our face, are we? Let's see who you are under there.' I tried to pull away out of reach, but she caught the veil and ripped it from the hat.

'Kitty!'

She turned to the others. 'She never bothered to come to Netta's funeral, but here she is dressed like a—' She broke off as the door to The Carnival opened and Fitzy came out onto the top step. He was wearing a black jacket three sizes too small for his bulk and there was a tall black hat balanced on his fat head. His rig looked like something he'd borrowed for the occasion. He raised his hands and the crowd buttoned it. The people who had been hammering on the door retreated a little way down the steps.

'You can't come in. Not now.'

I'd never been so happy to see him. For all that he was spoiled as a barrel of brandy run to vinegar, he still had a dangerous quality. The bare knuckler was never far under that pockmarked surface.

He shook his head. 'I'm sorry, but there it is. You'll have to go elsewhere to drown your sorrows.'

'Why not?' It came from the back of the crowd.

'Because I say so. That's why.'

'And what does Kitty say? The Carnival belongs to her, after all.' I recognised the voice immediately. Swami Jonah stepped out from the black knot clustered round the steps.

'Well, ma'am? She was one of yours after all.' There was

a tone in his question. Like the rest of them, it was clear he took exception to my mourning gear. I stared at Fitzy and he shook his head again. Beside me I heard Bella and Cissie mutter together. Bella crumpled up my veil and threw it down in front of me. 'And poor Netta not even cold in her grave.'

One minute they resented her for getting a solo, now they was buzzing about her memory like flies round a pile of shit. It came to me then that their feelings towards me weren't really connected to Netta's funeral.

Despite all my fine words and intentions, nothing could hide the fact that since I'd taken on the halls, everything had turned to dross. These people weren't my friends, they were my employees. And these days they likely didn't trust me as far as they could throw me. I was losing them all. I moved away from Bella and Cissie.

'Is the wake set ready in there, Fitzpatrick?'

He nodded. 'But I don't think, ma'am, that—'

I cut him off. 'Then open the doors and let them all in.' There was a muted cheer.

Fitzy removed his little hat. 'You don't understand, ma'am. There's—'

'No! *You* don't understand, Fitzpatrick. This is my hall and these are my people. We're here for Netta. Open up.'

He turned the hat between his fingers.

'That's an order. Do you hear me?'

'As you wish, ma'am.'

He moved aside and the crowd swarmed up the steps, with a good deal of pushing and shoving. A jug of liquor and a cold meat pie was worth more than Netta's dignity. I watched until the last of them had gone through and then I joined

Fitzy, who was still out on the steps. He waited until I'd gone through into the lobby and then he closed the doors and followed me.

When I pushed through the curtain and stepped into the hall the only thing I heard was the hiss of the jets. The mourners were silent as Netta in her fine oak coffin. Instead of gathering round the side tables where the jugs and platters were waiting, they was all staring at the lighted stage. Slowly, one by one, they tore their eyes from the painted screen that had been furled down to fill the entire space and turned to look at me. Their eyes glittered with a sort of excitement.

There was no doubting who it was sitting with her legs spread wide on the bar of that swing. Just to make it quite clear, in case there was ever a question in anyone's mind, there was a line daubed in red across the top.

The Limehouse Linnet has a greedy cunt.

Chapter Thirty-one

The large jagged letters had been slapped with a vicious force-fulness onto the canvas. Trickles of paint slid down from them into the scene below. But it did nothing to obscure the picture or the message. The glistening paint trails mingled with the bars of the cage around me, making the whole thing seem oddly alive in the limelight as the canvas swayed on the ropes.

The girl, grinning and arching her back on the swing, was naked. Instead of holding on to the bars she had one hand clasped to a ripe breast while the other was spread in her crotch where a pair of exaggerated and livid red lips, more like a gash than a woman's quim, opened wide to spew out a stream of coins.

As I stood there, taking it in, with all them crow eyes watching, a murmuring started up around me. I couldn't catch any words distinct, but I caught the meaning. The last green feather on my hat bobbed about in front of my eyes like it was trying to spare my modesty.

The murmuring came stronger. Someone over to the left stifled a laugh. I heard my name whispered excitedly over and again, the K and the T of it clicking and catching on eager lips like a nest of roaches rustling in a box.

The sound filled my head and a lead weight fell in my belly. The wide lazy eyes of the girl on the swing were mocking. I thought about Ma and what they'd done to her.

Vile pictures, obscene – the work of a madman. That was what Joey told me.

I marched to the stage, pushing through the clusters of whispering girls and sniggering hands. I went up the steps at the side and stood smack in the centre. The limelight shone up the vivid colours of my frock. What with that and the image looming at my back I'd never felt so cheap and degraded. I was stark naked in front of them, despite all them ruffles and feathers.

'Out!'

A man's voice parped up. 'We can still see it behind you. You can't make it disappear, ma'am.'

I recognised who it was from the accent. I pulled that bleedin' hat off my head and flung it to the stage.

'That a fact, Mr McCarthy? Because I reckon there's two of us here who can do magic and don't you ever forget it. I can make you disappear from my halls, quicker than that.' I clicked my fingers. 'As I understand it, there's not much call these days for disappearing pigeons, mind-reading, card play, knife tricks and dragon's breath sparks.'

Dragon's breath? It came to me with a clarity.

Lyco powder was the stuff we used in the halls for magical sparks and the like. Dragon's breath was what we called it on account of the fire and the noxious smell. It was what the box that came with Netta's blue dress stank of, along with Schalk's cologne.

I scanned the rows of people standing below me. Swami Jonah was leaning on the wall to the side. The candles flickering above made his bald head shine like the moon and picked

375

out the constellation of moles on his cheek. He stared back at me for a long moment, then he straightened up, turned his back and walked slowly out of the hall. His long black coat brushed the boards as he went.

I watched the moth-eaten drapes fall back into place behind him and something else fell into place too. Only it didn't make sense.

It wasn't the time to go chasing shadows through my head. Everyone in the hall was talking now. I saw the way their eyes moved between me and the obscenity hanging over my head.

'Sling it, the whole lot of you,' I shouted to make myself heard. 'And if I hear anyone spreading this around, there'll be consequences.' I caught Jesmond's eye and he looked at his boots.

'What about Netta's wake?' It was a woman this time.

I folded my arms and filled my lungs with paint-thickened air. 'I'm going to count to twenty and if any of you – apart from the Professor and Fitzpatrick – are still here when I get to nineteen, you won't have a job to come back to tomorrow. Is that clear enough? One, two, three . . .'

'I tried to warn you, so I did. I found it when I came back.'

Fitzy grabbed a jug from one of the tables set out for the wake and poured a stream of gin into a tin mug. He offered it to me and I took it. For the first time ever, I thought I saw a sort of sympathy in his face. My hand was shaking as I brought the metal to my lips. He poured another for himself and waved an empty mug at Professor Ruben, who shook his head.

Fitzy took a swig and rubbed the back of his hand across his whiskered mouth. He'd taken the ill-fitting coat off and was standing there in his shirt and breeches. Like me, that tired grey shirt had seen better days.

'I locked up myself. That . . .' He swung the mug at the canvas and gin spattered across the boards. 'That *thing* wasn't here when a party of us went to Brook Street to follow Netta's coffin.'

The Professor nodded. 'And there was no one here when I came earlier. You arrived just after me, Kitty . . . ma'am. I wanted to prepare a piece I'd written for her wake – a sort of farewell. But there was—'

'How did you get in?' I broke his words.

'I have a key. That's right, Patrick, isn't it?' He glanced at Fitzy who tipped back another mouthful and nodded.

'The Professor likes to practise when it's quiet. I gave it to him.'

'Who else has one?'

Fitzy shrugged. 'Me, you of course, ma'am, and Jessie.'

That made sense. Most likely, Netta had taken the key to The Carnival from Aubrey Jesmond for her 'sailor boy', Matthias Schalk, and he'd made a copy of it. But I still didn't understand how he'd managed to get inside the hall and paint up the canvas in the time they was all at Netta's funeral.

'With respect, you should have listened to me. That's not a vision they're likely to forget.' I heard the liquid rattle into the tin as Fitzy filled his mug again.

I went to the centre of the hall and stared up at the

painting. I held that tin mug so tight my fingers left dents in the cheap metal. Pain shot across my temples as I took in those curving black and red lines. It was humiliating and it was cruel. It was calculated to damage me in the most personal way. Fitzy was right. I doubted there was one among them now who would ever look at me quite the same way again.

'There was something, ma'am.'

I turned to the Professor. His big dark eyes looked sadder than ever.

'Kitty is fine. What do you mean, "something"?'

'Over here.' He scrambled down into the pit in front of the curved stage and pointed at the upright piano pushed hard against the apron.

'I tried to tell you earlier today when you came in with Peggy and the other man, Mr Lok, is it?'

I nodded and walked over to him. I leaned over the rail. 'What is it, Professor?'

'Here. It was everywhere – on the music sheets and even on the keys.' He pointed at the shiny red blobs scattered across the top of the piano. 'At first I thought it was blood, but then I realised it was paint, red paint. It was here when I came in earlier today. I tried to ask you about it, show you, but you were in a hurry to go up top.'

'So whoever did this was here overnight?'

'That seems most likely. And then they rolled the canvas up and out of sight.' He reached out and ran long fingers over the top of the piano. It was almost a caress and it put me in mind of Old Peter with his beloved cornet, Zhena.

'The paint had dried when I arrived. I was angry with the hands. I thought they'd been careless.' He stared up at the canvas. 'Who would do such a wicked thing? It's sick, Kitty.' He paused. 'No, more than that, it is . . . *verrückt.*'

I didn't need a translation, I got the gist from the way he thumped his hand against his head. I stared up at the picture again. Matthias Schalk had been working on it around the same time I was listening to my grandmother choke out her last breaths.

I thought of Ma and the Barons again and, quite unexpectedly, I settled on the image of Lucca's gun in my bag. Tell truth, there was a time when I'd never wanted to touch it, let alone use it. But that finicky girl with the high-strung principles had died as she huddled up to her brother.

From the rail I could see every detail most clear. The paint had dried and hardened so the curving scrawl of black and red glinted in the gaslight. Of an instant, the canvas juddered. We all flinched as the first, enormous, clap of thunder tore the air above the hall. Moments later, drops of water started to spit from above as the rain found a way through The Carnival's leaking roof. Some fell on the picture, rolling like fat tears down the coarse fabric. I watched the rain begin to pool in a creased pouch running at the bottom edge of the canvas.

'I'll get the hands to take it down and burn it.' Fitzy came to stand next to me. He leaned over the rail with the new-filled mug in his hands. I smelt the gin from it.

'We've had our differences, but . . .' He swilled the liquor around, careful not to catch my eye and I realised he was as uncomfortable as I was. 'You're losing them, ma'am. The fire, Netta – and now this . . .'

'Don't you think I know that?' I slammed my mug down on the rail, spilling gin over the brass and the wood. 'By the time news of that . . . piece gets out – and it will, I know them too well to think they'll keep their traps shut – me and this place will stink from here to the Isle of Wight. It will kill us.'

I stared up at the canvas again. Fitzy was right – that leering harpy wasn't a vision anyone could forget in a hurry.

I frowned and leaned closer. There was something else painted there, hidden in the fold catching the rain. Just above the crease there was a black mark. The weight of the water was pulling the material down so it showed clear. Anyone else might have taken it for a spatter of paint – after all, now I looked there was enough of it staining the boards – but to me that mark had a familiarity.

'I can furl it up and out of sight for now, so I can.' Fitzy breathed out heavily. 'No one deserves to be made a mockery of like that. Let me pull it away.'

I shook my head. 'Not yet. There's something I want to take a look at.' I went over to the side steps, climbed up and crossed the stage to kneel in front of the lower edge of the swinging picture. I set down the mug and reached out to steady it. Another crash echoed overhead as I held the canvas straight. I was right, there was a mark there, but it was more than that. It was a message, and not the sort of message just anyone could understand.

I rubbed raindrops from my eyes and my heart started to thump in my chest. The only other person I knew who could write this, let alone read it back, was Sam Collins.

Chapter Thirty-two

The mark was shorthand and it read:

Exodus Thirty-two send help

In the cab on the short ride back to The Palace it was too dismal to take out Joey's Bible and flick to the place. Through the little window I watched foamy water tumble in the gutters beside us. Sarah's 'George' had been right about building an Ark. In the past weeks a crust of filth had dried over London and now the drains couldn't cope with the sudden deluge.

Flashes of lightning lit up the interior of the carriage, showing up the rips in the leather where the straw poked through, the missing buttons on the seats and the scratches left by boot nails on the wooden floor.

There wasn't time to send word to Tan Seng. Besides, Professor Ruben made my mind up for me. Without my asking, he went to the street and flagged down a cab to take me home. As I went past him in The Carnival's lobby he shook his head, caught my hand and kissed it.

The cab stopped at the end of Salmon Lane and I pushed a handful of coins up to the driver. The rain was coming down so heavy that it caught my face through the slat to the box. The cab rocked on its springs and the horses tossed their big wet heads as I climbed down into the street. They wanted a roof over their heads and some nice dry hay. The driver, huddled beneath a sheet of black oilcloth, tipped his dripping cap and cracked his whip. Gouts of water spurted from the wheels as the cab rolled away.

By the time I reached the steps of The Palace the sodden folds of that cheap violet dress were clinging to my skin and caught around my legs. I could hardly see through the wet strands of hair stuck to my face. One of the double doors opened and Tan Seng appeared in the glow. He opened a wide black umbrella and ducked down the steps to shield me beneath its canopy. Together we scurried up and into the hallway.

'Kitty!' Peggy came flying down the stairs so fast, I feared she might take a tumble. Lok was just behind her. 'Where've you been all this time?'

I pushed the hair back from my face. 'Not now, Peg.' A pool of purple water was forming around me on the tiles. I smelt like a dog, an old wet one.

'Look at you – you're soaked through.' She frowned. 'The dye's coming off the dress – there are streaks on your face.'

I swiped at my cheeks and stared at the stains on my fingers as she went on.

'It was Netta Swift's funeral today, did you know that?'

'I do now.'

'They were expecting you. After you left The Carnival I only twigged what was happening when they started flocking together downstairs in the hall – all in mourning. I would have gone too, but the heat ...' She shook her head. 'I couldn't walk a mile to St Ann's behind her coffin. I got a pain and Lok brought me back here.'

'You all right, Peg? The baby...'

'I'm fine. It was the heat. Besides, all I could think of was you. Where did you go, Kit? You can tell us now you're safe home again.'

I shook my head. 'I'm going to my room and then...' I turned to Tan Seng. 'I want to see you and Lok in the parlour.' The brothers exchanged the briefest of looks.

'And you should be resting, Peg. It's late.' I reached out for her hand. 'We'll talk tomorrow. Not now. Please.'

'But...'

I shook my head. 'Tomorrow.'

I kicked the carcass of that stinking dress into the corner and sat on the edge of my bed. The dye leaching from the fabric stained my arms, my legs and my cotton shift. I pulled it off and over my head and tossed it across the boards to join the dress.

I reached to the lamp on the little side table, turned the flame as high as it could go and took Joey's Bible from my bag. I brought those marks to mind again and I was sure there was no mistake. It was Sam's shorthand.

Exodus Thirty-two send help.

Thanks to Nanny Peck, I recognised the first part as a book of the Old Testament, but, tell truth, not being the observant type, I wasn't entirely sure where to find Exodus. I rustled through the thin pages until I came to the Book of Exodus, then I flicked forward until I reached Chapter Thirty-two. I frowned as I ran a purple-stained finger over the cramped text.

2 And Aaron said unto them, Break off the golden earrings, which are in the ears of your wives, of your sons, and of your daughters, and bring them unto me.

3 And all the people brake off the golden earrings which were in their ears, and brought them unto Aaron.

4 And he received them at their hand, and fashioned it with a graving tool, after he had made it a molten calf . . .

My finger stopped over the last three words. I heard the scratch of Telferman's voice.

It is taken from the Old Testament, the Book of Exodus. I believe your own Bible refers to the 'molten calf' – an image worshipped in idolatry?

At the time he was talking about Houtman's paddle steamer. He reckoned it was badly named.

The story of the Golden Calf is not favoured by my people. I do not understand why such a name should be used for a boat. There are some who might consider it a blasphemy.

I pulled a wrapper gown around me, took up the lamp and went down the flight of stairs to my office, my bare feet slapping on the treads. The ledger I needed was lying open on the top of my desk. I pulled it towards me and scanned the rows and the dates. Since the moment I'd been summoned to Fraines Abbey I'd lost track of everything. And there was something else I'd forgotten.

I turned the page so sharp it ripped in two, but there it was, halfway down.

27th July Gouden Kalf out from Shadwell New Basin.

I'd marked it particular because I intended to send word to

Houtman that I didn't expect to trade with him again.

Christ! What was the date?

The clock in the parlour across the hall started to chime. Above the painted dial there was a crescent window in the case showing the date, the month and the shape of the moon. I snatched up the lamp and ran across the hall. There was a rustle from the shrouded cage in the corner and the sound of claws scraping on metal. Jacobin let out a string of profanities.

That, at least, was something that didn't surprise me.

I went to the mantle and held the lamp up to the dial, peering close to see the date. In less than an hour's time it would be the 27th of July, Houtman and his great black paddle ship would be leaving on the morning tide.

Another flare of lightning brought the room up sharp. Seconds later the clap of thunder came so loud that the drops hanging off the red glass candle holders at either end of the mantle chinked and rattled. Surely Houtman wouldn't take her out onto the river if this kept up?

'Lady?'

I swung about. Tan Seng and Lok were standing at the doorway, both of them carrying oil lamps. Tan Seng moved to the centre of the room and Lok went to set his lamp down on the low table beside the couch.

'You asked to see us.' The light from the lamp deepened the shadows beneath his eyes.

I'd intended to order them to tell me about the past. I wanted to know exactly what they were keeping from me about Lady Ginger and Ma. If they knew who my father was, I wanted his name from them and a lot more besides.

But now there wasn't time to talk. I pulled the wrapper tight around me, conscious that I was naked beneath it. Rain lashed against the window. It sounded like Old Nick himself was hurling fistfuls of stones at the glass. I was minded of that time when Matthias Schalk stood out there on the street, stroking the sharpened tip of his hawk-headed cane. It was the moment when I realised who had ripped Old Peter Ash apart and pulled the entrails from his body.

Send help.

The message was from Sam Collins and it was intended for me and no one else. But how on God's earth could he have hidden it on that filthy picture? Sam was clever, but I didn't have him marked for a fighter. Sweet Jesus! If Matthias Schalk had him . . .

I closed my eyes as the pain shot from nowhere and rippled out across my head, pulsing like waves against the stones of Shadwell New Basin.

It was what Kite told me at Temple Church: *others close to you will suffer.*

I hadn't even had a chance to get close to Sam yet. If anything happened to him . . .

I couldn't follow that thought through, scared of where it might lead me.

Houtman's boat had already taken a life. I thought of the body of that lascar boy mangled up in the paddle and the flecks of red in the yellow foam. I remembered what Ramesh Das told me.

Khunni is not a name, Lady. You are mistaken in that. It is a word. In our tongue it is the word for murderer.

I pushed the oil lamp onto the mantle and balled the heels

of my wrists into my eyes. I brought back that day at the quay.
Houtman had come ashore and was over near the barrels.
The horn had gone off, blocking out every other sound, and
the funnel let off a cloud of steam. Next thing the bald captain was leaning over the edge of the quay and poor Dalip was
thrashing around in the water, trapped between stone and
metal.

Murderer.

All along it was Houtman the other boy meant, not me.
Another huge thunderclap exploded over The Palace. The
lightning that came a split second before the burst was so
bright I could see it through closed eyelids. Jacobin started
up again under the sheet. I could hear his vicious little beak
plucking at the bars of the cage.

I opened my eyes and stared at the fabric-covered dome in
the corner. That parrot was trapped in the dark and so was I.

'Think, girl. Think!' I clenched my fists as I said the words
aloud. The tide! When was the morning tide? I took up the
lamp again and ran from the parlour back to the office. I had
a tide table in the desk, useful for when shipments came in. I
rifled through the drawer until I found it. I turned to the page
and ran my finger down the columns. I brought a hand to my
mouth.

'Lady?'

I looked up. Tan Seng was standing in the doorway. He
came closer and bowed.

'You require something of us?'

Chapter Thirty-three

We moved in single file down the unlit alley. Tan Seng went ahead and I knew Lok was tucked behind. I could sense him, even though I couldn't hear his steps. The rain was coming so heavy it was hard to see more than a yard in front of your face. Every so often, Tan Seng turned to reassure himself we hadn't been washed away.

He paused and looked back at me now, just as another sheet of lightning ripped the sky apart. For a second the dripping brick walls of the alley came sharp as a stage in the limelight, framing him as he stood there in his black breeches and oilskins. Rain slid off the sack slung over his shoulder.

I didn't suspect the pair of them possessed much in the way of London gear, so it came as a shock when we met in the hall. I was so used to seeing the brothers in their gowns and slippers that the sight of them standing there rigged out like a pair of regular dock boys was hard to take in.

Peggy watched us from the stairs.

Lok tied a small leather pouch to his belt and pushed it beneath the folds of his oilskin jacket. I bent to tie the laces of my boots.

'I don't suppose it's even worth my asking, Kit?'

I looked up at her. 'It's best you don't, Peg. When we've gone, lock all the windows, pull the shutters and bolt the doors. Go to your room, close up tight and we'll talk tomorrow.'

She stared at my breeches. 'Always tomorrow with you. Another costume, is it?'

I nodded. 'Something like that. It's easier to get about.'

'Get about where, exactly?'

When I didn't answer she came down to the hall and helped me with the cap, pushing loose strands up beneath it. The storm had made my corkscrew hair more than usually lively. Nanny Peck always said she didn't need to nail a strip of boat weed to the door to tell if a storm was brewing. She just needed to look at my thatch.

She'd have something to say about it now.

'There – you look a proper Tom.' Peggy stepped back and shook her head. 'These days you're keeping more secrets than one of Lucca's father 'fessors, Kit.'

I didn't answer that, neither. She looked over my shoulder at Lok and I swear she nodded as if to answer a question. I turned, but he was pulling his own cap down low.

Shadwell was a rough place in the day, but at night it was dangerous. St Paul's, over to the right of the alley, had the reputation of being the church of the sea captains. But it was the crews you should be wary of in these black streets. When they tipped out of the stand-ups after downing a skinful, there was generally only one thing on their minds. If they came across a woman out alone and they were capable, they'd take it. The streets round Shadwell were so notorious that even the penny tails wouldn't work them alone. Not so long back, I'd thought about trying to regulate the trade round here. I reckoned I could find a way to give them a sort of protection. That was at the beginning, when I was still as green as parlour paint.

Truly, the more I knew, the clearer it came to me that I couldn't make it different. As we crept along that alley, I thought of Dora crouched in her own sodden corner of Paradise waiting for the rain to wear her away.

I couldn't spin gold from shit. Turns out I wasn't the miller's daughter, whatever Sam might think. Of an instant, it felt as if there was a stone lodged in my throat. It wouldn't go down when I swallowed.

Normally the air here was full of tobacco, coffee and a hundred other spices mingling together. All I could smell now was overflowing drains.

We came to the end of the passage. Another flash of lightning showed up the greasy soot-blackened wall ahead. Generally, there were gaslights along this stretch, but the rain had doused the flames through the cracked glass of the lanterns. I needn't have worried about shipmates, the street was deserted. No one in their right wits would go out on a night like this.

Moments after the flash, a clap of thunder came so loud I could feel it rock the stones beneath my boots. A sudden gust of wind caught the edge of my cap and I had to slam my wet hand down hard to keep it in place.

High tide was at four in the morning, but surely no one would leave port in this?

The entrance to the basin was off to the left past the dock house, but we weren't going in that way. Even though half the customs boys who worked the docks were in the pockets of my skirts – or breeches on this occasion – they couldn't help us tonight.

If you didn't know different, you might have taken the street for a branch of the river. Torrents of water tumbled past the end of the alley, forming a pool at the grilled mouth of a gutter leading down under the wall and into the basin. The only way in was over the top. I waded into the stream glad of the breeches, even though they was stuck fast to my legs. A skirt would have taken up the water and weighed me down like an anchor. Lok and Tan Seng followed. If I had ever had doubts about their loyalty, those misgivings had been carried away with the rain. As Tan Seng stood there earlier in the doorway to my office I remembered the way he'd dealt with the cabman that night.

I should have trusted them from the start.

From somewhere nearby – St Paul's, I reckoned – a bell sounded. I tried to catch the chimes, but the notes were snatched by the wind. It was most likely a quarter, but I couldn't swear to it. It was past midnight when we left The Palace.

I pointed at the wall and mimed going over the top. Tan Seng nodded and shifted his bag from his shoulder. It rattled as he pulled it open and drew out a coil of rope.

Lok came to stand next to me and the two of us watched Tan Seng swing the rope above his head in a widening loop, before letting it fly up and over the wall. There was a metallic scraping noise. He fed the dripping rope back down through his hands and the scraping came again from the far side of the wall, followed by a dull clang. He yanked the rope hard and it stayed in place. He tested it once more, leaning back into the rain to let it carry his weight and then he sprang like a cat. Within seconds he was at the top, beckoning us to follow. He didn't move like an old man. Tell truth, I'd never seen anyone so limber.

I swiped the rain from my eyes and turned in amazement to Lok. He was staring up at his brother, holding his hat to his head with one hand.

'Good, he is good. Always. The rope trick.' He had to shout to make himself heard above the storm.

'Trick?' I looked up again at Tan Seng just as another sheet of lightning froze the scene into a moment of brilliance. Now he was balanced on the wall staring out over the basin beyond.

Lok sidled at me. 'Way back. When we first came to London we work in halls, Lady. Our talents were ... noticed by your grandmother.' His hands strayed to the pouch at his side. 'Now you go. I follow.'

Despite the shelter of the wharf houses, the boats lined up across the new basin bucked and tossed like teams of skittish dray horses. The wind whistled in the ropes and the eerie banshee pitch of it rose above the storm. A few lamps attached to the warehouse walls had managed to shield their light from the rain. Pools of yellow slicked the quay stones and splintered on the swirling black water.

The *Golden Calf*, or *Gouden Kalf* to name it right, wasn't hard to spot. But it wasn't easy to reach, neither. It was moored out in the middle of the basin, facing the entrance to the river and ready for the tide. It was the biggest boat there. As it rose on the incoming waves I got the impression that the paddle wheel winked at me as it reared and plunged again.

It was the only steamer in the basin. The other boats were sail ships of the old style. The *Golden Calf* rolled in the midst of them like a threat.

Lok landed lightly on the cobbles beside me and Tan Seng deftly loosened the rope, coiling it back into the sack. I saw now that there was a triple-headed, fist-sized grapple hook at the end of it. I flattened up against the bricks as the wind slammed a wall of water against us.

'What now, Lady?' Tan Seng twisted the damp plait that had come free from under his cap and forced it beneath again. His black eyes were bright and eager. Now it came to it, the pair of them put me in mind of fine instruments tuned for a performance. It was as if those two old men shuffling about The Palace together had been acting a role. Now, they were entirely themselves. I'd set them free.

I pointed at the *Golden Calf*.

'There – the steamer with the paddle wheel. We need to go on board.'

It was the third in a row of boats tossing and pitching about in the storm and on the fast-coming tide. They were linked together by ropes thick as a navvy's arm holding them to their place in the line. The ends of the ropes were wound around broken stone pegs strung out along the quay like rotten teeth.

'Mr Collins is there?' Lok stared over the churning water.

'Yes.' I nodded sharp, hoping I was right. But that's what Sam's message meant, didn't it? It couldn't be anything else. That lump in my throat hardened again.

'This way.' I headed off to the right, careful to keep to the shadows. If anything the storm was a friend, not an enemy. It kept everyone under cover, including us.

When we was close as possible we darted behind a stack of old tea chests lashed together. Sixty foot out lights moved on the deck of the *Golden Calf*. Someone stood at the bow with a lantern and there was another light bobbing about at the stern. A third, fainter because of the height and the swaying, was attached to the funnel.

There were at least two people on deck.

'Lady?' Tan Seng looked at me.

I chewed my lip, tasting the metal of soot in the rain. 'We can get on easily enough. I can climb across on the rope.' I pointed at the line running out to the steamer from one of the stone pegs on the quay. 'The water and the height don't scare me. And from what I've seen tonight, I don't imagine it will trouble either of you?'

Tan Seng bowed his head. It was an acknowledgement not a servility.

'The trouble is . . .' I faltered as lightning made everything clear as day in the split of a second. There were men out on the deck.

'How many did you see?' I rubbed the water from my eyes.

'Two men, maybe three, Lady?' Lok reached into the dripping folds of his oilskin.

'They are the trouble.'

We ducked as another massive clap of thunder made the tea chests judder.

'Not trouble.' Lok untied the pouch and produced a pipe as thin as a reed. He handed it to Tan Seng and then he delved deeper into the bag.

'See, Lady.' He dropped a handful of tiny black pellets into his damp cupped palm and nodded at the pipe.

I shook my head. 'No, I don't see.'

Lok took the pipe from Tan Seng and brought it to his lips. He aimed it at the *Golden Calf*, puffed out his cheeks and pretended to blow.

'Sleep comes quick.' He grinned at me.

No wonder my grandmother noticed their talents.

The last of the men must have dropped his lantern. The tiny glowing ball tumbled down the black side of the boat and disappeared into the swirling water. The only light clearly visible now was swaying at the top of the funnel.

I shielded my eyes and peered through the rain. Just below the line of the deck there were three faint flickers. They moved in time with the boat, the space between them never widening or closing. I reckoned they were windows of a sort running along the side. In addition to the men up top, there was someone below.

Lok sniffed and clenched up his hand to stop the unused pellets from being washed away. He stared at the boat. Tan Seng rattled out a stream of words I didn't understand and Lok nodded. He loosened the pouch at his belt and pushed the pipe and remaining pellets back inside. Then he wiped his hand roughly on the wet oilskin of his jacket.

'Not good, Lady. Sleep come.' I knew he meant to wash the taint from his skin. Whatever they were, those little black seeds must've had a kick like a horse.

After Lok had taken out that long bone pipe and shown me the pellets we slipped along the shadows at the edge of the quay until he was satisfied that he could take a clear aim. Me and Tan Seng flattened up against the wall as Lok moved forward to crouch behind one of the stone pegs. Now his plait had worked free from under the cap and the wind flailed it around him like a whip. I watched him raise the pipe to his lips. The way he shifted from side to side – his tiny body tight as wire – minded me of a cat juggling its bones for a pounce.

Of an instant Lok's head jerked back. A moment later the light moving at the front of the boat disappeared. I held my breath. Even though I wanted to wipe the rain from my eyes and my face, I couldn't move for fear of casting a jinx.

When no one on deck sounded a warning, Lok turned and grinned. He bent forward to guard his hands from the rain, filled the pipe again and lifted it to his lips.

He picked off the other two quicker than a child could count to ten on its fingers. It can't have been easy, despite the fact he made it look like it was nothing more to him than spitting on a rag when he polished up the silver at The Palace. Although we were less than forty foot away now, the angle of the boat and the way it rolled in the basin meant his marks were never still and never straight.

Lok raised his right hand and Tan Seng darted from the shadows to join him. The brothers crouched low, their heads bent together as they watched the boat. Rain shattered off their black rounded backs. Tan Seng turned and motioned for me to join them. As I tucked up close beside him thunder ruptured the air and another sheet of lightning showed up the rope stretching out from the peg stone across the water to the bows of the *Golden Calf*.

I nudged Tan Seng and pointed at the rope.

'I'll go first.' I mouthed the words on account of the storm, but he shook his head so violent that his cap slipped awry and the end of his own plait unfurled again down his back. He rolled it into a knot and forced it back into place. He pointed at himself, then me, then at Lok, who nodded.

I didn't have a chance to argue.

Without waiting for me to have a say in the matter, Tan Seng caught the rope in his hands. Then he was off over the edge of the quay, curling his legs up and over the rope and hauling himself along arm over arm. He moved off quicker than a circus boy. Truly, I found it hard to think of the man swaying on the cable as the ancient who fussed over my tea tray of a morning.

When he was halfway across, and dandling twenty foot above the water, he paused, freed an arm and gestured for me to follow.

'You go now.' Lok blinked as rain spattered across his face. 'You swim?'

I nodded. 'I'll be fine.' I flinched as lightning blanched his features. 'Can you swim?'

Lok wiped his nose. 'Like fish, Lady.'

I glanced over the water to the *Golden Calf*, took a deep breath and reached for the rope.

Chapter Thirty-four

Crossing the basin was the easy part. All them sessions on the ropes and the swing in Madame Celeste's attic had prepared me to perform in a cage strung up seventy foot over the heads of the punters. In all the time I was up there I was never scared, except for the night at The Comet when the plaster ceiling failed. And even then, when it was all over, the thing I remember most clear was the way my skin prickled and my head fizzed. I'd never felt so completely alive. It's a terrible thing to admit, but a part of me was greedy for the thrill of it. I knew now that Joey wasn't always to be trusted, but something he said to me in the Bedlam rang true.

Even during the most difficult times it was exhilarating. When I felt my heart beat so wildly in my chest that it might burst through my ribs I was glad of the pain.

I think I understood what he meant. It wasn't pain exactly, but I felt it too. Danger was a reminder that you were flesh and blood and breathing and thinking and moving about in the world. It made everything sharp and fresh as a new box of paints. Perhaps me and my brother were more alike than I cared to admit?

It took me a couple of minutes to haul myself across. I copied Tan Seng, hooking my knees over the cable and pulling myself arm over arm. The rain fell hard on my face, but there was nothing I could do about that. Halfway out

I felt the rope pull tight and dip lower to the water as Lok began his own crossing. I paused, clung tight and craned my head to see him ten foot behind and closing fast. He was lithe and nimble as his brother.

I started off again, conscious that the weight of two bodies made the rope sway wider.

'Lady!'

At Tan Seng's voice I twisted about and caught sight of one of them great black paddle wheels rising and then plunging again into the water. Of an instant, I thought of poor Dalip, his body jammed and mangled in the slats. It was as if the *Golden Calf* felt me there. As the boat rose again and bucked to the right, the wheel rode high and a deep, metallic scraping sound, so loud I could hear it above the storm, echoed from the hull. I tightened my hands on the rope and dragged my eyes away.

'Here, Lady!'

Tan Seng was hunched over the black edge of the boat. In the shadow I couldn't see his face, but from the faint pricks of light leaching out from a row of tiny glass roundels I'd seen from the quay I could make out where the rope threaded into a hole in the bow about four foot below him.

As I swung there, I tried to work out how to scramble up the steep metal side to join him on deck. I'm still not sure how Tan Seng managed to climb up on board, but I was grateful when he ran another rope down beside me.

Holding tight with one hand I reached out and pulled it to me. I wound my arms around it and carefully unhooked my legs from the cable. I hung there for a second, before spinning about and flattening the soles of my boots against the slippery black sides of the boat.

Once I'd got a purchase, it was easy to clamber up. Tan Seng hauled me over the rail and I scanned the shadowy deck as Lok joined us, dropping light as a moth to the boards. The rattling and whistling of the wind through the ropes of the old-style sail ships jostling around us in the basin was deafening. There was a dismal groaning and thumping too as their timber hulls scraped and bumped against each other.

Tan Seng tapped my shoulder. I turned back and he pointed at a dark crumpled shape lying at an odd angle across the deck a little way off. It was one of the men we'd seen from the quay. I went to crouch down next to him, reaching out to push the sodden collar of his coat away from his face. He was alive, but his breathing was slow. His eyelids flickered as he dreamed. A thin trail of blood ran from a tiny wound on his temple and down the side of his face.

Lok knelt beside me. 'Sleep long time.'

I peered back down the cluttered deck. I couldn't make out much beyond the funnel stack. Shadowy piles of barrels and crates lashed together along the boards made it difficult to be sure, but as far as I could tell there was no one moving about now. A platform midway down the deck showed chained double doors leading down to the hold.

A low hut-like structure, the wheelhouse most like, jutted out from the base of the funnel stack. Another slash of lightning, accompanied by an almost immediate crash of thunder, showed up the glass in the windows and an arched doorway. It was a way inside.

Send help.

I thought of the dim lights I'd see along the side of the

400

boat. If Sam was a prisoner here, they'd keep him hidden somewhere below. I thought of his unruly hair, his clever dark eyes and his rangy frame and I tried to muffle the thought of what Matthias Schalk might have done to him.

'They sleep long time.' Lok spoke again.

'Before we do anything else we need to make sure of that.' He raised his eyebrows doubtfully as I stood up.

I brought a finger to my lips. 'Keep close and follow me.' I reached out to steady myself as the boat pitched in the water. The deck was slippery with rain. A person could easily lose their step and end up over the side. One of the paddle wheels clanked and grated again like a warning.

The other men were easy to find. Both of them were slumped on deck, one still had a dead smoke clenched between his fingers. The trickle of blood tracing a path down the bristled cheek of the first and the thick-set neck of the second were silent testimonials to Lok's skill. Neither of them were Houtman.

I ducked as a sheet of rain smashed across the deck. Any other shipmates on board tonight would be down below. The question was how many of them were there?

I pointed at the arched door and beckoned the brothers close.

'We need to get inside, but I reckon we won't be alone.' My neck prickled beneath the jacket. I pulled at the oilskin. It wasn't the rain that made my skin crawl.

Lok patted the pouch at his side and made a swift gesture at Tan Seng who slipped across the deck to the wheelhouse. I watched as he crouched low and bent his head against the door beneath the glass pane. After giving it most careful consideration, he stretched up his hand to the round brass handle set into the wood. The door swung open, but Tan Seng caught it deft to stop the wind from throwing it back against the wall.

'We go in, now, Lady.' Lok's voice came over my shoulder. I turned – the bone pipe was ready between his fingers again.

It's an odd thing, but that wheelhouse seemed larger on the inside than it looked from the deck. As Lok closed the door soundlessly behind us and flattened his little body against the wooden wall it took a moment or two for my eyes to grow sharp in the dark. The wheel was over to the left and there was a stack of papers and charts. Over to the right there was a bundle of cloth and rags folded into a pile that might have served as a mattress.

The stink of oil and coal came strong, and there was something else in the air too, the sour stink of men who didn't go much on the dainties. I was glad to have a roof over my head again, and not just on account of the shelter. I needn't have worried about anyone hearing us moving about. The rain was falling so hard it could have been Barney Knuckle up there dancing a jig in his Lancashire clogs.

At first I couldn't see a way to go below, but after a moment, when I'd grown accustomed, I caught a faint glow coming from the edges of a trap in the boards. There was a loop of rope set in the middle to pull it up. I nudged Lok and pointed to the hatch, but he was already staring at it and turning the pipe in his hands.

Tan Seng padded across the wheelhouse floor and sank to his knees. He bent his head and listened like he did out on deck. He raised his hand twice and followed up with a chopping motion.

'There are two below us, Lady.' Lok rolled a couple of them black seeds between his fingertips and pushed them into the end of the pipe. He wiped his hand on his oilskin coat again.

'My brother will go first.'

They moved fast. As soon as I pulled the hatch open Tan Seng dropped into the room below. A second later Lok bent his head into the gap and took aim. His head jerked and the first pellet caught Houtman smack in the centre of his broad forehead. The captain reached up in surprise to feel the place where it bit into his skin and then he looked at the red on the tips of his fingers. He stood up abrupt from the desk pushed against the curved wall, sending his chair toppling to the boards. The muscles in his ugly jaw worked as he stared down at the old man crouching on the floor of his cabin.

Tan Seng's plait had worked itself loose again. The way it trailed down his rounded back made him look more than ever like a yard cat out for a scrap.

Houtman clearly didn't take him for a threat. A grin twisted across the man's lard-block face.

'*Wat hebben we hier?*' He pushed at his sleeve and came forward, balling his right hand into a fist the size of a butcher's mallet.

'No!'

I didn't mean to call out, but I couldn't help myself.

Houtman's bald head shot up. His pale eyes widened as he caught sight of me framed in the open hatchway just behind Lok, but by then it was too late. If he had something to say about it, the words didn't make it to his lips. Of an instant his eyes rolled in his head. His body crumpled and he toppled forward like all his bones had been curdled to a junket.

As he fell, his head caught the edge of the ladder steps. There was a shout from somewhere deeper in the room below. Lok ducked forward and his head jerked again. A yelp, a rattle of furniture and the thud of boots on wood, then, just like Houtman, a second man tumbled into view. There was a thump as his dark head met the boards just in front of Tan Seng, who turned to look up at us.

He nodded and pushed the head of the man spread out in front of him. He'd fallen flat on his face. There was blood pouring from his nose; the sticky little pool glinted in the dim light of the oil lamp swinging from the ceiling. The only other light in the room came from a small brass lantern on the desk.

Lok reached for the pouch at his belt and slipped the pipe back inside.

'Lady.'

He bowed his head and moved aside on the ladder steps to let me down first.

The cabin beneath the wheelhouse was about twelve foot long and wide as the boat. Part of it – the end nearest the hatch – was arranged as a sort of office. There were more charts spread over the top of a narrow desk. Houtman had clearly been consulting a tide table with the help of the candle lantern when Tan Seng surprised him. Now the book lay face down on the floor next to the fallen chair. The spine was broken and loose pages slid across the boards with the sway of the boat.

I reckoned I had something else to be grateful to the storm for. The captain wasn't about to ship out any time soon after all. He was sitting there calculating the next window.

The low space clearly served a double purpose. Rows of wooden bunks were bolted to the curving walls at the other end. The air was thick with the meat smell of unwashed men. Without going a step closer, I knew the scramble of stained yellowing sheets on the bunks had never seen a laundry tub. So far as I could make out they were empty. Then again, now I looked, there might have been a shape curled up there in the shadows of the lowest row. As the lamp swayed I saw there were ropes binding a humped form to the slats.

Sam?

I ran forward.

'No one else is here, Lady.'

I turned. Tan Seng was standing now. He pushed the plait back beneath his cap and spread his feet wide to steady himself as the *Golden Calf* pitched. There was a grating sound from outside as the paddle shifted.

'There's someone . . .' I faltered as the lamp swung again. The puddle of yellow light slicked across the bunks and showed plain that what I'd taken for a man was a roll of old canvas strapped to the slats.

I pulled off my sodden cap and let my own plait of hair roll down my back. If Sam Collins was truly here then where was he? I thought about the double hatches up on deck – perhaps he was down in the hold?

I went back to the ladder. To reach it I had to step over Houtman's body. He'd fallen at an awkward angle, one leg bent up beneath the other. There was blood seeping from the side of his head too. When he crashed against the steps he must have cracked his skull. I didn't feel bad about that. I stared at the brown freckles that spread across the back of his bald pink scalp like tea stains on a dish rag.

A red pool, much like a halo on one of Lucca's saints, bloomed around the top of the captain's head, lapping round the feet of the ladder steps. There was something else there too.

I bent for a closer look and stretched forward to run my fingers across the boards. I was right, there was another hatch here hidden in the shadow beneath the steps. I followed the edge with my fingers. A small square trap was set flush into the wood, but I couldn't see nor feel a way to pull it open. As the lamp overhead moved again, I caught the glint of something small and gold.

There was no handle, but there was a brass lock.

I straightened up, stepped over Houtman's body again and went to the desk. I searched through the papers, throwing them to the floor when I couldn't find what I needed, and then I pulled open the drawers, emptying the contents onto the boards.

Where was it? Where would he keep it?

Of an instant, I knew. That day at the quay – it wasn't coins he was jangling. It was keys. I knelt down beside Houtman and pulled his jacket open. He moaned.

I glanced up at Lok. 'How long does it last?'

He pushed Houtman's head with his foot and stared down

at him. The man grunted and his eyelids flickered like those of his shipmate lying out on deck in the rain. Now I saw the deep gash on his left temple where he'd caught the stairs. He murmured again and his right arm twitched, the fingers of the hand bunching and knotting themselves together in a way that didn't look natural.

'How long?' I asked again.

'Long enough, Lady.' Lok blinked. 'He will sleep long enough.'

I dipped my hand into Houtman's breeches pocket and felt coins. I pushed deeper and my fingers closed around a metal ring. I drew it out sharp and the keys jangled together.

One of them was small and brass.

I let go of the rope and stared up at the square of light overhead. I took a breath, but the fug stoppered my lungs. The hot, stale air had the tarry reek of a coal hole – one where something had died. Tan Seng moved in the hatch overhead and the shadow of his body fell across me. For a moment the dark was so dense I could feel it huddling up against me.

Seconds later a glow bobbed about above my head as he passed the candle lantern from the desk down on another rope. I'd insisted on going down first; as soon as we opened up that second trap I knew the gaping black hole was the last place we'd find any more of Houtman's shipmates.

Tell truth, I wondered about finding Sam too.

I reached for the lantern and freed it from the rope, then I turned and raised it high to show up the space. I stepped back in surprise. A great black wheel rose across the floor not six foot in front of me, half of it disappearing into a space below. Almost three times my height, the wheel was set with hundreds of little metal teeth, each one buttered thick with gobbets of oil. An array of other cogs and chains of varying size connected to it along with two metal shafts that stretched to reach each side of the boat. It put me in mind of the workings of a timepiece – one belonging to a giant from one of Nanny Peck's stories.

As the boat rocked, all that metal grated together and a hollow moan echoed off the riveted walls. I knew what it was straight off – the engine that ran the paddles. It was sleeping now, but when it was awake this place was the beating black heart of the *Golden Calf*.

There was a thump as Lok swung down from the hatch to land beside me. We'd agreed that Tan Seng should wait up top, while we went below. There was a scrape and the greenish flare of a Lucifer as he lit a stub of a candle. Arching shadows cast by the mechanism flickered on the curved walls around us. They swayed and moved in a way that minded me that we were below the level of the water down here.

I pushed the thought from my mind and held the lantern out. It didn't help, all I could see was that the blackness continued beyond the wheel. I turned. There was a wooden slatted wall behind us, with an opening to one side.

It was a struggle to draw breath down here, my lungs hung like lead weights in my chest. I tried to swallow enough air to fill them and something sour that wasn't coal clawed the back of my throat. I looked up. The hatch was still open but I couldn't see Tan Seng.

Even if I knew the men up top were set to sleep a fortnight I wouldn't feel easy. There was something . . . *dark* about the *Golden Calf*. I'd felt it that first time at the quay and the sense of it was coming so strong now it was like an itch. One I couldn't scratch.

Nanny Peck would have called it a presentiment. There was a time when I would have laughed at that and called it something else. I wasn't so sure now. The sooner we found Sam and got off this bleedin' boat the better.

'You go that way, Lok.'

I swung my lantern towards the gap in the wooden wall, the light slipping across the oily floor to show where I meant.

'I'll take the other side.' I pointed to the shadows beyond the mechanism.

'What if . . .' Lok frowned. He sniffed and started again. 'If he is not here, Mr Collins, what then, Lady?'

I didn't answer. If I did it might make it a truth.

I swung my lantern towards the gap in the slatted wall again.

'That way. If you find Sa . . . Mr Collins, call out. I'll do the same.'

I watched him disappear through the gap with his candle and then I turned to the wheel. I ducked beneath one of the metal arms that drove the paddles and stepped across the gap in the boards. Ahead of me now I could see another thin wooden wall, like the one Lok had just gone through. There was a dark gap over to the right.

The boat rocked and I reached out to steady myself on the wooden edge of the doorway. Behind me the workings of the wheel clanked and groaned with the movement. I held the lantern high. There was a sort of corridor ahead, a narrow passage lined with wooden partitions. The look of it put me in mind of the stalls you might find in a stable yard, but half the size. I moved forward and peered into the first of them. The light bounced off a mound of glittering coal heaped up against the bowed wall. There was a shovel buried in the pile. I carried on, but the next two stalls were filled with coal, same as the first. The stink of something left to rot was stronger here.

As I swung my lantern back to the passage there was a huge clap of thunder and the boat swayed about so violent I fell against the wall. The lantern dropped to the floor and rolled away from me, the flame dancing madly up the walls.

'No!'

I couldn't bear the thought of losing the light. I tried to catch it, but the boat rolled again and I stumbled to my knees. The lantern bounced and came to an upright halt against the edge of one of the stalls ahead. The flame inside the glass flickered and dimmed to a pin prick and I thought it would surely die, but then it gathered itself together and grew bright again.

For a moment I reckoned the light had disturbed a rats' nest on account of the scratching that started up. I paused expecting something on bony little feet to scuttle past me in the gloom, but then I heard shuffling, followed close by the rattle of metal and a scraping sound. Someone coughed in the stall now lit by the lantern.

'Sam!' I darted forward, catching the edge of the stall to steady myself. 'Sam! I'm here – it's me, Kitty.'

I snatched up the lantern and raised it high. A mound of

rags trembled in the corner of the stall. I had to cover my mouth and nose as I recognised the source of the stench of shit and piss that fouled the air. A bloody hand emerged from the folds and reached out to me. He was alive! I could feel the thud of my heart in my throat.

'Sam, what have they done to you?'

I ran to kneel beside him and took his hand in mine. 'I'm here now. I saw the message you left for me. It was a clever thing to do.'

Of an instant, his hand gripped mine so tight I almost cried out. He started to cough again, his body jerking beneath those soiled wrappings.

'I'll take you out of here, Sam Collins, but first, let's get you some air.' I reached forward to push the rags away from his head. As it came free he bent forward to cough again and I saw the dark hair matted to his scalp.

He looked up.

'No!' I brought my hand to my mouth. 'Christ, no!'

Chapter Thirty-five

'Fannella?'

Lucca coughed again as he tried to speak. I pulled the tattered blanket gently from his head and shoulders. His lips were cracked and swollen. Mottled bruises circled his neck.

'It worked.' It was barely a whisper. His head trembled as he stared up at me.

'*Perdonami, Fannella.*'

His good eye was bloodshot, the pouched skin around it smudged purple and green. I pushed the knotted hair back from his face. Tell truth, I was having trouble taking in what I was seeing in front of me. I stroked his cheek, as much to convince myself he was real as to comfort him. His skin was hot and damp to the touch.

'You're not meant to be here, Lucca.'

'*Perdonami.*' He repeated the word, then he bowed his head, raised my hand to his mouth and kissed it fierce, holding it there fast. When he spoke again, his lips felt like autumn leaves brushing against my skin.

'I . . . I'm sorry, Fannella, so very sorry.' It was less than a whisper. I had to lean close to hear him. He hunched up tight and a shudder went through him. I realised he was weeping. I wrapped him in my arms, cradling his head against my shoulder. Finding him on board was the last thing I'd expected, but seeing him again was the only good thing that had happened to me in the longest time. I didn't care about the state he was in.

'I've missed you so much.' I stroked his head. Beneath the lice and the filth I caught the familiar scent of him and it made me hold him closer.

'I'm here now, Lucca. It's going to be all right.' Of an instant he went rigid in my arms.

'You don't understand.' He pulled away and stared wildly at me. 'You won't . . .' A tear rolled down the good side of his face, leaving a trail in the grime. 'They forced me . . . you must believe me, Fannella. Tell me that.'

He wasn't making sense. The thought came to me that he might be burning up with a brain fever. I cupped his face in my hands.

'I'll tell you what, we're going to get you out of here.' My mind tumbled with questions, but answers could come later. The most important thing was to get off the boat.

'Listen to me.' I gripped his face harder. 'Can you stand?'

He shook his head and reached down to move the blankets aside. A manacle was clamped around his right ankle. A chain attached to it tethered him to a ring bolted to the wall of the boat. There was a circle of crusted blood where the metal cut into the skin. From the look of it, that manacle had been there some time. Beside us the flame in the lantern sputtered as the boat swung in the storm. The candle was little more than a thumbprint of wax now. I thought about the shovel along the passage. Perhaps I could use it to break the chain?

I stood up abrupt and bent to take the lantern.

'I'll be back in a moment.'

'Don't leave me.'

Lucca caught at my sleeve. There was dried blood on his fingers. I raised the lantern and the light fell sharp across his battered face. He flinched from me like I'd beaten him.

'Lady!' At Lok's voice I swung about so fast the candle flame almost died. I heard a bumping sound.

'Mr Collins, Lady. I have him.'

Sam! He *was* here too? I went to the edge of the partition and saw a faint glow from the far end of the passage. The bumping came again. I turned back to Lucca who was staring in the direction of the sound.

He looked up at me. 'Sam?'

I nodded. 'I came here to find him with Lok and Tan Seng. I didn't expect to find you as well.'

'Lady!' Lok's voice echoed again.

'He is alive?' Lucca was speaking more to himself than to me now. The drops of sweat on his forehead glistened in the lamplight. I was right about that fever.

'*Grazie a Dio.*' He whispered the words and the chain rattled as he drew himself up against the metal wall of the boat. He buried his forehead in his hands.

'*Vivo! Grazie a Dio è vivo.*'

I glanced in the direction of Lok's voice. If I left the lantern with Lucca, there was just enough light coming from Lok's candle through the gap at the end of the passage to show the way.

'I'll leave this here with you, Lucca. When I come back – and it won't be long – we'll get that chain off. We're leaving this place – all of us.'

I ducked beneath the metal shaft and stepped around the wheel. Lok was sitting cross-legged on the boards with his back to me. He wasn't wearing his shirt now. I could see the bony curve of his spine in the dim light of his own little candle stub. There was a ripping sound and he hunched forward.

I heard a low moan.

Sam was slumped against the wall. Several buttons were missing from the shirt that hung loose on his spare frame. Dark stains marked the shoulder and spattered the right side of the cotton. His feet were bare, like Lucca's. A red mark around his right ankle suggested he'd been chained for a time too. I couldn't see the top half of his face, just the tip of his nose and his mouth showed beneath the bandage wound loose about his head. Lok had torn strips of material from his own shirt to make it.

I knelt down next to them.

'What's happened?' I reached forward to the makeshift bandages, but Lok caught my arm and shook his head.

'Kitty?' Sam stirred and tried to sit up straight. He turned in the direction of my voice. 'Is that you?'

'Yes.' I reached forward again and squeezed his hand. 'I'm here, Sam.'

He tried to smile, but of an instant, he gripped my fingers as if the effort of moving the muscles of his face caused him pain. 'I . . . I'd like to be able to say, Kitty, that you're a sight for sore eyes, but under the circumstances . . . I am grateful to you and . . . Mr Lok, is it?'

I nodded, but realised he couldn't see me. 'Yes, that's right and Tan Seng is here too.'

'You got our message, then?'

Our message?

Sam's mouth tightened with pain. He released my hand and his fingers brushed gently over my shoulder, finding their way to the side of my face. I could still smell the tobacco on them as he stroked my cheek. A jolt went through me again, just as it had with Lucca a minute before, only this was a feeling I couldn't quite catch.

'What do you mean, Sam?' I touched his hand.

'They made him do it – everything. He is not to blame.'

Something thumped overhead. Brittle shavings of dried soot pattered down over us. I looked up to see Tan Seng peering down from the hatch. He moved aside and another face filled the space, a face I recognised.

Chapter Thirty-six

When I saw Hari up there framed in the hatch I didn't understand what was happening. It was only when Tan Seng moved into view to feed a length of rope down to his brother that I caught on.

Tell truth, without Hari's muscle I don't know how we would have got Lucca out of there. Sam could stand – just about – but Lucca now, he was frail as a stray that's been locked in an outhouse for a month.

When it came to it, I didn't need the shovel to break the chain that tethered him to the wall. Lok reached into his pouch and drew out a thin metal hook. He fiddled with the lock on the side of the manacle and it fell from Lucca's ankle leaving a scabbed and filthy ring. As I held the lamp high and watched him work the lock, the wiry muscles of his thin back flexing in the candlelight, I thought again about all them years the brothers had spent with my grandmother.

Once Lucca was free, me and Lok carried him out of that stinking stall and back to the space beyond the wheel. When he saw Sam he tried to speak, but his voice was lost in another bout of violent coughing. Sam turned his bandaged head to the sound.

'Lucca?'

I answered for him. 'He's sick, very sick, I think. He needs to get out of here. We all do. Can you shift for yourself?'

Sam nodded. 'As long as someone guides me.'

Lok swung himself up first and then Sam went. It was hard, but he was able to climb part of the way using the rope and then Hari reached down, caught hold and pulled him through the hatch. I had to tie the rope beneath Lucca's arms so he could be hauled up and out. When it was my turn, I climbed up easy enough.

The cabin seemed crowded now.

Houtman and his shipmate were still stretched out across the boards. I caught a look pass between the brothers. Lok shrugged, he stared at the bodies and his fingers went to the pouch at his belt. He pulled the ties to seal it up.

'We go.' Tan Seng pointed to the step leading back to the cabin on deck.

Hari rested the oars in their locks and reached for the metal ring hanging from the edge of the quay to pull us close to the stones. The rowboat tossed like a gin stop on the swirling waters of the basin. The rain was still coming hard, but the storm had moved on. Occasionally I caught the rumble of thunder and a distant ripple of light in the sky, but the worst of it had passed.

Lok and Tan Seng sat up front. The brothers crouched close scanning the shadows that lined the basin. We didn't take a light from the boat. Better to move in darkness, Lok said.

Lucca's head rested on my shoulder. He shivered against me, but I could feel the sick heat of his body through the rags and the damp of my own clothes. He was rambling. I couldn't make sense of what he was saying, it was all a jumble of English and Italian.

'*Lei è la figlia.*' He clutched my hand. '*Sua figlia.*'

'Hush now. Save it.' I stroked his head and tried not to think about that painting of me at The Carnival. Turns out it wasn't blood on Lucca's fingers after all. It was paint – red paint.

They made him do it – everything. He is not to blame.

That was what Sam said. I tried to sort it through in my head, but it wasn't the time for following black thoughts down dark passages. Sam was huddled in the well of the little boat, his back jammed up against my legs. I could feel the blades of his shoulders through the damp stuff of my breeches. Lok's makeshift bandage was still tied round his head. Occasionally he reached up to keep it in place. I saw his fingers trembling.

Jesus! What had happened to the pair of them?

I put my hand on Sam's shoulder and he covered it with his. I felt the warmth of his skin as he held tight.

'Lucca's burning like a firebox. What happened, Sam? How did you two come to be—' I broke off. There were small stains spotting through the scraps of linen bound around his head.

'Not now, Kitty.' He tried to sound like his usual self, but I saw him flinch as the boat bumped hard against the basin wall.

Hari called out. I looked up. Through the rain I thought I saw a light and movement above us. A moment later another fraying rope end came dandling down. The brothers scrambled up the slimy wall one after the other and then they reached down to take Sam's weight as Hari guided him to the side and lifted him up. With the shifting about, the boat swung in the water. I had to grip the side with one hand and Lucca tight against me with the other to stop us from toppling over. He opened his eye and scrabbled for my hand.

'*Edie.*'

Christ! He was so far gone now he didn't recognise me. Something that wasn't rain trickled down my face. Lucca Fratelli was the best and kindest man I'd ever known, or was ever likely to. What had they done to him to make him paint those pictures of me?

Because they were his work – I was sure of it.

The boat rocked again as Hari turned back to sign that I should go next. It was easy enough once I'd freed myself from the tangle of blanket and rags huddled against me. I used the rope to clamber up and was grateful for the hands that pulled me over the top.

A welcome party was gathered on the quay – a gang of lascar boys, a dozen or so, were waiting there with Lok, Tan Seng and Sam. They all bowed when I straightened up. Two of them held lanterns, the lights muffled and dipped so a dull yellow glow licked the stones at our feet.

There was a scuffle from behind and Hari hauled himself over the edge of the quay with Lucca slung over one broad shoulder. He made it look easier than carrying a sack of cherries. Once he was up top, Hari swung Lucca round into his arms and without a word or a pause he strode towards the gates leading out onto Fox's Lane.

I started after him. 'Not that way. He can't.' I turned to Tan

420

Seng. 'It will be locked, and anyway the customs . . .' Tan Seng shook his head.

'It is arranged, Lady. We go now.'

He took Sam's arm and began to lead him off in the direction Hari had just gone.

I tried to call out again, but strands of wet hair caught across my lips. I'd left my cap on the boat and now the plait had worked itself loose. I looked back at the lascar boys. There was only five of them standing there now. Above the sound of the rain I heard the bump of the rowboat against the stones down below and then the splash of oars. I went back to the edge and peered into the black. A faint prick of light was bobbing about. I frowned as it slipped out across the water towards the *Golden Calf*.

'Lady!'

I turned. Lok beckoned. 'This way.'

The gates to Fox's Lane were open. When we came level, two of my customs officers were standing there under dripping black umbrellas. One of them had come from his bed. The tail of his nightshirt flapped about under his brass-buttoned coat. They raised their caps, but never said a word or blinked an eye as we walked straight past and out into the lane.

I didn't get the chance to question it. Not then, leastways. Lok quickened his step and scurried forward, keeping Sam close at his side. I went after them. Over to the left the bell of St Paul's started to strike the hour. We turned into the end of the lane, but I couldn't see Lok and Sam clear in the shadow of that big old church.

I heard a single rap and a clattering sound and then I was

blinded as the lamps of a great black carriage flared up.

I froze.

The horses whinnied and jigged about in the traces as Tan Seng stuffed the rags that had blinded the lights into his pocket. Up top, a driver tipped the rim of a hat that shadowed his face.

'Namaste, Lady.' I whipped about, but the wind plastered my hair over my eyes. I forced it back to see Ramesh Das standing beside the steps to the open carriage door. He was wearing a low round cap sewn with beads that glinted in the lamplight and a long frock coat of the old style. Beneath it a dark tunic reached to his ankles.

He bowed. 'We will return to The Palace. Dr Pardieu has already been summoned.'

I pushed the flailing hair away from my face again. 'But how . . .? How come you're here?'

'Your friend, Mrs Tewson, carried a message to me this evening.' He glanced at Tan Seng, who was fussing with the carriage lamps. The scene in front of me brightened. The carriage, the horses, Ramesh Das and Tan Seng – they all came up clear as day. It wasn't Tan Seng polishing the glass that made the difference. From behind us there was a muffled boom.

Of an instant, the end of Fox's Lane lit up like Guy Fawkes. There was another dull crump and the grate of metal against metal. A shower of sparks peppered the air. The rain falling on my cheeks now was black with smuts.

'Do you remember, Lady, when we spoke of the boy Mehal?' Ramesh Das stepped closer so we were standing to-gether. I looked up at him.

422

'The boy who ran away – Dalip's brother?'

He nodded. Another unnatural spurt of brilliance filled the air above the basin. As the light faded, the hollows beneath his eyes and cheekbones darkened. 'Mehal is found again and protected. He told a most interesting story. You will recall the word *khunni*? You thought it to be a name, Lady?'

A shower of cinders pattered around us.

'It means murderer – that's what you said.'

Ramesh Das nodded again. 'Poor Dalip was murdered that day on the quay because he recognised Captain Houtman.'

I shook my head. 'I don't understand.'

'Dalip worked at night as a pot boy at The Town of Ramsgate. Sometimes he carried food to the tables and booths. The night before he and his brother went to Shadwell New Basin with you and Mr Fratelli, Dalip saw Houtman with Matthias Schalk. They were together in a booth. You will recall I told you that Schalk was known and feared?'

I nodded. 'You said he was a devil. You all keep a watch out for him, or words to that effect?'

'Indeed. Dalip recognised Schalk that night. And the next morning at the basin he recognised Houtman again.' He paused. 'Unfortunately, Houtman recognised him too. It is my belief that he could not allow the boy to live in case he told of this connection. Mehal saw the captain push Dalip into the water. Houtman knew he would be crushed and drowned.'

Ramesh Das stared over my head at the pulsing clouds.

'I shall not mourn the man's passing or that of his associates. It was their time.' He gestured towards the carriage steps. 'Come, we must go.'

I swallowed and tasted coal and tar and metal. Over the roofs of the warehouses standing between us and the basin the rounded underbellies of the rainclouds glowed and pulsed with an eerie orange light. The rumbling that came now wasn't thunder.

'What about the other boats back there?' I swiped rain and that bleedin' hair from my eyes. 'There must be people on them.'

'They will have cut Houtman's vessel from the line first, to ensure that the damage is contained.' Ramesh Das glanced up as another burst of embers spurted over the warehouse roofs like the fiery licks off a Catherine Wheel.

'In your Bible, Lady, when Moses returned from the mountain he gave orders that the Golden Calf should be destroyed. Let me see if I can remember the words.'

He closed his eyes.

'*And he took the calf which they had made, and burnt it in the fire, and ground it to powder, and strawed it upon the water.*'

Chapter Thirty-seven

The carriage halted at the end of Salmon Lane. The dark was thinning over to the east, but the globe of the lamp on the corner still flickered with a sickly light. The carriage door opened and metal steps fell to the cobbles. Hari bent forward to gather up Lucca's body and then he squeezed his bulk through the narrow gap and carried him back along the passage. Lok and Tan Seng went next guiding Sam between them. Before I followed I shifted to the edge of the seat so I could see Ramesh Das clear.

'Thank you.'

He bowed his head. 'I serve you, Lady.'

'Why?'

'Because a debt must always be paid.' He raised the tip of the middle finger of his right hand to his forehead and bowed again.

'What debt?'

He shook his head. 'You must go to your friends.'

I stood and stretched out my hand. It was covered with scratches and cinder smuts. He took it and raised it to his lips.

'Lady.' He stared up at me. The yellow light caught the amber of his eyes. They glowed like the embers of a fire.

'The doctor will be waiting.'

I nodded and stepped down to the street. The carriage moved off as soon as I set my feet on the wet cobbles.

Pardieu shook his head.

'All we can do is wait. There will be a crisis and if he rides the storm – note I say *if* rather than *when*, Lady – there will be a chance.'

The room was fugged with sickness and naphtha. Lucca moaned and twisted in the bed between us. The sheets were already sodden with the sweat pouring off him. I dipped a strip of cloth into the china bowl on the washstand and dabbed at his forehead. His eyes rolled back in his head and he started muttering again. I didn't understand what he was saying, but I caught the same word over and over.

Figlia.

Pardieu reached for his bag and rummaged about inside. I heard the chink of glass. I wrung out the cloth and dipped again. Lucca's fever caught in the folds and made it warm to the touch. Peggy had gone to fetch another bowlful. She was waiting up for us when we got back to The Palace. Pardieu was there too, flapping about the hallway like a tatty jackdaw.

I lay the strip of cloth across Lucca's forehead.

'Do you know what it is, this sickness?'

Pardieu shrugged. 'I cannot be sure. It could be any one of a number of similar conditions. If it is the nervous fever, there is hope. If it is the Irish fever . . .' He stopped delving in the bag, sucked on them big front teeth and stared down at Lucca in the way that minded me of a mourner at a graveside. The old crow was dressed for it. The scuff on his black shoulders lay so thick I could reach over and write my name in it. They made a good pair, him and the Beetle. It wouldn't have surprised me to find they had a side going as mutes, ready for business at the drop of a coffin lid.

'A tincture of laudanum, Lady.' Pardieu worried his buck teeth again. He brought a small blue glass bottle close to the oil lamp by the bed and pleated up his eyes to read the label. He nodded to himself.

'Six drops every three hours. Dilute it in water – if you can get him to take it down it will calm him and prevent the excretions.' He passed the bottle to me. 'Someone should be with him at all times. When he burns, wrap him in cool, damp sheets. If his stomach hardens and swells like that of a woman with child or if you see marks on his body, a red rash, spontaneous stripes as if he had been whipped across the back or chest, send for me immediately.'

'Why – what does all that mean?'

Pardieu didn't answer. He snapped the bag shut and reached to the bed to turn Lucca's face towards him. Lucca spluttered like the Thames at high tide was frothing in his lungs. Blood was crusted round his nose. He started to mutter again.

'I did not think him to be a family man, Lady.' Pardieu shook his head.

My eyes swam with tears that brimmed over and tracked a path down my cheek.

'Are you saying I should inform his kin? Only if he's that bad, I don't think I can send a message to Italy in time. Anyway, there's likely only his sister now that his mother's—' I broke off. I saw it clear. Lucca had never gone back home, had he? I remembered what he told me that day in the hall downstairs when he took off.

Gia cannot write. Someone must have written this for her.

427

Bait – that letter was bait. The person who wrote that letter knew that Lucca Fratelli had a heart as true as Big Ben. They'd used his goodness as a trap.

I stared down at his face. For all that his blood was bubbling like gravy, he was almost as pale as the tangle of sheets beneath him. Even the lattice of scars that usually showed dark on his olive skin was grey. It lay on him like a cobweb.

'Lucca!' I tried to swallow a sob, but the tears rolled free. I bent to kiss his forehead and felt the clammy heat rising from him. His hands clawed at the linen and that muttering started up again.

Pardieu caught my shoulder. 'I would not advise such contact, Lady.' He paused. 'When I talked of his family I was not referring to a sister – there, he said it again.'

'Said what?' I wiped the back of a hand across my eyes.

'*Figlia*. I believe it is the word for daughter. The word is close to the Latin *filia*.' He held his head to one side. His dirty yellow collar showed beneath the curtain of limp grey hair. He looked like a dog waiting for a bone after walking two yards backwards on its hind legs.

He smiled thinly. 'Of course, the classical languages are the *lingua franca* of my profession.'

I didn't even bother to ask him what that meant. I just took Lucca's hand in mine and held tight.

'I'm here. It's Kitty.'

'Does he have a child?' Pardieu's voice was dusty as his coat.

Jesus! I was about to say something sharp, but the door opened and Peggy backed into the room with a basin of water in her arms.

'How is he, Kit?'

I shook my head. 'Not good. And I don't think you should be in here with him. Not with the baby. Leave it and get off to your own bed. You've had a night of it too, by all accounts.'

She set the bowl down and started to fuss at the sheets that had come free.

'Lok told me what you were going to do. He was worried. He came to see me just before you went off last night and asked me to go straight to Ramesh Das and tell him everything. He said to wait until you were gone and then leave by the yard gate.'

She straightened up and her face creased with concern as she looked down at Lucca. 'I did the right thing, didn't I?'

I nodded. 'I don't know how we would have got Lucca and Sam off that boat without help. How is he? Sam?'

'He's down in the parlour waiting for you.'

'In the parlour! Shouldn't he be . . .?'

'He was insistent, Lady.' Pardieu crossed the room to un-bolt the shutters. Morning light was slipping through the cracks in the wooden panels. He folded them back and pushed the window open. For the first time in days there was a cool draught. The storm had broken the heat. Light bounced off the windows opposite and sliced across the room.

He turned back to us. 'I have given Mr Collins morphine for the pain, but not enough to cloud his mind. He refuses to rest until he has spoken to you. I . . . I have done my best. The wound is clean and freshly bound. Time will tell if an infection has taken hold.'

Peggy sat on the end of the bed. 'He says he wants to speak to you, Kit. He won't take no for an answer. I'll stay with Lucca.'

⚓

Sam was sitting on the floor leaning back against the couch. He was wearing a fresh shirt and his long legs were stretched out in front of him, bare ankles poking out from the end of breeches that didn't seem to fit. I reckoned they was borrowed from Tan Seng.

He turned when I opened the parlour door. Only one side of his head was wrapped in bandages now. Pardieu had bound a clean white strip over his forehead in a diagonal that didn't cover his right eye. His brown fringe poked out at the side and the stubble on his jaw was thinking about a beard. He struggled to stand but I darted over.

'Stay there.' I knelt beside him. 'You should be resting, Sam.'

He shook his head. 'Not yet – there's too much to tell. I need to do it now, while everything is clear and while I can. Besides, I'm not sure what might . . .' He ran his fingers lightly over the bandage. 'How's Lucca?'

'Bad. It's like he's burning alive . . .' I heard the crack in my voice. 'If the fever breaks there's a chance. Pardieu's upstairs with him. He says he's given you something?'

Sam nodded. 'Morphine – what a wonderful thing. The pain is still there, but it's as if it belongs to someone else. Your medical man hit the dose just right. My brain is sharp, but my senses are numb. In other circumstances I could almost appreciate the appeal of it.'

He pushed the stray hairs poking out from under the bandage aside so he could see me clear.

'Your eye, Sam, is it . . .?'

'We'll make a matching pair for you now, Lucca and me. We could be bookends.' He tried to smile, but there was a tic to the side of his mouth that told of the effort.

'Christ!' I stared at the bandage, trying not to imagine what was under the cloth. 'What happened on that boat, Sam?'

He moved his hand back to his lap and balled it to a fist.

'It didn't start on the boat, Kitty. It started the day you asked me to find out about Lord Denderholm and those other men. When I began to make enquiries it seems I stirred up a vipers' nest. You remember my friend at the Bureau?'

I nodded. 'The one who shouldn't have given you that piece you ran in your paper?'

'Oh come now, Kitty, or perhaps, under the circumstances I should call you Miss Peck? I think we both know it's *your* paper. You are the proprietress of *The London Pictorial News*, aren't you?'

I didn't answer, but that didn't seem to matter. I don't think he meant it as a question. He carried on.

'That friend went missing. He vanished without leaving a message or a trace. His family are distraught. I found out the day I last saw you and I felt . . . responsible. It made me more determined than ever to find out what was in that mysterious file at the Bureau.'

'And did you?'

Sam shook his head. 'They got to me before I got to them. Just by asking questions about Denderholm it seems I

431

attracted attention to myself. The wrong sort of attention.'
He paused. 'Do you have a smoke?'

'I . . . I keep some in the drawer in my office. I'll go and
fetch them.' I made to stand, but Sam caught my sleeve.

'No – don't go. Please.' He smiled, properly. 'You really are
the Bohemian, aren't you? Smokes and breeches?'

I hadn't changed since we came back. Tell truth, I hadn't
given my rig a thought. Them wet breeches were scratching
my legs so I'd rolled them up to my knees. Sam stared at my
ankles. Of an instant, I felt like I was naked sitting there next
to him. His shoulder seemed to burn against mine. I shifted
so there was a gap between us, but I could still feel him.

'Go on then, Sam. What happened?'

'I received a message at *The Pictorial*. Very cryptic it was
too – a clandestine meeting after dark. The gist of it was
that if I wanted to know more about the activities of Lord
Denderholm and the London Imperial Agency I was to come
alone to an address in Whitechapel.'

'That don't sound like a clever thing to do.'

He shrugged. 'As I told you before, I have a network of
trusted . . . friends.' He turned to me, his eye fox-sharp beneath those tufts of hair. 'I imagine that's something you
know rather a lot about?'

'I don't know who you keep company with, Sam Collins.' I
looked away.

'It's not the people *I* keep company with I was talking
about.' He let that hang there for a moment. I felt his eyes on
my face.

'The fact of the matter, Kitty, is that it's not . . . unusual
for me to gather information from irregular sources. The

message mentioned a financial transaction, so it didn't smell wrong.'

He pulled up his legs and circled his arms around his knees. 'I went to Angel Alley with a packet of money in my pocket. Your money, I might add. I arrived just before midnight as instructed. The lamps were unlit, but it's a poor place so that didn't strike me as odd. I was told to look for the sign for Galley's – a furrier's merchant – down a side passage. I found the passage easily enough, but it was so dark there I couldn't see the cobbles at my feet. I struck a light and made my way along. Someone spoke my name – it came from behind. I turned, but at the same moment I was shoved in the back. I dropped the match and fell to my knees. Something rough – a sack, I think – was pulled over my head. I struggled, but there was a blow. It knocked me cold.'

'Is that how your eye . . . how you lost . . . ?'

'No – not then.' He unravelled himself and started to trace a pattern on the boards with the tip of a finger. 'You have to understand, Kitty, I don't blame Lucca for what happened. In his position . . .' He shook his head.

'What do you mean, "his position"?'

Sam scratched his right cheek. I could hear his nails scraping through the bristles. It was like he was considering what to say next, ordering his thoughts. He took a breath.

'When I came round I was curled up on the boards of a bare room. I say "room" but it could fit into my office at *The Pictorial* four times over. Perhaps cupboard would be a better description? There wasn't a proper window, just a dirty pane set high in the roof, and there wasn't a chair to sit on or a pot to . . . forgive the indelicacy.

'When I moved, the pain in my back and head made me cry out. At first I couldn't understand, but after a moment or so it all came back – the alley, the attack. I gritted my teeth, pulled myself together as best I could and went to the door. I wasn't surprised to find it locked, but I rattled the handle anyway and called out. It was Lucca who answered. He was trapped nearby – along the passage in a room as small and dismal as my own. He didn't know how long he'd been there, but he told me it was pointless calling out or trying to escape. He'd already tried everything. He sounded broken.

'They left us alone for two days – I could tell from the window. I came to think of it as a luxury. Poor Lucca was in the dark. We talked to fill the darkness. It was . . . a way to distract him.'

Sam turned to me. 'I learned a lot in those two days. A lot about you, I mean, Kitty.'

I didn't rise to the challenge in his tone. 'Was Lucca ill, then?'

Sam nodded. 'He was weak, desperately weak. I could hear that. And the things they had made him do wore at his mind. He kept telling me over and over as if he was confessing to one of his priests. I think it was a comfort to unburden himself.'

He paused and worried at that knot in the boards again. 'Those pictures, Kitty, Lucca told me about them. He'll never forgive himself. He said they told him exactly what they wanted and forced him to work while they stood over him. When he refused the first time, they beat him. And they . . . they made another threat.'

I'm sorry, Fannella, so very sorry. It was almost the first

434

thing Lucca said when I found him on the boat. The thought that he had painted those pictures was like a knife to the belly even though I knew he wouldn't have done it willing.

Sam reached for my hand. 'He didn't have a choice, believe me.'

An unaccustomed warmth shot up my arm and bloomed deep inside as he twined his fingers into mine. I stared in confusion at my hand wrapped in his.

'You mustn't blame Lucca. They are . . .' Sam faltered. 'I thought I'd seen evil in my time, real evil, I mean, not the stuff of fairy tales. The stories *Pictorial* readers seem to like best prove that man is a base creature, but these two . . . I'm not a great believer in such matters, but if ever a man could be said to be lacking a soul . . .'

I looked up. 'You said "they" – two of them. Who are they?'

'Both northmen. Dutch, Danish, perhaps? One – the worst of them – very fair. Tall, pale eyes that made me think of a wolf. The other bald and built like an ox. Lucca knew his name.'

'You mean the captain – Houtman?'

Sam nodded. 'They came in the night, bound our hands and feet and took us in a carriage to the docks. And that was an odd thing, Kitty, that carriage was a grand affair, not some shabby street hack. They muffled the horses, pulled the blinds and lowered the lamps to make sure no one could see us.

'As we travelled, the fair one started to goad Lucca. He told him they had another commission. He said it would be something that people would remember and a message

435

for you. Lucca said he would never paint for him again, no matter what, then he spat at him, hit him straight in his eye.' Sam pulled his hand from mine and reached to the bandage. 'That was a mistake.' I noted the tremor in his fingers again.

'This other man – the fair one – did you ever see him with a cane? A silver-headed cane with a bird at the tip?'

'Yes.' Sam turned to me. 'He had it with him in the carriage that night and later when he—' He broke off. 'Who is he, Kitty?'

In the corner Jacobin started up. I stood, but instead of uncovering him I went to the window and loosened the catch to let some air into the room. I stared down at the wet cobbles.

'You clearly know him – the man with the cane.' Sam's voice was hard. I swung back to face the room. He was standing now. Beyond him I could see his shoulders and the pin holding the bandage reflected in the mirror, and I could see myself framed in the window, my hair ragged as a pigeon nest, my face covered in smuts.

'Who is he?'

My reflection looked away.

'He ... his name is Matthias Schalk. He works for ... someone I have dealings with.'

Sam laughed, a bitter sound, and folded his arms. 'Is that all you're going to tell me? I think I deserve—'

'Not now, please.' I crossed the room and reached for his hand again, but he kept his arms tucked across his chest.

It cut me. 'Listen, I will tell you everything, I promise, but just now I need to hear you out so I can fit it all into place.'

The lines round his mouth tightened. 'I imagine it's quite a tale?'

I stared up at him. The space between us now seemed wider than the Thames.

'Please, Sam, finish it. Tell me everything. If not for my sake, for Lucca's.'

That tic went off in his face again. He glanced at himself in the mirror, his eye moved to the bandage.

'There's not a lot more. I don't know why they took us to that boat, but I was grateful to get out of that room. They didn't bother to blindfold us as we went on board and they didn't separate us, not then. They took us down below deck, untied our hands and chained us to the wall in the coal store where you found Lucca. At first they left a candle lantern and that was a blessing. Lucca told me you both knew this Captain Houtman and his paddle ship. He said you'd traded with him. Is that right, Kitty?'

I looked at the boards uncertain how much Sam knew about my trades. I nodded. 'A . . . a lascar boy died that day. Dalip, that was his name.'

Sam was quiet for a moment, then he carried on. 'We talked about what the man – Schalk, is it?'

I nodded again.

'We talked about what Schalk said in the coach and Lucca swore he wouldn't do it. But I remembered what he said about the next painting being a message for you, and I had an idea. We could send you a message too. They could have come back at any moment, so I had to move fast. In the short time we were alone I taught Lucca how to write something that only you could read. I wrote it again and again on a

437

patch of board with a nugget of coal. I made sure it was brief and simple, something that couldn't be malformed by him or misinterpreted by you. Remember what I told you, the "X" is singular?'

I frowned.

'In the phonetic alphabet, I mean, Kitty. Do you recall that day in the Fields when we talked about the Bible and all those irregular words? Lucca said you knew the boat. I hoped that if you saw my message, Exodus Thirty-two, you'd know immediately it was me and where to find me. Find *us*.'

'And you were right!' I tugged at his hand again. This time he didn't pull away. 'You told me that thanks to the phonetic alphabet, you knew the Bible better than the Archbishop of Canterbury. I knew it was you straight off. But then, on the boat, when I found Lucca, I couldn't understand ... It was *you* I was expecting, not him.' I paused. 'You were apart when I found you, Sam. What happened after you taught him how to write the words?'

Sam's grip tightened. 'I don't blame Lucca. You must understand that.'

'Blame him for what?'

Jacobin's beak rattled on the bars of the cage behind us. Sam cleared his throat again.

'When they brought Lucca back on board after that last painting, Schalk said he wanted to play a game of chance. He produced a deck of cards and told us to cut. The highest would be the winner, he said. Neither of us was in a mood for gambling, but Schalk was ... insistent. We weren't in a position to refuse.'

'It was a trick all along. We chose the cards he always

meant for us. Lucca cut first, nine of Spades, and then I turned the King of Diamonds. Schalk started to laugh with the other man, Houtman.'

Sam rubbed at the coal smuts on my fingers. We stood in silence until I prompted him.

'Go on, the card trick?'

I heard him swallow so hard it sounded like something was caught in his throat.

'Schalk congratulated me on making the perfect choice. He took the card from my hand and went through the deck, picking out all the other kings. He laid them out on the boards between us and asked why the King of Diamonds was special. Lucca caught his meaning immediately. They'd made a threat already, at the beginning when he wouldn't do what they wanted. He started to whisper in Italian. I think it was a prayer.

'At first I didn't follow what Schalk was driving at, but then I saw it. The King of Diamonds is always shown in profile.'

I waited, but when he didn't explain I squeezed his hand. 'I don't understand, Sam.'

'He has one eye, the King of Diamonds always has one eye. Schalk said that it would be the loser's forfeit. A single eye.'

I pulled my hand free and brought it to my lips. Ramesh Das was right: Matthias Schalk was unnatural – and he was a sick-minded vicious bastard with it. Sam didn't look at me as he carried on.

'Houtman took hold of Lucca's arms and pinned them to his sides. He dragged him round and presented him to Schalk like a gift, but I shouted out and tried to come between them.

It was ridiculous, of course. I was chained. I don't know what I expected to achieve, but at that moment all I knew was that I couldn't stand by and watch.

'Schalk began to laugh again – it was an odd high-pitched sound. Not something I'll ever forget – and then he told us he was prepared to be merciful.' Sam was careful now to rinse any trace of emotion from his voice.

'He said that as I was the *winner* of the game my prize would be to choose.'

The clock on the mantle went off. The tinkling tune that always came before the chimes was a mockery of the scene running through my head. When it stopped, Sam finished off, speaking as light as if he were describing a breakfast.

'Of course, there was no question about it. I couldn't allow Lucca to become blind as stone. That would have been the wrong choice.' He paused. 'I think I'd like that smoke now, Kitty.'

Chapter Thirty-eight

I closed the door behind me and leaned back against it. I could hardly see the little office for the tears glassing my eyes. There was a time when I thought myself a pretty piece, twirling about in the cage decked out as The Limehouse Linnet, but she was a bird of ill omen. Everything and everyone she cared about ended up as damaged goods. And that's if they was lucky.

When I thought about Lucca and Sam, my heart pounded against my ribs like a farrier shoeing a dray horse. I loved them both, I knew that now – one as a brother, and the other as something more. Tell truth, I think I'd known it for a time, only I didn't allow myself to take it out and turn it around in the light. And now . . .

What now?

I'd brought Sam Collins nothing but pain. Anything he'd ever felt for me was likely as dead and buried as poor Danny Tewson. I rubbed my face. When I went back with the smokes, I didn't want him to see I'd been crying.

The boards overhead creaked as someone moved around in the room above. It was where Peggy and Pardieu were tending to Lucca. I stared up at the ceiling and tried to imagine how it was for him, kept in a lightless room and forced to paint them pictures. There were still things – a lot of things, tell truth – I didn't understand, but I was certain of this – he never made it out of London. When he went off that day he was caught in a snare, just like Sam when he went to Angel Alley. Kite's man had trapped them both, but how?

How did Schalk work it?

Under the stage at The Gaudy (before it burned to a hole in the ground) there'd been an old-time mechanism – a greasy network of cogs and wheels that moved things around up top. It took a deal of sweat and muscle to work the machinery beneath the boards, but the punters never knew a thing when a painted forest or a distant castle slipped into place. All they saw was what was right in front of their eyes.

I was in much the same position now. There was something else at work here, something I couldn't catch on to. Just when I thought I saw a twitch in the corner of my eye it vanished quicker than one of Swami Jonah's birds.

Another board creaked overhead and my throat went tight as a miser's pocket. If Lucca wasn't actually hammering on death's door he was reaching for the knocker to join the rest of them: Danny, Old Peter, Amit Das, Edie Strong, Dalip, even that poor vain cow Netta Swift. In a roundabout way I was responsible for the woman they fished out of the Thames, the one who carried that letter to Telferman.

Blood was painted so thick on my hands I might as well have killed them all myself. And it wasn't like it was over.

Joey was still folded away in his grim little cell at the Bedlam. I hadn't had time to even think about him, let alone how to get him out of there. What would happen if I didn't hand him over at the Barons' Aestas session? I couldn't do that, not to my own flesh and blood, but, then again, what else could I do?

It was hopeless. *I* was hopeless. Tears streamed down my face. They slipped round my chin and slid down my neck under the soiled cotton shirt.

I wasn't a Baron. I was a joke to them – it was sharp and clear as the limelight. They were playing a game with me, testing me to see how much it would take to break the wings off the foolish little songbird from the halls. For Lord Kite it went somewhere deeper. I knew – no, that's not right – I *felt* a darkness at the heart of all this that was about something more than power.

It was personal. I thought about Ma and what they'd done to her. I was aware of an odd sound something halfway between a sob and a wail. I clamped my hand over my mouth and forced it down.

I thought of my grandmother's little bundle of opium sticks and, God forgive me, I wanted one bad. It wasn't the taste of the smoke I needed. It was the nothing. I understood now why she gave me them that day. Lady Ginger's pain wasn't a physical thing. No, what she felt inside was her soul rotting away.

I went to the mirror over the little fireplace and stared at my face in the glass, noting the lines around my mouth that hadn't been there a year back. I daresay most people wouldn't mark them, but I could read them plain. My eyes were different too. The eyes of the girl in the mirror were a hundred years old.

I recognised the woman looking back at me.

I took up a brass candlestick, stepped back and hurled it at the glass. It crashed, bounced back and clanged to the stone of the hearth. For a moment nothing happened. The girl in the mirror froze, and then there was a splintering sound as a thousand tiny lines obscured her face. The glass clouded white like frost on a pane of a winter morning and then, very slowly, almost delicately it crumbled to the mantle, little glittering shards of it tumbling to the hearth and out over the rug and the boards.

In the sunlight from the window, the shattered glass at my feet glinted like fresh clean snow.

Cold and hard as a diamond.

I stared at the mess. My grandmother's splintered little voice repeated the words over and over. I bent to take up a pinch of the glass and pressed it hard between my thumb and the tips of my fingers until blood ran red and vivid against the smuts.

She was wrong. Lady Ginger was so wrong about me.

I was glad I burned them black sticks. I wanted to feel the pain. It reminded me who I was – the girl who was never afraid; the girl who went so high in the cage every night the punters couldn't see her through the smoke; the girl with a fierce bright spark burning inside her that could fire every hearth in Limehouse, maybe every hearth in the whole stinking City.

No, I wasn't my grandmother and her way wasn't mine. But she was right about one thing. If it took the last breath in my body to bring the Barons to their knees, I would give it. I was more than they knew, I wasn't Lady Linnet. I wasn't their creature.

I was Kitty Peck.

It was like an exhilaration. It was like being up on that swing in Madame Celeste's attic the very first time, when the pins fell free and my hair came tumbling loose.

The air in the room was stale as the fug that had filled my head for the last weeks. I let the splinters of glass fall from my hand and went to the window, throwing it open to let a fresh cool draught into the room. It felt clean on my face. I closed my eyes and gulped down a lungful.

There was a scuffling sound and I opened my eyes to see that bold little sparrow on the sill. It cocked its head to one side as if it was about to remark on the broken glass scattered across the boards behind me. If I'd had any crumbs handy I would have fed it.

I reached out my hand. 'You come back later, Edie, and I'll have something for you.'

The sparrow ruffled its dull brown feathers and then it took off again. I wondered if it was one bird or a whole family of them packed tight in a nest.

Family.

Something Lucca said on the row boat came back.

Edie.

I thought he was rambling with the fever, but it came to me with a clarity that he wasn't. And then there was that other word he kept repeating.

Figlia.

Pardieu said it meant daughter. Lucca wasn't rambling, he was trying to tell what I should have seen a long time back. I ran to the pile of ledgers stacked on the desk. Everything in Paradise, every shoddy business I'd inherited from Lady Ginger, was listed there; the people I ran, their trade and their value down to the last brass farthing. I knew their names, ages, occupations and where they laid their heads of a night.

445

I took the ledger for the halls and flicked to 'S'. Blood from the glass cuts stained the page as I ran my finger down the column until I reached 'Strong'. Poor little Edie's name had a line through it, but just above there was her mother, Brigid.

I followed the line across. Brigid Strong lodged at Palmer's Rents, off Broad Street.

That pain twisted into my temples again. I was a fool. It was right under my nose all along. The stink of lyco from the tissue wrapping Netta's blue dress should have told me. I flicked back five pages to 'M'. I found the name I was looking for, but by then I was certain. I ran my finger over the page.

Lady Ginger's words came to me.

Family, Katharine, it is always a simple matter of family. Remember that.

Chapter Thirty-nine

Michael McCarthy held the tin mug tight between his hands, but I could see it shaking. Not through fear, mind. I didn't think it was fear. He was careful not to look at me. Instead, he stared out of the dirty window beyond the brass rail of the crumpled bed. I could hear Brigid crying beyond the door. It was a fluttering broken sound.

Their lodgings – a couple of rooms apiece – were on opposite sides of the same first-floor landing at Palmer's Rents, but once you was inside it was clear they lived together. A half door in Brigid's bedroom, where we stood now, connected to the rooms occupied by Swami Jonah.

It was early evening. The sun had been wiped from the sky with clouds the colour of old dish rags. I'd asked Tan Seng and Lok to come with me. On the other side of the door they was sitting together at Brigid Strong's scrubbed deal table like a couple of Sunday visitors with nothing to say for themselves.

It was a snug little home she'd made. I dialled that as soon as I went through her door. China dainties lined the shelf above the hearth and the big wooden chair drawn close to the fire – the chair of the man of the house – had a blanket knitted from red and green wool thrown over the back.

It was when you looked closer you saw it hadn't been cared for in a while. There was dust on the shelves and the crockery was looped with cobwebs. The air was thick with cheap liquor and stale bodies. There was a coldness in there too that had nothing to do with the day outside. The sorrow in that room seeped into your bones.

Brigid's face was gaunt and sallow. Her grey hair hung in a knot down her back. When she opened up and saw me standing at her door she shook her head, but she didn't say a word. She turned to look back over her shoulder and shuffled aside to let me in.

Michael McCarthy had been sitting at that table when we arrived. There was a tin mug in front of him, but I knew it wasn't tea. He stood up unsteadily, glanced at the door and then at the brothers. If he was calculating whether or not he could conjure up an exit for himself, he decided on the latter.

'Come to pay your respects at last have you, ma'am?' There wasn't a snuff pinch of reverence in his slurred Liverpool.

I stared at Swami Jonah's long face and tried to catch a likeness. Without his robes and his turban he wasn't a man you'd give a second glance on the streets of Limehouse. He was tall and colourless. The only oddity about him was the fact the right side of his bald head was covered with little dark moles that tumbled down over his brow and onto his face. I remembered then that Edie had a mole high on her left cheek near the corner of her eye.

I looked back at Brigid, who was still standing near the door, rolling her hands over and over. She was almost invisible against that drab board wall. Something about her put me in mind of the crumpled shell left behind after a new-minted butterfly has spread its wings and flown away.

'Your business is with me, not her.' McCarthy saw me stare

at his woman. 'Look at her, she's . . .' He broke off as his voice thickened.

He cleared his throat and spat into the grate, a man again.

'It's me you want.'

'If you say so, Mr McCarthy.'

'We'll talk together then – just me and you. Through there?' He jerked his head at the door behind him.

'You'll be all right, Brigid.' He moved away from the table. 'Sit yourself down here – these men won't hurt you, will they?' The question was for me.

I shook my head. 'I give you my word.'

'This way.'

He picked up the mug and walked over to a wall cupboard by the hearth. He took out a brown glass bottle and then he went to the door and opened it wide for me to go into the bedroom first. He closed the door, leaned back against it and pulled the stopper from the bottle. I heard the liquor rattle into the tin.

'I've been waiting long enough. I knew you'd come, eventually. I won't offer you any. I don't think this is a social call, is it?' He rested the bottle on the boards near his feet and raised the trembling mug to his lips.

'You might as well sit.' I pointed at a chair pushed up against the wall. There was a shirt that might once have been white hanging over the back, the tails trailing on the boards. I knew it as one he wore for his act from the trick pockets hanging loose on the sleeves.

'I'm not taking orders from you. Not any more.'

I tried to imagine myself in his place. He didn't seem scared. Defiant – that's how he was. I curled my fingers tight around the handle of my bag. Tell truth, I didn't rightly know what I was going to do with him. All I knew was that I wanted some answers.

'Suit yourself. You won't be taking anything from me after today, Michael McCarthy.'

'Well, isn't that always the way of it, Kitty Peck … or whatever name you go by these days – Lady Linnet, is it? You do all the taking – and you couldn't give a tinker's shit for anyone else.'

I let the insult hang in the air. He wanted to pick at his wound until it bled.

'This is about Edie, isn't it?' I kept my voice low and even.

He stared direct at me now.

'You're not fit to say her name, you cold-hearted bitch.'

I swallowed. 'She was your daughter, wasn't she? You and Brigid – you … the pair of you?'

He took a gulp from the mug. As he moved I caught a wet glint in his eyes. I realised he was struggling to keep himself strong.

'We've been together for seventeen years now. It wasn't a secret, as such, but we kept it quiet. There was a girl back in Liverpool. We married young. In the eyes of the law she's still my wife. I wasn't free to marry Brigid, but she's …'

'She's your wife – good as, anyhow.' I finished for him.

'You think you know everything, don't you?' He rubbed the back of a hand over his face.

I took a breath. 'I think you killed Netta Swift. And there's some other things I've been thinking about too, but I want to hear it from you so I can fit it all together.'

'You killed my girl. Good as, anyhow.' He parroted my

own words back at me, slicked with sarcasm.

I shook my head. 'You're wrong. The fire at The Gaudy was an accident. I didn't . . .'

I stopped. I wasn't the one on trial here.

'Fifteen years old she was, just turned, and now it's like she never existed.'

Michael McCarthy balled a fist and thumped the door so hard that plaster fell from the ceiling. It coated his shoulders like the chalk dust he used to whiten his mangy pigeons.

'Magic – that's my trade, but I can't bring her back from the dead.' I flinched as he stepped forward and clicked his fingers in my face. Gin splashed over the rim of the mug and spattered the boards between us.

'Gone without leaving a trace on the world.'

His hand moved to his head, tracing the line of moles on his cheek. 'I've lost them both. Brigid's not been right, since . . . But you wouldn't know that, would you? Seeing as how you didn't trouble yourself to find out. You carried on flouncing around, giving your orders like nothing had happened when our girl was . . .' He stopped as his voice cracked. I watched his shoulders move as he fought to steady himself.

'That's the point, isn't it? We don't even know where she is. After the fire, me and Brigid, we didn't even have a body to bury. There's just a gaping black grave in the ground where The Gaudy used to be.'

I remembered something Lucca told me.

'The flowers – all them white flowers? That was you?'

'It was all we could do, and all we had to show our girl that we . . .' He faltered again. 'Brigid won't come now. She won't leave the Rents. Our Edie was nothing to you, but she was everything

451

to us. *Everything.* Our lives are empty – there's no future and the past has been stolen away. You want to hear it *all* from me, do you?' He tried to imitate my voice again, but the liquor firing his blood made Liverpool stronger than the Limehouse.

I nodded.

'I think I'll sit now.' He grabbed the bottle, pulled out the chair and sat down heavily in front of me, his black eyes locked onto mine.

'Why don't you sit too, ma'am? Or are you afraid of me?' He tipped back the mug.

'No – I'm not afraid, Mr McCarthy. I just want to hear what you have to say for yourself.'

'Before you pass sentence?'

I didn't answer. I sat on the edge of the bed.

'Go on then.'

I watched his face. A muscle twitched in his jaw.

He belched. 'Not in front of a lady.' He gave the word a nasty insolence and tutted.

'This is how it goes.' His eyes slid to the window again. 'I was at The Eagle on Cock Hill. It was just a couple of days after the fire at The Gaudy, but I already knew Edie wasn't coming back. The gin doesn't make the pain go away, but it swallows the time. I never had much call for it before, not like Dismal . . .'

He shook his head and took another swig.

'And then you came through the door bold as brass – all done up like a right fancy tot. I was surprised to see you alone in Broad Street and I watched you, making eyes at the barman, flashing your coin and all the while my little girl was . . .'

He wiped a hand across his mouth and swayed on the

chair. This wasn't what I expected. I'd never been to The Eagle alone, fact of the matter I'd never been there in company. It was a low sort of place – a stand-up where the drinkers are packed in so tight there's no room for seats.

As I waited for him to go on, something began to shape in my mind. I knew someone who most probably *had* been to The Eagle at the beginning of May, someone who looked a deal like me.

'You finished up smart and then you left. My head was swilling with gin and misery. But I saw one thing clear – I wanted to let you know what I thought of you so I followed. I saw you swishing away up the street like you owned the place and it came to me that there was something wrong in the world if you lived and my Edie . . .'

He looked down into the mug like he could see her there.

'I had one of the knives from the act with me. I generally carry one about – a person needs protection of an evening in Limehouse. You turned into a side passage and it was like a sign. This is your chance, Jonah, I said to myself.' He grunted and took a swig.

'I took aim and let fly. It hit you, I know it. I saw you go down and I was glad.'

Of an instant, it fell into place. It was my brother he'd followed from the stand-up, not me. I remembered what Joey told me when I went to the Bethlem. After he left Nanking Nancy's he said he was ashamed.

I went to a gin shop on Cock Hill. I think I spoke to someone there. When I left I was followed. There was a knife – I know that much. I saw it fall in the gutter. A silver knife with a bone handle.

McCarthy set down the mug, locked his fingers together and bent them back until his knuckles cracked.

'Of course, it was the liquor. I wouldn't have missed otherwise. Perhaps I convinced myself to see what I wanted? Two days later there you were lording over us all at The Carnival, not a mark on you. I hated you even more then – and I hated myself for failing.'

He leaned forward. 'I wanted you to feel how I felt. To know how it feels when everything you love, everyone you care for, is taken or hurt. And then I met a man who offered to help.'

His lips twisted into a sour smile. '"You help me and I'll help you, Mr McCarthy." That's what he said. We drank a toast on it.' He reached for the mug at his feet and raised it to me.

'*Proost!*'

I felt that cold whisper again on the back of my neck.

When I was small I had a toy that frightened me so much, Nanny Peck had to hide it away on the highest shelf of the cupboard in Ma's room. It was a Jack-in-a-box, only the Jack had outspread claws and the grinning red head of a devil. I remember the way that twisted little face grinned up at me as it flailed around, the wooden hands scratching against the painted side of the box.

At the beginning, I thought I knew where this was leading, but now I'd opened the box there were things springing out that were a thousand times worse than that wooden devil.

I stared at the drunken man in front of me.

'Matthias Schalk? Is that who you mean?'

McCarthy nodded. 'Mr Schalk was introduced to me by

Netta Swift. I knew he wasn't to her ... usual taste. But *you* know what Netta was like, don't you? We all do. She didn't ask questions – she just took what she wanted.'

He jiggled the mug and scratched at his wrist. The raw skin of his hands was cracked and blistered. His nails were long for a man and filed sharp – something to do with the act, I reckoned, them nails were for the cards, the catches on the boxes and the secret pockets in his clothes.

'Turns out Mr Schalk and I had something in common. A couple of weeks after Edie ...'

He scratched and started again. 'I was drinking one evening at The Lamb and he was there with Netta. She went off, but he stayed tight with me and we talked about my girl. I told him everything about that night on Cock Hill – how I hated you and wanted to see you die inside like me and Brigid. He listened to me most careful and then he told me he had some powerful friends who wanted to see you brought low. And he asked if I wanted to help him.'

McCarthy took up the bottle again and filled the mug to the brim.

'I wish to God I'd never agreed.'

He gulped down another mouthful and was silent for a moment.

'It was small stuff at first. I didn't feel right about what he asked me to do to Danny Tewson's girl, but at least it didn't hurt her, not like ...'

'Peggy?' That devil on a spring bobbed up again. 'You mean that was you? The shit on her step at Risbies, the business with the cat. The hair ...?'

McCarthy nodded. 'She was your friend, wasn't she? It was

like a game to him. Schalk. He knew all about you – everyone you cared about, anyway. I never understood why he wanted that lock of hair, or why he asked me to bury that ring in the shit, but he said *you'd* understand.'

He stared at me and I looked away.

'Then it was Lucca Fratelli.' I heard the clink of bottle on tin as he filled the mug.

I kept my voice flat as Hackney Marshes. 'Go on, McCarthy, you might as well tell me everything.'

He set down the bottle and plucked at some straw poking out from the tattered seat of the chair.

'Might as well.' He pulled the straw free. 'As a matter of fact I don't . . . didn't, dislike Lucca, but I knew how thick you two were. When Schalk said he had a particular use for him and asked me to help him with it I was happy to oblige. He said he wouldn't be hurt . . . that's what he told me then, anyway.' McCarthy rolled the dry straw between his thumb and forefinger until it crumbled to the boards. 'We had a long chat one afternoon in the workshops, Lucca and me. I'd asked him to freshen the paint on one of my properties and as he worked we talked about family, his family, mostly.

'When he got to the station that morning to take the boat train, I was waiting. I told him that you'd been taken ill and that he was to come back to Limehouse with me immediately. Very solicitous for your health I was. It was quite a performance, if I say so myself. Of course Lucca followed like a lamb – he'd do anything for you. I led him out to the carriage where Schalk was ready – and that was the last I saw of him.'

He tugged another straw free and I pulled at something he said.

'You said, you "didn't dislike" Lucca, as if he was something past. What do you mean?'

McCarthy shifted on the chair. 'As I understand it there's a boat. Your friend will be wrapped in oilcloth and resting at the bottom of the Thames estuary by now. That was the plan – it's what Schalk told me. Lucca's served his purpose.'

He grunted and drank deep again. 'We all have – me, Lucca and Netta.' He waved the mug and gin sloshed onto his shirt. 'Those paintings. I understand they were quite something to behold. I only saw the last one at The Carnival, but I hear they were all . . . very artistic. He was a rare talent, was Lucca.'

I couldn't hold it now. I stood abrupt, went over and slapped his face. It wasn't for my sake I did it. It was for Lucca. For what they made him do, and for the fact that the man in front of me had handed him over to them.

'Judas!' I spat the word in his face. 'No, that's not right, you're something worse. At least he did it for coin – there's something straight about that. You did it out of hate.'

McCarthy rubbed his cheek. He couldn't bring himself to meet my eyes when he answered.

'You're wrong. There was chink involved at the beginning. I had it in mind to start again. Brigid and me – I thought America might be the place. No memories for us there, see?' His eyes slid down to the mug. 'But you're right. It wasn't for the money. I wanted you to hurt like we did, here.'

He plucked at his stained grey shirt over his heart.

'But it went too far. By the time I realised what Schalk was . . . what he wanted me to . . .'

He cradled his forehead in one of his cracked hands.

'We tried to get out one evening. I thought I could disappear and make it stop. We don't have much, but I packed a bag and we left the Rents when it was full dark. You've seen her, Brigid, she didn't know what was happening. Schalk followed us. I don't know how he knew . . . Maybe he should be the magician, not me. He cornered us in Love Lane.'

McCarthy coughed and a little pool of greenish spittle slicked the boards in front of him. He stared down at it, wiped his hand over his lips and cleared his throat.

'He . . . he held that cane of his to Brigid's throat and told me that if I didn't carry on doing just what he and his friends wanted he'd rip her neck open and push that silver hawk so far down her gizzard he could hook out her lights. I didn't doubt him.'

He glanced up at me. 'And as you seem to know Mr Schalk, I'm sure you understand what I mean?'

I didn't answer. The satin ribbons of my bonnet tightened around my throat.

McCarthy turned the mug in his hands. 'It was all a mess. This . . .' he tapped his long nails against the tin, 'made it better some days, but mostly it made it worse. I couldn't think straight enough to see a way out. I blamed myself, but most of all I blamed you. It all started with you. All the black was in you. It was your fault.'

'That's not right and you know it. You're talking like a Bedlam.' I pushed his shoulder hard so he had to sit upright and look me in the eye. The chair rocked.

'You ever lost a child?' He stared up at me. The grey pouches slung beneath his eyes gave him the look of a carnival ghost. I took a step back. There was a sort of madness burning there.

'Jonah – that's my stage name, but by rights it's yours. That's what Fitzy says. I watched you all the time, wondering why a person like you was allowed to live when my Edie was . . .'

He lifted the mug and swallowed another mouthful.

'I followed you from The Carnival that day you went to see Peggy Worrow at Risbies. I saw you down in the hall and then I wanted to see where you went off to on your own. I watched you two together outside her lodgings and I saw her lash out. Do you know what I thought then?'

I brushed some lint from my skirt and sat down on the bed again. 'I'm not the mind-reader here, Swami Jonah.'

He rubbed the scabbed back of his hand against his breeches. 'I thought – there's another one who hates you, Kitty Peck. And then I felt a knife from the act in my pocket and I thought about my Edie.' He shrugged. 'You were too far away and I was too far gone. But I rattled you. I saw that.'

'You bleedin' coward, McCarthy. You could have hit Peggy!'

At least he had the grace to look guilty. 'Like I said, this . . .' he raised the mug, 'made my thinking as bad as my aim. That evening, at The Carnival, I went on as usual, but it was a mistake. There was an . . . incident.'

'Incident! You fell off the stage, Netta told me. You tipped over the rail, crashed into the pit and snored like a hog while your birds flew around and shat on the punters.'

McCarthy scowled at me. 'She told you that, did she, your fancy piece? She wouldn't let it go. Every time I saw her after

459

that night she made fun of me. They all laughed at me – Netta made sure of it. She couldn't let them forget it. She had a vicious tongue in her head, your friend, and she used it. That's why I didn't much care what happened next, not at first. We all knew how you felt about her. How you and she . . .' He held his head to one side. 'She told us all about you – the two of you, what you got up to together.'

He muttered something into the mug as he swilled the last dregs around.

'I didn't catch that.' Tell truth, I heard him all right.

'I knew you cared for her. That's what I said.' He stared at me and his eyes wandered off to the window again. I realised it was because he was so deep down that brown bottle he couldn't focus.

'Go on – Netta. What happened?'

'It was all arranged – I took delivery of *your* gift at The Carnival that day.'

'My gift? I never sent her nothing.'

He drained the mug and tried to fill it again, but the bottle was empty now. He peered down the neck like he couldn't believe the gin was gone and then he dropped it to the boards. It clanked against the chair leg.

'*I* know it wasn't from you, but no one else in the halls believes that. Schalk was very particular about the details. Netta Swift had to die on stage wearing that blue dress. Everyone was to think you sent it to her as a gift to celebrate her first solo performance. I was ready. Before taking it up to her I dusted the hem and the inside of the sleeves and the bodice with dragon's breath.'

'Lyco! That's what you used on her?'

460

Of a general rule you didn't need more than the smallest pinch to make a flash on stage. You didn't want to get it on your skin on account of the sores. That's why his hands were scabbed and why Marnie came out in a rash when she helped Netta with the dress.

'You must have used a bleedin' year's worth in one night.'

McCarthy nodded. 'I had to be sure, you see. It had to look like an accident. I told him beforehand about the smell – stinks of rotten meat, it does, when you use it in any quantity – so before he sent the dress to The Carnival he doused it in that cologne of his. When she opened up, Netta thought it was a gift all right, but despite what she said, she didn't think it was from you.'

He coughed and scrabbled for the tin mug at his feet. 'I think I'll fetch—'

'No – you'll finish your story first. The lyco – you needed it to make sure she'd go up like a Roman Candle?'

McCarthy coughed again. 'I couldn't rely on the flares, Netta was too experienced on stage to make that mistake. It was a simple thing to conceal a lighted Lucifer in the folds of the skirt, just before she went on. Sleight of hand . . . always a speciality of mine.'

Jesus! He was proud of his craft. I thought about the way Netta Swift died on stage. I heard her song turn to a scream of agony and I saw her black hair burn bright like a vicious halo.

Christ knows, she wasn't an innocent, but no one deserved that.

I wondered what Schalk had promised her. She must have been there that night when he forced Lucca to paint that picture of me up in the gallery at The Comet. She'd stolen the keys from Jesmond, after all. She was the first person to tell me about the other paintings too. She must have thought she was playing a clever game stringing us all along, including Jesmond.

Netta Swift was sharp as an oyster knife and slippery as the meat in the shell. But even she wasn't clever enough to see that Matthias Schalk was pulling her strings.

And I knew who was pulling his.

Can you be sure of anyone in Paradise, Lady Linnet? Think about that later, when you are alone.

That was what Kite meant that night when I met him at Temple Church. I thought he was trying to rattle me, but he was simply stating fact. I wondered who else he'd bought or bullied into his service. Something gnawed at the walls of my belly. This wasn't over, not by a long way.

I sat up straight on the bed and folded my hands tight in my lap.

'How could you see a woman suffer like that? The way she died . . . it was . . .' I couldn't find the right word as the fatty smell of burning flesh came back to me. 'She'd never done nothing to you, Michael McCarthy, not really, nothing beyond laughing at you. And even if you thought me and her were . . . together, it wasn't a reason to kill her.'

He swallowed. 'When it came to it I didn't want to do it, not even to Netta. I didn't have the taste for it, like I'd had a taste for the gin he bought me. But that night when we tried to leave and he caught us, he took Brigid and told me I'd never see her again if I didn't go through with it. I couldn't let him hurt her. Not that too.'

He started to hack again and it turned into something

between a choke and a sob. He wrapped his arms around himself and began to rock back and forth.

'He's a man of his word, our friend Mr Schalk, I'll say that for him. He gave her back after ... after what happened to Netta. But my poor Brigid hasn't spoken a word since.'

The liquor caught up with him now. He crumpled on the chair and then he toppled sideways from the seat to the floor where he curled into a ball. He covered his face with his scabby hands and started to weep.

I sat there silent and watched him. I thought about Netta and then I thought about Lucca and Sam and what his actions had brought them to. My hands locked together so tight I thought the knuckles might burst through the skin.

After a minute or two McCarthy quietened. He hauled himself up into a sitting position against the wall. I thought he was about to say something more, but he belched again. His body jerked and a stream of greenish liquid burst from his mouth, covering his shirt front. His head lolled slowly to his chest and I could see the moles across the top of his bald scalp. He started to scrape the boards with the long nails of his left hand. The sound of it made my flesh crawl.

The man sprawling in front of me deserved to suffer. As I listened to his drunken scrabbling I decided I'd make a public show of him that no one in Paradise would be likely to forget. The shadows in the room were deepening now as the last of the daylight crept away.

McCarthy started mumbling to himself. At first he rambled about Brigid and then seemed to be talking direct to Edie.

'. . . everything to us you are. Our little girl, our little diamond.'

I caught the echo of Lady Ginger in my head.

Cold and hard as a diamond.

'No!'

I said it aloud. McCarthy shifted to stare at me. There was no defiance in his cloudy eyes now, just fear and something like shame.

'Brigid had nothing to do with this. She's suffered for what I did. You need to remember that afterwards, Lady.'

Tears dribbled down his face.

Afterwards?

I stood up abrupt. 'What was in that bottle?'

'Gin.'

'Gin and what else?'

I snatched it up from the board and held it to my nose. The stink of rough liquor was there and beneath it another bitter tang – almond.

'Death.'

I heard the rattle of it now. McCarthy coughed some more of that bleedin' green stuff out.

'I served my purpose too, Lady Linnet. I don't deserve to live. I knew you'd come after me sooner or later. When you did, I wanted to give you something to remember me by. And you can remember Edie too, while you're at it. You might call it my last vanishing trick.'

He started to laugh, but it drowned in his throat.

Chapter Forty

I pushed open the door and ran to the side of the bed. I tugged at the ribbons and threw the bonnet to the rug.

'How is he?'

Peggy looked up. 'Better, much better, I think. His skin's cool to the touch now. Feel.' She shifted to let me sit on the edge of the mattress. I rested my hand against Lucca's face. He was calm and still and the sheets beneath him weren't sodden with fever. The circle of lamplight hugged the three of us close.

'Has he woken yet?'

She shook her head. 'It's no bad thing. I've been sitting with him ever since you took off.' She paused and I felt her eyes on me.

'You going to tell me where you've been or is that another one of your secrets, Kit?'

I thought about Michael McCarthy's body slumped against the boarded wall and the sound of a woman weeping. When I realised he was dead I didn't know how I felt. Part of me was glad on account of what he'd done, I'll admit it. But another part of me felt a terrible pity for him. I'd taken a thin blanket from the bed and draped it over him to hide the mess. I'd wiped his face and propped him against the wall. Then I'd opened the door.

I'll never forgot the look on Brigid Strong's face when I led her into that room.

Family, Katharine, it is always a simple matter of family. Remember that.

Only it turns out it wasn't a simple matter after all. In my experience that was the very last thing I'd say about family. I thought about McCarthy grieving for his girl and watching my brother dabbing it up as a frock in The Eagle – making eyes at the barman, flashing his coin.

That didn't sound like someone who was ashamed of himself, did it? But it sounded like Joey Peck. There was a time when my brother was everything to me. But that was long past. My family was gathered in this room. I stroked Lucca's face, pushed his dark hair away from his eyes and bent to kiss his forehead.

I sat back and took Peggy's hand.

'I . . . I did something I should have done a long time ago. I went to see Edie's Strong's mother.'

'Brigid?' Peggy stared at me. 'You chose a funny time to pay your respects – what with Lucca and . . .' She shook her head. 'It's not . . . I mean, with everything like it is here why would you go to her?'

I squeezed her hand tight. 'I had to. It was important. There were things that . . . needed to be said. Besides, I knew by then Lucca would come through. I was sure of it. I wouldn't have left him with you otherwise.'

I tried to smile, only it didn't come easy.

Lucca's fever had broken in the early afternoon before I went to Palmer's Rents. I'd sat with him for four hours, laying strips of soaked linen across his head and doing my best to untangle his limbs from the knot of sheets. Pardieu was right – the laudanum calmed him eventually and gave his body the chance to ride it out. At last he lay still and his breathing came steady in his sleep. That was when I knew I could leave.

Peggy had sat with him all the time I was with Michael McCarthy.

I glanced past her to the door. There was someone else I wanted to see. He was in another room across the hall.

When I went back into the parlour with the smokes, Sam had been sitting on the floor with his back against the couch, his bandaged head resting on his knees. It was only when I sat down next to him that I realised he was asleep. Pardieu's laudanum had finally run through his blood. Lok and Tan Seng had carried him up to the room next to Peggy's and helped me lay him on the bed. I closed the shutters so the light wouldn't disturb him and I put the smokes and another bottle of laudanum on the nightstand in case he woke in pain while I was gone.

When the brothers left the room I sat on the bed for a little while watching Sam Collins sleep.

We'll make a matching pair for you now.

The two men I cared most about in all the world had suffered because of me.

I let go of Peggy's hand and reached out to smooth Lucca's pillow. He murmured as I pulled it straight, but he didn't wake.

'Can you sit with him for a little while longer, Peg? I'm going to see Sam.'

'It's too late.' Peggy shook her head.

'What do you mean, too late?' The words lodged in my throat. 'He's not . . .' I couldn't even say it.

'Of course not, Kit. He's in a better way than Lucca.' A

great golden flower bloomed beneath my ribs. Of course, it was the lateness of the hour she meant. I turned away so she couldn't see my eyes.

'Don't worry. I won't wake him. I just want to see that ...' I just wanted to see him. That was the truth of it.

'No, I mean he's gone, Kit. He left about an hour before you came back. I was in here and I heard him on the stairs, so I went out.'

'You should have stopped him. He was in no state to leave.'

'I couldn't force him to stay, could I? He was down the stairs and in the hall before I could catch him. Off like a sight hound after a hare he was.'

My heart started rapping out so loud I was sure she could hear it.

'What did he say?'

'Nothing much – just that he had to get going. I offered to change that bandage for fresh linen, but he wouldn't wait.'

'Did he ... did he leave a message?'

Peggy stared at me. I saw the beginnings of an understanding creep across her face. She opened her mouth to say something but I looked away again, sharp.

'You get off to bed, Peg. I'll sit up with Lucca.'

It was only when she'd gone that I started to cry. I curled myself into a ball in the chair beside Lucca's bed and let the tears slide down my face. I stared at the flame of the candle lamp and didn't even bother to wipe them away.

I'd lost him. Sam knew exactly who and what I was now and he couldn't get away quick enough. I didn't blame him. I remembered a story book Joey had as a child – myths and legends from way back. Full of angry gods and punishments it was. There wasn't much love in it. One of the stories came back to me now, something about a king who made a wish that everything he touched should turn to gold. Turns out it was a curse not a blessing.

Everything I touched turned to dust.

I must have fallen asleep in that chair – the first real sleep in days. When I woke light was coming through the shutter boards and Lucca was looking at me. He smiled and reached out. He tried to say something, but his voice was barely a whisper. I took his hand and bent close.

'*Grazie. Grazie mille, Fannella.*'

I went to the bed, kissed his forehead and held him tight.

'I don't deserve thanks, Lucca.'

The Beetle stared at the bare boards in the gilded frame. If he wondered what had happened to the mirror, he didn't ask. When I came back into my office at The Palace the broken glass had all been brushed away. In the early morning sunlight I could see some tiny glinting shards lodged between the floorboards, but that was all Lok had missed.

Telferman sniffed and pushed his spectacles up his nose.

'I am glad you asked to see me this morning, Lady. I have something here for you ...' he tapped the battered leather case on his lap, 'and there is a matter of greater urgency.'

'No!' I leaned across the desk. 'Not today. That's not how this meeting goes.' I pushed the sheet of paper across the desk. 'Brigid Strong. I want her cared for. The best place that my money can buy. I want to know where she is and how she

469

is. I want regular reports. That's her address – written down there.' I pointed at the paper. 'I want her to be treated gentle and with respect. Is that clear?'

He pulled the sheet towards him and glanced at me.

'I understand that she is . . . that is to say, that she is associated with . . .'

'Mr McCarthy – Swami Jonah. Is that who you mean?'

He nodded. 'That is correct. I believe the two of them are . . .'

'Not any more they're not.'

Telferman stared across the desk.

'He's dead.'

The Beetle's eyebrows shot up, the straying grey hairs bristling like horns. 'Poor woman. First her daughter and now her . . . It is a great misfortune.'

'Something of that nature. I want him buried decent and I want Edie's name beneath his on his stone – she was his girl after all. You will arrange it, Mr Telferman.'

'Of course.' The Beetle picked at his yellow nails. 'This is very sudden. Mr McCarthy was always useful to your grandmother. His contacts were sound except in the case of . . . Ah . . .' He looked up and his nose wrinkled like he'd caught the scent of a good meat pie fresh from the oven.

'Captain Houtman – the contact came through McCarthy.'

'That don't surprise me.' I opened a drawer in the desk and took out a sealed envelope as the Beetle went on. 'And, of course, you are aware of what happened to Houtman's boat, the *Gouden Kalf*, two nights ago?'

I scrawled a name on the envelope without looking up. 'I reckon you already know the answer to that.'

I heard Telferman drum his fingers on his case. 'A most unfortunate accident. The lightning was attracted to the metal of the funnel. There were no survivors.'

'Did Mr Das tell you that?'

'Indeed, Lady.' Telferman nodded solemnly. 'Now, if I may, there are several matters—'

'Wait.' I handed him the letter. 'This is for Mr Das. As it is not addressed to you, I trust you won't open it. It will be best for you if you don't know what's inside. It relates to my brother.'

Immediately, he dropped the letter onto the leather of the desk top like it burned his fingers. He snapped open the case and I heard the rustle of papers as he filed it carefully away.

I promised Joey I'd get him out of Bedlam. The letter was the beginning of it.

The Beetle continued to rummage about. After a moment he pulled out a stack of ribbon-bound documents and a large rectangular parcel wrapped in brown paper. He placed them between us.

'These are for you – items from Lady Ginger. Matters relating to the estate and several other—'

I held up my hand. 'One more thing before I let you have your say. Are you familiar with the passages down by Bell Wharf Stairs?'

'Familiar is not a word I'd use, but yes, I know of them.' His eyes strayed to the documents. 'Really, Lady, I must—'

'What you must do is listen to me. There's a woman living in those passages. Her name's Dora and she has, *had* . . .' I corrected myself, 'a child, a baby. If she's still alive in that stinking warren I want her found and I want her to be given the same

471

treatment as Brigid Strong – medical treatment for her condition and a gentle place to live out the rest of her days. Is that all understood?'

The Beetle frowned, but he nodded.

Christ! It was nothing to me, any of it, but it was a start.

'Now – you go ahead. I imagine you want to tell me it's time for the Barons' Aestas session?'

Telferman shifted uncomfortably and shook his head.

'I am sorry, Lady.'

'Don't be. I'll be ready for them.'

'You misunderstand me. It is not the Aestas session that is a matter of immediate urgency.'

Telferman's little half-moon spectacles caught the sunlight from the window.

'It is your grandmother's funeral.'

Chapter Forty-one

The great black clock on the wall stirred itself, whirred and began to strike. The doleful notes were tuned to a falling flatness designed, no doubt, to express the most sincere condolence to passengers in possession of a first-class ticket.

I counted them – eleven. The train would leave in another half hour – 11.35 a.m., to be precise. The timetable never varied, apart from Sundays. It was regular as death. In the ten minutes we'd sat here I'd read all the notes in the leather-bound book left open on the table to assure grieving relatives that the body of their loved one was in capable, modern, hands.

It was clear to me as the face on the clock over the mantle that the London Necropolis Company understood the mechanics of death, but not much more. I had the distinct impression that if anyone had the temerity to weep a trap might spring open under their feet to remove the embarrassment.

Quiet, efficient, orderly. Everything here at Waterloo was designed to make a living from the dead. It was a factory of mourning. Just now my grandmother's coffin was rising from the depths of the building in the steam-powered lift. Once it reached platform level it would be transferred to a bier and pushed, with all solemnity, to the waiting train.

Not that I was inclined to weep, mind. Tell truth, I didn't

want to be here. I told the Beetle as much as he waggled his horns at me over the desk. But then I thought about it deeper and it came to me that seeing her finally laid to rest was a sort of ending.

And a beginning.

I tried to brush the yellow dust from my gloves, but it spread into a dirty brown smear across my knuckles. Pollen from the miserable white flowers drooping in a vase on the table where the book was set ready had fallen onto the black lace. The room was thick with the smell of lilies and beeswax.

I stood and crossed to the arched window looking down over the platform. The yellow glass of the roof cast a sickly pall over the train waiting below. As I watched, a spurt of steam rolled back from the engine swallowing the first and second of the four carriages lined up below.

I turned back to Telferman. 'Is it just us two?'

He looked up from the papers in his hand. He always carted his work about with him. 'She did not wish anyone else to attend her on her final journey.'

'Not even Mr Das – only he seemed . . .'

Fond of her was what I wanted to say, but it didn't seem quite the right word.

The Beetle settled the papers in his lap. 'I have no doubt he will pay his respects in his own way.' He glanced at the window. 'This is not for him. Besides, he does not believe in death – not as we would understand it, Lady.'

'I believe in it all right.' I sat down on an ebony-backed chair next to the window and stared at the lilies. The dusty balls of pollen hanging over the table were the only things in the first-class waiting room with a colour to them. The walls were covered in grey wallpaper with a swirling pattern – ferns or leaves. The marble of the fireplace was black, streaked with veins of white, and the padded couch where the Beetle sat was dark as his coat.

The smell of the lilies put me in mind of something rotten.

'What do you believe in, Mr Telferman?'

He shrugged. 'I was raised in the faith of my fathers. We do not speculate on a life beyond the one we have been granted. It is a mystery.'

'But what do you think?'

He stared at the window for a long time. 'I try hard not to think about it.'

I held my bag close. Inside, there were two rolls of paper tied with red ribbon. Tan Seng and Lok had given them to me when we left The Palace.

'For her, Lady.' Tan Seng had bowed once and slipped back down the stairs to the basement. Lok waited until his brother had gone and then he reached into his loose black sleeve to produce a parcel of green silk. He unwrapped it carefully to reveal a single, perfect ball of yellow petals – a chrysanthemum.

'For her, Lady.' He wrapped it again, passed it to me and nodded. Then he followed his brother downstairs. The green silk parcel was in my bag now. Tell truth, I wasn't sure what I was going to do with the rolls of paper or that flower.

We sat in silence for a minute or two. I caught the distant rumble of machinery and thought of my grandmother's coffin.

I stood and looked out of the window again. The platform was still empty. I was surprised. I knew the station had at least six other waiting rooms given over to various classes of mourner. I'd seen the signs down below as we came in through the gates under the arch and turned left into the grand and gloomy hallway. Those afflicted by first- and second-class bereavement were directed to waiting rooms up the wide staircase, while grief of the lower sort had its own entrance at the side.

I thought there was safety in the fact that the railway had turned death into a business enterprise. I'd expected more people to be waiting to catch the cemetery train with us today. Besides, if we'd arrived with Tan Seng, Lok or Hari, the officials of the London Necropolis Company wouldn't have allowed them up the stairs. At any other time I would have asked Lucca to come. I took a comfort from the thought of him sitting up in bed and sipping from a cup of weak tea when I left The Palace.

He was with me, mind, in a manner of speaking.

'How many stops do we make between here and Brook-wood?'

'None – the train runs direct. The journey is said to be very picturesque. The route was chosen for its tranquillity.'

I looked down at the platform. It was covered in steam again now, but when it rolled back there wasn't a living soul down there as far as I could tell. Not even a guard.

'Is she the only one on the train today?'

Telferman reached into his coat for his fob and I caught a waft of naphtha as he moved the cloth. He flicked open the case, pushed his spectacles down his nose and held it close to his eyes. He looked at the clock on the wall and adjusted the set of his own pocket watch.

'I understand that is one of the privileges granted to prime investors. Your grandmother held an early position in the London Necropolis Company. That has now reverted to you. You can, if you so wish, avail yourself of . . . '

He halted, as it came to him that availing myself of a funerary facility was the last thing I wanted to do. Telferman stowed the fob back in its garret.

'It is clear that you have not yet looked through the documents I left with you yesterday. If you had done so, you would have seen the true extent of your late grandmother's estate. Her investment portfolio has a considerable value. And her property, Fraines Abbey, for example—'

'I don't want it!' I spoke sharp and the Beetle twitched at me over the rim of his spectacles.

'I don't want none of it. It's tainted. You can start with that old house. Sell it and I'll find a use for the money.'

'This is not the time or the place for such discussion.' He sniffed. 'Your charitable instincts are to be applauded, Lady. But I must point out that you have need of considerable funds to continue to . . . organise the affairs of Paradise in the way your predecessor, you grandmother, did.'

'What if I don't want to do that? What if I have other ideas about organising the affairs of Paradise?' I mimicked his voice as I repeated his own words back to him. He turned away and brushed specks of dust from the top of the black hat resting on the seat next to him.

'I imagine the Barons will be interested to learn of your . . . other ideas, Lady.' He looked direct at me now. 'After the funeral we will prepare for the Aestas session. You must be ready for them. I believe the call may come any day now.'

Of an instant, the black crêpe dress clung to my skin. The stiffness of the material caught tight around my arms and waist. The high-beaded collar dug into the skin beneath my jaw and I could feel the smart of the blisters on my heels where the new black boots chaffed the skin through the stockings.

'What if I don't go?'

'We have already discussed this.' Telferman was about to elaborate further but the door opened. A small fat man in a long black coat with a line of brass buttons straining down the front stepped into the room. He removed his tall hat and bowed.

'She has been brought to the platform. Everything is ready.' His doughy face was round and pale and his little brown eyes looked like currants in the mixture. He blinked and bowed again.

'I have been sent to conduct you to the deliverance. Most of our valued guests find it a comfort to see their lost one accorded all dignity as they set out upon their final great journey.'

If you could bottle sanctimony and sell it by the quart, this man would coin it.

'Follow me, please. This way.' He flourished a gloved hand to the stairway.

⚓

I was surprised by the size of that shiny black coffin.

Even though I knew she was a shrivelled husk of a thing at the end, in my mind she was a deal larger than the box carried onto the train. If someone was to tell a person we was there for a child, they would have believed us. It took just four men to take her from the bier and carry her up the wooden ramp and into the mortuary carriage. They disappeared from view through the wide doors and the little buttoned man turned to me.

'The first-class accommodation is in the next carriage. If you wish to sit with your lost one, however, that can be arranged. There are no windows but the lamps are always lit.'

'We'll go to the carriage.' I didn't want to sit in the dark with a corpse between us.

The men reappeared in the doorway. They thumped down the ramp, unhooked it from the train and then two of them reached up to slide the black-lacquered door across. Once it was secure they joined the others beside the bier. There was some shuffling and clearing of throats. One of them sidled hopefully at the Beetle and then at me.

I knew what was wanted. I pulled open the strings of my bag and fished inside for the coin purse. It was lodged at the bottom. I'd been careful with Lok's silk-wrapped flower. I felt I owed it to him, rather than to her.

'For your trouble.' I handed them a sixpence apiece and they were satisfied. They doffed their caps respectfully and wheeled the bier back down the platform.

'The compartment is this way.' We followed Button Boy along to the next carriage. He reached up to open the door and three fancy metal steps rattled down the platform. He turned to the Beetle.

'When you reach Brookwood Cemetery Station you will be met on the platform. These are the papers.'

479

'I'll take them.' I plucked them from his hand. There was a printed image at the top of the paper and underneath it I saw her name, Elizabeth Redmayne, followed by a string of numbers.

'What's this?' I tapped the page.

'It is the device of the London Necropolis Company. We use it on our correspondence and our livery.'

He held out his arm so I could see the same symbol on the buttons. A snake swallowing its tail circled a skull and cross-bones. There were some tiny words there too.

'The Ouroboros is the symbol of eternity and this . . .' he pointed at the words, 'is Latin. *Mortuis quies vivis salus*. It means *A good life and a peaceful death*.'

I glanced at the Beetle.

'And the rest of it – the numbers here?'

'That is her plot.' He squinted at the numbers. 'Ah – I see she has a mausoleum.'

'A what?'

'A tomb has been constructed for her. From the number I can tell it is at the very heart of the cemetery. It must have been built in the early days of the company. Only our most valued patrons have such prime positions.'

A piercing whistle went off and a plume of steam rose into the air, obscuring the yellow glass roof. After a moment it folded down over the engine and began to billow along the platform towards us. The fat conductor held the door open.

'The London Necropolis Company prides itself on punctuality. The train is never late.' He rattled the handle, but didn't shift aside to let us go aboard. His little brown eyes strayed to my bag.

I reached inside for another coin. 'Here.' He removed his hat, bowed his head and smiled in a way that I reckoned was supposed to show his sympathy, but looked very much like a bilious attack. His pudgy hand closed over the coin and he stepped back. 'On behalf of the London Necropolis Company, may I offer condolence for your loss. *Mortuis quies vivis salus.*'

A good life and a peaceful death – that was it, wasn't it?

As far as I could tell, my grandmother hadn't had the benefit of either.

'Anyone there?'

I rapped on the shuttered booth again, but there was no answer. I turned to the Beetle, who was peering out through the station door. The sun was high in the sky, but there was a breeze. The sticky heat of the previous weeks had been washed away with that storm.

I went to stand next to him and shielded my eyes against the sharpness of the light. A courtyard led to a gravel path stretching out across a lawn to wide-open gates. Beyond them I could see dark green trees and clean white stones. Over to the right was a timber-clad building I took for a chapel. It had a spire, but it wore the look of something impermanent, like one of Lucca's stage sets.

There was a rumble as the train idling on the platform behind us shunted. A cloud of cinder-ash rolled into the little station hall.

'I thought he said we would be met on the platform.'

'He did. Perhaps we are early, Lady?'

I shook my head. 'Remember what Button Boy told us: "The London Necropolis Company prides itself on punctuality. The train is never late." And I reckon it's never early neither.' I looked back at the shining black carriage coming visible through the smoke.

'I know it was only a little box, but I don't reckon the pair of us could carry her off and shift her to the mausoleum she built for herself, wherever it is.'

The Beetle looked doubtfully at the train. 'Her wishes were quite plain. The interment was to be carried out before the minimum of witnesses. However . . . Look there.'

He pointed to the gates where a young man was running towards us.

As he drew level, he started to sort through the sheaf of papers in his hands. Some of them dropped to the gravel and were scattered about by the breeze. I darted forward to gather them up.

'Redmayne party, yes?' His whiskered face was red.

I nodded. 'We were told that someone would meet us here.'

'You must forgive me, there has been a misunderstanding. The men have gone to the north terminus. There seems to have been a muddle in the paperwork. I take it the deceased was not a nonconformist?'

I didn't know what my grandmother was. I didn't think it mattered much.

I quizzed at the Beetle.

'Her wish for the Anglican rite is stated in the will. I have it here.' He swung his case round.

'Are you a relative?' The man clutched at some more papers slipping from the pile.

'I am her lawyer. Marcus Telferman.'

'Excellent. That is a great relief. You can sign the casket from the train and complete the necessary papers. I am afraid we will need a new set for the recorder.' He turned to me now. 'And you are . . .?'

'This is her granddaughter.' For some reason I was glad Telferman answered for me. I handed the papers I collected from the gravel back to the flustered clerk. He performed a stiff, ungainly little bow.

'I must apologise, Miss . . .?'

'Peck, my name is Peck.'

'I must apologise, Miss Peck. This has never happened before. The company takes a dim view of unreliability. I am afraid Mr Telferman and I must go through the papers again in my office. Unfortunately, it is quite a distance from here – a walk of at least ten minutes or so to the far side. Brookwood is the largest cemetery in the world.'

He said it like he was presenting a marvel.

'Do you have the documentation?'

The question was addressed to Telferman, but I answered.

'If you mean the papers given to us at the other end, they're here.' I opened my bag and pulled out the sheet I'd taken from Button Boy. I was sorry to see that Lok's little parcel had come undone. There was a scattering of yellow petals now at the bottom of the bag.

The clerk took the sheet and scanned the details. He nodded. 'A fine mausoleum. The key, however, is also in my office.' He looked at me and I saw little beads of sweat on his forehead. 'This must be very distressing. May I suggest that while Mr Telferman and I make the necessary adjustments you compose yourself in the chapel? The pallbearers will be here soon to carry the casket from the train. I will send word to the chaplain that he is required today after all.'

I looked at the Beetle. I couldn't see his expression on account of the sun glinting on his half-moon spectacles. He moved them down his nose. 'I am happy to deal with it all. Do you wish to accompany us?'

The clerk shuffled the papers. 'When they arrive the pallbearers will carry the casket directly to the chapel. I imagine you would not wish your grandmother to be alone at such a time. Many of our ... patrons remark on the tranquillity of that sacred space.'

I felt the rub of the blisters on my heels. The thought of traipsing a mile through the forest of stones to watch Telferman sign a bleedin' document was ridiculous. Of an instant, the thought of sitting somewhere quiet and dim and cool was something more than appealing.

I made up my mind.

'I'll sit with her.'

The clerk bowed. 'It is unlocked. If you'll follow me, Mr Telferman.'

He swivelled about sharp on the gravel and started back the way he'd come. He seemed most eager to get away, but I supposed that time was money, even in a cemetery.

Telferman twitched his head at me and followed. I watched the pair of them pass through the gates together then I pulled the black net veil of my bonnet down over my face and turned to follow the path along the front of the station.

I wasn't one for prayers and such, but if there was a God and He was in a mood to listen to me, I thought I might thank Him for sparing Lucca and, while I was at it, I'd ask Him to take account of Danny and Amit and Edie and Netta and Swami Jonah and Brigid. There was someone else I was thinking of too. While I was sitting there I might mention Sam in passing.

I opened the gate and walked down the path to the door. The shadow was deep on this side of the chapel. I shivered at the sudden chill and felt the hairs rise on the skin of my arms under the black crêpe.

I reached for the handle and pushed. The smell of damp and old wood rushed out to me and there was something else there too. Something familiar. Before I had a chance to recognise the spiced leathery danger of it someone caught me roughly by the arm and dragged me inside.

The door slammed shut behind me.

Chapter Forty-two

They were waiting.

Twenty pairs of eyes turned to me. A trapped pigeon fluttered against the glass of a narrow window to the side. I heard its wings beat against the panes as surely as I heard the pounding of my heart. I swung back to the door but Matthias Schalk smiled and shook his head.

That cane of his rested against the wall. He took it up and flicked it casually – an instruction to move forward. I turned.

The Barons of London sat either side of the aisle, filling seven rows of bench pews in that simple wooden chapel. Lord Kite was standing at the altar in place of the chaplain. He was framed in the arch of the window, his white hair gleamed but his face was in shadow. Just in front of him in the aisle was a long, low marble table, the width and length of a coffin.

I couldn't move and I couldn't speak. My feet were rooted to the red and black tiles. I felt Schalk's hand on my arm, I tried to shake him off, but his grip tightened. I could feel his nails through the black crêpe. The chapel was silent except for the rattle of that bird and the sound of our steps.

As we walked down the aisle together I was aware of the bulk of him, but there was more than that. There was a sort of darkness around him too. Schalk towered above me, but it wasn't his shadow that fell across me. It was his soul.

No wonder McCarthy was terrified of him. I thought of

that poor cow Joey used as a messenger and what Telferman had told me.

The woman's tongue had been cut from her mouth and forced into a part of her body. Her left breast was found crushed in her mouth.

I glanced up at Schalk's face and looked away sharp when he grinned down at me. Cold blue eyes narrowed over cheekbones you could hang a coat from. It came to me that this was all a kind of madness – everything pulled inside out and stretched out of shape. We were stepping down the aisle like a pair at a wedding, only this was a chapel of rest not a church, and I was veiled in black.

As we walked I looked at them all through the spotted net.

Last time, in the candlelight at Great Bartholomew's, those faces hadn't quite seemed real, but now in the afternoon sun slanting through the milky glass I saw them for what they were. Grey men in black suits with their Sunday hats lined up on the Bible shelves in front of them. There was a sort of horror in their blandness.

It wasn't enough. I wanted them to look like the monsters I knew them to be. I thought of Ma and my throat burned.

I scanned the rows for Lord Fetch, the mound of flesh who served up his parable that night in Smithfield like he was sucking marrow from a bone. Since that afternoon at the Bethlem, I'd dreamed of him. I struggled awake gasping for air that didn't reach my lungs – and all I remembered was being smothered by the fleshy vastness of his stinking body.

If Fetch was here, I'd know it without seeing him. I took a deep breath, but all I caught was dust, damp and old greens. Beside the altar a display of pale, wilting flowers scattered petals and leaves across the tiles.

When we were level with the marble coffin table, Schalk released me. He nodded at Kite and turned to the first bench. The two men sitting there shifted along to let him sit. The heavy rings on their fingers and the golden hoops punched into their ears marked their trade. They moved as one because, to all intents, they were a single being. The Lords Janus came from the travelling people and they were joined. Two heads, one broad back and a tangle of limbs all buttoned neat in a tail coat.

I swallowed the bile that flooded my mouth.

Schalk sat next to them and tapped his cane on the brass rail fencing the altar as a sign. Kite turned his blind eyes exactly to mine. It was like he could see me standing there.

He bowed his bare head. 'We have come to offer our condolences, Lady Linnet, most of us that is. Lord Fetch could not be with us today. The journey would be too arduous for someone afflicted with such a delicate constitution. And I have accepted the apologies of Lord Vellum ...' He paused. Even though I knew it wasn't possible, his milk-white eyes roamed through the pews as if he was searching for someone. ' ... who has been detained by matters of state. When one among our number dies it is customary for us to gather to mourn his passing.'

I heard the rustle of stiff material as the Barons turned to look at me.

'Well?' Kite's voice came again.

'I ... I didn't know it was the custom. She never told me of it.' My voice came out higher than I intended.

'Ah.' Kite smiled. 'Please do not alarm yourself, Lady Linnet, *pacta sunt servanda*. You have no need to fear us. All is well – we are here for you. It is fortunate that I too am a prime investor in the London Necropolis Company. It seems there is a great deal that Lady Ginger did not tell you.'

The sun from the plain arched window at his back snatched up the silver of his hair. If I didn't know different I might have seen it as a halo. My hand tightened over the bone handle of my bag as I thought of Ma and what these men had done to her.

I thought of Danny beneath that ledgerstone.

I remembered the things I'd heard that night at Great Bartholomew's.

Most of the men sitting in the pews on either side of me looked like regular gents, but between them they held the sluice gates to the rivers of filth that flowed beneath London and beyond.

Destroy them, Katharine. You can end centuries of injustice.

My grandmother's voice came clear to me as if she'd climbed out of that coffin on the train and joined us in the chapel. It was an easy thing to say, not so easy to do. I knew I had to be most careful. They thought they held the winning hand, but Kite was wrong about something – my grandmother had told me about their greatest secret – the Vinculum. And I had the sequence to open it – whatever and wherever it was – from Joey.

I stared at Kite's face through the veil. I couldn't let them know I'd seen my brother. Although by now, if things had gone the way I planned, he'd be out of the Bethlem and well on his way. I didn't need to know the details, I'd simply asked Ramesh Das to deal with it – no matter how much it cost.

Marstin struck me as a buyable sort, but I reckoned he didn't come cheap. Same went for his friend Jeffries.

I took a breath to steady the fluting of my voice.

'Why are you really here? Is this the Aestas session?'

Kite shook his head. 'That will come soon enough. No – as I told you, Lady Linnet, we have come to pay our last respects. Have we not, brothers?'

There was a murmur of agreement. I could feel their excitement straining against the buttons of their mourning gear. They were no better than the punters who stood under that cage night after night.

I felt the jet-beaded neck of my dress tighten at my throat.

'That right? Only you didn't seem to *respect* her much – or the choice she made.'

Kite's stone eyes blinked. 'A funeral is a rite of great importance. It is the reading of the final page, the closing of the book – the ending.' He gestured at Schalk. 'It is a terrible thing when it is impossible to mark a passing. My friend has recently lost a brother.' He paused and I saw the tip of his pink tongue slide over his lips. There was a time when I found a rats' nest behind the planks of the back row of the gallery of The Gaudy. All them bald, blind bodies squirming against each other came to me now. I tried to master the shudder as he continued.

'I wonder, Lady Linnet, if you have heard of the fate of the *Gouden Kalf*? It was on your . . . estate after all.'

Kite's voice came smooth as the brushed black silk of his coat. I felt Schalk's pale eyes on me.

'You mean the paddle steamer struck by lightning at Shadwell New Basin?' I was careful to keep my voice flat.

Walk careful, girl, I told myself.

Kite nodded. 'My friend's brother, half brother to be precise, was the captain of that vessel. I believe you had dealings with him. His name was Houtman.'

'I ... yes, I ... know him – I took a shipment of gin off him.'

'His body has not, as yet, come to light from the wreckage. My friend, Matthias, cannot close the book.'

Kite waited for an answer. I turned to Schalk.

'Then I am sorry for your loss.'

I didn't mean a bleedin' word of it, but I kept my tone civil.

Schalk stroked the head of his cane. 'No bodies have been found. The storm must have carried them away.' He shot a glance at Kite. 'It would be a comfort to know what has become of my brother – and of the others on board that night. An ending.'

'And today is about endings.' Kite's voice was cold. 'Let us turn to the question of your own brother, Lady Linnet. When we last met I asked you a simple question. The time for an answer draws near.'

I shook my head. 'If that's why you're here, you'll go away with something real to mourn. How many times do I have to say this? I don't know where Joey is.'

By now that, at least, was true, I hoped.

Kite rubbed his thin pale hands together. 'Your obstinacy is unfortunate. Tell me, have you heard from your friend, Mr Fratelli?'

I stared at him. What answer did he expect? He brought his hands up close together beneath his chin like he was about to pray.

'Do you remember our conversation at the Temple Church? I remarked that you were often alone. It was by design, Lady Linnet. I have some . . . sad news for you – news of Mr Fratelli.'

And it came to me.

They didn't know what I'd done! They didn't know I'd saved Lucca and Sam from the hold of the *Golden Calf*. They reckoned they were dead along with Houtman and his shipmates. It was a power over them, but how could I use it?

I played for time to think, grateful for the net covering my face even though Kite couldn't see me.

'What about him?'

'He is dead, Lady Linnet.' Lord Kite grinned. His white eyes glinted in the slanting light from the window. 'He and another of your . . . acquaintances, a journalist, I believe. They were captive in the hold of the *Gouden Kalf* when it was wrecked in the storm. I told you that people close to you would suffer, madam, if you did not do as I wished. It is a simple matter – you must choose. It will continue until you give him to us.'

He paused and held his head to the side, calculating his next words.

'Matthias tells me the Italian cried like a child when he daubed those walls. Yes – it was your own loyal friend who betrayed you. What do you think of that?'

The doors at the back of the chapel bumped open and my grandmother's black casket swung into view. It was so small that the six men crowded round it almost tripped on each other's heels as they carried it solemnly up the aisle to the marble table. All the while my mind ticked like a clock.

Think, girl, think!

We watched them lower it. Then they stepped away, bowed and filed back to the door. When the door slammed shut behind them I turned to Lord Kite. I opened my bag and reached inside taking out a red silk 'kerchief. A handful of Lok's yellow petals scattered to the tiles.

'Do ... do you really want to know?' I made my voice broken and small, like I was on the edge of tears. I balled the 'kerchief in my hand. 'I think Lucca Fratelli's very much alive. When I saw him this morning he was sitting up in bed with a cup of tea – Imperial, I think it was – between his fingers. I'll ask him what he thought about doing those paintings, shall I, when I get home?'

I span around and began to walk fast to the door.

'Wait. We have not finished with you yet.' Kite's voice rang out. I heard the scrape of wood on tile as Schalk stood up abrupt from his pew.

I swivelled on my heels and flapped Lucca's ivory-handled pistol from the 'kerchief. Another shower of petals fell to the stones as I held it out in front of me, both hands clasped round the grip. The Barons rose up from the pews like a black wave. Schalk stepped into the aisle. He brandished his cane across his body.

I pointed the pistol at Kite.

'Well, I've finished with you, Anthony Carstone.'

A low muttering filled the chapel. Kite blinked.

'Surprised, are you? I know who you are and a lot more besides. I've finished with you, with all of you.'

Schalk started to walk towards me. I swung the pistol to him.

'Not another step.'

He kept on coming. There was less than twenty foot between us now. He turned the cane in his hands. There was a flash and a mighty crack as the pistol went off. The force of it threw me off balance for a moment. Tell truth, I didn't mean to pull the trigger. My fingers had tightened round the ivory grip as Schalk came closer.

The air filled with smoke and a firecracker tang. I heard something fall to the ground. It was the cane. Schalk was still standing five yards off, but now he was clutching his right shoulder. Blood seeped through his fingers. The muttering of the Barons came stronger, three of them stepped from the pews and into the aisle behind him.

I held Lucca's dainty pistol out straight in one hand and backed to the door. Schalk flexed his broad shoulders and rolled his neck. He moved his hand and examined the blood for a moment, then he shrugged like it was nothing more to him than the bite of a gnat.

He bent forward and reached for the cane.

'If you touch that thing, I'll shoot again.' I meant it. Christ! Lucca's pistol went off accidental, but I wished it had blown that black-hearted bastard to hell where he truly belonged.

I pointed the pistol direct at Schalk's blond head and ripped back my veil to see them all clear. The chapel fell silent. The men in the aisle paused, uncertain what to do. A couple of them glanced back at Kite who was still standing at the altar. The pigeon battered against the window again and then it took off across the chapel.

I carried on moving slow, careful not to blink or let the

gun tremble in my hand. I reached out behind me and at last my fingers found the latch of the door. I took a breath.

'As a matter of fact I'm pleased you're all here. You've saved me a deal of trouble. I won't be seeing you again . . . *gentlemen*. I won't be at your bleedin' Aestas session or any session after that. You're a joke, the lot of you, with your secret names, your made-up words, your *pacta sunt* whatevers and your play acting. That's what this is, all this rigmarole. It makes you feel more than you are, don't it? Makes you feel special? I reckon it makes you feel clean to dress your filth like a theatrical show. But it's real – don't you ever forget that, because I won't. It comes to something when a girl from the arse end of London can give a sermon on justice. I know what you are and I don't want none of it. Turns out I'm not the stuff a Baron is made of. And I'll tell you this for nothing – I'm glad of it. If I thought the smallest part of me was anything like any of you, I'd cut it out with my own hand.'

I yanked the door open. A gust of wind slammed it against the wall and sent leaves scuttling across the tiles of the chapel. Of an instant, that pigeon swooped low over the heads of the Barons and out into a dull afternoon.

I didn't turn. I kept the pistol trained on the aisle.

'If you send your dog Schalk after me, I'll put it out of its misery.'

As I backed into the light Kite called out.

'Do you imagine that you can simply walk away from us?'

'I don't have to imagine anything. I'm doing it right in front of you.' I took another step back. 'If you're waiting for me to nominate a successor then you'll be waiting a long time. And if it's the other way out, then I'm the one with the gun.

See – I know all about the rules. All them pointless made-up rules.'

'But there is still so much your grandmother did not tell you.' Kite's drawl came again. 'Do you remember, Lady Linnet, when we spoke of your father?'

I froze.

'He is here.'

The pistol trembled in my hand. I tried to steady it.

'You?' The echo of my question whispered off the walls.

Kite stepped down from the altar. The Barons parted as he walked to the end of my grandmother's coffin, grinding Lok's yellow petals beneath his black shoes.

'Not I, but he is amongst us.' Kite smiled and gestured at the men ranked around him.

'We cannot be certain. Perhaps it was Lord Oak, or Lord Iron, or Lord Silver, Lord Mitre, Lord Sable, Lord Ferrous, The Lords Janus . . . or Lord Fetch.'

That was the last I heard as I flung myself into the light.

Chapter Forty-three

I ran down the gravel path from the chapel and I carried on past the station, stumbling along pathways and through rows of pale carved stones and quivering spear-shaped trees. I didn't know where I was going. I was running blind.

I was grateful for the ache beneath my bodice as I fought to fill my lungs and for the stab of the blisters on my feet. They pushed the other pain from my head. At one point I tripped over a fallen stone hidden by ferns and crashed forward, warding off the jagged edge of a monument with my hands. Screaming tears opened in the lace of my gloves. I pulled them off, cast them aside and carried on.

At last I came to a place so dark and silent that I couldn't even hear a bird. It was a long while since this part of the cemetery had seen a gardener. Stone angels, their faces worn blank by weather and indifference, sprouted from clumps of nettles, and brambles scrabbled at the sides of marble buildings set at respectful intervals in what must once have been a lawn. Even so, the houses of the dead were a good deal grander than the houses of most of the living where I came from.

I stepped, panting, into a shadowed circular space and turned about slowly, staring down each of the tomb-lined pathways fanning out around me. There were twelve of them, one for each hour. I caught my breath as a dark shape slipped across an avenue, but then I saw it was the shadow of a tree moving in the breeze. I looked up into the oval window of grey overhead and felt the first drops of rain on my skin.

If I stood there long enough, perhaps it would wear me away like the faces of all them angels? I wouldn't have minded. If the rain could wash away the thoughts going through my head I would have stood there for a thousand years. Of an instant, the pain started up across my forehead. The world shattered into two halves divided by a wavering line that sparked and shimmered.

I crumpled to the steps leading up to a little plinth set with a sundial. I ripped off my bonnet and threw it down to the mossy gravel. After a moment, the breeze, which had sharpened to something with a bite, snatched at the spotted net and carried it off down one of the avenues. My eyes burned as I watched that bonnet, the fractured double version of it, roll and bump along the path.

It wasn't true what Kite said. I couldn't be. It wasn't possible.

The bonnet skittered up against a marble wall and lodged between some metal railings. The ribbons, multiplied by the fault in my eyes, flailed like the legs of a great black spider.

When they tested our grandmother, they took her daughter.

Joey's words came again, but now I heard a different story in them. I thought of that nightmare – the way I fought to breathe as the stench of Lord Fetch pressed against me. And I thought of him and Ma.

'No.'

At first it was a strangled whisper, but I said it again and again to make it true, ripping at the beads around my throat to let the air into my lungs. Somewhere between the tenth and the twentieth denial it became a scream.

It was the rain that brought me back. That and Telferman's voice.

I pushed the sodden strands of hair away from my eyes and watched the Beetle scurry towards me along the tree-lined avenue. He was doubled beneath an umbrella that bucked in the wind. He called again and raised a hand as if he thought I might bolt. I turned the little pistol about in my hand and waited for him to draw level.

'Where have you been, Lady? I have searched everywhere. We were forced to inter her without you.'

'We?' I stared up at him. The pain was fading now and the crack in my sight was nothing more than a ripple to the right.

The Beetle frowned. 'The clerk-custodian, the chaplain and myself. When we arrived at the chapel you were not there.'

'But who else was there?'

He blinked behind his spectacles and shook his head. 'The casket was ready, but the pallbearers had gone.'

'I didn't mean the pallbearers.' The hem of my dress flew up around my ankles. I drew up my knees and linked my hands around them. I pushed the pistol into the folds of the material to hide it.

'She was alone. We waited for some time, but when you did not return the chaplain insisted that the service should go ahead. I was the only person with her. The clerk – Roberts – went to gather the pallbearers and the hearse for the transfer.'

Kite told me to be wary of those around me. I looked up at the Beetle and felt the rain sliding down my face.

'Here. You must allow me.' He stepped closer to shield me with the umbrella. If he wondered where my bonnet was, he didn't mention it.

'You are wet through. I did not think that you would be so . . . affected, Lady. Forgive me . . .'

For once the smell of old naphtha rising from his cloth had a comfort to it. Marcus Telferman was my man, now, to his marrow. I was sure of it.

'Roberts is a fool. When we reached his office the paperwork was quite in order. He had merely mislaid a sheet. The mistake was his entirely. It was most irritating.'

He rustled about in his pocket for that fob of his. Careful to keep it dry he brought it close to his eyes.

'I am sorry, Lady. There will not be time to visit her mausoleum. The train leaves in less than a half. We are some way from the South Terminus.'

I sat up. 'Is that the only way back?'

Telferman nodded.

'Then I'm not going.'

He patted his pocket and shifted his spectacles to see me better. 'We will be the only party on the train. It is, *was*, a benefit of early investment. I believe there may have been one other funeral here today, but I saw the mourners depart in their carriages from the Pine Avenue Gate when I accompanied your grandmother's casket along to the Western Avenue. It was a large group. Roberts was with them by then. I can only hope he gave them better service.'

I stood up. Crystals of rain scattered from my skirt and Lucca's pistol tumbled to the gravel. I was lucky it didn't go off again. I glanced at the Beetle, who was looking at the pistol. His eyebrows were drawn so tight together the hairs might have tangled themselves in a knot.

I opened my bag and reached down. I stowed the pistol inside and snapped it shut.

'I think he did, Mr Telferman. I reckon Mr Roberts gave them the service they wanted.'

⚓

The Beetle was right, we were the only people on the train.

Even though I believed him, I was careful to check. Huddled beneath his black umbrella we walked the length of the platform three times to make certain. The last time, the driver and the fireman leaned out from the cab and watched like we was a couple of Bedlams out for a stroll.

Telferman didn't question why I wanted to make sure we were alone. Fact is, he hadn't said much since he clapped eyes on the pistol.

With less than a minute to go I allowed him to open the door to our compartment. He stood aside to let me go first. It was comfortable in there, you might even call it luxurious. A single gas lamp set between the mirrors above the empty seats opposite ours was already lit against the sudden gloom of the day. It was Nanny Peck's belief that summer rainclouds cast a darkness deeper than the winter variety. Looking out of the window at the drab platform it came to me she was right.

At 2.15 sharp the whistle blew and we moved slowly out of the station. I watched the rows of stones and monuments through trails of water sliding down the window.

He is amongst us. He is amongst us. He is amongst us . . .

The sound of the engine took up the words going round and round in my head. I shut my eyes, bent forward and covered my ears with my hands to stop the noise.

I felt Telferman's hand on my arm and looked up.

'We must discuss the Aestas session, Lady. Your parable must be ready.' He sat back. 'Today is perhaps not the day, but . . .'

'No.' I pulled up straight. 'As you say, today is perhaps not the day. And neither is the day after that or the day after that. You can number all the days from here to the end of time, but I'll never go among them again. After today, I'm not a Baron any more.'

The Beetle shifted uncertainly. The train rolled to the side as it veered left and he gripped the padded arm of his seat.

'You do not understand, Lady Linnet. As I explained, you cannot—'

I stopped him. 'I can do what I bleedin' like.'

Tell truth, I didn't know what I was going to do, but I knew this. 'And I'm not Lady Linnet, I'm Kitty Peck – and that's an end to the matter.' I turned away to the window. I felt his eyes boring into my back, but I didn't look at him.

I stared at the girl reflected in the glass and I couldn't tell the rain from the tears on her cheeks.

⚓

The train began to slow and then it juddered to a halt. I rubbed the mist from the window and peered through the steam. It wasn't London out there. We were in the middle of a sloping field. There were cows sitting beneath a tree at the far end.

'I thought you said the train didn't stop anywhere?' I looked at the Beetle now. He was fiddling at his nails. We'd been sitting in silence for the last quarter.

'It does not.'

'What's this, then?'

He glanced at the smeared window. 'Perhaps we are taking on water. That seems most likely, Lad . . . Miss Peck.'

Of an instant, the door to the compartment opened and the steps rolled down. My hand flew to my bag as a man wearing a tall hat climbed into view.

He hauled himself up the steps into the compartment and flung his hat onto the seat opposite before turning to me.

'Good day, Lady Linnet. May I offer my condolence for your recent loss.'

Lord Vellum pushed a lick of dark hair back from his forehead. He adjusted the tails of his black coat and sat down.

'And this must be your lawyer, Marcus Telferman, of Pearl Street. Would you leave us, please?' He gestured to the door. 'One of the men will help you down.'

I span back to the window. There were four men standing alongside the track below. I didn't recognise them. One of them tipped his cap. I pushed my hand into the bag on my lap and worked my fingers round the ivory handle of the pistol.

Vellum pushed the door wider. 'If you would leave us, please, Mr Telferman. I have taken the liberty of making arrangements for your onward journey. You will not be harmed. You have my word.'

I stood up, clutching the bag close.

'*Pacta sunt servanda* – is that it? The word of one Baron to another?' I heard the Beetle swallow. 'They've sent you to finish off today's business, have they? Why don't you take this back as my answer?'

I pointed the pistol in the bag at the roof of the carriage and pulled the trigger. The power of the blast threw me back into the seat, but I managed to right myself and keep hold.

'I'm not scared of you – any of you. It's you who should fear me. I'm not going to play by your rules. Sling it.' I motioned the pistol to the doorway. Its silver barrel poked out now through a scorched hole in the velvet.

Lord Vellum smiled. 'Another bravura performance. That is exactly why I want to speak to you . . . alone, if I may. Mr Telferman?' He raised a grey-gloved hand and pointed to the door.

'He's not going anywhere. I've got another four bullets. That's one for you and three of your men out there.'

Lord Vellum leaned back and folded his arms. 'I have four officers outside and another four waiting in the coaches in the lane – all of them armed. You may keep your gun, Lady Linnet, if it makes you feel safe in my company, but I would appreciate it if Mr Telferman left us while we continue *à deux* to London. I do not think it is a matter of choice, but I would prefer to act as a gentleman. I would offer that hollow Latin phrase, but the word of one Baron to another is worthless in this instance.'

He flicked at some invisible speck on his black sleeves and I saw the gleam of his gold studs.

'I am not a Baron, Lady Linnet. That is precisely what I wish to discuss with you.'

Chapter Forty-four

The door slammed. I watched Telferman walk across the field in the company of Vellum's men. The train whistled and the field disappeared in a cloud of steam. We began to crawl forward and it was a moment or two before Telferman came clear again. He'd stopped and turned to watch as we moved away. He looked small and dusty and frail and old.

'He ... he won't ... They won't hurt him, will they?' I was surprised to find a fondness for the Beetle I didn't know I possessed. If we came through this, I'd get him something better than a puffin for his collection.

I turned to the man sitting opposite. He was young, not above five years older than me, perhaps a little more, but that was all we had in common. It was clear from the gleaming studs on his cuffs, the sheen of his coat and a general sleekness to his person that me and Lord Vellum moved in very different circles.

There was his voice too. Something in the tone of it suggested he was on the edge of delivering the punchline to a great joke that only he was in on. I despised the easy assurance of his manner. What was worse was that I despised myself for respecting it.

He was a toff. I'd met enough of them in the halls to measure their worth in a blink. Lord Vellum was higher than anyone I'd met. If you cut him he'd bleed ink.

'Well? I asked a question.' I kept my hand clamped on the pistol.

Vellum smoothed his hair back from his grey eyes. This time it fell perfectly into place. He minded me of Sam if he could bother himself to get a decent trim. The thought of Sam caught me. I felt a hot rush beneath my ribs. And then I thought of the article in his paper. The story that led him into a trap.

The story with the picture of the man sitting in front of me now.

What did it all mean? I looked at the seat beside me. In the startlement, Telferman had left his hat behind. For some reason it made him seem even more defenceless out there in that field.

'You promise they won't hurt him. The Beet . . . Mr Telferman.'

'On behalf of Her Majesty's Government, you have my word, Lady Linnet.'

Vellum sat forward and I caught his scent. Lavender and something rich. He smelt of money.

'In fact, I am here today on matters of state.'

Wasn't that what Kite said back in the chapel of rest?

And I have accepted the apologies of Lord Vellum, who has been detained by matters of state.

I shifted the bag so the barrel of the pistol pointed direct at him across the narrow space between us.

'I've heard that already. You were late to the cemetery because of it. You've come to have your say now then, have you?'

Vellum pulled off his grey kid gloves and folded them neatly. 'There is a discussion to be had, but perhaps not the one you expect. Would you mind if I opened the window? There is a peculiar odour in the compartment.'

He leaned over to take the handle of the brass wheel set into the panelled side and wound the window down a little way. It squeaked as the pane moved.

The nostrils at the end of his fine cut nose flared. 'There was a cupboard at school where the masters kept their gowns that had a very similar aroma.' He smiled and I realised he was a looker. I despised myself again for thinking that.

'Now, I have a question for you, Lady Linnet.'

I shook my head. 'I thought the rule in polite society was ladies first. I've got questions for you. And I'm Miss Peck, Kitty Peck, not Lady Linnet.'

'Very well.' He nodded. 'Your questions, Miss Peck.'

I sat up straight. 'For a start, who is Lord Denderholm and what is the London Imperial Agency? And for that matter, who are you? Vellum's not your real name, is it?'

'Of course it is not.' He pushed the folded gloves into a coat pocket. 'Your first question is a matter of great interest to me. That is interesting.'

'I don't care about interesting.' I steadied myself as the train rocked. 'I want answers.'

'Then I'll give you some.' Of an instant, Vellum's lazy amusement disappeared. 'The very existence of the London Imperial Agency is a secret of state.'

'Well, it's not that secret if it can appear in a newspaper . . . with pictures?'

He arched a brow. 'Indeed. And it appeared in your newspaper, if I am not mistaken?'

I thought about Sam. Steady girl, I thought. I didn't want

to say anything that led him into more trouble.

'I didn't own it then, but . . .' I nodded.

Vellum stared out of the window. 'English summer rain. It has a beauty of its own. "But when the melancholy fit shall fall Sudden from heaven like a weeping cloud . . ." Do you know Keats, Miss Peck?'

'Keats the butchers on Bromley Street?' I didn't think that was who he meant, mind.

Vellum stared at me. 'Your newspaper, more precisely your friend Mr Collins, caused a great deal of damage. I grant you it could have been worse. I suppose we must regard it as fortunate the story was published within the privacy of the pages of *The London Pictorial News*. However, it was enough to unmask me.'

It came clear now. 'So that's why you took him, is it? That's why you tricked him into that meeting?'

Now it was Vellum's turn for confusion. 'Tricked him?'

'Don't come it with me. You set him up and now I know why. He was making enquiries. But he got too close, didn't he? Too close to you, Denderholm and the rest of them. That's why Kite's man got to him. The Barons wanted to silence him.'

I pushed a damp strand of hair away from my eyes. 'As you weren't there in the chapel earlier I've got a bit of news for you. I found them, both of them, Lucca Fratelli and Sam Collins, and I got them off that stinking boat. They're alive and . . .' I halted as I thought of what they'd been through. 'They're alive, that's all you need to know.'

Vellum looked up at the ceiling. The bullet had gone straight through leaving a smudge of black around the hole in the wood. He twisted a gold ring on his smallest finger.

'Again, that is interesting, Miss Peck. I was not aware of this – not all of it anyway. I knew your friend Mr Fratelli had been taken, but that was before my ... association with the Barons came to an unexpected conclusion. Mr Collins saw to that, but I was not responsible for what happened to him.'

'Are you saying you didn't set up that meeting at the furrier's – Galley's – to trap him when he asked questions about that article?'

Vellum nodded slowly. He kept on twisting the ring and staring at the ceiling. His eyes narrowed like he was seeing something up there and wanted to fix on it. The train whistle went off and we shifted hard to the left. I gripped a leather strap hanging off the wall, but kept the pistol levelled at him.

'Well?'

'It seems to me that your journalist friend might have done me a great favour.' Vellum looked at me now. 'He has confirmed a connection between the Barons and ... someone I have a professional interest in. Before today, I did not know this for a certainty.'

'You knew about Lucca, though? You just said so.'

'It was unfortunate, Miss Peck. There was little at the time I could do to help Mr Fratelli without revealing my hand. Your newspaper did that instead. The article, and more precisely the picture of me, made it impossible to continue my subterfuge.'

'Your what?'

'My act, Miss Peck. You are not the only performer here. Collins's error destroyed months of painstaking work. You have no idea what it cost.' Vellum looked sharply at the window. I got the impression he was trying to master himself before he went on.

'The existence of the Agency was known to a select few, until it appeared on page seventeen of *The London Pictorial News*. Mr Collins caused more damage than he could know.'

'But it wasn't his fault. It was an accident – a mix-up. His friend at the Bureau gave it to him by mistake.'

'Was it a mistake? Perhaps it was something more.' Vellum twisted the ring again. 'We live in dangerous times. The Agency will soon be engaged on important work. It will protect the realm, but first we must clear away the filth.'

'Listen.' I shook my head. 'I don't know anything about the Agency – nothing beyond that bleedin' picture and that name – Lord Denderholm. I don't understand why you're here. If you're not a Baron, what are you?'

'I am an instrument of justice.' Vellum reached into his pocket and produced a silver box. He opened it and took out a smoke. The way of it minded me of Sam again, except he didn't offer me one. He struck a Lucifer on the side and took a drag.

'Are you familiar with the labours of Hercules?'

'Not unless it's a dog act from The Hyperion.'

'You are most amusing, Miss Peck.' He batted at the smoke between us. 'Let me enlighten you. Hercules was a hero of Greek myth, famed for his strength. The gods set him twelve labours to atone for the murder of his wife and his sons. The sixth labour was to clear the dung from the Augean Stables in a single day. The stables housed a thousand cattle and had not been cleared for thirty years. Can you imagine the extent of the task?'

'I've cleaned the halls after a night when the Baltic boats have put in. I don't have to imagine it.'

Vellum's nose twitched. 'Indeed. London is full of filth. My job is to clear it away. Starting with the Barons.'

He took another drag and flicked the ash through the open window.

'It took a great deal of cunning to infiltrate them, Miss Peck. It took cunning to ensure that I was accepted into their number – lies, stories, bravado, betrayal . . .' He flicked the ash again, but this time I saw his fingers tremble.

'They tested you too?'

He didn't answer that. Instead he stared out of the window and carried on.

'In the end, as you know, it's always a matter of family. The Barons rarely appoint beyond their blood.'

I stared at the dusty top of the Beetle's hat as I thought of Ma again. It wasn't true. It couldn't be. If I allowed myself to believe that any one of those men was my father I'd go mad. No wonder my grandmother lost herself in opium. To see her own daughter . . .

I snapped my mind shut to the pictures that tumbled again.

'I'm not one of them.' I shouted it out loud.

Vellum's cool eyes measured me. After a moment he tossed the stub of his smoke through the window.

'I believe we share a common enemy. The days of the Barons are numbered. They are an anachronism, a nightmare from the past. We live in a modern world and London is the centre of that world. There are many who envy that position.'

He broke off as the whistle came again. The train reined

itself back and began to slow its pace. I glanced at the window, but all I could see out there now was rain and trees.

'Where are we?'

Vellum took up his hat. His long fingers traced a pattern on the flat silk crown. 'We are at my destination. Yours, however, is the London Necropolis Terminus at Waterloo, a journey of some fifteen minutes from here.'

The train idled along for a minute more until it came to a stand. He stood up and reached into the top pocket of his coat. Immediately I shifted the gun, but he smiled.

'You are unharmed. You will be met at the station and taken to your house off Salmon Lane. I do not advise you to travel alone. Your man, Telferman, will also be returned, safely, to Pearl Street. You have my word.'

'What sort of a word is that?'

'The word of the Crown.'

'But what about the Barons? I don't understand.' I stared up at him. The pistol and the bag were lying flat on my lap now.

'The Barons are as fleas on the back of a dog compared to what is coming. But fleas carry disease and that weakens the body. They must be eradicated so the body is strong and ready to fight. Here . . .'

He passed me a white card.

'You have questioned me, now I have a single question for you. Will you work with me, Miss Peck, to destroy them? You need not give me your answer now.'

He reached for the handle of the door. I caught the rich clean scent of him again before the stink of coal and soot came rolling through the open door. I heard the rattle of the steps as they folded down and I saw movement – shapes moving about in the steam outside.

Vellum gave me a curt nod and swept his hat to his head. He turned to the door and disappeared into the steam, but his voice came back.

'If your answer is yes, seek me out.'

Epilogue

Tan Seng was waiting at the top of the steps to The Palace.

I wasn't unnerved by it now. One of the girls at The Gaudy had kept a dog that ran to the door and barked for ten minutes every night before her man came home. It didn't make no difference what the time was, that dog knew his master's mind the moment he made it up.

I felt the old boy's eyes on my face and wondered what I looked like. A wreck, is my guess, what with the soot, the steam, the wind and the rain. What had Vellum, or whatever his real name was, made of the wild girl sitting opposite him on the train, pointing a gun at his vitals?

'Lady.' Tan Seng bowed.

'No!' I was on the verge of telling him to call me anything else, but it could wait. 'No – there's nothing I want, thank you.' I tried to make it sound like a reply to a question he hadn't asked. The images in my mind were forcing themselves on me now. Ma in that dress. Ma with the Barons. Netta in that dress burning to a cinder. Swami Jonah slumped against the wall. Lucca and Sam gambling for sight on the turn of a card. It wasn't just pictures. My head was full of voices too – all of them clamouring for attention – those I lost, those I hurt, those I hated . . . those I loved.

I glanced at the stairs. I should go straight to Lucca and Peggy. She was sure to be sitting with him. I crossed the black and white tiles, steadied myself on the rail and began to climb. It was like hauling myself up a mountain. I stopped halfway to push off my boots. There were gaping holes at the ankles of my black stockings where the stiff new leather had worn weeping blisters into my skin. I stacked the boots to the side of the stairs and left them there.

At the second landing I heard Peggy's voice through the door to the bedroom and I caught Lucca's cracked laugh. It turned into a cough, but then he said something and Peggy chuckled. Next thing the boards creaked and she was clucking like a hen. The pair of them were comfortable and, for the moment, they were safe.

I reached for the handle. My hand was covered in smuts, the grimy skin torn by brambles. I pulled back sharp. If I went in there now, I'd take the darkness with me.

I turned away and headed up another flight to my room and my bed. I needed the sort of sleep that drags you down so far that nothing disturbs you. The sleep so deep and black that not even the nightmares find a way in.

Of an instant, I remembered Pardieu's laudanum. I'd left a tiny bottle of the stuff on the nightstand beside Sam's bed. I slid a look at the stairs in case Tan Seng or Lok might be there, but I was alone.

⚓

I sat on the bed. There was still a dent in the pillow from Sam's head. From the rumples on the sheets I could see where he'd lain. I ran my fingers over the creases as if I could feel a trace of him there. I'd lost Sam too, but at least there was a comfort in the fact that he'd walked away from The Palace of his own accord.

It was a comfort of the sort that brought tears to the eyes. I cupped my forehead in my hands. If Sam had any sense – which I knew he did – he'd open a distance between us as vast as the Atlantic Ocean.

There was a soft thud as the velvet bag slipped slowly from my lap to the rug. The edge of Vellum's card poked out through the scorched hole made by that shot on the train. I reached down, opened the bag and took out the stiff white square.

33 LITTLE SANCTUARY

That was all, I flipped it over but the other side was a blank. It didn't mean nothing. I threw it down to the rug and looked to the small green bottle on the nightstand. It was still there where I'd left it out for Sam if he needed it, but now a folded sheet of paper was propped against it. It was addressed to me; just '*Kitty*', nothing else.

Of an instant, something inside me knotted itself up tight and hard. Of course! That was the way of it, wasn't it? He couldn't go without having the last bleedin' word. I snatched up the note and flapped it open. There wasn't much to see.

2 John. Verse 5.

It was written out straight, not in shorthand, the sloping letters formed careful and clear. Sam had underlined 'Verse 5'. Another of his Bible references.

I stared at the sheet trembling between my dirty fingers. I was sick of clever games. I let it fall to the floor where it came to rest face up next to Vellum's card.

2 John. <u>Verse 5</u>.

The words taunted me. I slipped off the bed and went quietly across the landing to my own room. I'd hidden the little Bible Joey gave me in a linen drawer. I drew it out and flicked through the pages, pausing when I came across the place where he'd scratched out the code for the Vinculum. I folded the tissue-thin paper down to mark it and then I carried on searching until, eventually, I found Sam's reference.

I ran a finger down the tight-packed column. As I read, my heart began to thump so loud under that black crêpe bodice I thought it would bring them all running.

And now I beseech thee, lady, not as though I wrote
a new commandment unto thee, but that which we had
from the beginning, that we love one another.

When I was reading it through for perhaps the eighth or ninth time, the evening sun slanted through the window, turning the room and everything in it to gold.

To be concluded in *Kitty Peck and the Parliament of Shadows*.

Acknowledgements

If you've followed Kitty's progress so far, you'll have noticed that the world is closing in on her. The past casts a long cold shadow and dark new secrets lurk round every corner. Despite the fact that the story you've just read is set during the fetid summer of 1881, a friend who read the first draft commented that I managed to make it feel as bleak as winter.

I took this comment from Lisa R. (mentioned below) as a compliment.

I'm not a summer person. In fact, I think I might be one of the very few people who experience a lowering of the spirits when the days grow longer and the sun climbs in the sky.

By the end of August each year my chilly little heart flutters at the thought of the gloomy evenings, lamp-lit rooms, log-stacked fires and opaque black tights that lie ahead.

If you have read this on a beach during a heatwave, I do apologise if, just occasionally, I made you shiver. (Although I'll take that as a compliment too!)

As usual, I could fill several pages with the names of everyone who has supported and encouraged me, but I will try to be brief. First I'd like to thank my excellent Faber & Faber editor Louisa Joyner for her excitement and advice, Tamsin Shelton for her forensic eye and, importantly, Hannah Griffiths for her wisdom and general brilliance.

I am so grateful to friends from every part of my life:

518

to Lisa R. – my ever-enthusiastic first reader; my work colleagues in SPAB attic – Ali M., Felicity M., Pippa E. and Sophie M. (who are definitely not mad in the Mrs Rochester sense, and who manage to keep me sane when I'm juggling deadlines!); my oldest friend Leah W.; my university 'coven' Rachel G., Jo C. and Jane S.; my twin school friends Helen F. and Sue S. and, of course, my wonderful agent Eugenie Furniss – one of the only people I know who shares my deep appreciation of all things wintry.

Finally, as ever, thanks to Stephen, who makes everything possible.

Kate Griffin, 20 November 2016
(my legs are encased in opaque tights
as I type in a gloomy lamp-lit room)

Also in the Kitty Peck series

ff

KITTY PECK
AND THE MUSIC HALL MURDERS

Shortlisted for the CWA Endeavour Historical Dagger

LONDON, 1880

In the opium-laced streets of Limehouse the ferocious Lady Ginger rules with ruthless efficiency. But The Lady is not happy. Somebody is stealing her most valuable assets – her dancing girls – and that someone has to be found and made to pay.

Bold, impetuous and with more brains than she cares to admit, seventeen-year-old seamstress Kitty Peck reluctantly performs the role of bait for the kidnappers. But as Kitty's scandalous and terrifying act becomes the talk of the city, she finds herself facing danger even more deadly and horrifying than The Lady.

This thrilling historical mystery takes us deep into the underworld of Victorian London. Take nothing at face value, for Kitty is about to go down a path of discovery that will have consequences not only for herself, but for those she holds most dear . . .

ff

KITTY PECK
AND THE CHILD OF ILL FORTUNE

LIMEHOUSE, MARCH 1881

Kitty Peck, a spirited but vulnerable seventeen-year-old, is the reluctant heiress to Paradise, the criminal empire previously overseen by the formidable Lady Ginger. Far from the colour and camaraderie of the music hall where Kitty once worked, this new-found power brings with it isolation and uncertainty. Desperate to reconnect with Joey, her estranged brother, Kitty travels to Paris. Reunited at last, she is unable to refuse his request to take a child back to London. Within days of her return it's clear that someone has followed them, and this someone is determined to kill the child . . . and anyone who stands in their way.

Kitty Peck and the Child of Ill Fortune is a fast-paced historical mystery with breath-taking twists and turns that takes us from the decadent, bohemian world of late-nineteenth-century Paris to a deadly secret at the heart of the British Empire.